FATAL CIRCLE

LINDA ROBERTSON

Pocket Books

New York   London   Toronto   Sydney

A Division of Simon & Schuster, Inc.
1230 Avenue of the Americas
New York, NY 10020

This book is a work of fiction. Names, characters, places, and incidents either are products of the author's imagination or are used fictitiously. Any resemblance to actual events or locales or persons, living or dead, is entirely coincidental.

Copyright © 2010 by Linda Robertson

All rights reserved, including the right to reproduce this book or portions thereof in any form whatsoever. For information address Pocket Books Subsidiary Rights Department, 1230 Avenue of the Americas, New York, NY 10020.

First Juno Books/Pocket Books paperback edition July 2010

JUNO BOOKS and colophon are trademarks of Wildside Press LLC used under license by Simon & Schuster, Inc., the publisher of this work.

POCKET and colophon are registered trademarks of Simon & Schuster, Inc.

For information about special discounts for bulk purchases, please contact Simon & Schuster Special Sales at 1-866-506-1949 or business@simonandschuster.com.

The Simon & Schuster Speakers Bureau can bring authors to your live event. For more information or to book an event contact the Simon & Schuster Speakers Bureau at 1-866-248-3049 or visit our website at www.simonspeakers.com.

Cover design by John Vairo, Jr., photos © Masterfile & Trevillion

Manufactured in the United States of America

10 9 8 7 6 5 4 3 2 1

ISBN 978-1-4391-5680-3
ISBN 978-1-4391-7694-8 (ebook)

"The vampire told me you are the only one who can instruct me," I said.

"Help me, Beau," I continued. "Tell me how to protect myself."

For an interminable minute the owner of Wolfsbane and Absinthe sat unmoving, thinking, studying me. Then he laughed. He rose from the stool and returned to the curtain, pausing to glance at me before pushing through, still chuckling.

He wasn't going to help. I started for the door.

"Where are you going?" Beau called, holding the curtain open.

"You're not going to help me."

"But I am."

"Why are you laughing?"

"If you only knew, doll. If you only knew." He waved for me to follow him into the back and let the curtain fall.

Praise for *Vicious Circle* and *Hallowed Circle*

"Linda Robertson's second urban fantasy is an instant classic, featuring a refreshingly wise and likeable heroine."
—Affaire de Coeur (5 stars)

"Well-developed supernatural characters, mystery, and a touch of romance add up to an out-of-this world thriller."
—*Romantic Times* (4 stars)

"Hallowed Circle is near perfection. . . ."
—Book Lovers Inc. (4.5 stars)

***Fatal Circle* is also available as an eBook**

Don't miss these Persephone Alcmedi books . . .

Vicious Circle

Hallowed Circle

Available from Pocket Juno Books

We do not, most of us, choose to die;
nor do we choose the time and conditions of our death.
But within this realm of choicelessness,
we do choose how we live.
—*Ambition: The Secret Passion*, Joseph Epstein

This one's for my own wolfy bad-boy rocker, Jim.

Thank Yous:

Red-Caped Hero Thanks
Paula Guran
I'm upgrading you from the usual "margarita thanks"
to the Hero's Cape for this one.

Java-n-Chocolate Thanks
Michelle, Melissa, Laura, Emily, Faith, Rachel, and Tracy
To my writing group, the Ohio Writer's Network (OWN)
for reading, critiques, support, and the friendship.
It's priceless.

High-Frequency Thanks
Billy Nyte & Syrinx at NRRRadio.

Cookie Monster Thanks
Shannon & Co.
For reading and sharing baked goods. Yum!

Tour du Jour Thanks
Scollard. You always have answers.

Reverent Gratitude
For the Many-named Muse. You still *rock*.

Extra Thanks
To the copyeditors, reviewers, and bloggers and tweeters.
To Jolly Rancher because your Hot Cinnamon candy is
inspiring. And to Zocalo for excellent food and service.

CHAPTER ONE

My living room clock read two-forty-six A.M. It was no longer Hallowe'en night, but All Hallows' Day. Or, as some called it, All Saints' Day. But it was no saint who held me in his arms—it was a wærewolf.

"I think you'd like my apartment, Red." Red. That's me. Persephone Alcmedi to the rest of the world. Seph to some. Red only to Johnny, my not-exactly-Big-Bad-wærewolf. "It has that open-living concept."

I wasn't fooled. "It's a glorified dorm room, isn't it?"

"If by 'glorified,' you mean it has a private bath-room, then yes." Johnny sniffed, affecting annoyance. "Something I sacrificed when I moved in here."

I'd had to forfeit my home's vampire defenses three weeks before to save a friend's life and Johnny had tempo-rarily moved into the third-floor attic room—for protec-tion purposes only. The defenses had been reinstated, but he'd remained. He being the epitome of "tall, dark, and handsome," I hadn't complained.

"C'mon." Johnny's deep blue eyes glittered seduc-tively. His voice dropped low. "Nothing's more romantic than a bachelor pad."

We'd both had a hell of an evening. Words like "hectic" or "demanding" didn't begin to cover it. But evidently I was the only one suffering from fatigue.

His band, Lycanthropia, had played at the Hallowe'en Ball. Johnny was the vocalist and guitarist for the techno-goth-metal band and he'd given his all on stage. He should have been as exhausted as I was.

Of course, I'd made quite an effort on that stage, too. I'd fought and killed a fairy in front of hundreds of witnesses, who'd applauded afterward thinking it part of the Hallowe'en show.

Killer fairies and rock'n'roll: that was only a small part of what we'd dealt with this evening.

"Do you honestly want to show me your apartment *now*?"

"My one bulb is burned out so there's not much you'd actually see." His lean-muscled arms slid around me. I felt so grounded and safe in his embrace. "But I promise, what you feel will make up for it."

What Johnny wanted was crystal clear, and so was the reason he thought going elsewhere was a good idea. I'd already mentioned my fears about the rest of the household learning we were intimate, so he was trying to keep the secret. At his apartment we could have assured privacy and we wouldn't have to retire to separate bedrooms as we had to here. Cuddling and sleeping together after sex would have been nice.

Apparently, to him, if we weren't actually seen together we had plausible deniability. Not that my live-in grandmother—Nana—would ever believe that we'd visited his apartment in the middle of the night just so he could give me the nickel tour.

Nana and my nine-year-old foster daughter, Beverley, were asleep in their bedrooms—each just a hall's width from mine. The old saltbox farmhouse had paper-thin walls. Even the layers between the second-floor ceiling and attic floor lacked the ability to dampen noise. I'd heard Johnny playing his guitar up there when his little amplifier wasn't even cranked up to "1".

Still, there were things he didn't know. "The *lucusi* is coming here at dawn, Johnny."

He pulled me closer. He'd gotten a shower after the show, washing off the smell of sweaty leather stage clothes and leaving only the cedar and sage that was his unique scent. "Had to try."

His breath on my neck was warm, his voice just rough enough to catch in my ear and send a tingle down to my toes. Parts of me were suddenly insisting they didn't qualify as weary. It made me reconsider the definition of tired. "It's just so far to drive. All the way to town, only to turn around and come back here by dawn."

But people in the throes of new love did crazy things like that.

Did I just think the L-word?

"You could fly."

He was right, I could. Due to my performance a few days earlier in the Eximium, a high-priestess competition, I'd been inducted into the powerful *lucusi* led by the Eldrenne Xerxadrea that was due at dawn. A real witch's broom was one of the membership perks. "But . . ."

"You don't want to fly?" He nuzzled my neck.

"It isn't that." Running my fingers through his long

dark hair, I looked up—way up, he's six-foot-two—and let him see I wanted him, too. "I have a better idea."

"Do share." Another nuzzle.

"There's only one place in my house with any kind of privacy and soundproofing." Tiptoeing, I kissed him lightly before saying, "Your kennel."

"Oh, that is *sooo* hot." He ran his hands up and down my backside and couldn't suppress his grin.

Carrying a lit jar candle and blankets, I led him outside and around the house to the cellar. Johnny pulled the slanted metal doors open and I descended the concrete stairs.

While Johnny shut the doors behind us, I placed the candle in the middle of the floor and spread the blankets over the fresh straw on the floor between the cages. I glanced into the shadows at the door of the rearmost steel kennel. This was where his beast was unleashed, where the animal in him took over. A shiver of desire ran through me.

When I heard Johnny's footsteps had reached the bottom stair, I asked over my shoulder, "I don't suppose you could help me out of this costume?"

He stopped in his tracks.

I tugged on the lacings of the bell-sleeved velvet midriff bustier—part of my costume for the Ball—and smiled.

"Actually—" His voice was a little higher than he intended. He stopped to clear his throat and started over. "Actually, I can help with that." He was by me in an instant, deftly working the knot. Seconds later, the fabric loosened and I took a satisfyingly deep breath. Then his skillful fingers touched the bare skin at my waist, thumbs drawing little circles. "Anything else I can help you out of?"

"I'm not technically out of this."

"Oh," he said softly. "My bad." He began loosening the lace-up strings even more. "Up or down?"

"Definitely *up*."

He was so gentle, moving so slowly, careful of my hair. He was just removing my shirt, but he made it sensual, as if he were rubbing lotion all over me. Tanning lotion. The cellar was suddenly so warm I could have been standing in summer sunlight. The bustier fell onto the blanket-covered straw at my feet.

As I kept my arms raised, Johnny placed my hands on the bars atop the open cage door, and squeezed my grip to indicate I should let them remain there.

His warm fingers traced every contour of my arms, slowly descending until he could brush my hair away from my ear on one side. He put the line of his body against the back of me and nuzzled against my ear. While he sucked gently on my earlobe, his hands shifted toward my breasts.

A trembling resonance fluttered up my spine. Heat was building low in my abdomen. Sensations jolted through me like electricity, and all thought of tiredness fled.

Abruptly, the cellar door creaked open and crashed loudly against the ground outside. "I locked that," Johnny muttered.

Someone was coming down the steps. We turned to see who—

Menessos.

The vampire descended with an elegant gait and casually inspected the cobwebbed space, all but ignoring us. My aura could feel his breath and the warmth of his skin. *At least he's fed.*

The heat. The energetic desire. Had it been Johnny's ministrations or the vampire's presence that caused it? Menessos's presence had stirred a similar reaction in me at the Eximium, but Johnny stirred my proverbial flames pretty damned well all by himself.

Menessos had played Arthur Pendragon in my dreams long before we'd ever met. With his walnut-colored hair in carelessly regal waves and his trim beard, he resembled a king of times past. Of course, in those dreams he wore medieval clothing; seeing him in a suit—probably Armani or something equally expensive—still seemed odd to me.

Amusement lit his features when he saw my hands covering my breasts. He averted his gray eyes and donned an apologetic expression. "Pardon my interruption." Menessos sat down on my dirty cellar stairs with no more regard for his designer slacks than if he were seating himself in a cozy chair. He then placed his elbows on the step behind and let his legs stretch out before him.

It didn't look like he was planning on leaving any time soon.

"How'd you get in here?" Johnny demanded as he repositioned himself to shield me from Menessos's view. He stripped off his overshirt and gave it to me. "She reinstated the wards. And I locked the cellar door."

I shot my arms into the shirt's sleeves and started buttoning.

"I have my ways." The vampire was smiling; though I couldn't see him from behind Johnny, I could tell by the tone of his voice.

"Forget how," I said, pushing past Johnny. "Why?"

"I'd like to have Xerxadrea's hanky. The one with my blood." He added, "Please."

"Why do you want it?" I asked.

"She nearly lost it once already and the fairies could"—he flashed a glance at Johnny—"use it against me, magically. To keep that from happening, it must be destroyed. I prefer burned."

"Déjà vu," Johnny said. "I'm sensing a theme here. Red keeps ending up with things that are dangerous to you, and you want them burned. First the stake. Now the hanky. I bet it was some firebug like you who started the whole witch-burning thing way back when."

"Fire destroys. Water cleanses. Air distributes. Earth absorbs. All equally effective at releasing the threat, but fire is the fastest, surest method." Menessos crossed his ankles; the movement caused my aura to ripple like the surface of water.

At the Eximium I'd shielded using something akin to the witch hand-jolt—a "friendly" way to assess someone else's power—and found I was able to reduce the effects of the vampire's presence. I drew that jolt-shield tight around me as I darted back into the kennel and bent to pick up the discarded bustier. I'd tucked the hanky in my costume earlier and hadn't even considered it when being undressed. I searched the velvet top. The hanky had remained in the bustier.

"Here." I held the crusty fabric before me as I approached him.

Immediately on his feet, Menessos snatched it from my fingertips. He crouched by the candle and held the dirty square of dark fabric over the flame until it had caught, then tossed it to the floor. The harsh shadows caused by the candlelight gave his face a crazed appearance as he whispered, leaning in to be certain every scrap of fabric was consumed. Thankfully, the fabric burned quickly— but I couldn't say I was thankful for the smelly smoke it left wafting about the cellar.

"Now you should go," I said. We'd already established that both of us knew the bond between us had inverted and I was the master. He had to obey. Or so I hoped. It was my strong suspicion that he wasn't going to prove an obedient servant.

"Hold on, Red." Johnny jerked the pull chain on the overhead light. It was a harsh hundred watts. "I want the vampire to explain how he got past the wards."

Good question.

Menessos stood. Directing his reply to me, he said, "Perhaps the details are not meant for your lover's ears?"

"Perhaps you're wrong." Johnny was obviously not going to back down, even for someone who'd kicked his ass a few weeks ago.

"It's a magical secret, and should be hers to share. Or not."

"Oh." I realized Menessos meant his binding to me superseded the wards I'd created. "That."

"What?" Johnny asked.

Knowing he needed to feel he was one up on Menessos and to be shown that I trusted him, I said, "The binding allows him access." While that was true, it wasn't the *full* answer. I hadn't yet explained to Johnny that Menessos was bound to me, and not the other way around.

"Figures." Johnny pointed at the stairs. "But now you *can* go."

"Wait." I waved at the smoky air to encourage it up and out into the night. "If, despite the wards, you can enter because of our binding, does your binding to the fairies follow the same principle?"

A gratified expression registered on Menessos's face. He'd recognized my question as somewhat insightful and seemed pleased. "I am not certain. That is the second reason for my presence: to stand guard over you until your perimeter wards can be rebuilt."

Johnny crossed his arms for bouncer-perfect emphasis. "I can protect her."

"Yes, but with your pants off and your other head doing all the thinking, perhaps it is best to let me have that responsibility for a night."

Exasperated, I angled myself between them with my palms out like a boxing referee. "I increased my wards after Aquula was here." A mermaid water fairy, Aquula was one of the four fairies bound to Menessos—and the only one who didn't resent the connection and wish him truly dead and gone. In fact, she'd actually swooned at the mention of his name.

"Your wards are strong, Persephone, but now that you've killed one of them you must not take the chance. You require something specifically antifey. Xerxadrea and her talented *lucusi* are preparing it even now."

"They let me fly home on the broom and they didn't say anything about it."

"Of course not. But I am certain they saw you home safely, whether or not you were aware of it. Xerxadrea and

I discussed all of this at the Ball. I left early, as you may recall. I did so in order to make arrangements that would allow me to comply with her request."

Curious. "What was her request, exactly?"

"That I come here and watch over you until they had the wards up—"

"You could have stayed outside and done that," Johnny said under his breath.

"They're not coming until dawn, Menessos," I said matter-of-factly. "You'll have to leave before then."

"Or perhaps you would be so kind as to allow me to stay down here for the day?" Menessos gestured to indicate the cellar. "It's not exactly what I'm accustomed to, but on more than a few occasions I've been forced to sleep in worse accommodations."

"Sleep." Johnny sniggered. "Yeah. We'll call it 'sleep.'"

Menessos spread his arms in a show of conciliation. "I assure you. I came only to protect my interests."

While my mind easily replaced the word "interests" with "master," I was certain Johnny's mind had inserted "property." I needed to tell him the truth. Now was as good a time as any. "Johnny—"

"Persephone," Menessos interrupted before I could go further. "Half of my objective has been accomplished. Will you allow me to make it a complete success? Let me keep watch so that you may rest and know all in your home are safe this night." Something in his voice pleaded with me. "Please, rest. Sleep."

I had been about to tell Johnny that Menessos wasn't the master here. If the vampire could read my thoughts he might be keeping me from telling so he'd remain one up on Johnny. Male ego games weren't meant to be understood by women. Menessos was also being very courteous and wording things as if to ask permission. It was unlike him and I was suspicious, but this was preferable to a pissing contest that would sooner or later develop into fisticuffs. Johnny could be told tomorrow. "But you have to go before dawn," I insisted to Menessos.

"I know where I belong, Persephone."

I pivoted on my heel and was ready to leave, but Johnny stopped me with a gentle clasp of my shoulder, turning me to face him, studying me and searching for any sign I was being given a mesmerizing vampire command. To reassure him that wasn't the case, I stroked his arm. "It's okay." I moved toward the steps. "C'mon."

Menessos added, "And you, Johnny. You need your rest, as well." He didn't use a dog reference. My suspicions were soaring.

Johnny reiterated, "I can protect her."

"Yes, and you *will* protect her, if this war is fought. In the meantime, if you want to be foolish enough to claim no rest in my presence, so be it, but do not be foolish enough to let your place at her side grow cold."

Because my senses were amped up by the binding with Menessos, I could smell things like never before and, just then, the vampire's insinuated threat riled the wære. A musky testosterone scent filled the cellar. Luckily, neither did more than glare at the other. As for me, the mention of war had knocked all thought of sleep from my mind.

Johnny took my hand and preceded me up and out into the night. Menessos extinguished the candle and tugged on the pull chain to turn off the light. He followed us, pausing to shut the cellar door behind us.

We walked silently around the house to the front porch. November's eager fingers had chilled the air. A mist was settling in. The bannerlike leaves of the fodder-shocks rustled lightly at our approach, sounding like stiff paper scrubbing together. The jack-o'-lanterns' tea lights had burned out hours ago and their dark faces seemed sad. *Yup. Hallowe'en's over.*

Johnny opened the door for me. Menessos came around the corner slowly, intently staring across the cornfield.

Inside the house, my feet headed directly for the stairs, but I lingered with my palm on the newel post's ball finial. I didn't want to go to my lonely room and climb between cold sheets and sleep alone. What I wanted was Johnny's warm body next to mine, and the security of his arms around me.

A few days before, I had felt overwhelmed because it seemed impossible to balance my new life with all its myriad complications, let alone being the Lustrata and somehow bringing balance to the world. Now my own actions were the catalyst for a war.

How the hell am I going to fix this?

"Stay with me on the couch, Johnny?" I asked.

"You bet." Johnny lifted my hand from the finial and led me into the living room. We'd left an end table lamp on, and he sat near it, on one end of my tan corduroy slip-covered couch. Johnny and I had made love there. Once.

This room. This couch. Our first and, so far, only time.

Shortly after the intimacy, I'd been confused and hurt that he might have betrayed me with some women at a gig. He hadn't, but at the time his supposed unfaithfulness had been such a concern. Not that we'd discussed exclusivity with each other or anything, but it was the kind of thing I expected and thought was understood. Now, infidelity seemed pretty insignificant compared to war.

When he sat, my hand fell away from his. I turned in a slow circle. This space was my sanctuary, filled with all my Arthurian books and posters. Over the mantel was Waterhouse's painting *Ariadne*. A very impractical thank-you-for-not-staking-me gift from Menessos. The security system for the valuable artwork was supposed to be installed this Friday.

So many things had changed in such a short amount of time.

"Wanna put your head in my lap?" Johnny asked teasingly.

Some things, like Johnny's constant innuendos, weren't likely to ever change.

My exhaustion was reaching complete and the weight of my worries filled the room, threatening to suffocate me. Johnny could probably feel it too. He was trying to ease away the heaviness with humor.

I faced Johnny with a genuine smile. "You wish."

"I certainly do."

I gave him a mock scowl.

"Okay, okay." In one motion, he turned out the lamp and moved the couch pillow onto his lap. "Now?"

I laughed and it felt good. "Now."

As my feet carried me forward, a silhouette crept across the picture window behind Johnny. It was Menessos taking a sentinel's position on the porch, but I could feel his presence, feel how he yearned to be the one inside comforting me.

CHAPTER TWO

It was nearly dawn. Freshly showered, wearing clean blue jeans and a long-sleeved creamy yellow T-shirt with some beaded embellishment around the scoop neck, I crossed to the edge of my porch, yawning. Even with the chill in the crisp air, the mist had held on, giving the morning a sense of magic.

The ground was wet with cold dew that soaked the hem of my jeans as I went to check the cellar door. Not to verify Menessos's presence—the warmth caressing the underside of my sternum assured me he was still here. As expected, the door was secured from the inside as if people were huddling down there to escape a tornado. There were no people down there, however, only one insatiably obstinate vampire. There might be no storm to shelter from, but the cellar offered protection from the even more dangerous, for him, daylight.

Johnny's footsteps *shush*ed through the grass as he rounded the corner.

"He's locked himself in down there," I said.

"Wolves in your attic and corpses in your cellar." Johnny's hands rested on the black denim at his lean hips.

"Just another glorious day in 'Ohio: The Heart of It All.'"

I scanned over his long fingers, up the heather gray of his long-sleeved jersey to the black waves of tousled hair and the dark lines of his Wedjat-tattooed eyes.

My arm slid around his waist and directed him toward the front of the house. "I have a nagging feeling that this is going to get ugly before it's over, and we'll be appreciating any break we can get. Even if Menessos is the one giving it to us."

He hung his arm across my shoulders.

When we rounded the house, I could see the east. There were thick clouds promising rain overhead, yet the first glimmer of true sunlight glistened on the less-cloudy horizon, and reflected off every damp particle floating in the air like a haze of glitter.

In that enchanting moment, six broom-riding witches in a V formation drifted down from the sky to land in my yard. It's not every morning a girl sees Elders in street clothes. Xerxadrea, the eldest, was in the lead position and, apparently, a red, white, and navy blue velour jogging suit was the flying outfit of choice for ancient Eldrennes.

Every one of the witches wore some type of dark jogging suit and white sneakers. All wore goggles that any steampunk fan would love.

It made me want to race up to my closet and throw out the few jogging suits I was guilty of owning. Mine were solid pastel colors, though, stylish and cotton, and I'd never once considered wearing them with Red Baron goggles.

Johnny leaned close to my ear and whispered, "I never

would have believed those old ladies could sit a broom. At least not without stirrups, handlebars, and broad bicycle seats attached."

I elbowed him in the ribs. They could probably hear him.

"Merry Morning to you, Persephone." Xerxadrea pushed her goggles to her forehead. Her raven landed on her shoulder. It had been perched in a nearby tree, watching.

"Merry Morning to you, Eldrenne."

Xerxadrea had pallid skin, almost as white as the long braid draping over her shoulder. Only the splotches of pink above her sunken cheeks gave her any color. Most notable were her blind eyes, covered with a thin, bluish film. "You remember Ludovika, Jeanine, Celeste, Silvana, and Vilna-Daluca?" Though Vilna-Daluca was also an Elder, Xerxadrea was among the eldest, and she was afforded the name and title of Eldrenne. The rest were high-ranking high priestesses.

"Yes." I silently repeated their names to myself again.

"I have news," Xerxadrea said. Her voice was thin and a bit breathy. "The Witches Elder Council convened in emergency meeting last night after word of the fairies' threat of war reached them. They recognized the Hallowe'en death of the air fairy as a sign of the Lustrata's return."

I nodded. It had to happen sometime.

"The Elders have begun trying to make contact with the fey to see if they can negotiate a peace. It may buy us some time. I will keep you advised as this progresses, but"—Xerxadrea extended her hand, receiving a satchel from Celeste—"on with the purpose of our visit." From the canvas bag Xerxadrea removed four iron spikes, each topped with a huge black stone. My first thought went to onyx, but this was too shiny. Witches Armor. Better known as jet. She supplied one to each of the four priestesses. "Go," she told them.

"What are they doing?" I asked.

"We are setting you a perimeter."

"I have wards."

"Not," Vilna-Daluca said, "like these."

Reaching into the satchel again, Xerxadrea brought out a palm-sized iron candle holder, at least that's what I thought it was when she thrust it at me. Accepting it, I saw it was round and had an ornate latticework rim with four little spikes. Next, she offered me an obelisk-shaped piece of jet that fit perfectly into the square indention in the base. After surrendering the satchel to Vilna-Daluca, she said to Johnny, "You should jog up the road about a hundred yards or so. And you," she said to me, "need to come with us."

Johnny prowled across the lawn, passing two witches headed for the front corners of the property. Witchcraft and sorcery both stirred energies that could cause a wærewolf to go into a partial change. Xerxadrea had courteously cautioned Johnny to stay clear until the spell work was done and posed no threat.

"Here," Vilna-Daluca said, stopping us in line parallel to the front door, but about twenty feet out.

Shoulder to shoulder, we faced the street. Xerxadrea smelled like harvest spices and the scent of anise and nutmeg filled the air as she spoke.

Iron spikes, fire-forged
Empowered and engorged
With defensive protection
    and offensive rejection
    Of fairy strike.

She tapped the ley line, and its response caused the hair at the nape of my neck to prickle. The other two witches had gone to the rear corners of the yard. Behind the house, one of them called out, a wordless sound of defense. Before me, the witch in the northwest corner gave the same cry and stabbed the iron spike into the ground. Then the woman to the northeast, followed by the witch in back. Finally, the witch who had started it gave her cry again, and I knew the ley power had completed the circuit of my property, at least the part that wasn't cornfield. I owned twenty acres in total.

The obelisk thrummed, a light but steady vibration, one I could readily detect. Both of the witches with me gave a cry and threw their hands up into the air. My skin crawled as the ward rose up like a wave, and crashed down on the other side, pushing through and under to make an invisible cylinder of protection.

The Eldrenne set it spinning, and her gestures seemed to indicate she was adding power from the line in small amounts. When she was satisfied, she drew an equal-armed cross in the air to seal her magic.

"It is done," Xerxadrea said happily. "You can check its power level with this." She patted the obelisk. "If it feels weak, refuel from the line."

Tramping along, using their brooms like walking sticks with floppy bottoms, the group rejoined and headed for my porch. Gently grasping Xerxadrea's age-spotted arm, I held her back. "I have to tell you something. And I want it to be a secret between us."

"As you wish."

Johnny was jogging toward us. I felt a little pang knowing I should have told him this before I revealed it to Xerxadrea. "Weeks ago, Menessos marked me. Afterward . . ." We'd be here all morning if I gave her details. I went with the short version. "Somehow, I flipped it."

"You transformed a stain into a hex?" "Stain" was the slang term for a vampire's mark, but a witch's mark was also known as a "hex."

I swallowed. "Yes."

"*She* tested you, and you passed." By "she" Xerxadrea meant the Goddess. "Nothing I wouldn't expect of the Lustrata." The corner of her mouth crooked upward. Evidently this came as no surprise to her.

"My question is this: he wasn't held out by my wards. Will this one you just set be any different?"

"Yes and no."

I wasn't sure how to phrase what I wanted to ask next.

"Come, come, Persephone, I know you have questions," she said.

"The fairies who are bound to him, can they use the binding they have to him and get through?"

"Through your former wards, yes. This"—she gestured all around—"no. We've specifically empowered it against fairies, using iron and Witches Armor. He cannot call them here. He was supposed to tell you that."

"He did . . . sort of, but I wanted to confirm it."

"What about the ley line?" Aquula had ridden the line and appeared to me in the grove. "What if the other fairies ride it and show up here?"

"They could. We cannot block them from using the line. You're safe inside." Blindness notwithstanding, Xerxadrea—who had never been here before—released my arm and once more headed for the porch. Her pet raven leaped from her shoulder and landed on the porch rail, cawing. Johnny had passed us and was now observing from the doorway.

"Okay. About this war then . . ." I wanted guidance and advice.

"All in good time." She patted my hand.

Vilna-Daluca called out, "What's for breakfast?"

Until she asked, I hadn't equated their dawn services with my being their hostess. As a solitary, I hadn't any cause to practice coven etiquette. "Well." I shot a worried, pleading look at Johnny. Even if this Mother Hubbard's kitchen cupboards were bare, that wærewolf could whip up a feast.

"I'm on it," he said, winking at me. He opened the door as they advanced onto the porch. "I hope eggs and pancakes will do?"

At the steps, Xerxadrea did her witchy-mist thing that was fast becoming her trademark to me. The fog enveloped her lower half and she rose up gently and smoothly. If Nana could do that, I'd worry less about the wear and tear the stairs did to her knees.

"Ruya"—Xerxadrea said the name of her raven—"will

remain out here." She added her broom to the collection leaning just beside the door.

I reached for the door but, hearing the popping of gravel under tires, stopped. Lydia's mud-splattered pickup rolled up the driveway. She'd been the interim high priestess for Venefica Coven, when their former leader went missing. It was because of Lydia that I'd participated in the Eximium: she had nominated me to take the priestess position. Thankfully, the competition ended with Hunter Hopewell gaining the title and not me. Lydia was also the previous owner of this house and land.

"Lydia's arrived," Xerxadrea said.

"How do you do that?" I asked.

"Do what?" She used to add "child" to the end of her sentences. I wondered if she had stopped saying it because I was now a part of her *lucusi*.

"See," I blurted out.

"Sorcery, of course." She smiled enigmatically.

I knew that, but had hoped to get more of an answer. Since she didn't offer, I didn't press.

Lydia slid from the big truck easily and approached us. Her hair was twisted into her usual bun, and she wore a corduroy dress and flat-heeled boots. She bid us a proper greeting and apologized for being late, citing her chickens had gotten loose. "Is Demeter awake?"

Her question reminded me that Lydia and Nana used to be friends—and that, according to Lydia, they had parted on not-so-good terms. "Probably. She claims the crack of dawn is her new alarm clock."

Taking a deep breath, Lydia nodded. "If need be, I'll go."

"Let's hope that isn't the case," I said, holding the door

open for Xerxadrea. Her warm, soft hand rounded my arm, obliging me to stay with her as we entered, but I managed to keep the door politely ajar for Lydia.

The rattling of dishes met our ears as we proceeded down the hall. The witches had gathered in the dining room around the big table, which seated six easily. After seeing Xerxadrea to a padded chair, I added the middle leaves to the table. With enlisted help, we moved the bench and two chairs from the dinette in the kitchen to fill in. The table would now seat ten—assuming Nana would join us.

To spare Nana's knees, I'd promised to have the dining room renovated into a downstairs bedroom and add a bath. However, if, as a member of the *lucusi* or as the Lustrata, I was going to have pow-wows around my table with any regularity, not having this space might be a problem. *Maybe I'll ask Xerxadrea to teach Nana that mist-magic thing.*

About that time, Nana, Beverley, and Ares came down from the second floor. Herding the Great Dane puppy out the front door to do his morning business, I stopped them there in the hall and asked, "I thought you two were going to sleep in today?" Last evening Beverley had been kidnapped by fairies. They had tried to kill her, but Menessos's quick action had saved her. To me, kidnapping and attempted murder were definitely grounds for a day off from school. "How about we call the office and say you have a tummy ache from eating too much candy? Then you can stay home."

"But I want to go." Beverley's smile was bright.

Before I could even try to dissuade her, Nana assured

me, "We talked about it upstairs." She was trying to see into the dining room; the chatter was drawing her attention.

"I won't say anything to anyone, Seph," Beverley chimed in. "I promise."

Beverley was dressed and ready. Insisting she skip school would sound ludicrous, so I let it go. Ares came back to the door. I let him in and held his collar so he didn't take off and knock little old witches from their chairs. "All right," I conceded to Beverley. "Take Ares to the garage and feed him so he doesn't bother our guests, please."

Because Beverly kept saying "kibble," the growing-into-a-behemoth animal allowed the child to guide him down the hall and past the strangers he unmistakably wanted to sniff.

Taking Nana to the dining room through the living room, I said, "Nana, perhaps you'll remember Xerxadrea?"

"It has been a long time, Demeter." They shared a polite word or two. Then, "If I may introduce the rest?"

"Please do." I remembered their names, but allowed the Eldrenne to continue the introductions because I wanted to gauge Nana's reaction to Lydia.

Xerxadrea indicated the high priestesses as members of her *lucusi,* then lastly said, "And this is Lydia Whitmore."

Until then, Nana had been consummately playing the crotchety old crone with a bit of elderly befuddlement, busily digging her cigarette case from her robe pocket, giving the effect of barely listening, fostered by half-hearted nods as each name was spoken.

But at Lydia's name, she stilled. Slowly, stiffly, Nana

turned. She squinted as if her eyes were going bad, but they weren't. This was her expression of contempt. It was usually reserved for the mention of nursing homes, bingo, and antismoking laws.

The painful silence wore on, as fragile as a soap bubble.

"Hello, Demeter."

Nana lifted a cigarette to her lips and lit it without taking her stern stare from the last-arriving guest. She took a drag and, from the corner of her firm-lined mouth, blew smoke at the ceiling. I was convinced that just then she could have chewed up tin cans and spit out nails.

"Lydia Whitmore," Nana whispered, not having removed the cigarette, "is speaking to me?" Her whisper was a lit fuse. A short one. "After fifty-six years?"

Lydia stood slowly. "I'll go."

Nana jerked the cigarette from her lips and gestured with it as she spoke. "Oh, no, Lydia, sit! Stay! Eat the food from my granddaughter's table." There was sarcasm and a threatening, seething rage in her gravelly voice. Nana shuffled into the kitchen, glaring at Lydia all the way.

A second later, I followed, speechless.

Because Beverley was standing at the counter eating, I didn't ask Nana the obvious. The kitchen was filled with the smells of breakfast, and Johnny was moving pancakes onto a platter. To the kid's delight, he flipped one through the air to land on her plate.

In minutes, all the food was ready and Johnny shoved a platter of scrambled eggs at me. He lifted the other serving dishes, piled with pancakes and sausage links, and headed to the table with a nod for me to follow. As he placed them before the wowed assemblage of witches, he swiped a hotcake from the top and rolled it around a link. "I'm going to run Beverley to school." He bit into the food even as he left the room. "I'll be right back," he added from the hallway, just before the two of them went out.

"Thank you," I called, glancing at the clock. It was eight-twenty-five already. The sunrise was so late in the fall!

He'd gotten me out of the kitchen and back to my guests, but I was a hopeless hostess. I didn't know what to say or do. *Apologize to Lydia? Apologize to Nana?* Around me, the women were filling their plates and digging in. They weren't waiting for me to fix something; I hadn't done anything wrong. "Sit down, Persephone. Eat with us," Vilna-Daluca said.

I sat. I heard the engine of Nana's LeSabre cough and rev. *I should be taking Beverley to school.* Already, this was upsetting our routine. While I was sure Johnny had made Beverley a lunch, I doubted he had included one of the sticky-notes from the joke book in the cupboard. *She's my responsibility.*

"Is it even safe?" My voice was soft, but it was enough that the movement and chatter around the table ceased.

"Is what safe?" Vilna-Daluca asked.

"For Beverley to go to school today? After all she's been through, losing her mother and with what happened last night. Maybe she should stay home."

"She has the necklace on," Nana answered from the kitchen. "The fey cannot touch her."

I twisted in my chair to see her. "But should she go? Did she sleep? Is she—"

"I spoke with her," Nana reassured me again.

I left the table. My stomach couldn't tolerate food right now anyway. Drawn to the kitchen where I could be almost alone, I opened up the joke book. The sticky-notes had joke questions on the front, answers on the back. I should have remembered before they'd gone out the door. Such a small detail, but it had become clear these meant something to Beverley. She read the joke to the other kids at the lunch table. It was winning her friends.

"My life is getting in the way of her life being *normal*." It was never my intention to see how much this child could be expected to tolerate, but damn, she seemed to be taking it in stride better than I was. *Maybe I'm not good enough to be a parent.*

"Persephone." Nana's voice was soft.

Stuffing my despondency deep down and plastering on an "I'm okay" expression, I grabbed the carafe because it was the only thing within reach. "Coffee?"

She snorted and said, "Sure," then came and leaned on the counter beside me. I poured two cups, and neither of them was my favorite Lady of Shalott mug. We drank in silence, side by side, listening to the chatter that had picked up again in the next room.

Before I'd finished the coffee, Johnny returned. He entered by the front door, passed through the living room and dining room, checking on the gathered witches and inquiring if they'd had enough to eat. They claimed they had and complimented him on his culinary skills. Someone remarked, "Your pancakes are as fluffy as a cloud."

"Well, you would know," he replied, "flying around on brooms like you do."

He came into the kitchen and, seeing Nana and me, wagged the empty platters and whispered, "They didn't leave a crumb," before stacking them in the sink. "I thought only wæres and teenage boys had claim to the appetite crown, but damn, those seven little old ladies can chow down!"

"There's still coffee." I lifted the carafe again.

He took it and poured himself a cup. Derisively, he asked, "So what are we going to do about the corpse in your cellar?"

"Corpse?" Nana echoed, voice hollow.

"He means Menessos."

"He's *here*?"

"Yes." The chatter in the other room had stopped.

Xerxadrea appeared in the doorway. "You must make Menessos tell you the truth."

"Finally!" Johnny exclaimed.

"Huh?" I asked.

"I'm not the only one who thinks Menessos is a liar." Johnny grinned over the edge of his mug.

"Do not add implications to my words, young man," Xerxadrea snapped. "I insinuated nothing of the sort." Though her patriotic velour jog suit was quirky, her formidability was undeniable. "Menessos is many things," she went on, her voice firm but without the condemnation. "He embodies things you fear, things you envy, and things you cannot comprehend, but he is not a liar." Before Johnny could protest, she raised a hand and added, "Oh, you can argue he twists facts to suit himself, but what he truly does is so much more than *that*. He can instantly take all the information he's acquired and accurately discern which words—and what order—will produce the best advantage for his purposes."

"My bad," Johnny muttered. "He's not a liar, he's a manipulating ass."

Again, I couldn't intervene because Xerxadrea was quicker.

"Omitting the unaccommodating words doesn't make him a liar or an ass. It makes him a *master*." She pointed at Johnny. "Perhaps you would learn a few things if you would but try to see beyond your own conflict, and see his."

Johnny's silence couldn't disguise the fact that he resented her scolding. It was conveyed in his raised chin and rigid spine.

Xerxadrea continued. "His perception has been transformed by eons of blood. He has worn the fabric of this world for so long it's threadbare and holds no mysteries for him now. He has mastered the patterns. Whatever moment in time you're bitterly clinging to and trying to alter . . . it's merely a thread to him. He can sever it as easily as he can fray it into a hellish and frantic existence for you. Or he can reweave that thread, making those seconds produce an outcome to fit the necessary and inevitable truth he uniquely sees, and it is *that* truth of which I spoke."

She gestured to me, and held out her arm.

"Take me to him, Persephone. We must speak with him privately, you and I."

CHAPTER THREE

Being that she was an Eldrenne, I didn't argue with her or point out that talking with a vampire during the day should be impossible. She'd have a way around it or she wouldn't have suggested it. So, though I shared a glance with Johnny, I simply obeyed. As I led Xerxadrea carefully off my porch, Ruya cawed softly. Xerxadrea whispered back something I couldn't understand.

"He's locked himself in down there, Xerxadrea."

"I can tend to that."

So could I, but she was the one wanting in, so I'd let her do the unlocking.

At the cellar door, we halted. While the clouds overhead warned a cold rain could fall any second, I could feel his presence like a warm summer sun kissing the skin of my chest.

Xerxadrea's strange eyes shut and her hand rose before her, gnarled old fingers quavering as she mimed feeling along the underside of the door. Her face pinched up, and she whispered a single, sharp word. I felt a snap of ley power just as she sliced through the air like a sideways karate chop.

She nodded at me. "Now."

I threw open the newly unbarred door then reached for her arm, but she had mist drifting around her ankles. I held back while she glided down the precarious steps. I followed, seeing the strange vapor dissipating when her feet safely met the cellar floor. *Nana definitely needs to know that trick.*

I jerked the pull chain on the overhead bulb. Menessos had lain in the spare cage to die. He was utterly still.

Xerxadrea approached him, pausing at the open door. I watched, guessing she would tap the ley line to somehow make the vampire awaken in the day.

"You found her," Xerxadrea said grouchily.

Menessos sat up. "And before you did." He stood, brushing straw from his tailored suit.

I was shocked. My senses had not detected her tapping the line at all. I hadn't heard her whisper magic words or anything else. Maybe she'd multitasked when opening the door.

"She'll give me the hanky back and I'll transfer Ruya to you."

He exited the kennel and placed his hands lightly upon her frail shoulders. "That bet was made decades ago! I demand no payment. You need Ruya now." He tenderly stroked her white hair and part of her long braid. "I named her as the prize only to hurt you, then. And now I have no interest in hurting you."

"Your wounds have healed better than mine," she whispered.

"Which is why there is no need to hurt you now. I am . . . *sorry,* Xerxadrea."

They had a bet about finding the Lustrata? And the hanky was a means for him to collect his winning? "You outed me as the Lustrata to her during the Eximium?"

Xerxadrea spoke over her shoulder. "I didn't know which contestant it was. At first." A thought seemed to occur to her. "I told you he fancied me once, as he fancies you."

I'd thought she had been implying they were lovers or that he'd wanted her for his court witch. I'd mistakenly believed her lofty position in WEC signified her resistance to him. That wasn't what she'd meant at all. "He thought *you* were the Lustrata."

"Long ago," he said, caressing her wrinkled cheek.

"Better you than me, Persephone." She turned back to Menessos. "I wagered and I lost. Promise you will be good to Ruya."

"I burned the hanky, Xerx."

"Why?" she demanded.

"I didn't want to risk the fairies claiming it."

Xerxadrea pulled away from him. "That was an accident." For the first time since I'd met her, she sounded as old as she truly was.

"I know." His tone was gentle, blameless.

Xerxadrea made no reply.

Into the silence that had enveloped us, I asked, "How did those fairies come to be bound to you?"

"It is a very long story."

"I'm patient." That was a lie, but he was going to tell me, one way or another.

"Do you know the story of the curses in the Codex?"

"Yes. Una was a priestess who had two lovers. Some

new guy came to town telling of another god, fell in love with her, then cursed the three of them when she wouldn't have him."

"There's much more to it that was not in the Codex. Una and her lovers sought a way to break their curse," he said. "With their magic, they searched—" He stopped, obviously looking for the right words to explain something I probably wasn't going to understand anyway. "They searched various astral planes and eventually discovered the fey race. The fey were seeking a new world to inhabit."

"Why?"

"The fey had made some bad decisions in their own world and were trying to correct them." He waved it off like a minor detail.

"Don't be vague, Menessos. I have a war to stop. What bad decisions did they make?"

"Truly, it does not matter." The vampire began to pace. "Una and her lovers agreed to let the fairy-kind into this world—but, in return, they wanted their curse broken. The fey did not know how to take the curse off, but promised to teach the trio higher magic, sorcery. As part of the bargain, the fairies also agreed to protect their magic rites. The four fey royals were bound to Una and her lovers personally—the most powerful protecting the most powerful—until such time as they discovered a way to break the curse."

That ancient "curse" had actually resulted in a pair of highly infectious viruses—vampire and wærewolf. The science stole the story's mystical flavor. I said, "And there is no cure so . . ."

"The irony of it all," Menessos said, continuing with the story, "is that Una and her lovers also had a secret. It was unbeknownst even to them. They were not aware of the full extent of their curses; they only came to know as the years passed. You see, the fey believed their binding to the three would end when the mortals died . . . but one of them was no longer mortal."

"The vampire," I said.

The elusive explanation hit me. The question that had surrounded him since we'd met, was answered. I gaped blankly at him, thunderstruck.

Menessos was able to perform sorcery. He didn't stink like other vampires. Xerxadrea hadn't used the ley to rouse him when he should be "dead" while the sun was up.

"You." I breathed the word more than said it.

His foot scraped along the cement floor as he shifted his stance, but he said nothing.

"You were *there*? You let them in, you—" I could hardly breathe, and my heart was pounding in my chest. "You were the first! And you never . . . never died."

Menessos was still *alive*.

CHAPTER FOUR

"Thousands and thousands have given their lives to share my curse with me, but none among them know what the two of you now know," Menessos said.

It was incomprehensible. Almost. Xerxadrea had said he'd worn the fabric of this world until it was threadbare. She'd said eons. I hadn't taken it literally.

"The fairies who were bound to me are their royalty, Persephone. They have sought to break their ties to me as eagerly as I once sought to break my curse. When the witches agreed to use elementals as their magical protectors instead with the Concordat of Munus forty years ago I vowed not to call on them myself. The Concordat had no bearing on me but my promise was a gesture . . . It helped keep peace." Menessos looked at Xerxadrea. Something unspoken passed between them.

Peace. Balance. What I—as the Lustrata—was supposed to bring. One way or another my role was to act as the catalyst through which humans, witches, wæres, and vampires would learn to accept each other and coexist in peace. Not that anyone had told me specifically how I was supposed to do this.

Destiny sucks.

Menessos turned to me. "I kept my vow, Persephone, until the night I joined your magic circle to save your friend Theodora. They would have sensed my use of sorcery. They mistakenly assumed it meant I would start calling them again. Now they will stop at nothing to break their binding to me."

"So you're confirming our suspicions that these fairy royals are devious geniuses. They did all this—invading witch turf, kidnapping Beverley, trying to steal the handkerchief—in order to involve the witches. Why?"

"To get them to hand me over. If the witches don't comply, the fairies will start a war."

"Why would they need the hanky, too? I mean, the other actions were enough to ensure their warmongering."

"If they couldn't succeed through their outwardly manipulative ways, then"—Menessos spread his arms then let them fall—"with enough of my blood, they could try to succeed through covertly manipulative ways."

Xerxadrea cocked her head oddly. "Or perhaps it was simply opportunity. The hanky . . . the fairy attacked me searching for it."

"True," I said. I'd witnessed it.

"Oh my. He didn't attack me and accidentally find something he could take advantage of. He was actively hunting for that hanky. He knew it existed."

My breath caught.

The fairies shouldn't have even known.

"How?" Menessos demanded, voice tight with rage.

"Someone at the Eximium must have told the fairies," she said. "Among the contestants or Elders, there is someone in contact with them, someone we can no longer trust." She made a fist. "We need to find out who. We cannot afford an inside menace."

"Xerxadrea, we weren't to speak of the details of the Eximium. Blood was taken from each contestant to seal the spell. That can be used to find out who is talking about it."

"That I will do." Xerxadrea's mouth formed a thin, hard line.

"I will have Goliath investigate, as well," Menessos interjected. "He will find out who has betrayed us and silence them permanently."

"Hold on, Menessos," I said. "Let the witches handle this. They have the means to do so through the blood seals. Goliath doesn't." Goliath Kline was, among other things, Menessos's second in command and head of security.

"She is correct, Menessos," Xerxadrea said. "Moreover, with the bloody cloth gone, *that* threat to you is destroyed. The threat remaining within our ranks is to Persephone . . . and to those she must protect."

Beverley. Nana.

Menessos tilted his head and raised one walnut-hued brow. "If the threat to her is in your ranks, perhaps she'd be better off in mine."

Xerxadrea considered it for a moment and then started nodding her head. "Now there's an idea."

Uneasy, I looked first at one then the other. "What?"

"Erus Veneficus," Menessos said.

I knew "Erus Veneficus" meant "Master's Witch."

Some witches became servants of vampires, but doing so didn't go over well with WEC because their loyalties were indisputably divided.

"Yes," Xerxadrea repeated. "It would force the council to cut her off." That sounded like a very bad thing to me. "And it would reinforce the idea that you are the master, not her."

Menessos shot me a surprised look.

"Yeah, I told her." Then I asked Xerxadrea, "Why is it important to reinforce that?"

Though I asked Xerxadrea, Menessos answered. "If we show the world that you serve me, and make even the fairies believe it, they will think I commanded you to kill Cerebrosus and blame me."

"Okay. Not that I'm not grateful to have them pointing their little fingers at you instead of me, but what difference does that make?"

"To kill any fairy royalty is punishable by torture and death."

"Torture and death?" *Cerebrosus was bound to Menessos. He was a royal. I killed him!* "Oh, hell." My gut went so cold.

"Exactly."

"Going after you, Persephone, doesn't give them what they truly want, but they've already used you once to put WEC in the middle," Xerxadrea said. "If we use you, too, then the negotiations will go much easier for the witches."

"How so?" I didn't like being used once, let alone willingly signing up for a second go-round.

"What they want is me, truly dead, in order to release them from their bonds," Menessos said. "They'll jump on the chance to demand that WEC turn me over to them."

"And WEC can pressure her to deliver you in order to gain the council's favor as the Lustrata." Xerxadrea's expression was delighted. "This will work."

"Hold on," I said to the Eldrenne. "I'm *not* going to deliver Menessos to fairies who will kill him!" I turned to the vampire. "Hell, Menessos, just let them loose. Sever the binding and let all this be done!"

"If it were that simple, I would have done so already."

I'd had the option to be unbound from Menessos— and chose not to be. Fear rose up like a hand around my throat. The words croaked out, "Why isn't it that simple?"

"They are bound in my *life,* Persephone."

As I began to feel that there was no way out of this, my panic exploded. "My life was bound to you, initially. Just do what I did—"

"Persephone!" His soft voice calmed me. "You clung to who you are, Persephone. You couldn't pay that price," Menessos said. "What makes you think I *can*?"

The hammer of realization finally hit. Inverting the binding would simply mean the fairies would sever it by killing Menessos. I was his master, but my ignorance showed just how unready I was to truly fill the role. I struggled to cage my fear and tuck it away somewhere deep.

Menessos gripped my arms, a soothing gesture, sincere and innocent, but my shields were down. At his touch my body resonated and filled with warmth as if syrupy sunshine were pouring into my bones. My soul answered: *mine.*

"Their deaths would sever—" I didn't finish the sentence as I realized what that meant. "Aquula." Menessos nodded solemnly. The mermaid fairy had acted to aid me and she was in love with Menessos. I couldn't kill her; I couldn't ask someone else to. Even to keep Menessos alive. My teeth clenched.

"Persephone."

"No," I said, resolute. I drew Menessos into my arms wishing I could protect him as easily. "I cannot let them take you from me."

Menessos savored my embrace triumphantly. I felt as if some piece of me that I'd become accustomed to having absent had just been replaced. We fit together so comfortably—

"I am flattered you are so eager to protect me," he whispered.

Xerxadrea, who'd been quiet for the last few minutes, interrupted. "Come, Persephone. It is time we went above."

Menessos slipped out of my arms and returned to the kennel, to resume pretending he was dead. Or maybe it was true sleep he sought. He'd been up all night. This was the schedule he normally kept.

With the cellar door shut, I led Xerxadrea around the house. She whispered, "We have to make a good show of this for my *lucusi*. I trust you understand your part."

"I do."

"He must make you his Erus Veneficus as soon as possible. You must leave this place to convince the fey." She was speaking and moving hurriedly, as if in an angry huff. "And tell him he must contact the media and have them cover it."

"Why make it public?"

"It gives us cause to publicly separate ourselves from you." We started up the porch steps. "Using the media always makes things more convincing." With a flick of her wrist she sent both of my doors slamming open. "You are henceforth ostracized!" she shouted, and pulled away from me as she entered the house. "Witches! We are leaving."

The chatter in the house ceased. Johnny's footsteps sounded in the hall. Nana was on his heels.

"Everyone must sever their ties to you now, Persephone," Xerxadrea said irritably. "Everyone!"

"But she's the Lustrata!" Johnny countered, coming to my aid.

"Perhaps," Xerxadrea snorted. "But no witch of such lofty acclaim would sully herself as an Erus Veneficus!"

She fixed her filmy eyes on me; I shivered and could not speak, even to make a show of defending myself.

"That vampire has a hold on you, a grip crushing tight! I believe you can fight free of it. Because of that, I will hold the Council back for as long as I can to give you time to make that fight. They normally put an EV under the Faded Shroud, but with you claiming to be the Lustrata they will not be easily pacified. My guess is they will call for you to be Bindspoken, child."

The *lucusi* were filing out between us, reclaiming their brooms and stepping off the porch.

"Of course, once Menessos is destroyed," Xerxadrea added, "there will be redemption."

"You're afraid, aren't you, sorceress?" Nana's defiant, don't-argue-with-me tone made everyone take notice. "And I know why. Facing the fey—the very creators of your beloved sorcery—you're sure to lose. That would be too humbling for the likes of you."

For an instant Xerxadrea smiled; then the smile faded and she didn't back down. "This must be, Demeter. And well your eyes know it. Even you will separate yourself from her before this is over."

"If your skills aren't good enough to keep you from running away at the first sign of difficulty, you're not worthy to stand in the presence of the Lustrata, let alone stand in her home and partake of her hospitality." Nana waved her arms as if shooing a bunch of clucking hens. "I'd make you retch up your breakfasts if it wouldn't make a mess. Out. *Out!*"

CHAPTER FIVE

Nana's rage was frightening, but as I sank onto the couch all I felt was numbness. Not only was I on the brink of a war, my best allies were cutting me off. I understood what was being done, and why, but still my stomach was twisting into knots that cut off all emotion.

"Pretty convincing, don't you think?" Nana was *beaming*. Smoke, left in the wake of Xerxadrea and company's departure, swirled around her head like a nimbus of doused anger-flames. "The highlight was seeing Lydia retreat. Oh, I've waited years to bust her ass with a dose of reckoning."

I squinted at her, confused. Seemed she knew what was going on. But how? "Are you scrying again?"

Before she could answer, Johnny interrupted. "Red, she said Menessos had a crushing hold on you." Johnny was more sober; he'd bought the act.

The protrepticus buzzed in my jeans pocket.

I'd forgotten all about it. A dead cell phone turned into a magical device powered by my aural energy, it connected only to Xerxadrea and her *lucusi* via a spirit who lived inside it. In life, the spirit had been Samson

D. Kline, the defunct Southern Baptist preacher and the brother of Menessos's next in command, Goliath Kline. As the ever-changing ring tone sang through the denim I recognized "Renegade" by Kansas.

Thunder rumbled in the distance and the rain began to fall. Taking the song and the rumbling sky as conclusive evidence I was about to get angry—Sam always pissed me off—I snapped the phone open. "What is it, Sam?"

"You played that perfect!" He laughed so hard that even on the little screen I could see his stomach flab jiggling like Jell-O under his light blue polyester suit.

"Played it?" Johnny joined me on the couch, leaning to see the screen.

Sam smoothed his bad Donald Trump comb-over and went on. "Xerxadrea is very pleased."

"Like we give a shit about whether or not she's happy!" Johnny spat. "After what she just did."

I put my hand on his arm. "She's cutting me off but it's not because of Menessos. It's to protect me. There's a possible inside threat."

"A possible inside threat?" Johnny repeated.

Nana's beam turned quizzical.

I explained what had happened in the cellar the night before, although I left out exactly what Johnny and I were doing when Menessos showed up. "The hanky Menessos burned represented a blood oath he had made to Xerxadrea at the Eximium. Someone who knew of that hanky told the fairies about it. That someone had to have been present at the Eximium. It could be a contestant, or it could be one of the Elders—two of them are in her *lucusi.* This 'mole' may intend to do more damage, so cutting me off from the group protects me from that possibility."

Samson loosened his tie even further. "It is not a 'possibility,' the danger is real. Everyone here will have to cut you off, too."

Nana's rage returned, but this time it was the real thing. One hand fisted and the other jabbed the air toward Sam. "You lyin' stripe-ed-ass snake!" She pronounced words with more syllables than they were supposed to have. Her declaration was ten times more hostile with a half-burned cigarette still dangling from her lips. "That is not true!"

Sam's fingers mimed the motion of making a puppet talk to mock her as she spoke. "They'll use your safety to compromise her!" He added in a quiet grumble, "You old biddy."

"Ha!" She jerked the stub from her mouth. "She knows better than to let worry for an old woman—whose life has been lived—keep her from her task."

No I don't. "Nana. I couldn't let them hurt you."

Johnny stood and paced. "They just put up new wards. And if the gestures mean what I think they mean, it's above and below as well as around. This place must be safe."

"It *is* safe," Sam agreed. "While you're here."

"I can stay put," Nana said.

With a self-satisfied smirk, Sam hooked his thumbs under his lapels and his fingers galloped on his chest. "But the kid has to go to school. Outside the wards. Five days a week."

That made the shoulders of both Nana and Johnny slump in defeat.

Home school, I thought. But I couldn't confine Beverley here. That seemed cruel. She deserved a normal life. Normal, for Beverley, meant public school.

I didn't want to be a vampire master's witch-at-court, and I *really* didn't want the crap that came with it, such as the risk of being Bindspoken. But even more than that, I didn't want my family to come to harm because of me. I set the phone on the table, still open, and stood. "I have to go away and be inducted as Menessos's Erus Veneficus."

Nana sank into the chair. "No."

"That's what the old witch said was all the trouble. Why would you go ahead and do whatever that is?" Johnny asked.

"It means she'd be the witch at the beck and call of the vampire, before all his court," Sam answered.

Johnny shook his head. "No way."

"Johnny."

"She said his grip was crushingly tight on you! He's reeling you in more! Can't you see that?"

My nails raked through my hair. I needed to tell him the truth *now*. But not in front of Nana and Sam.

"She *will* be safe there, in his house," Samson said.

"Safe? Surrounded by bloodsuckers?"

"Safe from the fairies," Sam clarified.

Johnny exuded defiance. "How is it safer there than here with the wards?"

"The vampire's house is surrounded by asphalt and is made of iron. Two things the fairies can't tolerate. Here, twenty acres of rural farmland. Fairy heaven."

Their conversation was fast enough it kept me from interrupting. Johnny ended it by snatching the phone and smacking it closed. I think he wanted to throw it across the room, but he knew it couldn't get too far from me. He handed it to me almost reluctantly.

"It'll have to be a public ceremony," I said to Nana.

"Oh, my god," Johnny cut in. "He does have a hold on you!"

"He does not! She said that to make the rest of what she said convincing. If you'll let me explain it to you—"

Nana interrupted, "A public ceremony is dangerous, Seph."

My head was reeling.

"Sam just said she'd be safe there. Do you mean she's not?" I could count on Johnny to jump on any angle that might keep me from Menessos.

Nana answered, "Not all the Lustrata's enemies are fey."

"Maybe we can use this," I said, "to draw those enemies out." I bit my lip, considering. "But Nana, as soon as we make the announcement, you have to go to the press and make it public that you're renouncing me over it."

Before she could protest, Johnny did. "No one will care about that! What grandmother wouldn't renounce her granddaughter when she becomes the Erus-thingy-witch of a vampire?"

"If the fairies believe we've had a falling-out," I said, "they'll be less inclined to try any repeat kidnappings."

Nana snorted and crushed the filter into the ashtray. "The fairies won't believe, 'Oh, I'm so disappointed in her, I never want to see her again.' It's too simple."

A lump rose in my throat trying to keep me from saying what had to come next. I swallowed down. "They'll believe it if you out me to the media." That silenced them both. "The true identity of the Lustrata, to those in the know, will be revealed."

"You didn't want that," Nana said.

"Which is why it'll work."

"No." Nana shook her head. "You're not just saying, 'Hey, here's your chance!' to Menessos's enemies and human opposition in general. You're telling the Lustrata's enemies where to find you and opening the doors."

"But it's shutting the doors on you and Beverley becoming leverage used to get at me."

"That's *too* dangerous, Red." Johnny's voice was tight. "That could get you killed."

"Exactly. It's not information Nana would give lightly. It should be proof enough that we are truly through with each other. She's practically inviting someone to kill me."

She smacked the arm of the chair. "I won't do it!"

"Nana, you have to." *Goddess, I hope I know what I'm doing.* "It's the only way to buy your safety and Beverley's."

"Buying our lives with yours is too high a price." Nana sank back into the cushiony chair. "Going public is the last thing you wanted," she croaked softly. "Now you're giving it up to make yourself a target."

Her tone left me squeezing back sudden burning tears. "I'm the one taking action, it should be my risk. Not yours. I'll give it up gladly because that's better than you or Beverley getting hurt." My voice had gotten husky. "The advantage of making myself the target is *knowing* I'm the target. Believe me, I'll be taking down names."

Johnny crossed his arms. "I won't cut you off. I won't abandon you. I have no ties for them to exploit."

I had to be honest. "Your career with the band could be ruined."

He paused, but just for a second. "I don't care. That Tarot reading Demeter did weeks ago said I'd have to sacrifice something in order to gain something else of greater value." He gripped my arms as Menessos had done in the cellar. "I pick you."

His gesture, too, was sincere, and I felt protected *by* him, not protective *of* him. I expected the Domn Lup to ably protect himself as well as me.

"How can you be sure about this?" Johnny squeezed just a little more.

"The witches have absolutely no presence in Menessos's haven." I slid the protrepticus into my pocket. "So whether it was an Elder or a contestant, they're cut off from me and that will keep me from being an easy target."

"Red, the witches don't worry me."

"They should. Many of them fear the Lustrata will make things worse for witches. They'll work hard to stop that from happening. Someone has already taken action, sharing info with the fairies. When I'm inducted into the vampire's court, that's a ceremony they have no cause to want to see. If any of them show up, we'll know something is awry."

"Yeah, I know you can handle that. But the vamp will have all the time in the world to manipulate you. Can't you be safe without having *another* tie to him?"

"Johnny, please trust me, he does not have a hold on me." I tried to let him see in my expression how valid that statement was. "This is a minimal tie, considering. And I have to talk to you about the stain. It's different than you think it is." The fewer people who knew it was a hex, the better. "Perhaps upstairs?"

He brightened considerably. "Alone in your bedroom?" He leaned down for a kiss.

"Sheesh." Nana stood and shuffled off to the kitchen with her ashtray.

Johnny's lips were soft, but he hadn't shaved this morning. The stubble was rough on my skin in a good way. My fingers trailed over his cheeks. When the kiss ended, he said, "I am your protector. Where you go, I go."

"You'd follow me to Menessos's court?"

"I'd follow you into hell, Persephone."

My thoughts ran to Nana's Tarot reading he'd mentioned. Hermes was the Magician on the last card, the final outcome. The Magician was an inner guide that sometimes directs one to perilous and wearisome places, but only to point out the potential one has.

"Havens probably have rules like covens and dens do. No matter what, we'll find a way for you to be there. My acceptance of the title will be subject to your acceptance there, too." In one version of the mythology, it was Hermes who rescued Persephone from the underworld where she was the prisoner of Hades. Maybe Johnny would be the one to get me out.

"Actually," came Menessos's voice from the hallway. "The Erus Veneficus is allowed a pet."

CHAPTER SIX

"How the hell—" Johnny sputtered. "Didn't that old witch tuck you in before she left?"

"As a matter of fact"—Menessos gave him a sly smile—"she did not."

"The sun's up!"

"But behind those thick rain clouds." Menessos wiped at his wet shoulders. As if on cue, lightning cracked like a whip and a boom of thunder echoed. The rain responded: the light sprinkle became a downpour.

"Fucking great," Johnny muttered.

He must have thought Menessos was making a display of his power. And boyfriends generally didn't like other guys showing off in front of their girls. *Yup. I used the B-word.*

"I will have my people make the announcement immediately." Menessos ran a hand over his rain-damp hair; the waves had tightened into curls. "I'll see to it they commence preparations immediately. May I use your phone? The battery seems to have died on my cell phone."

"In the kitchen." I pointed. He walked down the hall.

Johnny turned his back to the painting over the fireplace and crossed his arms.

"I won't let him reduce you to a pet," I said.

"There has to be a way around this. Living with him can't be the only solution." His jaw was set. "The wære aren't a part of this at all. You'd be safer with them, a neutral party. Besides, they owe you. You've kenneled anyone who ever needed it."

"Opening my cellar door to protect people on the outside isn't the same as asking the wære to shield me from the fey."

"She's right, Johnny," Nana said. She must have vacated the kitchen when the vampire entered. "Wærewolves have no investment in this. Staying out of it costs them nothing, while aiding her might cost them a great deal."

Johnny rolled his shoulders and let his arms straighten until his stance held less tension, but I saw it for what it was: a *pose*. "I could declare myself the Domn Lup."

It was not a suggestion he made carelessly, so I considered it. But my heart knew it wasn't the answer. "That would still only end with forcing them into a situation that would cost them." Before anything else interrupted my telling him what he needed to be told, I moved toward the stairs. "Come on. Help me pack."

My bed was still made from yesterday. The box the costume had arrived in still lay open on it. With a light shove, I pushed the box onto the pillows. I dug my suitcase from the closet and plopped it onto the bed, unzipping it open. The underwear from the dresser would go in first. *Mustn't forget clean undies.*

Johnny shut the bedroom door behind him. "You're really going to pack up and move in with the vamp, just like that?"

"You packed up to avoid having to drive Nana's LeSabre."

"Touché. But guess what I took the kid to the bus stop in?"

I tossed cotton panties into the suitcase and strolled up to Johnny. "Thank you for that." I curled one finger into the belt loop of his pants. "Let's be clear: moving 'in with the vampire' and 'into the vampire's haven' aren't the same things. And, it's temporary." I tugged gently on the belt loop. "You are coming, right?"

"Nope."

I went wide-eyed.

"I mean, what you're fondling and tugging on is only my belt loop and that's not nearly sensitive enough to make me—"

"Johnny. You know what I meant."

He grinned. "Of course I'm coming with you."

To continue the double entendres, I added, "I don't mind coming first."

"Oooo, nice one."

"Score," I said. "One to one."

He pretended to chalk our points onto an air score-board. "Let the innuendo wars begin."

"Bring it on."

His arms encircled me and he whispered in my ear, "I'll always put your needs first."

I would've relished his embrace, but— "Hey" I said, shying out of the hug while letting my hands linger at his waist, "I need to tell you something. I've been neglecting telling you because the fewer people who know, the better. This is the first time I've had a chance to tell you. I can trust you to keep a secret, right?"

He straightened defensively. "Is there any reason to think you can't?"

"You did steal and replace a certain magic stake, a decision that led to Sam's death and Nana and Beverley's abduction."

Duly reprimanded, he relaxed his posture again. "It seemed like the right thing to do and for the right reason, Red. I had nothing to do with what Sam chose to do."

It was a valid point. "No matter what, you can't reveal this. Ever. Even if it seems like the right thing to do."

"Okay."

"Swear it."

Johnny snorted. "I haven't heard it yet."

"*Swear* it."

"Fine. I swear I won't ever reveal the secret you're about to tell me. Unless it has something to do with Jimmy Hoffa's disappearance, Jim Morrison's death, or events on the infamous grassy knoll."

That was probably as good an oath as I'd ever get. "Do you remember when I told you that I'd figured out my troublesome issue with the stain?"

"Yup. You told me not to 'let any stab of jealousy wound me.'" He semisang the words I'd used. I poked him in the ribs. "What? I used it in some lyrics."

I should have known. I squeezed his waist with my fingers. He was so solid and firm muscled. I regretted Menessos's interrupting us last night. "When I took

Vivian's stake into my hands . . ." I considered telling him the whole of it, but I'd put off these words too long already. *Short version.* "I flipped the binding. I didn't know it at first, but it's become very clear. Menessos isn't my master. I'm his."

Johnny blinked at me as that sank in. "You mean—"

"Yeah," I said when he didn't go on. "I'm not stained, so I'm not going to be manipulated by him. He's hexed. I have power over him."

Johnny launched into laughter. "Then there's no need for you to become that tiara-wearing heiress-thing."

"E-R-U-S. Air-oose. And, actually, there is. We have to keep everyone else thinking that he's the master."

"Why?"

"The fairies will want to hold him responsible for my actions anyway. If he's the master, he's responsible for my actions. It serves the purpose. And it's my charge to keep things in balance, including the vampire balance. He's perceived as a very powerful master. If he's outmastered . . . you see all the trouble that would follow?"

"Sure, but why should we care if his cronies know you're even more powerful than he is? That benefits you."

"Lower vampires with a desire to move up might challenge him. It could cause an unending parade of challenges—"

"So?"

"So that wouldn't help the balance."

"Pendulum's gotta swing, Red. Things may be better when the smoke of charred vamp bodies clears."

I ignored the jibe. "Still, I'm his master, Johnny. I'm responsible for his safety, like I am for Beverley's."

"Uh-uh," he said firmly. "Not 'like' Beverley's. She's a kid. He's a master vamp. He can take care of himself."

"The fey are going to try to kill him. I can't sit idly by and let that happen. I can do something about it. I'm the Lustrata, I'm supposed to do something about it."

"You do the right thing, for the right reason." He pulled me close again. "That's my girl." He stroked my hair and we just held each other. "Who else knows you're the boss?"

Downstairs, through my thin floor, I heard the phone ring.

"Menessos knows, of course. Xerxadrea. You." My totem animal Amenemhab also knew it, but he was my counsel and no one else's. He didn't need to be on the list. "I know this sucks. I just can't risk Beverley having to suffer because I wouldn't step up to the plate."

"And what if it's you that she needs here, not Demeter?"

What am *I going to say to her?*

"Persephone!" Nana called.

Johnny released me and I opened the bedroom door. "Yes?"

"Telephone."

"Take a message."

"I tried. He insisted there was little time."

I went out and down the stairs. "Who is it?"

Nana shrugged. "Dunno. But the walking corpse went back to the cellar," she said as I passed her. *Good.*

In the kitchen I lifted the receiver to my ear wondering where my cordless was hiding. Probably between couch cushions. "Hello?"

"Is everything all right?" It was Jimmy Martin, editor for my "Wære Are You" column.

"Yeah, why?"

"It's Wednesday, your column is due, and I didn't get it yesterday like usual."

Oh, hell. On top of all my other worries, I still have a job. "Just polishing it up right now, Jimmy. It'll be in your in-box in less than an hour, okay? I promise."

I spent the next hour furiously scolding myself for forgetting about it and putting my notes together into a readable column. The only reason I got it done at all was because I was doing a series on wære parenting and this was part three. A premise and supporting notes were already compiled. Still, it was far from my best work.

It was just after four when the front door shut loudly, announcing Johnny had dropped Beverley off. He had to go work on guitars, some German order that came in, but he planned to be back at dusk to go with me and Menessos to Cleveland.

Beverley stopped at my bedroom door on her way to her own. Her book bag dragged behind her and the usual boisterous fourth-grader energy was absent. Everything about her was evidence of how tired she was. "Have a good day?"

"Yeah. I have some math to do."

"Give me a few minutes and I'll help, okay?" I was finishing up my packing.

"I don't need help, I know how to do it. Why are you packing?"

"I have to go away for a few days."

"Where are you going to go?"

"To Menessos's."

Sinking onto the edge of the bed, I patted the spot next to me so she'd come and sit with me. "Remember when we carved the pumpkins and had our safety talk about handling knives?"

"Yeah."

"What's rule number one?"

"Safety first."

"Right." Damn, this was hard. "See, the fairies are mad about one of them being killed—even if it was in self-defense. They're making threats. So, in order to keep that safety rule, I'm going away to make sure you and Nana are safe.

"Just a few days?"

"I hope."

Her fingers fidgeted, but she said nothing.

"Beverley?"

"What about my birthday? Will you be back for that?"

Shit, I'd forgotten! Her birthday was the ninth, so I had eight days. "I don't know how all of this is going to go, so I can't swear I will be here on your official tenth birthday, but I can promise I'll do everything possible to be here."

"Okay." She played with the zipper on my suitcase. She didn't seem convinced.

"What is it?" I prompted.

"Will we be safe here, without you?"

"Those witches put in new wards this morning, it is very safe here. But you still have to wear the necklace when you leave—"

"I won't forget that again."

I put my arm around her shoulder and squeezed to reassure her. "Then yes, you'll be safe."

Over the side of the bed, her feet swung and clunked together at the heels. "What about Johnny?"

"He's coming with me. And there's one more thing."

"What's that?"

"I remember how mad you got when Vivian said mean things about me, so I'm telling you now: as part of keeping you safe here, Nana is going to tell some newspeople that she's very mad at me. She'll probably say mean things like she never wants to see me again." I leaned in to whisper. "But secretly, everything's okay. She's pretending, so everyone will think she's mad. You have to pretend it, too, if anyone asks."

Beverley squinted. "Why?"

"I doubt anyone will pester you over this, but if anyone besides Nana talks to you about it, just say you're never talking to me again. If they pressure you, just say you don't want to talk about it. Can you do that?"

"Yeah."

"You won't bring it up or mention it to anyone?"

"Geez. No. I didn't talk about fairies today. Just like I said."

"Beverley, you are amazing." I hugged her again. "I'm going to miss you while I'm gone, kiddo."

She squeezed me tight. "You will be back, right?"

"Count on it. And I promise you this: when it's over, we are having the biggest party for you. Johnny will make the cake and we'll invite all your friends from school, okay?" I made a mental note: *weather permitting, find ponies for riding.*

• • •

Assessing my magical supplies and what I wanted to take with me, I decided the bloodstone would be an excellent choice. Good for increasing courage and for alleviating unnecessary fear, it was also a stone of power and victory. I lifted it into my palm. The vibration was a bit weak. I had a quartz crystal that was well charged. I picked it up with my left hand. Calling energy out of it, propelling it through me, wrapping it with my need for courage, I pushed it into my right palm and charged the bloodstone. Just as I finished, Nana walked in.

"I'm going down to fix dinner."

"Okay. You cook and Beverley and I will clean up. Deal?"

"Deal. Anything special you want?"

"Whatever" almost came out of my mouth, but I caught the shining in her eyes. She wanted to make me dinner. "Any of your colcannon left?" Nana had made her delicious, if not quite accurate, version of the mashed-potatoes-and-cabbage dish for Hallowe'en.

"Leftovers?"

"It's your specialty. I'd love to have that before I go."

She nodded.

"And Nana? Promise me you'll only make the most necessary trips on the stairs?" I'd taken her scrying crystal and hidden it in a shoebox in my closet, but that didn't heal the damage to her knees. Scrying always took a physical toll. "And promise me, no more scrying." The look I gave her said I knew she'd used alternate means to look into the future without the crystal.

"I promise."

She shuffled from the doorway. I added the bloodstone to the items I was packing, then retrieved the scrying crystal and packed it, too, shoebox and all. She was pushy enough she might rummage in my room while I was gone and find it. She could still scry with a glass bottle and blessed water, but I was praying she'd not be tempted.

Though mashed-potato dishes are on my list of comfort foods, my emotionally traumatized stomach couldn't handle much for dinner. Afterward, Beverley and I cleaned up the kitchen together. Then, as I brought down my broom and my suitcase packed with magic supplies as well as clothes, Beverley carried the toiletries bag for me.

The sun would be setting in about twenty minutes. We had a little time. "Packing's done. Homework's done. Should we play 'go fish'?"

"Sure! But you have to do the voices."

"What voices?"

"Johnny never says just 'go fish,' he says, 'Git yer pole 'n git down to that there yonder crick!'" She imitated his impression of a hick perfectly. Then she switched to British for, "Or, 'Blimey, old chap, you need to retrieve some fish from the market.'"

Twenty minutes later, we were giggling uncontrollably at ourselves when Johnny came in, leaving the big front door open. The screen door snapped shut but let a swirl of cool autumn air follow him. "Sounds like somebody's stealing my act." He came to hug me. "You get that math done?" he asked her.

"Yup."

They traded high fives.

"You ready?"

Before he could answer, Johnny's cell phone went off like an air-raid siren. He jerked it from his pocket. "Sh—oot." He changed his expletive for the child-safe version. Nana had once threatened to start a swear jar.

"What is it?"

"I completely forgot. The band is doing a radio interview tonight."

Though he'd earlier professed to be choosing me over the band, I wasn't about to insist that he do so. I was confident he'd juggle it expertly until the time came when he absolutely could not avoid it any longer. "What time?"

"Eight." He pushed buttons on the phone. "I can just make it." His expression was imploring. "I can't crap out on the guys. I set this up."

I wasn't exactly fond of the idea of going alone into the vampire's haven, but I wouldn't make things harder for him. I hoped he never had to "crap out on the guys." I nodded.

"That's okay, Johnny," Menessos's voice heralded from the doorway as the vampire strolled through. "You can join us later, whenever you're done." He flashed his delighted and pointy grin.

CHAPTER SEVEN

While Menessos gave the location of his haven to Johnny, I changed into my freshly washed copper Henley shirt and added my brown blazer. They dressed up the jeans a little. I had to admit, this kind of felt like I was meeting his family. I wanted to make a good impression, even though I knew the notion was ridiculous.

When I came downstairs, Johnny hugged me, planted a quick kiss on my cheek, and whispered, "This thing runs until ten. I'll get to you ASAP." Then his lips pressed mine. It might have grown into something lustier but Beverley giggled and we both broke it off.

I escorted him outside. The rain was gone, the sky clear, but it was cold.

Johnny pointed to the duffel bag on the porch. "That's my suitcase." It was pretty big, as duffel bags went.

"I'll take that with my stuff."

"Make your minion carry it for you."

"Johnny."

He affected innocence and shrugged. "It's heavy."

"*Riiight.*"

His lean arms encircled me with another hug and he

whispered, "You're the boss, Red. Don't be afraid to make him know it."

"I'm not." The hug ended too soon. "I'm not a fan of going in there alone, but I'm not afraid of it, either."

He tweaked my cheek. "That's my girl."

Like a good boyfriend, he left me with a toe-curling kiss that sent fireworks sparkling up and down my spine. "I'm sure we'll have our own room at the haven," I whispered. "There's some perks to our temporary relocation."

"How am I supposed to talk coherently about band shit while my brain is stalled on that promise?"

I tapped his temple lightly. "Duh. Think with *this* head in the studio." I added, "Innuendo point for me."

He chalked it onto the air scoreboard. "As soon as I get to you, though, the other one's taking over." He finished with a low and lusty growl in my ear.

When his motorcycle roared up the road, I went back inside. Nana leaned in the dining room doorway, smoking and giving Menessos the stink-eye. He appeared a bit sheepish. "What did I miss?"

Neither offered an answer.

Beverley spilled the beans. "He complimented her on her shirt."

"That's it?"

"She told him not to try any weirdo vampire crap."

"Oh." The moment went awkward. "Well. I hate long good-byes, so let's get this over with."

Nana put her cigarette in the ashtray and came forward, open armed. "It's the right thing for the right reason, Nana. It will all work out."

"I believe you." She patted my back.

"The contractors are supposed to come and give quotes about the remodeling. Their days and times are written on the calendar. And there are enough sticky-note jokes inside the book cover to last for three weeks . . . I don't think I'll be anywhere near that long, but just in case. Use them and it'll be kind of like I'm still here."

Nana backed away. My attention went to Beverley. Unenthusiastically, she came toward me. I crouched to receive her hug. "I'll be thinking about you, kiddo."

"I miss you already."

"Likewise." When this embrace ended, I held on to her arms, being as earnest and sincere as I ever was. "I will be back. And that party will happen."

The onset of her tears brought mine flooding up like the dam just broke. "I gotta go." I stood, hefted my bags, and left.

With everything tossed in the trunk of my Toyota Avalon, we climbed into the car. Menessos got in the back. Seeing my displeasure revealed in the rearview mirror, he innocently asked, "What?"

"I am not your chauffeur. Get up front."

"I'm sorry, Persephone. Habit." He settled into the passenger seat.

At the end of the drive, I flashed my lights at the pair of silhouettes on the porch waving. "To I-71, right?" My voice was thick, still fighting tears. *Damn it. Enough with the weepiness shit!*

"Yes." It soon became clear that Menessos only gave directions on an "as needed" basis—which also kept the car uncomfortably silent. His method, though not very satisfactory to my detail-seeking self, would still get us there.

I considered my present state. *This can't be hormones. My Depo-Provera shot isn't due until Yule.* The nurse, aware of the timing, had teased about it being my gift to myself. *This is just an outlet for stress. Don't think about it as leaving home. Talk about something, anything!* Shoving that emotion away, I asked, "Is there an Internet connection at the haven that I can access to do my column?" I'd packed my laptop.

"Yes. High-speed Wi-Fi. You are welcome to use my desktop if you'd care to."

About to insist that I didn't want to impose, I stopped myself. *Do masters worry over imposing upon a servant?* I wondered if strong emotions made one a terrible master.

"Thanks. I'm used to the laptop."

More silence.

"Tell me about your vampires," I asked.

"All vampires . . . *all* of them, everywhere, are mine. My curse has become theirs. And I mourn for them as equally as I delight in them. They are my children's children's children."

I took a breath in order to rephrase.

"Do not misunderstand," he went on, "I never created life in the womb of a woman. But I brought forth my kind with a relentless and undeniable seed. It brings death and rebirth into a new kind of life. And yet as I watch them, my offspring, so many of them waste the gift they have been given."

I felt like I should cue Bach's "Toccata and Fugue in D Minor" after that little speech. I tried again: "I meant the vampires at your new haven. What's it like?"

He sulked for a heartbeat or two. "Masters run their

havens like mini-kingdoms. Their word is law. Not all observe the *same* laws, however. In my private haven, none are allowed to spoil the gift they have received. You will find evidence of my dominance, but . . ."

"But?"

"I care for them. Genuinely. I believe most of them truly care for me."

It is *like meeting his family.* He didn't elaborate further, so I asked, "What are your laws?"

"My laws are based on respect for and compliance with my supreme authority." He twisted to face me. "I believe you are beginning to understand how the people around someone with power come to expect things of that someone. And not just trivial *things.* They expect protection, they seek their leader's favor. My laws are simple and firm, my rewards are quick and generous." With wry pleasure he added, "And I do enjoy being in charge."

That didn't surprise me at all. What did surprise me were his directions right to Public Square, the center of downtown Cleveland.

"I'm better acquainted with the history of Chicago and New York, but I am told that in the light of day you can still see the letters spelling out 'May Company' atop this building."

"Your haven is in an old department store?"

"Technically yes, but specifically no."

"What the hell does that mean?"

"The department store was ground level and several stories up. This particular building, interestingly enough, goes deep into the ground, more than you might expect. Do you know the local history?"

"Not really."

"Care to venture a guess at what is down there?"

"Subway tunnels?" *I don't want to live in tunnels and room with rats.*

"No. Beneath is a long-neglected theater, barely more than a ruin. We are, of course, modifying it to accommodate our needs. It would have been a shame to destroy a beautiful structure, so the terrible state of disrepair was truthfully an advantage to us."

"Aren't you being a little Anne Rice Theatre-of-the-Vampires . . . minus Paris, of course."

"Underground real estate is always hard to find. Especially in a big city on a lake. Our choices were limited."

"Right."

He directed me to pull over in front of the building, basically at the intersection of Euclid and Roadway, where a trio of men stood—men blatantly advertising they were the dangerous sort. My instinctive reaction was to drive the other way, fast, but Menessos got out and greeted them. They gave acquiescing nods, and I realized they were servants. More than that, they were vampires.

"You two, conduct the bags from the trunk to the appropriate rooms. You, park the car and return the keys to me."

I popped the trunk and got out. Before either of the vampires could reach inside the Avalon's back end, I removed my broom. "I'll take this myself." I quickly retreated.

Following Menessos, we approached what was basically a wall of particle board, with one rough-cut opening for a standard windowless steel door in ugly primer gray. KEEP OUT was spray-painted on the wall in bright colors and with graffiti artistic-style letters. Centered on the door was a circle of black, with the stylized fang symbol—six gleaming white teeth, the outer two were fangs. Like the universal symbols differentiating men's and women's bathrooms, this image indicated a vampire establishment. A governmental regulation meant to protect the innocent public, of course. It was a sign I knew to avoid, but I wasn't avoiding it this time.

I'm about to enter a real vampire haven.

I had expected the gray door would be locked, but Menessos reached for the knob and opened it with a turn.

Before Goliath and Menessos crossed my path, I considered the undead anathema, and *I* avoided them. I wasn't about to be converted by the new "Vampire Executives" campaign—which was trying to soften their image from demonic bloodsuckers to lawyer-type bloodsuckers.

What's funny is they see that as an improvement.

Both Menessos and his next in command had shown evidence they were above-average violent offenders. Yet, I had seen both offer kindness and tenderness as if they were still *people*. It was hard to believe.

And here I was going into Menessos's world, his haven. There would be *a lot* of vampires.

Like Krispy Kreme doughnuts at a Friday morning office meeting, I didn't stand a chance.

"After you, Persephone." He indicated for me to enter.

Had we been going into a normal public place, the "chivalry isn't dead" gesture would have been more appreciated. Not knowing what to imagine on the other side of this under-construction vampire domain, my steps were hesitant.

A single light, the only illumination, beckoned me away from the empty, echoing department store entry toward a separate structure to my left. As I neared, the structure was revealed as an old ticket booth. Through the filthy glass, I saw a metal-caged bulb dangling from a now-exposed beam in its ceiling. The eerie glow was enough to make out that the booth was faced with deep cherrywood paneling and ornate molding. A thick coating of dust obscured the details.

It wouldn't have surprised me to see a cobwebbed skeleton sitting inside that booth. The sound of distant pounding and power tools could easily have been mistaken for rattling chains and rapping spirits.

Menessos led me past the booth and through the dingy lobby behind it to a short hall where we passed a boarded-up elevator. We descended a wide stairway opposite the elevator. Occasional bare light bulbs screwed into once-elegant wall sconces provided minimal illumination. My fingers followed the wooden railing until I realized it was not only dirty but rotting and splintery, as well. Many of the iron spindles were missing.

The farther we went, the worse it became. *I might have to use my broom to clear the way.*

The stairs were covered in dust and debris, although the center portion was cleaner from obvious travel—and I could see why people were staying to the center. The walls were black with grime and mildew, the paint and paper peeling like diseased skin. It smelled moldy and musty, and underlying that was the damp odor of rusting metal. *This is what abandonment smells like.*

The staircase rounded down a quarter turn and a hallway stretched to either side. The ceiling here was as bad as the walls. The tiled floor was dirty, cracked, and broken—furthering the haunted-house atmosphere.

Menessos stopped and looked both ways thoughtfully.

"Are we waiting on ghostly traffic to stop so we can cross?"

The dim light caught the gray of his eyes, making crescent moons of them and the effect transfixed me. He said, "I am just trying to decide which way I should take you."

Accustomed to Johnny's innuendos, I found that his words had my mind flashing on various sexual positions. *Stop it. He's not Arthur.*

"This way." He led me to the left, past this level's boarded-up elevator, and down a longer flight of steps. It, too, curved and was dilapidated in disgusting ways. We emerged into a lobby. Three sets of double doors were spaced along the wall on the far side. The centermost pair stood open with enough light streaming through to illuminate a considerable number of mostly large boxes sitting in the lobby.

Beyond the door, amid the sounds of construction, a female voice shouted, "Damn it! They better be furred out in ten minutes!"

Menessos strode ahead of me toward the open doors, but I guardedly kept three steps behind him. It wasn't a full moon and if people were furring out—

As I peered around the door frame I saw a room covered in the expected layer of dust, but this was *new* dust from the renovation that was evidently in full swing here. The area was brightly lit with work lights. The shouting woman stood at a podium near the doors. She was slender and wore a turquoise tank top, black jeans, and work boots. Her black hair was woven into a waist-length braid. Her bare arms were lean but bore obvious muscle tone. Bracelets rounded each wrist.

In front of her, the theater "house" was a study in contrasts. Portions remained dilapidated, but just as much was fresh and new. All the seating in the orchestra level had been removed. Its gradual rake had been leveled and what appeared to be black marble was being installed as flooring. The stage—I could see right under it—was held up by a new framework. There were men under it, grunting and hammering and sweating.

Vampires working and sweating? I realized most of the workers' shirts actually did show signs of wetness under the armpits. *So these aren't vampires but Beholders. A lot of them.* My count topped twenty.

"Did you hear me? Where are those carpenters?" The female voice again.

"They went to get drinks," came a static-laden reply through a two-way radio on the podium.

The woman grabbed the handset. "Mark," she replied, no longer shouting. "I don't care if they take their break early, but they didn't check with me. I intend to stay ahead of schedule."

"They checked with me. I meant to tell you." He sounded apologetic.

After releasing an aggravated sigh toward the ceiling, she continued. "There's nothing elegant about cinderblock. I want it furred out and I expect to see the drywall hung by dawn."

"They'll get that done. It's this exterior wall I'm worried about."

They sounded like a married couple disagreeing about which work needed to be done on the house first. He wanted structural issues fixed; she wanted the aesthetics addressed.

"The bricklayers will be here tomorrow," the woman replied.

The man's voice came softer, saying, "If I had a dollar for every tomorrow . . ."

"Then you'd be funding this job."

Speaking of the guy paying for this, I located Menessos to the right of the doorway I still hadn't passed through. He was only a few feet into the room and no one seemed to have detected him yet.

The man said, "The pyramids couldn't have seemed as impossible as this, Seven."

Seven?

"The pyramid builders didn't have jackhammers or cranes. So I don't want to hear the word 'impossible' again."

Before she had a chance to speak again, Menessos softly said, "Seven."

The woman turned. "Menessos!" She approached him with open arms and he accepted her embrace. "I worried when you did not return last night."

"All is well," he said.

Not quite mollified, she looked him over to make sure. As she performed her inspection of him, I made an inspection of my own. Her dark hair was pulled back into a single long braid. Her eyes had bright blue irises that darkened at the outer edges. The coloring gave her eyes the impression of glowing. Paired with high cheekbones and perfect proportions, hers was a striking face—even at the thirty-something she was. In this environment it didn't surprise me that she wore little, if any, makeup. *Her lashes couldn't naturally be that lush and full, could they?* The bracelets with bright blue-green stones that matched her tank top, however, *did* seem odd for a work zone.

She's definitely a vampire. And from his words, the guy she was talking to, too.

She caressed Menessos's biceps. "I hope she's worth all the efforts these men are making. I'm dealing with enormous amounts of whining."

"I heard that," the man called from the ceiling opening.

She laughed; it had a melodic and playful quality. *Doesn't seem so dangerous. Maybe this* will *be okay.* My sassy smart-ass self had stood up to Menessos and Goliath as necessary. Perhaps that boldness would serve me well here. Even if I was horribly outnumbered.

Menessos maneuvered her hands into his and held them. "She is definitely worth it." He gestured to the doorway. "Let me introduce you."

"She's here? All I can smell tonight is wood dust and sealant!" She searched for and found me, half hidden behind the door frame. "You're not timid, are you?" she called with a laugh. It was said without aggression, but the question bore a challenge nonetheless.

That made my feet move. *Be bold.* Marching forward, I put on my most amiable smile. "No. Just cautious."

"Persephone, this is Seven."

"Interesting name," I said, and I extended my hand and shook hers with as much confidence and strength as she put into it. No limp-fish handshakes here. Cold, definitely, but firm.

"As is yours." Her hands went to rest on her hips.

She was clearly capable and had taken my usual pose. I gave her a brownie point or two for that. I decided to keep her talking about herself, if I could. "So you're in charge of the renovation?"

"I am." She seemed very pleased that I acknowledged her authority in the task. Unfortunately, she wasn't willing to give me any more details about herself. "Any special requests for your chambers?"

My chambers. I would be staying here, in the midst of this disaster area trying to be brought back to life. "Requests? From what I've seen so far, finished would be nice. And clean." *At least it's not tunnels and rats.*

Seven's reaction was enigmatic. "It's not finished, but you can give it the once-over. This way." She was petite, much shorter than I, but despite my longer stride, I had trouble keeping up with her as she walked through the house.

"You've done a massive amount of work already," I commented as I followed her up steps that led up to the left side of the stage. Menessos was right behind me.

"Yes, it's quite an undertaking, but not *impossible*." She smiled as she stressed the last word.

Crossing the brightly lit stage, Menessos gestured at an open framework slightly upstage. "I thought the screens were going up tonight?"

"They are. They're over there," Seven said, pointing at a row of boxes that, according to the labels, held large flat-screen display monitors. "The rest of the crew has gone to the Blood Culture. They should be back any minute."

The Blood Culture was a bar for vampires, and its owner, Heldridge, could've been the poster boy for the "Vampire Executive" PR campaign. I'd met him at the Eximuim and he definitely had the bloodsucking-lawyer-type persona.

As I understood it, the blood bars paid cash to donors. Around here, many of the donors were nurses and staff from the Cleveland Clinic and University Hospitals—who enjoyed the supplemental income. The bar then resold the blood like any other retail operation.

Seven guided us into the stage-right offstage wing and through a maze of stacked lumber, stage lights, and other material. She opened a door in a cinderblock wall that opened into a rectangular space. The far wall soared up two stories. Two doors pierced it. One at floor level, the other opened onto a small landing atop a flight of metal stairs.

"This area was used as the green room when they did live shows here." Seven indicated the space around us. The room was gray. Floor and walls. She started up the stairs to the upper door. We followed. "I know, it's not green. That's just the theatrical term for any room used by the performers as a sort of lounge area close to the stage.

"Here we are," she said from the landing. She tapped in numbers for the keyless electronic lock and opened the plain steel door, went in and hit the light switch.

The first thing I saw was a broad stone fireplace centered in the finished room. *Finished.* I almost cheered. Seven had said "not finished"; she'd meant "not furnished." The walls were solid, the ceiling and floor complete. I allowed a small sigh of relief to escape my lips. Seven could take it for appreciation.

The stacked stone rose up fifteen feet, like a giant support column. The bottom was open to the front and back. To the right of it, a black-granite-topped bar separated a small kitchen with stainless steel appliances and pale cabinetry from the rest of the space. The opposite side, except for a pair of dark mahogany tables and wrought-iron lamps, was empty. There were black-lacquered doors in the wall to my left, leading, I guessed, to a bathroom and a closet.

Small spotlights focused on a large empty steel security frame attached to the leathery brown, textured wall. A perfect location for Ariadne. Too perfect.

How long does he think I'm staying here?

The floor throughout was pale oak. Glossy black molding gleamed at the top and bottom of the walls. The ceiling was painted a soft wheat. I moved further into the room and noticed a circular portion of the ceiling behind the fireplace was recessed. Intrigued, I drew closer. After leaning my broom against the stone fireplace column, I discovered the interior was a dome painted like a night sky with wispy clouds.

Not a hovel at all. So much more than a hotel room. My "chambers" were a very comfortable apartment.

Beside me, Seven flipped another switch. Pinpoints of light began to glow in the dome "sky," little fiber optics twinkling like stars. "Wow."

"I was thinking this for the furniture," Seven said, offering me a design board she'd picked up off the kitchen bar. Pictures of furniture, swatches of fabric, and a pair of professional sketches suggesting layout were all fastened to the board. A large black four-poster bed would be placed under the dome, with sheer black curtains hung around it. Curtains of a heavy opaque fabric would hang from burnished brass rods running from the side walls to the centered stone stack of the fireplace, effectively dividing a sitting area with two chairs and a black leather sectional angled around an entertainment center. She'd accented the black and brown theme with blues that would rival her eyes for brightness.

"What do you think?" She leaned subtly into my personal space and inhaled deeply. She was trying to "taste" my mortal scent.

Determined not to be annoyed, I smiled and said, "I love it. Everything is so dark, but I know it will feel cozy." *Now if we could just move it to a building that wouldn't be crawling with vampires . . .*

"This area used to be six dressing rooms, a bathroom, and a hallway." She circled me, pointing. "I had it gutted and completely remade. These walls, the floor, and the ceiling have been reinforced with steel arcs, cinderblock, and concrete. No creature is coming in here, unless you open the door."

"And the fireplace flue?"

"Asphalt on the roof, iron grille at the exterior top. Any antifey wards between, you do yourself." She circled me like a shark, her slow, predatory vampire grace indicating a change I didn't like. "The door is the only way in or out of this room—it's set in a reinforced frame and is made of solid steel."

"We can post guards, if you would like, but I doubt it will be necessary," Menessos said. He'd held back, but now he moved in, intimately close. His nearness caressed my aura, but he hadn't evoked his usual heated response from me. "Everyone inside the building is loyal to me. Still, some may express jealousy for the attention you will receive."

His fingers wrapped loosely around my arm and his thumb pressed to the bend of my elbow, on the vein. He leaned close enough that his beard brushed my cheek.

Seven was watching with a level of intensity that made me even more uncomfortable.

Menessos nuzzled close to my ear, near the veins in my neck, and whispered, "With your living blood so warm . . . the interest is unavoidable, but no one would dare harm you, for none would risk my wrath."

His voice was like warm silk on my skin. Even without his metaphysical push toward desire, I was enticed. Still, he did not provoke that lust heat through my body. And he could have.

Meanwhile, Seven still circled.

It was this kind of shit that made me nervous to be in the company of vampires. So nervous, in fact, that the first idea that struck me made my mouth open. "Then why bother with guards?" I asked. "Nobody wants the boring duty of standing outside a door, right? Your people will think I'm weak and afraid."

"Aren't you?" Seven asked coolly.

Her glowing irises were neon bright, but I'd counseled myself to be bold. "Don't mistake my caution for fear. I am mortal, yes, but Menessos just said there's no reason to be afraid."

Seven's stalking ceased and she announced, "Your witch may survive after all."

"Not only is she brave and quick to assess others," Menessos replied as his hand trailed down my arm, "she is beautiful and powerful, as well." He threaded his fingers with mine. Finally, warmth rushed through me.

Seven must have sensed it and took it as a cue. She moved toward the door. "I hear the crew coming in. By your leave, Boss?"

"Of course."

I hadn't heard anything before, but as Seven left, laughter drifted through the open door as did the sound of many footfalls. When Seven shut the door, Menessos stroked my cheek, gently aligning my face with his. Our lips were so close. "You are so captivating."

He stared at me as if he could see all the way through me, to the burning desire in my very core . . . burning for him.

"Your very presence here soothes me and invigorates me. Your voice and your eyes are, to me, the bright reassurance that a summer day is to you." His thumb stroked my neck. "In your company I feel as if the world is warm and bountiful."

His words, offered like a bouquet of summer color, held the trembling timbre of a first date, as if each syllable were felt with such deep intensity, striving to mean *more*.

He kissed my cheek, so softly. "My world is more tender with you in it."

His words, a breath in my ear, gently urged my spark of desire to rise up and blaze white-hot.

CHAPTER EIGHT

No! I raged at myself. *Refuse his influence! Deny him the power to stoke these flames into more than I am willing to let them be.*

Our bond, I'd learned, afforded him a measure of automatic compassion from me, and it was difficult to suppress. This, however, was base instinct responding in knee-jerk reaction to his call. It was up to me to stay mentally alert to his manipulation. Not just to keep my head lest I panic as I had in the cellar, but I realized that if I gave in to the passion he kindled, my regret would be fierce.

I expect exclusivity from Johnny and I owe him nothing less.

The heat within me began to cool.

Features wilting with rejection, Menessos slipped his attention to the side. His fingers gently combed into the hair at my temple. The strands fell free of his touch. I shivered.

"The Beholders will continue to work in shifts throughout the day." He sauntered away from me. "My people will work around the clock. All will be completed in the hall in two days' time. We will have the ceremony Friday."

His matter-of-fact shift reminded me that, like it or not, I was going to be here for several days at the very least.

"May I take you to dinner? There are many fine restaurants in the vicinity."

"I ate with Nana and Beverley."

"A diminutive portion."

"What makes you think that?"

His lip twitched. "Think? I know this to be true. I am very attuned to your body."

Twenty minutes later, we were outside and I pointed to the restaurant next door—the upper half of an old, finned Cadillac sat atop an out-of-place attempt at a formal entry. A neon sign graced the lintel. "There?"

"Decidedly not."

"Not good?"

"I wouldn't know. But the manager emphatically communicated his dislike of our kind. I therefore forbid my people from visiting those premises. He will find his registers lacking for his misjudgment."

"Okay. Where, then?" I buttoned my blazer.

Waiting for him to answer, I took in the crisp lines of his suit. He'd changed out of the one he'd worn when he slept in the hay in my cellar. All of his suits were cut to complement him as only the best garments can, but tonight there was something especially masculine about him. He wore no tie and his linen shirt was neither tucked nor fully buttoned. I appraised his self-assured gait, and the competent way he scanned both sidewalks ahead of us and behind, gauging every facet of our environment.

No matter how docile he seemed, underneath he was a predator.

No matter how modern he seemed, underneath he was ancient.

He'd lived *thousands* of years. He'd experienced almost all recorded history from the dawn of civilization until now. Yet, he strolled along with me, hands unassumingly in his pockets. Seemingly content.

"What was the moment you realized nothing would ever be the same?" I had to ask.

He stopped under the House of Blues marquee and considered.

"Many times I felt despair at what I had become, but always Una and Ninurta were there to comfort me, as I was there for them." Until then, he'd spoken while gazing sincerely at me, but there his words faltered and his focus fell past me—and not as an indication of lying. I sensed his heartache rising to the surface. "We grieved," he said. "Like a child's song sung in rounds, it was the same melodious grief, overlapping at different intervals, but always together. We'd loved together, and we'd been cursed together. We were strong together. For a time it seemed it would always be so. My day of reckoning came when Ninurta took his own life."

"Ninurta?"

"He bore the curse of the moon."

"He killed himself?" I touched Menessos's arm. "I'm so sorry."

"Una and I tended his body, bore him to the tomb." He sucked in a lungful of cool night air.

I waited; he was staring up Euclid but was lost in

memory. The Lake Erie breeze, though light, packed enough chill that I could see my breath in the air. *And Johnny is on his bike in this.* I wished my blazer were a little thicker. A cup of hot coffee would have been nice to drink *and* to hold. "What happened after you buried Ninurta?"

Still fixated on something up the road, he answered, "Guilt enveloped Una in a continuous embrace. Our curses had spread before we learned how to control ourselves through magic and sorcery. She was certain the world would be destroyed by our spawn. For her, I killed vampires and wæres alike, trying to correct our mistake. But the bloodshed could not purchase her peace. I tried to kiss away her nightmares, but my arms could not offer any comfort that was as constant as her regret." He checked the roadway in a sweeping glance that brought him to face me. "Una's dark hair turned silver. I knew she would age and die and finally be free of her shame. I was glad for her. But I had to watch her die and bury her alone. And I have been alone ever since."

I felt a deep sympathy for what he had endured. "But you aren't alone."

His elbow pushed out for me. "Take my arm, Persephone, and we will go forth."

"Hmmm?"

"A local slogan." He smiled. "Go fourth-with-a-U— for an area on Fourth Street, where there are many restaurants. It is past the season for eating out of doors, but it remains a destination for the locals."

I allowed him to lead me. My concentration circled around his story, without awareness of where we were going. As we strolled down a road blocked from traffic, however, my thoughts returned to the here and now. He guided me past the various venues, including a comedy club. Then he ushered me down a quaint brick alley.

Multicolored party lights zigzagged over our heads. A bench sat under the next building's fire escape, from which hung a sign that read: ZÓCALO, MEXICAN GRILL & TEQUILERÍA.

The hostess showed us through the brightly colored space to a table next to a beautiful iron railing, placed the menus for us, and left. We sat. There were gorgeous brassy lanterns hanging all around. A curved stairwell led down to more seating and the kitchen. It was lovely.

I am sitting in a Mexican restaurant in Cleveland, Ohio, with the original *vampire.*

Opening the menu, I fixated on the ornate lettering, seeing the page like art. My mind couldn't focus on the words.

His native tongue is Akkadian, Old Babylonian, from thousands of years ago. He still lives, suspended in time, as if he'll be thirtyish forever.

Forcing my mind to the words on the menu, I scolded my sullen self for having girlishly pathetic worries like being "forever changed by the experience." Menessos couldn't go back to things as they were, either. I wondered if he had wanted to.

How does he deal with it?

"Are you all right, Persephone?"

"Yes. Why?"

"You're practically glaring at your menu."

Yeah, at least here I have choices. "Tell me about the fey we're facing."

"Such talk will keep."

"But we have to make plans."

"Planning is best done on a full stomach—yours isn't—and to be effective, it must be done in secret."

I laid the menu down and looked at him questioningly.

The waitress took my posturing as a sign and came for my hurried order of diet cola and chile relleno.

The light from a neon sign at the bar glossed the vampire's walnut-colored hair with a reddish glow. His beard balanced his face, his square jaw, and afforded him a hint of history, as if he belonged in the armor-clad times of the past. But his times were much farther back. As he scanned the bar, the neon light cast its red sheen on his beard, too: it seemed soaked with blood. "Wærewolf bartender," he whispered. "Another in the kitchen downstairs. Do you not smell them?"

I sniffed. "Now that you mention it . . ." I'd dismissed the scent as that of two-by-fours from the theater, but this was quite different. It lay low, underlying the smell of savory food. Something not *of* the restaurant, but *in* it. Something woodsy, like the cedar part of Johnny's scent, but missing the sage.

"Ahhh. You need to take heed of these things, Persephone."

"So I don't say something they shouldn't know."

"Correct."

"Do you really think they'd listen? That they'd tell anyone?"

"Are you willing to take the chance?"

The waitress set the diet cola in front of me. "Chile relleno's coming right up."

I waited until she had gone. "You've molded patience into an art, of course. There's no sense of time running out for you, is there?"

"No."

"Childhood seems timeless, but hours of play pass in minutes. Bedtimes sneak up on you. Is that how it is for you?"

"Moderately. I suppose that childhood is as good an analogy as another. Children live gloriously seeking the next challenge, hunger incessantly, and growing old isn't a concern."

I laughed quietly.

"Becoming an adult means becoming accustomed to the scheduling of events. Rising to a new challenge that could define one's life becomes a wearying negative. Personal growth takes its place behind maintaining the money flow that feeds the schedule." The fingers of one hand rippled a bored staccato on the table. "Being wealthy is a better analogy. Wealth alleviates the concern for basic survival and creates the environment for growth."

The waitress returned with my plate. The deep green poblano chilies were stuffed with asparagus, zucchini, tomato, and strips of peppers. It smelled scrumptious.

"Why do you choose not to eat meat?"

I stabbed my fork into the food. "As any starving college student can tell you, meat's expensive. Cans of protein-rich beans aren't. Just kind of happened, I guess."

"With your ties to Johnny, that will probably change."

Over the last few weeks the meat Johnny had prepared in my home had smelled delicious and I had more than once almost given in and eaten some. "What ties?"

"You've bonded with him, too," he said curtly.

I stopped with the fork halfway to my mouth.

"How to explain this without using your *other* titles here in public? What you are and what he is, imprint upon each other. It is not yet a formal bond like other bonds you're experienced with, but similar."

"Yet?" I put the fork down.

"Eat."

"Explain."

"In private, I will. We will have our privacy sooner if you do things my way."

When we left the restaurant, it was not quite ten P.M. but it felt much later. Johnny wouldn't get here for another hour or more, so I strolled slowly. "The days are getting so short," I said. The sun had set today at six-twenty-three.

"This season permits a longer life for vampires."

That made the cold somehow more fitting, forcing people safely inside, but I didn't say that aloud.

We made our way into the theater using the same path as before, but this time we passed fewer cardboard boxes. Now there were nearly forty vampires and Beholders working about the room. The hammering ceased when Menessos and I entered. They stared at us as we crossed to the stage.

We'd been gone about an hour, enough time for them to have set in another quarter of that gleaming black floor. The underarea of the stage was blocked halfway across, too, and apparently Seven had had time to tell everyone the master was running around with the brave new Erus Veneficus. At least he hadn't held my hand and led me through the theater. I'd walked by myself like a big girl. *My hurrying was meant only to keep up with him. Not a rush to get through and away from all the fangs. Really.*

Atop the stairs, Menessos tapped in numbers for the lock—hmm, I needed to know the code myself—and opened the heavy door for me. With the exception of the empty space on the wall for a painting, everything from the design board Seven had shown me was now set up and arranged. My suitcase and toiletries bag rested at the foot of the big black bed beside Johnny's duffel. They'd even started a fire.

"They did all of that out there—and this—in an hour?" I dropped my blazer on a chair and went to warm myself near the flames.

"It was merely moving and placing furniture, Persephone. You must have somewhere to rest tonight."

Even as he spoke, the work resumed in the theater beyond. The hammering echoed as if several dozen carpenters on meth were out there.

Menessos shut my door, and the noise was immediately silenced. I studied the three different locking mechanisms on it. Bolts at the top and bottom of the door, another at mid-level—in addition to the automatic electronic lock, of course. Very industrial. "Now, about my knowledge of the fey that could assist you . . ."

"How about we start with Johnny?" I wanted to know about the ties Menessos mentioned at the restaurant.

His voice lowered. "How about we start with*out* Johnny?"

Though my back was turned to the fire, warmth slithered across my aura; it was an invitation duplicated in his smoldering eyes.

I drew my shields around me. "Why do you bounce back and forth between humanizing yourself to the point of making me feel sorry for you, and then play Mr. Dangerous Sex-Starved Vampire?"

Amused, he said, "I am not sex starved."

"It's annoying and it'll get old, fast, if you keep it up."

The heat abated, but was still present. "My apologies, Persephone." Standing at the end of the granite countertop, he reached into a decorative azure blue bowl and lifted one of the crackled glass orbs. Even as he inspected it, twisting his wrist, I could feel it as if his fingers were flicking over my aura. "Do you not like having your flesh kindled?"

I recognized and resisted this, strengthening my shields even more, but my body still responded to it. "Wasn't that made clear with the word 'annoying'?" The breathlessness of my voice pissed me off. So did he.

"The birth of a master is a *sensitive* time." After replacing the glass orb gently, he moved casually nearer and the temperature in the room rose noticeably. The heat, the caress of my aura, his voice, it all triggered a yearning for him, I craved him, needed him. And if he was attuned to my body, he damn well knew it.

I retreated.

He stopped six feet from me. "Persephone, this is what it means to be the master of a vampire."

"No wonder vampires struggle to rise through the ranks," I muttered.

"It is quite pleasurable, isn't it? Erotic."

It reminded me of working with the ley line. At first touch, the power of the ley scalded, but as the touch lingered it became euphoric. Addictive. "What perks do you get from it?" No breathlessness in my voice. Only anger.

"Because you are mortal, I hear your heart begin to pound. I watch your cheeks flush with warm, fresh blood as desire overwhelms you."

Suddenly he was right behind me, as close as he could be without touching me. My aura snapped tight around me, shielding me while his power rubbed against that intangible defense and created a metaphysical friction that stole my breath again.

"Here, surrounded by those I master, I am stronger. Oh, Persephone . . ." There was an edge to his tone, a sharp reminder, yet he spoke my name rapturously. "I know what you are feeling, for I have felt it. I have fed upon it. And now, I nourish you with it."

His fingers stroked my neck, and the barrier between us was no more. I smelled hot cinnamon and I melted against him. His touch molded me against him, his lips brushed my cheek. "Taste the power I give you."

The first time Menessos kissed me—in the circle when we'd saved Theo—his kiss had been as fragile as the edge of a toasted marshmallow. Not this time. His mouth covered mine forcefully, his arms surrounded me. My rebellious body took over, encouraging him. Lips parting, I welcomed his tongue. His embrace tightened. My hips pressed into him.

He ended the kiss and whispered, "I must." His mouth lowered onto my neck, and time slowed.

The vampire's lips found the thudding pulse of my vein. I felt the needle tips of his teeth, pressing. My skin broke—the shafts of his fangs pushed deeper. I felt each millimeter of him entering me as definitively as sexual penetration. It hurt like losing my virginity had hurt. It was painful and yet it was perfect.

With his tongue pressed at my new openings, he sucked, tugging the skin of my neck gently into his mouth. My hips pressed harder against his groin and my body answered his demand. I bled for him and I felt . . . *potent*.

Mine!

He was mine. Mine to command. Mine to protect. Mine to have if I wanted. Sustained by my energy, Menessos was mine to feed as well.

CHAPTER NINE

I awoke to a night sky with twinkling stars in it over my head.

"Holy shit!" The sound of Johnny's astonished voice came a second before the dull thump of the heavy door shutting.

Does everyone but me have that door's damned combination?

Realizing I was on the bed, I sat up in a rush. I was alone. My clothes were still on. *Good.* Feeling my neck, I touched a bandage. *The bastard bandaged me?*

Scooting to the edge, I kicked the sheer curtains aside. My feet hit the floor and I stood—

Dizziness made me immediately sit again. I called out, "Back here." The heavy curtains had been shut, separating the two spaces, and the fire burned low in the hearth.

"Lemme figure out how to lock up," he answered. "A lot of vamps out there."

"How many?"

A glass of orange juice sat on the bedside table. Eagerly, I downed half of it to the chunking sound of metal defenses engaging. We were supposed to take advantage of our aloneness. I gulped more, to the beat of Johnny's approaching footfalls. *C'mon, juice, kick in.*

"Probably thirty vamps, fifty or sixty Beholders."

More than there had been earlier. Or more than I had seen then, anyway. Or Johnny could smell them in unseen places like Menessos had smelled the wærewolves at the restaurant.

The thick curtain parted and light from the other room glowed behind him. It suited the sunny demeanor he was exuding. "At the main doors, I was convinced this whole place was a dump, and then I'm led to this ritzy little abode, with the hottest woman I've ever seen waiting for me in the bedroom."

He entered the room and the curtain fell shut behind him, plunging us back into the dark like an eclipse. I immediately preferred this; the darkness seemed to energize me. "Wow." He pointed at the dome. "The stars are out."

I snorted in amusement.

"Bet that cost him."

"Bet it didn't affect his bank accounts a bit. How was the interview?"

"Cool! It's this NRRRadio station. They run it out of a house in Westlake, and it's got this professional-yet-laid-back atmosphere. Web-based setup; the site has a window with a live studio Webcam in one corner and a chat room in another. People posted questions for us. The DJ, Syrinx, was awesome. Let us kinda take over the flow of things once we were used to everything."

As if the DJ'd had any choice.

Johnny clapped his hands and rubbed them together.

"This is all very romantic, stars, cozy fireplace, and all. Very romantic, indeed, if you ask me—which you didn't." Stopping before me, he reached out to my chin and lifted. "All this place needs is a little music. Guess we'll have to make our own." He bent and kissed me softly. My lips felt bruised, but I didn't want him to think I was holding back. When it ended, Johnny straightened and licked his lips. "Mmmm, orange ju—"

By the light of fake stars, he detected the bandage.

Instantly the sunny demeanor frosted over. He didn't need an explanation. Tension flared, then doubled, tripled. He moved away. "Don't." I caught his arm, felt the bones resetting under my grip. Anger was giving him power to change. I held on. "Don't."

He stopped. Voice quavering and low, on the edge of a growl, he said, "Give me one good reason."

"I'm the master—"

"Not of me!"

With an irritated shove I released his arm.

He didn't move; my attempt to push him away must've struck a nerve. He didn't leave.

"Let me finish?" He didn't object; perhaps he'd realized I was explaining, not commanding. "Being a master comes with certain responsibilities."

Johnny lurched away, giving me his back. He was breathing hard. "Fuck!" he shouted into the air.

"You know how the protrepticus feeds on my aural energy?" An almost imperceptible nod indicated I had at least some of his attention. "It's with me constantly, but I use it so seldom I don't really notice the drain." I drank the last of the juice and set the glass on the table. "This isn't so different. Think about it. I've been drawing on his energy. I just didn't realize it. Many times. When I ran in the field, when I sparred with you, when I confronted the fairies. Maybe more. I hexed him over three weeks ago, Johnny. He was due . . . a . . . a recharge. And aural energy alone wouldn't satisfy him."

Johnny watched me. Seething. The fire glow behind him gave an orange edge to all the black he wore. He could have been a living ember. Even the dark blue of his eyes seemed to reflect some of the burning color. The breath he drew in made me think he was about to rage, but when he spoke, his voice was even. "How often will he get his due?"

"I will keep it to a minimum. Believe me."

"I believe you. But I'm wondering why you don't sound even a little distressed or pissed off about it."

He was right. I didn't. I was indifferent because, on some level, I had to have known this was inevitable. *Right?* "Wouldn't do me any good to be pissed off. Anger won't change this. It is what it is."

After deliberating with himself, he came and sat beside me on the bed. He was still too rigid, but as he opened and closed his hands they were normal, not furred and clawed. "Red, do you want this?"

It had to be difficult for him to accept, as Nana would say, "another tom slinking around the cathouse." I had to give him kudos for not totally going Neanderthal on me.

I remembered Sammi and Cammi Harding, the bank heiresses who'd been escorting him backstage after Lycanthropia's Rock Hall showcase. One of them had kissed him. Seeing it had hurt me. Deeply. If our roles were reversed right now, I wasn't sure my reaction wouldn't be Neanderthalish. *How very unfair for someone so concerned with justice and balance to be.*

I wondered if, when he officially ascended as Domn Lup, it would change him. Anyone would be permanently affected by such authority, the weight of unpleasant decisions and alliances. I guess we were both learning to accept these things that neither of us could change.

I answered him with the truth. "I need you both."

Johnny tucked my hair behind my ear, and his finger ran gently over the exposed bandage. "Promise me that, analogywise, I get to be considered the twelve-cylinder sports car you drive too recklessly and too fast, say . . . a Ferrari 599 GTB Fiorano in Daytona Black."

"I'm even imagining black leather upholstery."

His lopsided grin was adorable. "Of course. And the vamp gets to be considered the detestable but law-required insurance policy with the irritating premium."

I laughed and moved into his lap, stretching my arms around him. *Don't ever change.* "You are definitely my only ride."

"Oooooo. You're revvin' my engine."

"Your whole analogy deserves a few innuendo points."

His lips brushed mine like flower petals at first, then as he strayed to my cheek, it seemed he became aware that he was on the side Menessos had fed from and shifted roughly to the other side. I hoped it was because he was concerned for my covered wound, not an objection to putting his lips where Menessos's had been.

Guilt rippled over me. The master/servant bond had taken over and I had failed to rule it. In that state,

I might've yielded and made love to Menessos . . . and yet Menessos hadn't taken advantage of me. *As if drinking without permission were somehow* not *taking advantage.*

Johnny eased me from his lap into the middle of the bed and slipped away from me. "Don't go," I said, reaching for his arm and coming up with only sleeve. My mind had wandered, my kisses had surely been lacking. He stood beside the bed, studying me. I said, "Stay with me." I wanted to convince him my heart was in the right place. Moving onto my knees, I kissed him and caressed him all over. But he wasn't responding. "Hey. I'm trying to rev that engine you're so proud of."

He kissed my forehead. "You gave blood tonight, Red. I can't take anything more from you." Yet he spent the next thirty seconds taking his clothes off. I moved over to lie on the near side of the bed and enjoyed the show.

"Gee, mister, you sure are good at sending mixed signals."

"Can't sleep unless I'm naked. Move over." I moved. After throwing down the covers as far as he could, he lay down and pulled just the sheet over him.

I tugged the sheet down in playful increments.

"Get naked and get in here beside me already."

He might have changed his mind about intimacy, but as I stood to undress, my vision went starry and my knees went weak. I caught myself, but he'd seen. He patted the mattress next to him. So I had to remove my jeans the unsexy way: on my back. I threw the denim to the floor as if it were the source of my trouble and snuggled up to my rock'n'roll biker-boyfriend.

With my head resting on his shoulder and his arm

wrapped around me, contentedness enveloped me. Cuddling, even without the afterglow, was peaceful. How unexpected, to find serenity here, deep in the earth in a vampire's haven with growing numbers of undead beyond my door.

I'd given blood and reassurances tonight, because that's what each of them needed. As I lay there, I wondered, did I have what *I* needed? I couldn't readily name anything I lacked.

Except answers. To questions like, how could I lie here feeling contentment when there was a battle brewing?

I can lie here because I believe there is a way to win. Somehow.

Dragging my nails lightly across Johnny's chest, I snuggled tighter against him and let the feeling of security in his arms take hold. I cast aside my worries and slept.

CHAPTER TEN

Pounding on the door awakened me. It sounded like someone kicking.

Wrapping up in the sheet—Johnny lay on his stomach sleeping—I hurried into the front room. The kicking continued in trios, with pauses between. The clock on the stove read eleven-twenty.

As I reached the door, during one of the intervals, I heard an exasperated voice shout, "Just open the fucking door already." At least I thought that's what the muffled voice said.

"Who's there?" I asked through the intercom.

The female voice answered, "Risqué." She didn't use the intercom but shouted through the door. I barely heard her.

Not sure I wanted to open the door for someone who wouldn't use the techy device let alone someone named for being daringly close to impropriety, I asked, "And why are you kicking the door?"

"Because I'm holding your heavy-ass breakfast tray."

Oh. Good reason. I worked at the strange locks and opened the door.

"Finally." Risqué barged in, blazing past me like a five-foot inferno. She marched toward the kitchen. Mounds of blond ringlets hung down her back and bounced as she walked, hitting the top of frilly orange boy shorts that left her shapely, tan legs bare—legs that seemed long despite her lack of height. "Thank Hell your groceries are going to arrive today," she said belligerently. "Boss said there's no food in your kitchen, and to be sure you and the wolf-man have enough to eat." She shoved the tray onto the counter. "So there you fucking go." She turned, showing me a disparaging frown and big eyes—the color of which matched her fire-engine-red lipstick. It stunned me silent.

Offerlings and Beholders are the humans accepted into the vampire's court. The former for their beauty and the latter for their muscle. Risqué might not be entirely human, or she might just have a thing for albino rabbit contacts, but either way, she was scary and beautiful. If pressed, I'd have pegged her as an Offerling.

Offerlings get two marks at the outset, so even new Offerlings outranked longtime Beholders in a vampire's court. An Erus Veneficus outranked any Offerling. Status: reason for her irritation with me. She might have benefits above every Beholder in the building, but my newly arrived self represented a dose of comeuppance—hence, she was carrying my tray. Menessos had mentioned there would be jealousy and her behavior fit. *And he also mentioned he was not sex starved.*

Risqué gave me the once-over and evidently disapproved of my sheet. "Do *not* tell me you're going for the Greek goddess morning-after look. Ugh."

I decided her hair reminded me of powdered eighteenth-century hairstyles, but with less height and even more ringlets. She had ringlets in front, too. They—and nothing else—covered her breasts. More or less.

"Boss put clothes in the closet for you, you know." Those startling eyes squinted up angrily when she spoke. "I'm sure there's a nice Vera Wang robe in there."

Letting her get to me would be a mistake. I walked to the kitchen bar. "Mind your tone, Risk."

"It's Risqué. *Ris-kay*. And he told me to tell you about the clothes."

I lifted the silver lid on the tray. Eggs, sausage, bacon, pancakes, oatmeal. *Mmmm, oatmeal.* In a tone that could've been used to inquire about salt, I asked, "Did he tell you to be a bitch, too?"

"No. That's just part of the delivery service." Her scowl was fantastic, but lowered brows were an intrinsic part of such an expression. Her brows didn't lower. Instead of curving down on the outside to frame her eyes, they rose above her temples and seemed to join with her hairline. The not-quite-human theory was gaining.

"Do I smell bacon?" Beside the now-dark hearth, the curtain parted and Johnny emerged, wearing only jeans. He hadn't bothered to zip them all the way or button them, so the patch of dark hair under his belly button showed.

"Ooooo. Yes, darlin', you do," Risqué said, tone shifting to a Texas drawl as sweet as pecan pie. "But I will personally take your order if what's on the tray ain't enough to satisfy you."

He reevaluated the scene in a glance that was well

aware of her short-shorts, shapely legs, and, uh, ringlets. "Yeah, I've got an order," he said, hungrily.

"Tell me." Risqué shimmied her shoulders a little, resettling the blond curls so the tips of her pert breasts peeked through. Her nipples were too red, and I wasn't sure if that was a sign of abuse or a trait related to her eye color. She moved away from the counter and toward him as if to greet him. "What's your order?"

"Get out." At the last moment, Johnny angled and graced her with that rude shoulder bump that punks do to people on sidewalks. With their varied heights, it was more of his elbow bumping her shoulder.

With a loud "hmpf" of protest, she spun on her heel and left.

As the door shut, Johnny zeroed in on the bacon.

Thankful she was gone, I said, "I'm glad you're up."

Lifting three slices, he stopped to check his jeans front, then shot me a grin. "Huh. It was there when I woke up. Guess she scared it away. Just let me refuel . . ." He bit into the bacon.

"I meant *awake*."

"But that's not what you said. You're refueling, too, right?"

"Oh, yes."

While he searched for a plate, I tied the sheet ends and sat at the bar with my oatmeal. The sausage smelled so good. "Menessos insinuated that I had bonded to you, and that because of it I'd probably want meat."

He snickered. "I suppose you want two innuendo points now?"

"Of course. I can't hope to win this little contest, but

I don't want to give the impression that I've given up, either." I lifted my spoon. "Do you know what he's talking about?"

"Nope."

"Do you know the lore of the Domn Lup or any mystical bonding-type stories with wæres?"

"Oh, I've heard some stories about wære bondage but I don't think that's the same thing." He served himself a hearty helping of everything but the oatmeal. "And I don't know how you survive without meat." On his fork, he held a curiously shaped sausage link. "Wanna bite?"

After studying it and seeing how much grease was on it, I said, "Not really."

"One bite." He held the fork at me insistently. "You get an innuendo point for it."

"For biting it, not sucking it, right?"

"Right. Oh, and nice one, now I'll give you two points." He watched me with more interest than he should have, but after I'd "mmmmed" appropriately, he didn't push for more. "So what's on the agenda today?"

I shrugged. "Eat. Shower. Wait for Nana's announcement, I guess. I'm hoping that sometime soon we'll hear from Xerxadrea—if not, we may have to make a conference call on the protrepticus—and get our plans for dealing with the fairies in order."

"Sam will coordinate that, right?"

"I intend to insist."

"Well, all that sounds like stuff to do later. I've got a plan of my own in mind, and this one will keep you from pacing the floor here."

• • •

I thought the "not pacing" idea was going to convert into a suggestion of shower sex followed by more sleep. Actually, I was hoping for that. But Johnny, oddly, had something else entirely on his mind, though it did involve wrapping my legs around him.

We rode around Cleveland astride his Harley. Before we took off, he explained it was a Night Train and that my seat was called a badlander and bragged on the motor in terms I couldn't understand. He also proudly showed me the custom paint job—black and silver wolves— which he'd done himself. Guitars, he said, were painted with automotive paint.

We let the sun warm us at red traffic lights and then had the November air cool us down again when the signals turned green. We cruised University Circle and stopped for coffee at Arabica where I asked whether or not he needed to see Doc Lincoln, the vet he'd coerced into helping a fellow wære in need, about his apparent lack of libido. Johnny, of course, insisted his libido was fine and mentioned again I'd already been drained by "the fang-face." He promised after the ceremony we'd celebrate.

It was nearly three o'clock when Johnny parked the bike outside a bar called The Dirty Dog.

I indelicately wrestled myself off the motorcycle and strolled up to the establishment that had unquestionably inspired the term "seedy beer joint." Even from the outside it was conspicuously not a quaint tavern or an upscale martini bar. I barely made out the neon Corona sign in the front window—the glass was *that* grimy.

The inside wasn't any better. The smoking laws may have been new, but cigarette smoke had had many years to permeate the wood and furniture, and to tarnish the ceiling into what those folks who name paint colors might have called Urine-Stain Yellow. And that particular term might have been helpful in naming the odor of the place, too.

Inside, the tight, galleylike hall had a series of booths to the right that had to be older than me. Each had a poster showcasing a different beer from the Great Lakes Brewery. To the left was a long bar and a silent Wurlitzer jukebox. An old man sat at the far end, hunched over a glass. His hair was thick and white, buzzed short, and he wore a predominantly red tartan plaid flannel shirt with sleeves cuffed to show the thermal underwear beneath. He was the only person here. At our approach, he cocked his head just slightly our way and arched a single white brow.

"Johnny?" The long, stubble-covered face twisted with genuine glee. His smile was full of long, stained teeth. "Johnny! Haven't seen you in years, m'boy." He slid from his seat, a cane in hand.

"Hey, Beau."

They clasped each other's forearms in greeting. "Who's the doll?"

"Beauregard, this is Persephone. But that's a lot of syllables, so I call her Red."

"Ahhh, Red's easier on the tongue. As easy as she is on the eye." He held his hand out to me.

I took it firmly for a good shake, but he instantly jerked away.

"Jesus!" he grumbled, shaking his appendage like it hurt. "She's a witch!"

"Yeah." Johnny drew out the word as if confused.

I hadn't jolted him.

Beau lifted his cane and poked Johnny in the thigh with the tip. "Could've warned an old man!" He hobbled around the bar. His one leg didn't bend, and I wondered if Beau, like Nana, had bad knees. "What'll ya drink, doll?"

"We're not here for a drink, Beau," Johnny said.

Beau stopped. "You wanna see *him*?"

Johnny nodded.

"They call you in?"

"Nope."

Only Beau's eyes moved then, as they angled toward me, then sank down to his opening and closing hand. To Johnny he said, "Upstairs. You remember the way? Better knock first."

Johnny left, but my attention lingered on Beau. "How'd you know I'm a witch?"

He continued to tighten then loosen his fist. He snorted, then jutted his chin in Johnny's direction. "Better catch up to him."

I left, fighting the urge to hurry to catch up. Johnny was waiting for me, holding open a tall, thin door. "Stay close," he whispered, and went up ahead of me. The stairwell was narrow. The building was a physical representation of lean times. Every step creaked. It smelled of decaying wood, like a rotten cedar chest—cedar!

Wæres. The Dirty Dog. *Duh.*

Atop the landing, there was a short hall and a single door.

Johnny knocked, practiced being patient, and knocked again, more forcefully.

I felt the floor shake; someone was moving beyond. Someone big.

The door opened. The person who came into view was a head taller than the door frame, and three times as broad as Johnny. His dark, curly hair was thick and short, like a wire brush. The Hawaiian shirt he wore was loose on his giant frame, but the blue and orange pineapple and surfboard print wasn't doing him any favors. Tan pants were raggedly cut off below the knee. Apparently it had been a long, long time since his socks and sneakers were new. Whatever color they'd started out they were both a dismal gray now, and had been for a long time. "Hey, Hector."

The big man was still and silent long enough that I had time to wonder, *Is he in the WWF?* and move on to, *How the hell does he get out of this building?* It was hard to believe that he'd fit down the stairwell.

"Johnny Newman."

That surprised me two ways: his voice was soft, and very few people seemed to know Johnny's last name.

"Ig taking visitors today?"

"I'll ask."

The man ambled across the dark, high-ceilinged room; his size made his movements seem clumsy and overdone. He slid open a pair of pocket doors and passed through. To Johnny, I mouthed the question, "Ig?"

"Ignatius Tierney," he whispered back. "The *dirija,* the local wære supervisor."

At that odd word, I remembered Johnny telling me some of the secret side of how the wære world was structured. I also recalled that he'd not wanted to reveal his at-will changes to these people. That ability meant he would certainly be crowned as the Domn Lup—Wolf King—and he was in no hurry to be burdened with the responsibilities. Similarly, I hadn't wanted to reveal to the Elders that I was the Lustrata. We were both smart enough to know that making claim to such a position held not only power, but myriad obligations, too.

Destinies are destinies because they are inevitable.

Is that why we're here?

Johnny began to fidget. As for me, I was breathing deeply of the aromas around me, sorting through them. Woodsy, but not quite cedar. This was more juniper, maybe cypress. And something was mixed with it . . . either a heady wine—which wouldn't have surprised me with the bar downstairs—or ambergris.

Hector returned to view, and motioned us on. I followed Johnny, shutting the door behind us. The floor planks gave the slightest bounce. The blinds were drawn, keeping it dark.

Johnny stopped abruptly just inside the doorway.

"Never show up on a good day, do you?" The words were slurred and thick.

I peeked around Johnny's shoulder and saw a man sitting in a hospital bed. Ig's cheeks plumped, well, *one* did. He'd had a stroke.

"When?" Johnny asked.

Ig gargled saliva. I think it was supposed to be a laugh. "Two days ago." He waited then said, "Hector." Pronouncing the name involved massive amounts of phlegm. "Tell them."

"There's a clotting issue with his blood."

Johnny's question came quickly. "But the full moon will heal it, right?"

Hector's chin dropped to his chest.

"No," Ig said.

The instant Johnny looked at me, I knew what he was thinking: a transformation would heal this. Though the natural full moon was twenty-five days away, we'd gotten around that before.

"Tell them all of it," the *dirija* insisted.

"It keeps happening. He gets a TPA treatment·and heals to this stage immediately. This stage, no better. And it happens earlier and earlier with each moon cycle."

"We just had a full moon four days ago," I said.

Ig nodded. "S'pposed to be dead."

I'd have guessed Ig to be maybe forty-five. His face was speckled with freckles and his pale red-blond hair was just starting to thin. With lashes to match his Irish hair, his green eyes seemed big. Except for a drooping eyelid and the nonworking side of his mouth, he appeared to be a man in his prime. He patted the bed. "John, sit."

Johnny crossed the room, and Ig spotted me for the first time. "Who's the woman?"

"That's Red." Johnny sat on the edge of the bed.

Ig acknowledged me with a sniff of the air in my direction. That was when I saw that under his half-buttoned pajama shirt he wore a long silvery necklace, probably platinum or white gold. The thick links of herringbone chain held a large Y-shaped centerpiece, and while I didn't clearly see it, I was certain it was a wolf's head. "Beautiful. But not wære."

"I'm a witch." Get that tidbit out of the way this time. Beau's reaction still had me puzzled.

Hector immediately eased away from me as if he were backing away from a wild animal. "Dangerous company to keep." He outweighed me by at least two hundred pounds. He was a foot and a half taller than I. And he was backing away from me in fear. It seemed ridiculous, but it was actually the smart thing to do.

"She's cool, Hector. A bunch of us kennel at her place." To Ig, he added, "I didn't know about this." He gestured at the bed's frame as if that would convey the words he didn't want to say.

"What brings you?"

"Her."

"Back to the woman." Again, Ig considered me, but this time it made me feel that closing and buttoning my blazer would have been appropriate. "Why?"

"She's going to need the help of some wæres."

"What about those who kennel?"

"Just my band, a few friends. Not enough."

Ig scowled just a little at the word "band." "Who'd she piss off? WEC?"

"There's a lot going on, Ig. More than I can say. I came to ask if you would help . . . but you've already got your own concerns to deal with."

"Must be important. You'd not have come back otherwise." Ignatius took Johnny's arm. "There's only one way now." Gravely, he said, "Take my place."

Johnny recoiled and stood. "No!"

Discouraged, Ig's hand fell to the sheet, and was still for an instant, then it clenched and his features distorted defiantly. "I'm going to die anyway. Todd will be *dirija* by default. And he won't help you."

I didn't know who this Todd was, but the vibe in the room indicated that nobody here thought that was a good thing.

"Should be yours, John. If you're *dirija,* help is at your command."

Johnny shook his head back and forth slowly. "I can't," he answered. "I won't. I don't want to be a *dirija*."

"Ha!" Ig struggled forward, half of his body noncompliant. Hector moved to help him but the wære lord shouted wordlessly and the big man stopped. We were forced to watch long, awkward minutes of him using his right arm to jerk the useless left one into his lap, then drag his left leg across the bed to the edge so he could try to sit where Johnny had sat. The left arm fell out of place twice and Ig raged each time. It was sad and wretched and terrible. It hurt me to see him fight with himself for such a simple task.

When Ig finally had his body where he wanted it, he was breathing as if he'd just finished a marathon. Ferociously, he said, "Talk of what *you* want? *I* don't want to *live* like *this*!"

Ig stabbed a finger at Johnny, pointing, and his fury continued. "Your past may hide from you, but you can't hide from your future. Tear this agony from me! Take it now, I'm ready. Spare me this indignity!"

Stricken, Johnny rushed from the room. I could do nothing but follow.

Ig's howl of anger followed us down the stairwell.

CHAPTER ELEVEN

Johnny didn't say a word as he passed Beau, he just flew by, threw open the door, and stormed up the sidewalk to the Night Train, straddled it, and turned the ignition. My feet were planted on the sidewalk. I didn't know what to say to him, but I wasn't getting on the bike with him yet.

He understood and shut it off.

His hands left the grips and rested on his thighs. His head fell back, as if the sunlight might burn away his misery and pain. The bright rays kissed his skin, gleamed in his hair, and glistened on the earrings and brow rings. He still hadn't shaved, but the extra scruff suited him.

I waited.

"The first time I changed, Ig was there. He'd crossed my path at a deli, scented me. He didn't recognize me, so he knew I was either a new wære in the area breaking the law by not registering with the pack, or I was flat-out a brand-new wære. He had me followed." Johnny brought his skyward face down and his countenance was tight with emotion. "After the park, I was lost. I didn't know who I was . . . but I knew who I wanted to be. I chose the name Newman because I was a new man. And then I found out I was infected. Whether or not I was a wære before the park, I may never know. But I had to deal with it like it was new. Ig was there for me. He's been like a father to me."

Someday, he would have to reveal to the wære community that he was Domn Lup. But not today. Today he was reeling because his father figure was dying. "C'mon," I said, swinging my leg over the bike to sit behind him. My arms circled his waist and I laid my head against his shoulder.

He gripped the handlebars. "Where to?"

Last night we'd just cuddled, I'd needed rest. Today, I thought I might know the answer he needed. "Let's just ride."

Surveying the theater, I had another awe-filled reaction. The large display screens were now wired into the upstage framework and a logo like the one on the gray-primer door floated around in each screen, spinning and flipping. The marble floor was now finished.

A large circular dais covered with thick black carpeting was now situated downstage center. A big chair was centered on the dais. Accented by ornately carved wood, it had a thronelike appearance, but the padded seat, back, and arms made it look comfortable, as well. An angled beam of amber light focused on the chair shifted slightly. I glanced up. Someone was adjusting the stage lights above us.

We moved farther into the room. When the workers

observed us they stopped and stared at us. One of them, a giant of a man whose height and girth would top even Hector's, was carrying a divan all by himself across the stage. He wore a Cleveland Browns football jersey and dark blue jeans. He became aware of the quiet, saw us, and set the long piece of furniture down and stood like the rest.

Johnny took one of the pair of steps situated at either side of the proscenium to stage level. As we crossed the stage, we neared the colossal-sized man who'd single-handedly carried the divan. When I glanced back, he was following us off stage.

If we continued on into the little alcove, we'd be vulnerable. And trapped. I tapped Johnny on the shoulder. "We're being followed."

Johnny turned. "You need something?" Johnny's shoulders squared.

The big man had eyes as black as pitch, but his round face and thick arms were tanned to what Nana would call "brown as a biscuit." He used one massive hand to lift his shirt a little to reach into his rear jeans pocket. Then, he offered me a cream-colored envelope, a little larger than four-by-six inches. My name was written in black with calligraphic flair on the front. The back flap was bordered with gold. Its elegance was somewhat lessened by squashed corners and a slight bend. "Boss said to give you this." He spoke slowly and his inflections hinted at southern locales. It made his deep voice pleasant to hear.

I accepted the envelope. "Thank you. What's your name?"

"Mountain."

"Thank you, Mountain. You're certainly getting the renovations done fast. It's really amazing."

He bowed his head and backed away. "Thank you, Ms. Witch." Before he disappeared through the doorway to go back to work, I saw a straggly ponytail of black hair that fell past the ends of his long shirt.

Ms. Witch?

I opened the envelope and handed it to Johnny. A gold-bordered correspondence card bore the engraved letter *M,* also in gold, at the top. Below it, in the same beautiful penmanship, was written:

> *The access code for your chambers has been changed. 1109—your foster daughter's birthday. Now only you and I know . . . unless you share this information.*
>
> *—M*

I handed the note to Johnny as we climbed up the stairs. He read it, smirking, until, at the upper landing, we discovered brown paper bags sitting atop a large cooler. "The groceries," I said.

We put the food away. I was happy with the pasta and frozen vegetable selections, but Johnny mumbled about needing more than salt and pepper for spices.

There were still questions from earlier rolling around my brain. "Can I ask you something?"

"Just did."

I hit his arm with the box of spaghetti. "Beau said he hadn't seen you in years. Is he not normally around?"

"If things are still like they used to be, he has a shop,

but keeps odd hours there. When he's not at the shop, he's at the bar." Johnny headed for the door to get the cooler. "It's me who hasn't been around in years."

Ig had used the words "come back," hadn't he? "Why? If Ig's like a father to you . . ."

"Like most fathers and sons, Ig and I had our words. He's wanted me to be his second since he met me. He wanted me to learn how it works, to be ready to, one day, take full authority. But I wanted to front a rock band. We butted heads." He set the cooler down at the end of the bar and took a deep, deep breath. "He's still adamant that I lead his pack. Only now, I can't just assume the role through rank, I'd have to kill him for it."

I was only a little stunned to have this bit of wære culture confirmed. "How does murder fit into the equation? Wolf packs in the wild don't work that way, do they?"

"No. But people are people." He transferred lunch meats and cheeses to the refrigerator. "Strength leads. If one will yield, the fight is over. But that doesn't happen much."

"And Ig won't yield because he wants to die."

Johnny nodded. We finished up the chore in silence.

Then I couldn't help it anymore and had to ask. "Why hasn't this Todd killed him for it?"

"Everyone loves Ig. Anyone who killed him for power would be hated by the rest of the pack. Who would want to rule where everyone hated him?"

I leaned on the counter. "But you can wait, then fight Todd?"

"I don't want it."

I showed him a soft and patient countenance. He'd

have to take his place of power eventually. Just like I would, too.

"What I do want," he purred, coming toward me, "is a kiss."

I quickly jumped up to sit on the counter. "*Just* a kiss? I still feel cheated from last night."

He unashamedly assessed the height of the counter, put on a thoughtful expression, tapped his chin, and reevaluated the distance before nodding approval.

"Come here." I put emphasis on the words so they wouldn't sound like a dog command but like a lover's suggestion. It won me the boyish smile I adored.

When he neared, I hooked my ankles behind him. "You're trapped."

"That's what you think." Johnny backed up, hauling me to the edge of the counter. I threw my arms around his neck to keep from falling. His hands cupped my bottom and he asked, "Who's got who?"

"You win," I said, punctuating it with a victory kiss. "You have me."

He put me back on the countertop and changed the victory kiss into the passionate kind, beginning to—

His fingers brushed the bandage on my neck and, immediately, he broke away. "Yeah. Just a kiss."

"Johnny." My heels hit the cabinetry with a dull thud. He was heading for the door. "You're just locking that, right?"

"Nope." His voice had just a hint of tightness.

"Where are you going?"

"To see if the Beholders will award me any brownie points for helping out." The door shut behind him.

Sigh.

It made sense to make friends with the vampire's underlings, build camaraderie and all. But that subtle tension in his voice suggested Johnny had some emotional stuff he intended to sweat out. I still thought my idea was the better one, but that implied tender emotions. He wasn't able to accept my affection until he had released the angry emotions roiling inside him, and for that, he needed to perform sweaty *man work*. There weren't any trees to cut down and chop up for firewood here, but there were plenty of hammers to swing and nails to pound.

Bored and meandering around the room, I pulled my laptop out of my backpack and placed it on the desk. *Columnist work.*

For over an hour, next week's column was my center of attention. *No more being late.* It was number four in the series on wære parents, and my thoughts kept drifting to Ig and Johnny. I'd already roughed out the basic article, but added a new slant: how the wære community can come together like a family to protect the newly—or unknowingly—infected, and thereby protect the community at large. I couldn't send it to Jimmy Martin, my editor, yet, but I needed to take a break and then read it with fresh eyes, so I made notes for the following week's column and checked email.

Out of habit I checked the local weather hoping Beverley had remembered her jacket this morning. The link was the Channel 43 page, which also gave me area headlines in bullet points. The line "Vampire Court Growing; Bad News for Local Family" caught my eye. In seconds the video loaded and I hit play.

After the channel's news intro, the screen filled with footage of Nana standing on our front porch, leaning on the rail. Not surprisingly, a cigarette burned between her fingers. She was in need of a visit to the hair salon. The snow-white beehive had to go. It aged her in the worst way.

Back before Hallowe'en, Beverley had commented that if Nana would dye her hair black and put a buckle belt around her head, she wouldn't even need a witch hat. That one comment had said more than I could have in weeks of pointing out older celebrities on TV and saying, "That style would be good on you."

The camera zoomed in on Nana, but the reporter's voice-over was talking about Menessos moving his haven to Cleveland, saying, "While that's good news for the local economy, it is bad news for one family in particular." The station's logo and *DEMETER ALCMEDI* appeared underneath her and the reporter went on. "Today you learned that your granddaughter is set to become the Court Witch of the Regional Vampire Executive, Menessos. The Vampire Executive International Network public relations people tell me the position is one of prestige and power, an honor. Conversely, the Witch Elders Council PR department tells me it is a misuse of power and a position of shame. What is your reaction?" The reporter's microphone shot into frame, in Nana's face.

"Persephone has always been strong-willed, always made her own decisions. But this one . . . I can't abide. She's abandoned me, like her mother did."

Like my mother? My chest tightened with actual pain.

"She's gone to gallivant with bloodsuckers, to use her

power in service to the *undead*. Witches should respect the life of their power more than that. She, most of all."

"'She most of all'? Why do you say that, Ms. Alcmedi?"

Nana put the cigarette to her lips, then blew smoke into the wind. Her hands were shaking.

"Ms. Alcmedi?" the reporter prompted.

She didn't acknowledge him, but her voice came small and thin when she spoke. "That Hallowe'en Ball the other night, up at the Covenstead . . . that was *her* smashing that guitar on stage. That was my Persephone! I taught her better than to squander her gifts on the whims of a gods-be-damned vampire." They beeped her words out, but I knew what she said. She stubbed out the cigarette on the porch rail and then fixed the reporter with grim resolve. "She better never come back here." She measured him up and down with a sneer as deep as the Grand Canyon. "Same goes for you." She shuffled inside and shut the door.

Oh, my Nana is sooo good!

"Like her mother" was probably the single most-convincing thing she could have said. And it was accurate, except that when my mother left me with her, I was a little younger than Beverley.

I indulgently watched it twice more—the report ended with a triple replay of the most important seconds of the fairy-smashing video—then I made myself stop. This was doing nothing but hurting my heart and there was no way I could work on the column now. Johnny's idea of working off the emotional turmoil appealed to me. The place was spic and span. No need for cleaning and scrubbing yet. So, I shut off almost all the lights and went out the door. I may not have wære strength, but there had to be something I could do to help.

In the main hall, some were cleaning the floor, and others were arranging tables on the side already clean. As soon as I appeared, however, all working stopped in waves as they became aware of me. Even Johnny stopped. He glanced around, but remained quiet. Guess, like me, he was waiting to see what would happen next. The seconds ticked by. I couldn't stand it. "Mountain," I called.

Mountain had been single-handedly carrying a green futon couch onto the stage. He set it down gently, as if it weighed no more than a folding chair.

"I would speak with you."

He bowed his head and came forward.

Not sure what I wanted to ask, I hesitated.

"Where they cannot hear, Ms. Witch?" he suggested.

"Yes."

"This way." He led me back into the green room and shut the door behind us. "They can't hear us here."

"Why do they stop working when I show up?"

"You're going to be EV and that's how they show respect. They face you so you can see their eyes."

I liked the way he shortened the title and made it sound like a name. "And if I want them to continue?"

"You say 'continue,'" Mountain answered.

"And if I want to help?"

He chuckled. "The EV doesn't labor."

"What if I want to—"

From behind me, near the stairs, Menessos laughed. "Do not tease him."

I turned just as the lower door, the one beneath mine

and Johnny's door, clicked shut. Mountain turned for a quick retreat. "Mountain," Menessos called.

"Boss?"

"My newest prize. Yes?"

"Of course, Boss." Mountain left.

My anger stirred. "I was not teasing him."

"I know." Caught in a lie, the vampire seemed embarrassed.

"Is that *my* blood flushing your cheeks?"

"It is." In a blur he climbed the stairs and stopped before the door to my room. He glanced over the railing, then started punching in the code. "Join me?"

"I prefer we not be alone in my room again."

"Very well." Menessos opened my door. "You can stay out here." He proceeded inside.

Of course I followed, shoving the door open and marching quickly into my nearly dark chambers. Emerging from behind the door, Menessos slammed it shut and restrained me in a crushing embrace.

"Let go."

"I just wanted to remind you that of the two of us, I am the stronger."

"Duh. Let go."

"Oh, Persephone! Do you so loathe my arms around you?" He danced me around the entryway. "Bliss still doesn't have to be a difficult thing to find."

Sparring with Johnny, I'd been restrained in a similar fashion, minus the dancing. It had made me feel like I'd failed. My new goal was to keep from being caught in this position ever again. I went rigid in his grip. "Take your bliss and shove it."

"I refuse to believe you mean that."

"And I refuse to put a lot of faith in your words."

His confining embrace loosened a fraction. "Why?"

My mouth clamped shut. I wasn't going to offer anything to him freely.

He leaned in—I flinched—and whispered, "It is most fun when you are difficult."

I feigned a swoon. "Dear Diary, the top three least attractive qualities in a man are: patronizing me, the use of intimidation tactics, and conceitedness."

"Tell me why your faith in my words is lacking."

Like this, I couldn't break free. He had control over my body, but not my mind. It seemed like a Freudian reversal. So, the chances of him letting go were less if I didn't cooperate. "You said you'd explain how I'd bonded with Johnny. But you didn't. What you did was lure me in to get me alone so you could feed."

"You say that as if it is a reprehensible thing."

"Manipulating me *is* a reprehensible thing."

Again, he laughed. "I meant the word 'feed,' dear Persephone. I am a vampire. Separating people from pints of their blood is how I survive."

I refused to make eye contact. I had answered; he should have let go or loosened more or *something*.

"Do not be angry at things that must be so. And ponder not how to alter such things."

Through my clenched teeth I growled, "Release me."

The glow of the task lighting glinted in his steel-gray gaze as he whispered "Command me, Persephone. If you can."

CHAPTER TWELVE

My authority over Menessos was clearly not such that just to speak an order meant he had to obey. My hands fisted at my sides.

Again, he dared me. "Command me."

"I already did," I insisted. I considered head-butting him, but it would hurt me more than it would him. *And besides, a big goose-egg bruise on my forehead would be lovely for tomorrow's televised ceremony.*

He kissed my forehead tenderly. "You spoke angry words, witch, that is all. Angry words are often powerless words. Make me feel the weight of your command. Make me see your power, and believe the threat of your anger. *Rule me.*"

"No."

"No?"

"I will not play your game."

"This is no game. Your dominance over me is not real unless you make it so." His chin lifted so his fangs were right before my eyes.

Two months ago, I would have been terrified. Not now, however. "You want me to pretend to be your servant because that keeps you in power out there." I gestured with my nose toward the door and the haven and world beyond it. "But then you challenge me to prove my power in here. You get off on the power games, and are trying to play both sides."

"I am not playing, dear Persephone. I *am* on both sides. You have put me in this awkward position. We must invert the truth and play master and servant beyond these walls. There is no room for ambiguity with the foes who will be watching. Some of them may suspect it is a ruse. We must both know our places, unequivocally."

"Damn it, I get the point already! Will you just tell me what you want me to know and skip the stupid demonstration?"

He sighed as if conceding. "When I have met weak masters, I have disposed of them hastily."

"Are you worried about some vampire coming to town and trying to take over your haven?"

"No. Those havens of which I spoke infiltrated from the inside."

I squinted at him. "This is already your nest."

He squeezed me tighter. "And I dispose of any threats inside it. What if I want to kill Johnny . . . can you control me enough to stop me?"

That was it. Tired of the fearmongering and the bullying, I opened my fists, I drew energy into my palms and gripped his ass. In a heated whisper, I commanded him, "Release me," even as I let the power of a witch-jolt hit him.

His body spasmed under my touch, but he did not let go. He held me tighter and put my backside against the counter.

My tactics reversed. Like transferring energy from one gemstone to another, I drained energy out of him, dragging it deep into me.

Instantly, his arms left me. I was standing on my own so abruptly that, without the counter to support me, I'd have stumbled.

"You learn quickly." Menessos reclined on the couch, legs stretched along the cushions, ankles crossed.

I crossed my arms and gave him a petulant look. "Wouldn't this be easier if you'd just give me the damned textbook or something?"

His amusement lasted a fraction of a second then he covered it with bottled seriousness. Eau de College Professor. "One learns most effectively when the lesson is experienced in the flesh."

I stopped leaning on the counter and walked purposefully toward the door. "I think I'll go ask Mountain some more questions."

Menessos shot to his feet and intercepted me before I reached the door. "You came close to making a profound mistake out there." He made a face and adjusted his slacks. "Customarily there is an Erus Veneficus and an apprentice who is learning protocol from her mistress. You are lacking that training. I see now how a brief lecture would be beneficial."

He crossed his arms and looked arrogantly professorial. "Unlike the Lustrata who bears the burden of balance, an Erus Veneficus should be carefree, cosseted. You never lift a finger to do any kind of work unless it is at my direct behest, and believe me, if there is an advantage for me, I will command you to action. Aside from that, you are at my left hand, a representation of arcane power applicable day or night. Outside of court, as necessary, you tell others what to do." He pointed at the kitchen. "You are theoretically not even to cook for yourself. I included this because I have told them that Johnny is doing the cooking."

I tucked my fingers into my jeans pockets. "He probably will. He's quite good at it."

Menessos's expression changed to snide amusement. "How masculine of him."

"How childish of you."

He kept pushing. "The wære working with the Beholders shows his place is equal to theirs—far beneath me."

"No." My fingers left my pockets to perch on my hips as I arched my back just a little. "His place is beneath *me* . . . or in any other position in my bed." It was a low blow, but he had threatened Johnny's safety and I wasn't going to tolerate that. "Otherwise he's at my right hand."

My words, however, had no apparent effect on Menessos.

"Actually," he said in a droll tone, "in court I am at your right. He may, however, sit upon the floor at your left."

He was making sure I knew the rules of his court. I intended to make sure he knew where I stood. "Outside of your court, Johnny is my right hand. And that leaves you to be the left, I suppose."

"He is not my equal *here*."

"Of course not. Your people call you 'Boss.' His will call him 'King.'"

With inhuman speed, Menessos was right in front of me, close but not touching. "Yes, he is the future king of wæres, but he is laboring for *me*. What would his pack think of that? Will they accept a king who labors for a vampire?"

This maintaining-the-balance thing was proving to be at least as difficult to maintain between these two males as it was going to be with witches, vampires, wæres, humans, and whoever else was involved in the universe. "Your ego is about to take over the building." I side-stepped him.

Menessos held me back, forced me to turn around. "You do not understand."

"I understand that if I order him to stop working with them, it allows him to refrain from the labor without costing him his integrity. His show of equality will stand. Your people will not forget it."

Menessos sighed in exasperation. "I told you, in this place, the equilibrium is maintained only by my dominion. In this place, you must *both* choose behaviors that do not challenge it."

"How could my calling him back upset anything?"

"At worst, they will credit his constant attending to you as evidence of an appetite I cannot satisfy. At best, they will claim I've grown . . . permissive." He said that last word as if a foul taste accompanied the uttering of it. Another tremor of anger rippled through him. "A spoiled Erus Veneficus will not be well thought of."

"Let me get this straight: I'm not to be caught doing any work but somehow I'm also not to be thought of as spoiled?"

"You are to be pampered, Persephone. There is a difference." He still hadn't let go of my arm. His other hand, though trembling with anger, rose and smoothed my hair. "You must be even tempered and show that you appreciate your new status."

"Or?" I squared my shoulders.

"Or they will question you, and then me. Already they sense a change. I have told them it is the new city and the unfinished haven. They think I am weakening."

I jerked, wrenching free only because he allowed it. "Are you?"

He scowled at me.

"Is that why you stole my blood?"

Menessos walked past me, leaving my way to the door unhindered. From where I stood, the kitchen lights cast him in silhouette, a luminous glow around the dark figure; he could have been a statue of stone, except for that bright edge glinting with life. "I must drink of you. The court must see the evidence."

"That's not the only reason."

"No." He didn't face me. "The death of the fairy had consequences."

"I'm not stupid, Menessos. Stop dancing around the truth! I know every binding has a price. But you took from me without my consent—"

His bark of laughter cut me off. "You would never have given it freely!"

My face hardened; I was truly hurt that he thought so. "You don't know that! Before we saved Theo that night, you said I was an uncommon woman." I snorted. "You should have been honest. You should have given me the chance. Now you'll never know for sure, will you? But you have your neat excuse and that's good enough for you. Isn't it?" I shouted at his back. "That's *not* good enough for me!"

"The death of the fairy, through his binding to me, *did* weaken me." He finally looked me in the eye. "I have desired to know the taste of you since I first saw you. Since you burned the stake, however, I have *needed* to taste you."

"Is that why you insisted I rest at the farmhouse? So you could feed from me in my sleep? As if I wouldn't notice the marks?" My anger was growing hot. Fast.

"You have drawn on me and I have given according to your need. Alone with you last night, the first time since just before you altered the mark I placed on you, I could not resist." As further excuse he added, "I saw to it you were well fed first. I took only what I had to have."

The pitiful justification infuriated me. "Do you not hear yourself? You *planned* it!" I wished I could take that moment back and make him ask, make him do it the right way. If I could, I'd draw that power back to me and see if he could take it again.

I could feel the buzzing power he had drawn from me like the vibrating energy of a stone thrumming in my palm. Though I wasn't touching him, I recognized the magnitude and character of it as my own. That electricity was there inside of him, as was my hex.

"When have I *not* accepted the responsibility thrust upon me?" I demanded. "When have I drawn the line and said 'no, this is too much'? I am your master! I accept what that means, Menesssos! The good and the bad." I called that energy to surge to the surface. "And it's time you did, too."

Wind swirled around us. Power crawled over his body—my power, manifest in scribbles of white-blue light. *Discharge, escape back to me!* My hands cupped before me, ready to catch it. Reaching his sternum, the energy leaped like lightning. An arc of electricity zapped into my palms. I gasped, holding the power like a water hose, feeling it fill my aura as if I were a glass filling with icy water.

It put Menessos on his knees, panting and swaying.

CHAPTER THIRTEEN

"**E**nough!" Menessos cried.

I twisted and squeezed the power, stopping it—as if making a kink in a garden hose that stopped the flow of water—but I could easily reopen the flow between us in the same manner. I commanded, "You will ask, when you are in need."

He nodded, panting. "I will ask."

"You will not threaten Johnny again."

"I will not."

"And you will not harm him."

His lips pressed together.

"You will not harm him!" I unkinked the cord.

Menessos shouted, "I will not!"

I shut down the power flow between us.

Menessos caught the couch with his arm and managed to keep from falling over.

I stomped closer. "Did you *feel* that, Menessos? Did you *see* and *believe* that?"

"You are a marvelous quick study," he said between breaths.

Someone knocked on the door.

Feeling absolutely invigorated, I went to answer it and pressed the intercom button. "Yes?"

Mountain's voice replied, "I've brought the prize."

Menessos climbed onto the couch and whispered, "Stall, if you will."

"Just a minute," I said into the speaker, but did not move. When Menessos nodded at me I opened the door.

Mountain entered with a paper-covered painting. "Shall I hang it, Boss?"

"Please do." Menessos sounded normal.

Striding to the wall, Mountain placed the wrapped frame against the end of the couch, and reached up to the steel framework on the wall and turned it. The metal screeched intolerably for an instant, then the security frame was vertical.

It's not Ariadne *then.*

He unwrapped the package but the face of the frame was covered with white gauze. Mountain hung the picture, adjusted it straight, then set about connecting wires under the lip of the security frame. "Five . . . four . . . three . . ." he whispered, then jerked the gauze down, just as a field of blue static buzzed in front of the painting and dissolved.

"*The Charmer?*" I asked, gaping at Menessos.

"You do like Waterhouse, correct?"

Mountain flipped the switch for the accent lighting and left us. Portrayed in oil, a woman sat on the edge of a pond with a harp. At her feet, fish were swimming near to hear her play and sing. Her hair was dark, her skin pale, and her dress was a blue that matched the accent colors Seven had chosen to trim the room.

I couldn't look away from it, but my mind was racing.

Menessos—with his infinite wisdom—had been trying to weave this juncture to highlight his authority, then punctuate it with this extravagant gift. His ability to provide a valuable work of art as a decorating accent was supposed to make me feel indebted.

Johnny insisted the vampire gained his greatest advantage with his expert use of manipulation; Xerxadrea claimed Menessos's ability to weave events to meet his desired eventual outcome was his best—and most dangerous—talent.

My arms crossed over my chest. He hadn't exploited me this time. I had risen—*grown up?*—and somehow proved myself the stronger. He was probably regretting having hung the "prize" here. I turned away from the painting to see if there was a sign he was conceding this point.

Damn him.

Xerxadrea was right. He was nothing but smug—as if he had just lavishly rewarded my forced growth.

Menessos left shortly after Mountain, saying his people were rising. That was fine by me.

I figured the Beholders would work Johnny hard while they had him, so I decided to fix some dinner. No one would see my little rebellious act of self-sufficiency, but it made me feel better. With a pot of water on to boil for pasta, I rinsed the green peppers.

The protrepticus rang. Gounod's "Funeral March of a Marionette"—the *Alfred Hitchcock Presents* theme song.

"Hello?"

"Got a call from Xerxadrea coming in," Samson said.

"No insult, tonight?"

"Of course not, my lady," he said sweetly.

My lady? Not "little girl"? That piqued all my intuitive warnings.

"Hello?" Xerxadrea said.

"Hello. Can I speak freely?"

"As freely as you dare."

We're not the only two listening . . . Crap. I need to set up a time and place to strategize.

"I trust you now understand that what has transpired had to be, Persephone?"

"I'm going to be made EV tomorrow evening, so yeah." I took some broccoli and celery out of the refrigerator.

"Have you seen the news?"

"Yeah. You, too, I suppose." I wasn't about to let her and who-knows-who-else know our side of things. I separated the celery stalks and rinsed them off.

"For what it is worth, I am sorry things have had to go so far, Persephone. But we can still rectify this. I am certain you can repair that relationship if you put things right."

"I *am* becoming his Erus Veneficus."

"I have news that may change your mind. WEC made contact with the fairies."

"And?"

"Their demands are simple: they want Menessos dead. No negotiation."

We knew that. I shook the vegetables over the sink and placed them on the cutting board with the pepper. "What was WEC's response?" I picked up the knife.

"They agreed."

"What?" I put the knife down. *No sense taking extra risk of spilling my blood in the haven, huh?* "How can they agree to that?" I gave her the easy argument and cited the Rede: "*An' it harm none.*"

"*An' it harm some, do as ye must,*" she replied. "He's already dead. What else are they supposed to do? They have nothing to bargain with. An all-out war means both sides lose."

If I'd had any doubt about others listening, that sealed it. She knew he was yet alive. "Since both sides would lose, that means they're bluffing. WEC should call their bluff."

"The red fairy is not bluffing. I fear she has gone mad."

I took a deep breath. My uneasy emotions were building, casting a shadow that darkened my view of the situation. *Too much of that lately.* What was happening between WEC and the fey was necessary. Both sides were posturing and saying what must be said. "So WEC is buying time to prepare?"

"As are the fairies."

"So why are you calling me?"

"To convince you to deliver him."

"*Riiight.*"

"We know that as a pending Erus Veneficus, you are already bound to him, and that such a task will be difficult. However, you are also unique in strength. We are confident you will have the opportunity to seize control, and we expect that when opportunity arises you will take advantage of it. Officially, you are hereby duly notified: WEC commands you to deliver the vampire Menessos to the location known as Headlands Dunes on Lake Erie at dawn this coming Sunday."

That was way east of Cleveland. "And what do I get out of it?"

"They will count compliance with this command as proof that you are the Lustrata."

"And if I refuse? Perhaps it's in my best interest to not give them such proof. Even without the Erus Veneficus business, they wouldn't all be on my side."

"That's very true. If that is your decision, the Council are deliberating, weighing the risks of angering the Vampire Executive International Network by taking him themselves."

As if they could. "Sounds like avoiding one war only to start another."

"WEC can negotiate with the vampires more easily."

"With blood."

"Exactly. That does seem to render the least harm. The fey will take many lives in a war, or a single life to avert it. If the latter comes to pass, it may cost WEC some blood, but our blood can be regenerated."

"So basically you're saying that the Witches Council has already sold me out, and that the vampires will likely do the same to him—if there's a benefit in it for them."

"Yes."

So we're screwed. "The only way I can actually benefit here is if I save WEC the hassle of those negotiations, and deliver Menessos for them, thereby saving them their blood."

Gravely, she said, "Yes, child."

Child. "You don't think there's a chance that he's important enough to them to protect?"

"He's lord of the northeastern quarter of the United States, he's in their major hierarchy, but he's still replaceable. However"—Xerxadrea cleared her throat—"if they owe him favors or he has some secret information he can use to blackmail someone who could make a difference, perhaps they might rally to his aid."

She was giving me suggestions in code.

"But such unrealistic notions, if factual, would save him and cast you to your knees begging for mercy in an Elder's Court, and it wouldn't be mine."

That sounded decidedly terrible. "You're guaranteeing me that my compliance will earn me WEC's favor?"

"It's the best deal you're going to get."

I considered all this information, the options she was displaying for me. "Xerxadrea, do you honestly think the witches could take Menessos?"

"I doubt it would be easy, child, but I'm certain they can take him. They're prepared to have you Bindspoken to do it."

CHAPTER FOURTEEN

The protrepticus went to static, and when I checked the little screen, it was blank. The dread shading my view of the situation darkened even more. Fear tingled on my spine. I wondered how the Bindspoken ritual was performed, how many witches it took to achieve it. *Does it hurt?*

I returned to chopping up vegetables, and the weight of the knife in my grasp felt reassuring. Still, I jumped when the door flew open.

Johnny came in. He shut the door, scanned the room as if he hadn't seen me, and called out, "Lucy, I'm home," doing a surprisingly good impression of Desi Arnaz.

I really wanted to play along and not think about WEC's threat but I hadn't a clue what Lucy would reply to keep it going.

He came to the kitchen area. "Whatcha doin'?"

"Well, I've been told that the Erus Veneficus has a duty to be pampered and apparently being pampered does not include cooking, but you know me."

"You're a rule breaker?" He feigned shock. "What happened to 'the right thing for the right reason' bit?"

Making big, innocent eyes at him, I said, "Helping myself is the right thing when the reason is my own hunger and that of my hardworking man's."

"Ooooo." He planted a kiss on my cheek, slipped behind me, and copied the gesture on the other side. Suddenly the knife was in his grip, not mine, and he was chopping the veggies more skillfully than I could. "Tuck your fingers just under like this," he said, showing me his technique, "and keep the tip of the knife on the cutting board at all times. You have more control that way. You try."

He set the knife down, and as I picked it up again, his hands went to my waist. I finished chopping the rest of the peppers while he kissed the unbandaged side of my neck and whispered, "Good. Now, isn't that better?"

"Yeah."

"So what are you making?"

"Pasta and veggies."

"Meat?"

"Whatever you want."

"Heh, heh, heh." His warm touch rose up my sides, not tickling, but moving so his fingers could just stroke the underside of my bra. "How about breast? Chicken breast, that is." And then he was gone, getting meat from the refrigerator. In minutes he had the pasta in the boiling water, and was preparing to stir-fry the meat and veggies in separate pans.

"One pan," I said.

"You sure?"

"Yes." A little chicken would be okay. He poured olive oil in the pan then added the sliced meat, stirring it around with a wooden spoon. "Aren't you tired?"

"Yeah. I mean, we knew those Beholders work hard and fast, but damn."

"Let me cook then. You supervise."

"No, I got it."

Since he was taking over, I went to sit at the bar side.

I considered telling him about my run-in and power struggle with Menessos, but that could lead to the threat Menessos made and I didn't want to add to Johnny's stress today. I'd gotten Menessos's promise and that was good enough.

He put the wooden spoon down. "Is that another what's-his-house painting?"

"*Water*house. Yes."

"Figures."

"Don't you like it?" I rotated my chair to examine it again. "The color works perfectly in here."

Johnny checked it again. "Yeah. I guess it's all right."

I spun back. "It's 'all right'? Straightlaced and geeky little museum curators would get into fistfights over that painting."

"Can we get that on pay-per-view?" Laughing, he added, "I remember a boxing match that Ig took me t—"

I waited for him to finish, but he didn't. The pan on the stove was now receiving his complete attention.

"And?" My elbows rested on the counter.

"Guy got knocked out in the third round." His tone was even.

The rest of the cooking was done in silence. When Johnny served up two scrumptious-smelling plates and set them on the counter, he said, "I've decided that"—he lifted a bottle of white wine—"Ig can't help us and the pack is going to be reeling so it's best to just leave them alone." He dug around in the drawer and came up with the corkscrew. "We'll find another way." He opened the wine, poured two stemmed glasses, and put them on the counter for us. He came around to join me and took his own seat. "There's always another way, right?"

I smiled. He smiled back, but his eyes were somber and sad. He wanted me to agree with him. His father figure was dying, and I definitely understood why he wouldn't take action to become Domn Lup through ending that man's life. I wasn't close to Aquula, but I wasn't willing to take her life—even to save Menessos's.

Still, he couldn't avoid his destiny forever.

On one hand, I wanted to push him toward it. I felt desperate for help to save Menessos. The pack would have to do as Johnny bid them if he claimed that leadership. On the other hand, this wasn't my only option for aid. Xerxadrea had pointed out another avenue to pursue.

But between those hands was my heart, and it recognized that right now Johnny was clinging to the last bit of control over his life and his decisions. If I pushed him, in any direction, it would only make this moment ugly when it didn't need to be. All I truly needed to do was support Johnny. "Right."

We ate in silence, but with my last bite I couldn't resist nonchalantly bumping his leg gently with my foot. He bumped back in kind, and soon we were having a contest under the bar countertop like two bratty siblings. When my next turn came, he twisted his rotating barstool quickly away and slid out of range.

"No fair!" I cried, but he wheeled on me, spinning my seat. "I just ate!" I protested. After he sent me around three full times, I was laughing and squealing objections. He stopped me abruptly and I nearly tumbled from the stool, a bit dizzy. He watched me laugh, nakedly admiring.

"What?"

Johnny didn't answer; he leaned in. His mouth, those perfect, just-full-enough lips pressed to mine. That sweet tightening of low muscles gripped me deep inside, squeezing desire through me.

I buried my fingers in his dark curls and kissed him. His hand on the small of my back, he drew me to him. His heated touch started a chain reaction. In seconds, all my inhibitions had burned away.

He lifted my shirt up, breaking off the kiss long enough to yank it over my head. Inching my bottom to the front edge of my barstool, I wrapped my legs around him and leaned back, arching my spine. My head fell back as he unfastened the front-hook bra. A shrug and the bra dropped to the floor. I swiveled my hips, twisting the stool, to grind against him.

Johnny gave an appreciative growl and his hands stroked my thighs. When his fingers left the denim and touched my bare skin at my waist, sensations rocked through me. He traced my ribs, then lightly caressed the skin where my breasts rounded up. It tickled and teased. My nipples hardened, aching for his touch.

I arched my back further, begging wordlessly for more. My reward was the tip of his tongue flicking, wetting my skin—just enough that the cool air of the room made me even more aware of how I yearned for his touch.

Johnny unbuttoned the top of my jeans.

He released the zipper with maddening slowness. I couldn't wait for him to be inside of me. "Please."

Deftly removing my shoes, he freed me of my jeans and panties at once, then glanced disapprovingly at my socks. I bit my lip, then shifted my legs until I could hook toes in the top of one sock and push it off, then repeated for the other.

Lowering my feet to the footrest on my barstool, I leaned forward, reaching for him. In a heartbeat, his shirt had joined my clothes on the floor. My eyes took in the tattoos, the lean hard chest, the contoured abs. I reached for his belt buckle.

"No," he whispered, and shoved the plates and glasses away. He scooped me up and set me on the black granite countertop. It was cold and I couldn't suppress a shiver.

With a masculine look of approval for my little shiver-shimmy, he stood there between my knees and unfastened his belt, unbuttoned his jeans, and opened the zipper with excruciating slowness. I watched, waiting and ready. So ready. He pushed his jeans down and exposed his smooth, hard cock.

I whispered, "Give it to me."

He didn't. He pressed closer and kissed me, his usually soft lips now firm and urgent. His tongue searched for mine. He tasted like sunshine, like sweet heat, like sugar boiling into rich caramel.

My legs wrapped around him again, scooting me to the edge of the counter. "Just a taste," he whispered, and dropped to his knees. He ran his tongue over me until my legs were quivering. I gasped as my every nerve jolted in response. It was so good, I was so close, but this wasn't enough.

"Please, Johnny, I want you inside me."

He stood, adjusting himself.

I couldn't wait another second. Not even to be teased. I squeezed with my legs, trying to thrust him into me. But he stood firm, not letting me. He gave a very male little laugh. He was in control this time.

He rolled his hips, his cock rubbing up and down my wet labia.

Putting my hands far back, I stretched over the counter, arching up so his movements hit at the right angle, rubbing my clitoris in a way that felt so damned good. I sighed.

Then he pressed inside of me.

The breath I'd just squandered rushed back as I gasped. He grasped the counter on either side of my buttocks, and I squeezed my legs around him. He had an instant rhythm, thrusting hard and deep, retreating more slowly. I relished the retreat, but it was the harsh thrusts as his body pounded against me that rushed me to the edge.

I rose up and held his face in my hands, staring into his Wedjat-tattooed eyes. His gaze fell, and I followed it down, watching as our bodies joined, seeing how he filled me up.

That did it for me.

I fell back across the counter, arms spread wide, knocking the wine over. Cool liquid poured under me, spilled into my hair. One glass shattered on the floor but I didn't care. Ecstasy roiled me. The wine made the granite slick, and Johnny used that to his advantage. Instead of holding the counter, he held my hips, pulled and pushed me, fucking me fast.

I couldn't cry out, my voice was lost in the electric tremors shaking me. It was glorious. The theater could have fallen down around us and I wouldn't have cared as long as he didn't stop. I didn't even care when Menessos flashed through my mind, when I felt him tap the hex and taste my pleasure with me. He savored my wanton disregard like a piece of candy on his tongue. He laughed and I felt the heat of his breath in my ear, felt the sting of his fangs in my neck, felt his fingers on my flesh.

Words whispered through my mind. Menessos's voice. Latin, a chant ending with: *in signum amoris.* Those words left my own lips, in whispered sighs. *"In signum amoris. In signum amoris. In signum amoris."*

Johnny growled as pleasure claimed him.

Together we rode the bliss to its end, panting, entwined, and gratefully ensnared in each other's arms. It was beautiful.

Until I realized Johnny was kissing my sternum and whispering, *"In signum amoris . . ."*

CHAPTER FIFTEEN

Johnny carried me to the bed and we spooned until he was snoring deeply. Then I slipped away, hoping to sneak out. *Yeah, finally a chance for cuddling after sex and I'm leaving.*

He roused and sleepily asked, "Where you going?"

"To shower." To keep it from being a lie, I went and showered. The wine had matted my hair anyway. By the time I'd finished, he was sleeping soundly, so I found the soft, white couture robe that Risqué had mentioned. I donned the robe and its matching slippers, intending to creep quietly from the room.

The industrial door and the noise beyond it was going to be a problem, but I had to find Menessos and confront him about this. *Bastard. I put him in his place, and at his first chance, he's harassing me in a new way.*

Releasing all the bolts and then twisting the handle, I opened the door. I slithered out fast and shut it as quietly as possible.

I hurried down the stairs and to Menessos's door where I knocked loudly. I was going to get an answer about what had just happened. Plus Xerxadrea's warning about being Bindspoken gave me a second line of questioning to pursue.

No one answered the door. I tried the knob. Locked.

Stalking through the green room and into the back-stage area, I found a Beholder washing out paintbrushes in a deep sink. His jeans, T-shirt, and work boots were spattered with dark paint. He was wiry, but his upper body bulged with lean muscles.

"You there."

"Yeah?" He glanced up. His eyes were an unusual green-gray-brown, and conveyed a brokenness that made me uncomfortable, like the eyes of a pit fighting dog. When he recognized me he stood straighter and said, "Yes, my lady?"

"Do you know where Menessos is?"

He bowed his head. "Follow me."

Tromping around the theater wet-headed and wearing nothing but a robe wasn't quite what I'd had in mind, but I couldn't back out now. We passed into the theater. I saw Mountain carrying thick bolts of fabric on either shoulder, but the bulk of the crew was vampire. My guide gave a shrill whistle. Everyone stopped and came to a respectful attention.

Seeing that the nearest half-dozen of them were scent-ing me, I called out, "You may continue." The painter led me through the house, past Seven at the podium—she gave me a distracted nod—and into the lobby. We went up one flight of now-cleaned and restored stairs to the hall. At the end of the hall to my right, two pale and lean vampires stood on either side of a cherry door with an ele-gant polished brass knob.

"The future Erus Veneficus would see the Master," the Beholder said, and bowed, leaving me with the vampires. Both seemed formidable and fierce. One could have been a skinny Viking; the other could have been a Zulu warrior. If an expression other than "badass" happened to take either face, neither of them would have survived.

They waited expectantly, radiating the threat of being hungry and on edge. I had an urge to throw my arms up and shout "Boo!" but that probably would have gotten me killed.

"May I go in?"

"Always," the Zulu said.

The Viking opened the door for me. He breathed in as I passed, scenting me like a ravenous wærewolf standing outside a steakhouse on Friday night.

Inside, the room was like a gentleman's library, cherry paneling, dark leather-upholstered furniture. A full suit of armor stood in one corner, relics and weaponry of ages past in glass museum cases. A newer, gleaming dagger with wicked curves rested in a case upon the desk Menessos sat behind. He smiled up at me as smug as a Cheshire cat.

Stopping between the two guest chairs before his desk, I demanded, "What the hell did you do?"

"I have been in here for hours, tending my administrative duties, taking a few calls, approving orders, payment on other orders, and—"

"I don't see any paperwork." His desk was empty except for decorative items and a closed laptop sitting on an unmarked blotter.

"I completed it just before you arrived all lovely in that

robe and smelling of wolf." The look in his eyes made me truly understand the meaning of "devour." "Your cheeks are flushed. I might think I'd embarrassed you but your hands have risen to perch defiantly on your shapely hips, so"—he steepled his fingers—"I conclude the flush is more anger."

"We both know I can force answers from you, Menessos. Don't make me."

"You are not attempting to threaten me, are you, my dear?"

He'd just turned my anger switch from "almost" to "on." I fought to rotate it back. "Must everything be a struggle?"

"Life is a struggle."

"I've been here a little more than twenty-four hours, and already I am sick of the damned games you play. Every time things appear clearly established, you pull some new stunt. I may walk away from it having learned something, but it's wearying nonetheless. Is there never a moment of contentment for you?"

The predatory, masculine countenance returned, and his eyes became glistening pools of gray. He rose and came around his desk as he spoke. "We all fight for what we achieve and what we want, don't we?" He settled into a lean against the front of his desk, then lifted a tendril of my damp hair, admired the bandage, and reached toward my neck. In the next instant, he ripped the wide Band-Aid free.

"Ow!" I tried to slap him. He restrained my wrist.

"I know how this works, Persephone." He dropped the bandage into a waste basket. I tried to pull my wrist free;

he held on. "I know how *you* work . . . and then you 'pull some new stunt' and I find that truly, I don't."

The skin on my neck was burning from the rough bandage removal. When he didn't continue, I muttered, "Glad to know the feeling's mutual."

"But that's just it, the 'feeling' isn't." The tone of his voice was laced with a despondency that touched my heart.

Enough of this. Every time he ignited my rage, he followed it with stirring my heart, or vice versa, shifting until my resistance was gone and my anger was fully triggered. *Let's skip ahead this time.* Intending to invoke the power pull, I visualized it and felt the charge of energy materialize—

Menessos jerked on my arm, yanking me easily into his embrace, and sank his teeth into me.

I screamed and, my concentration lost, dropped the attempt.

He raised his mouth from my neck and stood straight, but his grip stayed vise-tight. He hadn't fed, just reopened the wounds or made new ones. Drops of my blood stained his lips, ran into his beard. "You may have the means to drain my energy, but I can drain yours, as well."

A trickle of blood slowly rolled down my neck.

Menessos came at me again. I feared he would bite me again, but he smeared blood from his lips across my cheek and whispered into my ear, "There's much more to mastery than simply holding the upper hand." He jerked the collar of my robe open, exposing my neck and breasts, and bent, licking where the blood had run.

I hadn't dressed fearing that doing so would wake

Johnny, but now I was wishing I'd taken that risk and put on more than the robe. I growled, "I still want answers."

"And I still want what Johnny has." Menessos fondled my breasts. He licked at my neck as a lover would, though the blood flow was fading.

My body was well satisfied, but even so, his touch was filling me with renewed yearning. I stepped backward to be out of his reach. It took more of an effort than it should have. "He doesn't get my blood. You do."

The vampire leaned once more against his desk. "He doesn't want your blood!"

"But you do. You need blood to survive."

"Ah, but I have Beholders and Offerlings to feed me. I wouldn't starve because you denied me blood, nor will I survive only because you gave it."

But you do need mine because I'm your master. I didn't want to flaunt that tidbit unless he pushed. "You're comparing sex to blood?"

"Both feed certain hungers."

"Menessos. I think what you get should be more valuable to you."

"Why? Because it doesn't require such vigorous interaction?"

I refused to let that comment sting. "You said you weren't sex starved. So what is this truly about?"

"Johnny gets more than sex."

Aha. The sorrow in his voice beckoned my pity. I couldn't deny it, but I could fight it with reason. I went forward and put my hands on his cheeks and tried not to think about the fact that my blood was yet on his chin. Earnestly, I said, "Menessos. I am not Una."

That statement had an effect.

I felt the stirring within him cease and he stilled to his core. He sidestepped away from me and strolled to the suit of armor. His back remained to me. "You said you wanted to know about the bond between the two of you, of the imprint. I thought you would figure it out for yourself with my nudge."

"So you admit you did something."

"Through the hex, I used your passion like a ritual."

"You can't mark him through me." *Could he?*

"No." He took a handkerchief from his pocket and wiped at the blood on his mouth and chin.

"You can't make me hex someone else." I wiped blood from my cheek with an unseen part inside the robe's sleeve.

"No."

"Then what ritual?"

"It is a *link,* but without a master. As if the two of you have bonded on equal terms." He crumpled the hanky and shoved it into his pocket. "As mates."

"Like a m-marriage?" I stammered.

"You sound bewildered by that notion. You love him, don't you?"

My mouth was open. I clamped it shut.

Over his shoulder, he said, "You're not an intemperate woman, Persephone. There are emotions between the two of you, or you would not have imprinted in the first place."

All my warning flags were snapping in storm-brewing winds. "Basic rule of magic: you don't perform magic for another unless they have asked you to. It's wrong."

Menessos chuckled softly. "That is *your* religion talking."

I needed to get myself and this conversation back on track, but he'd opened another door and, while he'd likely done it on purpose, I couldn't resist peeking through. "Are you suggesting my religion is not yours, as well, vampire-wizard? At the Eximium, I saw Hecate reach for you. I heard her tell you to be forgiven. What was that all about?"

Menessos twisted around. "What did you say?" Rushing back to me, he didn't wait for an answer. "Say that again."

I backed up, bumping into the desk. Menessos gripped my arms. "What did you say?" he demanded.

Obviously, I had information he badly wanted. This was an opportunity to make that work for me. "Answer all my questions completely, and I'll answer yours in kind." As an afterthought, I added, "How forthcoming you are will directly dictate how forthcoming I will be."

"No energy threats, just questions and answers?"

"If these are rules both sides will keep, then certainly."

"Agreed." He pressed his body to mine, nuzzled my ear, and licked again at the blood drying around the wound he'd reopened. "Ask away."

My body's yearning renewed. I struggled to form my lucid question.

"And no manipulative foreplay."

"As you wish." The vampire returned to his desk and seated himself behind it.

He gave in too easily. Or, perhaps not. Mentioning I wasn't his ancient inamorata seemed to have—at least temporarily—dampened his passion. I'd take what I could get. I sank into one of the guest chairs. "What ritual did you work over us without our permission?"

"As I said, you are more fully bonded."

"For what purpose?"

"I thought the two of you would come to understand on your own, by sharing a more fulfilling union. I told you bliss doesn't have to be—"

"Hard to find. I remember. And?"

"You will share a mental connection, knowing each other's moods more readily, empathically. If there is an emotion strong enough, like fear, it may call to the other—a benefit that, as your other role becomes clearer and more advanced, you may find as worthwhile as the more physical one."

If he meant being the Lustrata was dangerous, that wasn't a surprise. I crossed my arms and my legs. "And what's the bonus in this for you?"

"Bonus?"

"You told me earlier that 'if there is an advantage for me, I will command you to action' and apparently you were commanding. All your altruistic claims aside, he's a wære and what you dared was very dangerous."

"With all that you are to me, for you to be bound to all that he is to become, I benefit. And with what he is to become, wizardry isn't as much of a threat." Menessos projected nothing but sincerity. "You must be safe, Persephone. I have acted only to increase his ability to provide protection. Think of it as a gift."

He had an angle that, while I didn't approve, I understood. "Speaking of protection." My crossed arms fell. "I spoke with Xerxadrea. Are you possibly willing to share your secret with the vampire—what are they now?—lords or executives?"

"They are presently preferring the term 'executives,' but in my company you may use whatever term you like. And no, I am not willing to share."

"Even if it would mean they came to your aid?"

"If they were to come to my aid, then too much would change, and nothing would change at all."

"What does that mean?"

"It means perceptions would change, people would think the situation different than now, but it would not be." He shook his head and stared off at one of the museum cases. "The world would have a target to blame, and an immortal sage to be hounded by museums and historians, begged for explanations of the eons. And I wish to be neither of those."

"Enough to risk dying?"

With a steady stare, he said, "Yes."

I couldn't breathe; tension squeezed me like a vise. I stood. "Don't put it all on my shoulders to save you. You have to do something, too!"

He also stood. "I am not putting it all on you. Believe me, I am being proactive about this." When I didn't respond, he asked, "Has WEC tried negotiating yet?"

"Yes. The fairies will not negotiate."

He began pacing behind his desk. "Is there a time frame?"

"Headlands Dunes on Lake Erie at dawn this coming Sunday."

He nodded.

"As Xerxadrea said, the council wants me to deliver you. Barring that, they're giving consideration to asking the Vampire Executive International Network for approval to take you, a debt they'll repay with their blood."

"If you deliver me, what are they offering?"

"They recognize me as Lustrata."

He stopped and considered it. "Not a small offer, WEC endorsement. But they still cannot force witches individually to believe it, or to like it. Depending on the influence of the higher-ups, and their take on what you represent, they could either undermine you with propaganda, or build you up with it. They could use the threat of repercussions to lessen opposition to you, or the punishments they dole out could be inconsequential." He stroked his beard thoughtfully. "That offer could be good or bad. What's the threat if you don't?"

I sat again. "That was my other question for you. Xerxadrea said I'd be Bindspoken."

His shoulders squared and his hands dropped, clenching. "They wouldn't dare!" Then his chin dropped. "And yet . . . they just might."

"How does that happen?"

"I do not know, exactly."

"They can't do that from afar, though. Right?"

His fists loosened as he considered it. "No."

"Is there anything in the Codex that can protect me?"

"Yes." He nodded and came around the desk and rested one hip on it, directly in front of me. "But first you're going to have to go to Wolfsbane and Absinthe."

CHAPTER SIXTEEN

"What's Wolfsbane and Absinthe?" I leaned toward Menessos and gripped the arm of his chair.

"I will tell you that, after you've answered my questions about what you saw at the Eximium." Still leaning on his desk, he crossed his arms.

Damn it. Did I play stubborn? Hoping that playing along would win me some points, I conceded as he had, saying, "As you wish."

He nodded, then became as solemn as I had ever seen him. "Tell me again, in detail, what you saw at the Eximium."

"Just as Xerxadrea started to announce what her test would be, she spoke of Hecate. I felt the touch of Her power, and a light formed behind Xerxadrea. I could smell raisin and currant cakes. Then you sat up straighter. Did you see Her, too?"

"I remember what seconds you speak of, but I saw nothing. I heard an owl screech." His hand slid up to stroke his chin.

"I didn't hear that."

He was intent. "What did She look like?"

"She was beautiful, and haggard. Then at the Ball—"

"You saw Her at the Witches' Ball, as well?"

"Yes. After everything was over with Beverley. Xerxadrea took my arm and then . . ." My words trailed off. I reclined in the chair, remembering. Twice Xerxadrea had been the catalyst of my seeing the Goddess as Hecate. I had also seen Her as a mustang and as a woman in my meditations. As a child, I saw Her once when alone in a cornfield.

"Then what?" Menessos moved to the chair next to me. He perched on its edge, leaning close to me.

"I was with Hecate. Her face seemed to grow old, then grow youthful in seconds. Her eyes were so strange. They were eyes of the moon, eyes that had stared into the sun for eons." She'd said I would seek Her and find Her, when I was ready to see my own soul. But I wasn't going to tell Menessos about that.

"And what of me?"

"She gave Her Blessing to us, to the witches that hear Her. 'Witches mine,' She said. As She came forward, She reached out to you and said, 'Be forgiven,' as She passed and—"

"Touched my cheek." Menessos sat back.

"Yes. You felt it?"

"Like the moon had kissed me." That made him smile and sigh. A visible amount of relief swept over him then his relief transformed into seduction. "I know who and what you are, Persephone. And you are right, you're not Una. But, I yearn for you."

Not this again. "Menessos."

"Una saw visions of the Goddess, too. And so did—so did the second Lustrata."

I was gearing up to relaunch my protest, but this information made me curious. "What kind of visions?"

"Much like yours, I'm certain. They left her awestruck and inspired. Both former Lustratas explained their visions to me, but these incidents, though compelling, do not foster the same fervor in those who hear the tale as they do for those who are a part of the encounter."

I shared my agreement with a nod. My thoughts skipped back to this Wolfsbane and Absinthe. *If I am Bindspoken, there will be no more visions.*

Menessos touched my arm. I peered into his eyes. "Kiss me, Persephone. Kiss me and I will let you see the Codex."

I made an irritated face at him and stood so I could look down at him. "I know you've lived longer in times when women were mere chattel than you've lived in times where women had rights and liberties, but that's where you are *now*. Either you're with me and you share information I need without demanding whorish behavior from me, or you're not on my side."

"There is nothing whorish about your behavior."

"A kiss in trade for valuable information is."

"Don't I deserve some recompense for what I provide?"

"You get my blood."

"For my loyalty."

I stomped my foot. "And loyalty means you share valuable information!"

Menessos laughed out loud.

"What?"

"No matter what else time and circumstance has made of us, I am still a man and you are a beautiful woman. I do not need to draw you a picture, do I?" He gestured toward the rear of the room. "Actually, there is a painting back there that depicts it." He indicated a gilded frame that held the image of a pale woman in luminous and falling bedclothes astride a man in a rumpled bed.

I rolled my eyes.

"If I gain your kisses with information I provide, I will endeavor to always have information you need."

This subject needed to be resolved so we could come to some kind of mutual understanding, master to servant, vampire-wizard to Lustrata, and vampire executive to Erus Veneficus. "I need to know how to protect myself against being Bindspoken, and if you give a rat's hairy ass about me, you'll help me because you care and because it's the right thing to do."

"I care, Persephone. I care for you deeply." He stood. His fingers caressed my arm. "Do you care for me?"

"Yes."

"Then why such a fuss over a kiss? Did you not enjoy kissing me?"

"Twice we've kissed, and twice I've been *un*willing. You wound me up in your power when we saved Theo, and you manipulated me with energy here before you kissed me and fed from me. Maybe kisses are trivial to you, but they aren't to me. They're personal and intimate and not given so freely as you'd like."

He inched nearer. "Have you forgotten the kisses after you tended the injury Goliath's brother inflicted? I won those with poetry."

Okay. I *had* forgotten those.

"I am wounded that you did not remember."

"Menessos, fine, you've made advances on me and I know you're interested. I get it. And in spite of all the kindnesses you have shown me, in spite of destinies running in sync, I'm not a player. That's not my lifestyle. It seems to be yours, so go, do your thing, but don't waste your time on me, and for pity's sake stop trying to coerce me. I don't want to go where kissing like that will lead me."

His expression went all male. "Where will it lead?" His caress slid down so he could take my hand in his.

I did not clutch his hand in return. "You said you wanted what Johnny had."

"I did. And I do. But I will not take it from you forcibly. And I could have."

That was true.

"Just a kiss, Persephone. Agree to just a kiss now and then, not from your servant, not from the master of the Erus Veneficus, but as a reward for service in aid of the Lustrata."

It sounded logical, if not innocent, and it wasn't like kissing him had been unpleasant. It had been damned nice, in fact. But that logic disrespected Johnny and betrayed his trust. He didn't deserve that.

"Johnny doesn't even need to know."

"Hold on there!" He must've tapped into my thoughts. "You would rend his already jealous heart further?"

"No—"

"Then he does not need to know."

I pulled my hand from his. "I'm not agreeing to this, Menessos." Hands on hips: my punctuation to the statement.

"He may be your protector," he said, curling his fingers around the robe's knotted belt, "but I am your guide. You have to let me lead." He jerked me to him.

I shoved away and removed his fingers from the belt as I spoke. "Whatever. You share information because it is the right thing to do, or don't. Either I die, or I'll be miserably Bindspoken forever. If either of those things happen, I won't have much need for a guide, now will I?" I pivoted on my heel and left.

It surprised me that he would let me leave and say nothing, but he did. The guards reacted only with sniffing—my wound was scabbing over, but it was freshly opened. Six steps down the hall, Menessos's door opened again. "Persephone. I have had an idea, concerning the matter we were discussing, and the location of the place you need to go. Rejoin me for a moment longer, won't you?"

I stopped and considered. The guards were watching with interest. "Of course." There was no other viable answer that would maintain the pretense. And though I could likely find out what and where Wolfsbane and Absinthe was on my own, his simply telling me would be easier.

When the door closed again, he gestured to the guest seats before the desk. I sat in one and he took the other. "You are right."

I waited.

"If ever our lips meet again, I want it to be because you wanted them to. Not because I influenced you."

Sure, when it sounds like it was his *idea, it's a good thing.* "I am glad we can agree on that."

"Wolfsbane and Absinthe is in the Arcade. If you enter by the Euclid Avenue doors, it is just inside on the left. You must speak with the owner, he'll probably be the only one there, but in case he has hired someone, insist on talking only with him. Tell him I sent you."

"I can do that. Then what?"

"Tell him of your threat. He is the only one I know of who can instruct you in what you must do."

CHAPTER SEVENTEEN

The following morning, Johnny and I slept in until ten. He didn't seem aware of my short absence and went happily about making breakfast. I silently rehearsed how to ask him if he'd been aware of the magic Menessos had inserted into our lovemaking, but he exuded such happy contentedness that I didn't want to ruin it by pointing out the vampire had interfered.

Once we had eaten—I ate a whole slice of bacon all by myself for his entertainment—he had to go. He had to assemble a special-order guitar at the Strictly 7 ware-house, then cover the one-to-six shift at the music store where he sold guitars.

It was raining so we found and questioned Mountain who kindly sent another Beholder to play valet and fetch my car. Johnny would take the Avalon to work and, since the Arcade was close by, I'd walk.

After a soak in the tub, and a thorough inspection of all the expensive clothes Menessos had filled my closet with, I decided on jeans from my suitcase and a long-sleeved white cotton shirt with some decorative lace at the low collar. Remembering how the lake effect chilled the air here, I added a black fleece hoodie under my brown blazer.

Mountain was waiting in the green room, lying on the green futon couch I'd seen him carrying before. He sat up. "Boss said to show you out the back way, Ms. Witch." He yawned.

"Were you sleeping?"

"Yes, but it's all right."

"Let me go the way I know. You get some rest."

"Can't do that."

"Why?"

"They're hanging things high in the theater, best to avoid going in there right now. Don't need them trying to be formal with your presence and falling off ladders and such."

"Oh. Right."

He strolled across the backstage. "This way." He showed me to a huge service elevator, opened the gate, and stepped in. "This is how the stage sets were brought down for touring shows."

This theater hadn't been used in decades. I stopped before getting onto the elevator. "How old is this elevator?"

"Boss had it all replaced, it's dirty and beat-up because we've hauled so much debris out through here. Takes a toll."

I conceded and he shut the gate. We started up. "I don't mean to contradict the Boss, but when I asked you those questions, I wasn't teasing you. I honestly didn't know." I didn't want him to think I was mean.

"Haven rules are confusing at first." The elevator

lurched to a stop and he opened the gate. "This goes up another floor to what was the storage area of the department store, but we'll get out here. Boss said it'd be good for you to know the back way around." Mountain led me through hallways, then up the steps to the ticket booth. It had been cleaned and decobwebbed, too.

"I know where I'm at now."

"I'm to escort you, Ms. Witch. For safety's sake."

He'd showered since his shift ended and his long ponytail was still damp. The Cleveland Browns jersey had been replaced with a wine and gold Cavaliers jersey with a long-sleeved black T-shirt under it. I felt guilty at being the cause for him to miss his rest; he was undoubtedly tired. I intended to keep this outing as short as possible. "Okay. But when we're not on vampire turf, call me Seph. All right?"

"Deal."

Mountain opened the door, and, thinking he was being gentlemanly, I moved to go through. He held up a hand. "I go first. To make sure it's safe." He checked outside, then gestured for me to come through.

Mountain was ever watchful as we made our way down the street, but strolling in silence seemed rude. "So what's your story, Mountain?"

"Grew up a farmer's son. Wanted to do anything but work a farm. Got in at the steel plant. Twelve years later, my father was dead, the farm was chopped into a subdivision, and the steel plant shut down. All I could get was a job flippin' burgers. Boss offered better benefits. I donate blood and work hard. In return, I'm fed, I have a roof over my head and a bed that fits me. And like he promised, I never get bored."

"He works you hard."

"I'd rather have something to do than nothing to do." He paused. "What about you? What are you giving up to be at his side? If you don't mind sharing, that is."

"I don't mind at all." I told him about my land, thinking he'd find that interesting. "I have twenty rural acres. I just live in the farmhouse and rent the acreage to farmers who've planted corn on it. I'm hoping that taking this role will actually assure me the chance to go back there safely."

The sun was hidden behind the rain clouds but the precipitation had stopped falling so my hood stayed down. Still, the breeze was stealing a few extra degrees from the day. Having added the hoodie was a stroke of genius on my part. "Do you ever feel afraid around all the vampires?"

"No. They taunt all the Beholders, especially the new ones. Called me Bloodmobile at first since I'm so big. Still, what the vampires dole out is less humiliating than being the fat man working the grill. They have harassment laws, but what's a twenty-year-old shift manager supposed to do about the customers—spoiled teenagers— spouting cruel comments at the cook?"

There was something off about the notion that taking what human teens dished out was worse than what vampires might do. "So how'd you come to be called Mountain?"

"With my mark, my strength increased. I'm almost immovable."

I didn't doubt that. "Do you think he'll turn you?"

"Don't want to be a vampire."

I was surprised. "Most of the Beholders want to be vampires, though, don't they?"

He didn't answer immediately. I saw a sign that identified this as Superior Avenue. "Hey, aren't we supposed to be on Euclid? Menessos said the place I'm going to is just inside the Euclid entrance."

"The Superior entrance is much prettier."

I meant to keep it short to benefit him, and here he was choosing to go the long way to benefit me. He was a big sweetie. "As long as you know where you're going."

Farther down the sidewalk, he answered my prior question. "Some Beholders want to be timeless immortals, I guess. I don't know why."

"I thought that was standard. Why don't you want it?"

"I know my place. I've seen the bottom, and seeing it, feeling that low, leaves scars. I'd rather die than go back there, and when I say die I mean real death. Not undeath. My place isn't anywhere near the top. Why would I want that to go on forever?"

"You're not afraid of dying."

"No. But yeah, the Beholders who are desperate to become vampires, they are. You can see it in their eyes. That's why he won't make them."

"Do they know he won't?"

"Most of us know that won't happen. We're just strong men who've lost our place in society. Some were homeless and had nowhere else to go. Some were fed up with the unjust corporate bubble. Some couldn't break in. Others couldn't break out. A couple couldn't handle a breakup. A few just broke down." He flashed a wistful half-smile that disappeared as quickly as it came. "A lot of broken people in the Boss's stable. But hard work, and the ability to perceive what the real goal is, garners rewards."

My confoundedness was genuine. "Huh."

"What?"

"I don't know. To me, it seems that taking shelter with vampires would only be an alternative end to an already self-destructive cycle. I hadn't considered that people could find a new beginning and a safe refuge with a vampire."

Mountain tipped his head toward me. "Do you know why we call him Boss?"

"No."

"We aren't slaves. We do honest work and are compensated fairly."

I nodded.

"Here we are." I followed his gesture and I stopped in my tracks. All the beautiful characteristics of stone were showcased in one elegant façade. Above and to either side of the arch were six smooth columns with ornate capitals, creating vertical lines. An elaborate frieze and layered, rough-hewn stones created horizontal lines. But it was the giant masonry arch, the flair of femininity, that tied it all together and commanded attention. Like a woman who knew how to adorn her curves, the stones of the arch were edged with fascinating and intricate details.

I'd lived near here most of my life and never realized that close by there were gorgeous reminders of how much care and talent people used to put into architecture. "Mountain, thank you."

"For what?"

"For bringing me up Superior. I wouldn't have wanted to miss this."

His cheeks dimpled with a wide grin. "You're welcome . . . Seph. C'mon."

Mountain opened the doors and led me inside, where I halted again to take in the scene. The interior was as sophisticated and eye-pleasing as the exterior. "Wow."

"The two buildings here are joined by this five-story Arcade. The glass skylight is over three hundred feet long. There are eighteen hundred panes of glass up there."

After filling my sight with the long dome of the skylight, I took in the details before me. The four balconies all had wrought-iron rails that incorporated brassy street lamps. Along the walkway, broad-leafed plants thrived. Everything was marble or brass or gold, and the doors of the shops were glossy wood in keeping with that golden tone.

"It's one of the first indoor shopping malls in the U.S. Opened in 1890," he added. "And was funded by several people, but the most famous of them was John D. Rockefeller."

"How do you know all this?"

"When the Boss first came to Cleveland scouting for places to install the haven, I came with him. Research was my day job for a few weeks. Good libraries here. Did you notice the griffons?" He pointed up at the heads jutting out from the top of the uppermost level like drainage spouts.

We crossed the Arcade, with one level below us—a food court—and two levels above. Many of the shops were vacant, but that couldn't dampen my awe.

Finally, at the far end from where we'd entered, Mountain pointed toward a door. "I'll wait for you here."

He settled into a spindly chair at a marble-topped table near the railing. I hoped the chair was cast-iron.

The first door this side of what had to be the Euclid entrance, just as Menessos had said, bore the words WOLFSBANE & ABSINTHE in gold and black letters that tried to glisten, but had seen too many days to have any gleam left.

The knob nearly twisted itself in my palm, and a brass bell clanged to announce my arrival. Inside, the aromas were all I'd come to expect from a witchery supply shop. Near me were racks with slogan-laden tees and a few flouncy shirts—clichéd witch garb. Thick columns held up a high ceiling, and the mosaic tile of the Arcade gave way to wooden flooring inside. It creaked softly under my feet.

It was the back wall, however, that hooked me and drew me in. A wall of tall old shelving with large glass jars, labeled and most cobwebbed, holding every kind of dried herb, flower, nut, seed, and root imaginable. To the right were various-sized scented candles, vials of essential oils, and a plethora of incenses and incense burners. All these scents mingled with the metallic tang of large iron cauldrons and the earthy smell of brooms made with various kinds of straw and wood. My nose didn't know if it should sneeze or just relish the overloading odors.

I went farther in. There were bins with tumbled and raw gemstones, cases with wands, crystal balls, Tarot decks, and jewelry. There were Goddess statues, small animal statues, gauze bags, bells, and spools of ribbon in all colors. Laden bookshelves dipped in the middle like swaybacked horses, displaying a few dozen titles as well as stylish journals ready to be filled. Near the register was another clothing rack, taller, with a dozen empty hangers and a single rather gaudy orange velvet cape lined with a fabric showing owls and bats in flight. Something smelled like peaches.

A hand parted the pair of purple curtains behind the register, but whoever it was remained shadowed within. "May I help you?" A male voice, deep and commanding.

What was the line from The Wizard of Oz? *"Pay no attention to the man behind the curtain."* "Are you the owner here?"

"You come to make a sales pitch?" he asked grouchily. "'Cause we don't want no coffee machines, no free magazine displays, and no scouting cookies, either."

I blinked stupidly for a second. "No. None of that. I was told to talk to the owner."

"By who?"

"I'm not about to reveal that to someone who won't even show me his face."

A small-statured man with a long gray beard and hardly a hair atop his head stepped from behind the curtains. His moustache was curled up on either end like the villain in cartoons. He wore a blue button-down-collar shirt, a bulky gray cardigan, and black pants. Thick glasses, oblong and wire-rimmed, sat on his round nose. The left lens had a crack running low across it. They made his eyes look blurry.

My mind was trying to figure out how such a short man could have such a deep voice. "Are you the owner?"

He laughed. "So you were sent to ask something of the owner of Wolfsbane and Absinthe, were you?" His voice and chin lowered. He pointed at me with a single long finger bearing a long ring of yellow zircon. "You're after the *wyrd*," he said slyly, as if his words affirmed him as a mystical guru.

I really hated it when salespeople of any kind stereotyped a customer. That kind of thing had no place in true witchery and yet too often I found playgans (my term for people "playing pagan" for all the wrong reasons) using the sagely soothsayer persona to make a sale. "Obviously, the person who sent me was wrong. You're a fake." I headed for the door.

Just as I neared the clothing rack next to the door, I heard, "He may be, but I'm not."

I knew that voice. It stopped me. "Beau?"

He came into view, buzzed white hair seeming brighter for all the rich wood tones and dim lighting here. Not unlike the first time we'd met, he wore a plaid flannel shirt with rolled sleeves revealing thermal underwear beneath. This time, the flannel print was blue and green. He tapped the ashes off a little cigar and put it back to his lips. He punched a button on the register and the drawer popped open. "Maurice, go have a cup of coffee." He provided the bearded man a five-dollar bill. "And drink slow."

Maurice took the bill and seconds later passed me as he left the store.

"What do you want, doll?" Beau called as the bell on the door stopped clanging.

I slowly made my way toward the register again. "Do you remember me?"

"Yeah. Johnny calls you Red. What do you want?"

"Do you own this shop?"

"Yes. Why?"

"I was sent to ask you something."

"Johnny send you?"

"No. Not him. And I had no idea I'd find you here."

He brushed the ashes off the end of his cigar—I think it was the source of the peachy smell—and laid it beside the register. Taking his cane from somewhere just inside the purple curtains, he moved stiffly along the counter toward a stool. "You need some kind of . . . *herb*?"

Something about how he said that made me think he was asking if I was here to buy pot. "Um, no." But I didn't truly know what I was here for. "Or at least I doubt it."

"What?" He squinted at me as if the sun were in his eyes, the way Clint Eastwood did in the spaghetti Westerns before he drew his gun. "Who sent you?"

"Menessos."

"So you run with wærewolves and vamp-execs?" He dropped his head down and shook it. Then something seemed to occur to him that made him still. He looked at me, and from under the bushy white eyebrows, it wasn't quite friendly. "What did he tell you?"

"That you were the only one who can instruct me in what I must do."

Beauregard didn't ask the obvious. He just kept staring at me.

"I need to protect myself against being Bindspoken."

He laughed, the irritated, I-bet-you-do kind of laugh, and jabbed at something behind the display case with the tip of his cane. "I've seen the news, doll." He continued poking his cane at whatever was on the floor. "And I've seen YouTube."

I leveled my chin and said nothing.

"I know why WEC wants you Bindspoken. I know what you are, and what you're here for. I even know what you're trying to do." Beau stared at me. "The Lustrata is a promise and a threat. The promise of justice and balance, but there's also the threat of making things worse by failing in her task. Twice before the Lustrata has failed. They'd rather keep things as they are than risk them getting any worse." Beau shifted on the stool. "Are you going to fail, doll?"

"If I'm Bindspoken, we'll never know." It wasn't an answer, so it didn't surprise me that he didn't comment. "Help me, Beau. Tell me how to protect myself."

For an interminable minute he sat unmoving, thinking, studying me. Then he laughed. He rose from the stool and returned to the curtain, pausing to glance at me before pushing through, still chuckling.

He wasn't going to help. I started for the door. Again I made it as far as the clothing rack.

"Where are you going?" Beau called, holding the curtain open.

"You're not going to help me."

"But I am."

"Why are you laughing?"

"If you only knew, doll. If you only knew." He waved for me to follow him into the back and let the curtain fall.

CHAPTER EIGHTEEN

The back room of Wolfsbane and Absinthe was dark and had aisles created between rows of industrial shelving filled with boxes and small crates. There were two dark doors to the right, both shut. My tongue seemed immediately coated with dust—before I even opened my mouth.

"Marco," I said softly.

"Polo," Beau shot back.

I caught sight of him then, like a shadow, moving down the left row, and followed.

"Help me." He leaned his cane against the back wall and started lugging a crate from the bottom shelf into the pathway. "The lid." Together we hefted the wooden lid up, but when my hand slipped and touched his, Beau recoiled and lost his grip. The lid crashed down on his foot. He didn't so much as move his foot, he just wiggled his fingers and then made and unmade a fist as if I'd shocked him.

"Beau . . . are you okay?"

"Yes, hell, just don't touch me."

"I didn't mean to." The memory of his reaction to my handshake hadn't left me.

"Is your foot okay?"

"Yes, why?"

"The lid hit your foot. Hard."

"Did it?" He shook his hand in my direction as if waving me off. "Prosthetic. Don't worry about it."

He had a fake leg. No wonder he used a cane and walked stiffly.

He dug around in the crate. Packing peanuts cascaded over the edge. "Here it is." More packing peanuts rained to the floor as he lifted out an antique jewelry box. He opened its glass door, pulled on a drawer within, and removed a key. He offered it to me. "Hold this." He replaced the jewelry box as he'd found it then relieved me of the key. "Pick up those peanuts, will you?"

What was I supposed to say? He was old and had a prosthetic leg.

When I'd scooped up the peanuts and replaced them, I hefted the lid into place.

"Missed a few," Beau said.

He was right. Several had hidden between the lid and the crate. So, when I was certain I'd gotten every last piece of the crackly foam stuffed inside where it belonged, I dropped the lid shut and proceeded to shove the crate back under the shelving by myself. It wasn't easy and he didn't offer to help.

Smacking my hands together jarred most of the dust from them and, hopefully, it indicated "job done," too. "What's the key to?"

"This way."

We revisited the public portion of the store. Beau opened a case and flipped up the felt liner on the bottommost shelf, revealing a lock. He inserted the key, lifted the shelf up, and pulled out what could only be described as a wooden briefcase. Punching the register, he dropped the key into the drawer and shut the register again. "In the office."

I hoped this rigmarole would be over soon.

He twisted the knob on the closer of the two doors, yanked the string hanging from the overhead lamp, and a murky forty watts did little more than illuminate the dust floating in the air.

Beau put the briefcase on the desk. I studied the item before us. The hinges were rusting, and the wood had a nice patina to it. Then Beau reached into his pants pocket. He brought out a key ring that any janitor would have been proud to carry. There were at least forty locks in this world that Beau could open. Planting my backside on the rusty metal folding chair across from the desk, I hoped he knew which one he needed.

After the first three keys didn't unlock it, he confided in me that he hadn't opened this briefcase in over ten years, and that he'd completely forgotten about it until I'd brought up protecting myself. Beau hadn't struck me as the absentminded type, but as the seconds relentlessly ticked by, I found myself willing to reconsider.

Three full minutes later, I heard the lock click and Beau mumbled, "Of course that's the one."

He spun the case a quarter turn, then opened it. I expected both sides to lie flat on his desk and reveal two traylike halves, but my guess was wrong. This "briefcase" opened flat, but more like a pop-up book. Fragile paper of brilliant colors created a scene of unicorns, griffons, phoenixes, and dragons.

Beau rotated the base slowly so I could see every side.

I had never seen such a beautiful pop-up piece of art. In the center, four larger images of the legendary creatures stood posed as if they were on family crests, each supporting a portion of paper that created an origamilike cube. I realized from the colors and art that each beast stood for one of the four elements: earth, air, fire, and water.

"Do you like it?"

"I've never seen anything like it. I knew of various symbols used by witches to represent the four elements, but never have I seen these creatures used as such."

"They are more than *representations*. They are earth incarnate, air incarnate, fire incarnate, and water incarnate."

I shook my head, disagreeing with him. "Elementals are spirits."

"Why?" Beau challenged. "Because that's all you've ever known them to be?"

"Yes."

He harrumphed. "The spirit of an element is an elemental, and elementals are embodied in the flesh in these creatures. Haven't you talked to the vampire who sent you here about this?"

"No."

His surprise was genuine, but faded quickly. He grumbled, "Of course he leaves it to me to tell you. Bastard."

"Tell me what?"

He gestured at the pop-up. "That's what all this is about."

I knew he didn't mean the art itself.

"The fairies really came here for one reason: to steal this world's elementals. They'd destroyed their own. That's why they made the deal with Menessos and his buddies way back when. Fast-forward a few thousand years; the fairies are sick and tired of being at the witches' beck and call. They offer up elementals to guard the magic circles. WEC agreed." He shook his head. "He was behind the Concordat, too, I'm sure of it." He paused. "The elementals are there, in the fairy world. So long as the door's open, witches can still access the elementals—like your spirit in astral travel is just a spirit and not your body, so is the spirit of these elementals when they guard your circle here, from afar."

I wasn't sure I believed this. "Unicorns, dragons, griffons, and phoenixes were all really real and were of this world?" And Beau knew Menessos's secret, too. Maybe not the part about being alive, but he knew enough.

"Once upon a time." His smug look grew more self-satisfied as he added, "That's how we know *of* them, but what we know is *all* screwed up. They're gone so there's no proof except what people used to know, data passed from person to embellishing person over millennia."

"That's fascinating, Beau." *But what's this got to do with protecting me from being Bindspoken?* I plastered on my politest expression. "Did you make this?"

"No. But it's been in my family for generations." His voice quavered just a bit at the word "family."

"You okay?"

He nodded, studying the paper spectacle between us.

It was an opportunity, so I asked, "Why does my touch hurt you?"

"You're a witch."

"And you run a witch's supply shop. You are a witch, too, aren't you?"

His whole face seemed to harden into stone. "Not any-more."

Sweet Goddess. "You're Bindspoken?"

"Going on sixteen years."

No words came to mind other than "how" and "why," but neither of those were any of my business.

"I keep the shop just to piss the wrinkly old bitches off."

A laugh tumbled out. I couldn't help it. It fit: crotchety old man with a cane, running a witchy shop with a fake front man to basically give the finger to WEC.

"And helping you, doll, will gall them even more."

"So you will help?"

"This ain't no tea-party centerpiece." He indicated the paper between us, then placed his elbows on the desktop and leaned into the display, his stony eyes sparkling. "And you're going to owe me for helping you."

"What do you want?"

"Before the next full moon, you come back here and we'll discuss it then."

"I won't commit to anything—"

"You don't have a choice if you want to avoid what WEC is planning for you."

Couldn't say I liked having my nose rubbed in it.

"And I don't have a choice, either," he admitted. "I have to help you. If you're Bindspoken you can't help me. Reach into the paper box at the top," Beau said. "Take what's inside."

Only one side of the box was attached. My fingers delved gingerly inside, brushed something.

A flare of heat rocked me, and I withdrew. It wasn't

sensual heat like Menessos sought to enflame me with. This was like what Nana had described as a menopausal hot flash. I wasn't touching the stone anymore but the reaction continued, heat growing, spiking, rolling up and down my body. Sweat beaded on my upper lip. "Whoa."

"What is it?" Beau asked.

"It's hot."

He laughed out loud and slapped his thigh. "It likes you."

"Likes me?"

"That's how it used to greet me. It's had a long time to be alone, I thought it might have lost some zing, but apparently not."

"Some 'zing,' you say?"

"Just take hold of it. It'll calm down."

I wasn't convinced. My expression told him so.

"If it didn't like you, you would have felt nothing."

I reached in again, more determinedly. What I came up with was a dazzling pendant the size of a Reese's Cup, but if it had been chocolate, it would have melted in my hot palm immediately. "Fluorite?"

Beau nodded. "From before it had such a name."

I knew that fluorite was considered a "newer" stone in the witching community. I had heard of a farmer who acquired some previously untilled acres south of my land, and when he tried, the plow kept hitting stone. He'd realized why it had been previously untilled, and had been angry until word got around and "someone" pointed out that if he'd collect the large chunks, he could sell them to a rock dealer. He hadn't known there were such folks as rock dealers. His gratitude culminated in my choice of the pieces; I had a large hunk of the raw stone's pretty inter-locking cubes on my bookshelf at home.

Harvesting the stones paid more than the crops he'd have sown that first season. And now he had prime fields.

The pendant's thin, flat circular disc had a variety of pale colors: sea green, lavender, and ice blue. It was set into a ring of flames, the kind usually depicted around a symbolic sun, but these flames varied from gold to silver to copper to iron. *Greetings,* I thought to it and put my salutation into a pulse through my palm.

The temperature of the room, for me, returned to normal. "How do I use this?"

"Wear it, doll. Put it on a chain and wear it."

"That's it?"

He cocked his head. "Not 'it' as in that's all. You know better than that. I'd say activate it, but I think your touch already awakened it to life."

I heartily agreed. "What, exactly, is its purpose?"

"It is a talisman of power, an amulet against harm, and a charm of invisibility."

Okaaay. "Invisibility is good. Hide me from WEC?"

"If someone tries to target you with magic, the magic will miss."

"Could be dangerous for those around me?"

He nodded. "Could be dangerous if you're hurt and someone's trying to heal you with magic. It'll miss, too."

I studied the little pendant. "It's quite pretty."

"The fluorite represents both the face of the sun and the moon. The gold and copper rays are the sun, the silver and iron ones are for the moon."

"I've never seen anything like it, with that duality."

"Wait'll you see what it does during an eclipse."

I was going to have to check my almanac. "Beau, I want to be clear. Are you giving me this or am I borrowing it?"

"It's a little thing the Lustrata ought to have about her neck, doll. Let's leave it at that."

"Thank you."

"Don't thank me yet. There is, however, one more thing you must do."

"I'm listening."

"No charm is infallible, not even one as powerful as this. Any token can be removed from you. Though I'd hate to think the Lustrata might let that happen, if you're wise you'll do something more permanent."

"Like what?"

"Displace a few pieces of your soul."

CHAPTER NINETEEN

"What?" On my feet, I stared down at Beau, incredulous.

"It's not as bad as it sounds."

"N-not as bad as it sounds? Not as bad? What the hell, Beau? It's—"

"It's a binding ritual."

"Fuck," I whispered, plopping back into the metal chair. Noticing Beau's questioning look, I added, "I've dealt with enough binding issues lately." Sarcasm helped make my point. I thought.

Beau seemed unimpressed. "Suck it up, Lustrata."

I sat straighter, took a deep breath, and readied to give him a speech he'd not soon forget.

He beat me to the punch line. "Do you want to fulfill . . . and survive . . . this destiny of yours, or not?"

My lungs deflated. "Of course."

"Then you have to pay the price. It's gotten worse with each incarnation. Each time the stakes are higher, and the enemy's investment has grown stronger. If you fail, it will be worse for the next one."

"How do you even know that?"

He gauged me steadily; I maintained an air of firm expectation. I wanted an answer. Finally he said, "I had cause to do an enormous amount of research."

"What cause?"

"We'll discuss that before the next full moon."

I hated being inveigled. "You were researching the Lustrata?"

"I researched everything. I help you solve your problem, and you'll help me solve mine. That's fair, isn't it? Balanced enough for you, O Bringer of Justice?"

I could do without the sarcasm and with a lot more information. "I'd like to know what you want me to do to help you."

"For now, protect yourself. Don't let them seal your magic in. Place a piece of your soul with someone else, and take a piece of someone else's soul into you."

"How do I do that?" I demanded. "And how does that help?"

"Menessos knows how. It's in that old book of his."

My breath caught. "Menessos sent me to you to find out how to do whatever it is I have to do. Wait—you know about—?"

"The Trivium Codex? Yes, I know of it. And he sent you to me so I could tell you what you didn't want to hear or wouldn't have believed if *he* told you. It's all in the book."

"You're telling me to give a piece of my soul to the vampire?"

"No, I'm telling you to give up two pieces, and to receive two pieces."

"I need to give him two pieces of—"

"No, give two people each one piece."

I blinked.

"Catching on, doll? The trade-off must be done at one time—the three of you together. Convincing Johnny will be thorny at best."

"Johnny's a wærewolf. No magic."

"Johnny's Domn Lup, doll. He *is* magic."

"What?" *Magic? And how does he know Johnny's Domn Lup?*

"Those tattoos. Someone figured out what he was long ago. And whoever it was had him tattooed as a . . ." He struggled for the right words. "It's not so dissimilar from being Bindspoken." He leaned back in the chair a moment. Closed his eyes. Opened them and spoke rapidly, as if he'd found what he wanted to say in some mental dictionary. "Instead of outside forces permanently hardening and sealing your aura to sever you from the energies of the universe as with Bindspeaking, this is more like convincing your magic to relinquish its power into the art and colors of the tattoos. It has the perk of being reversible. Johnny has to persuade the tattoo artist who locked the power up to unlock it."

"You never told him this!"

Beau shrugged. "He can't remember where he came from, let alone when or where the tattoos were given him, or by whom, so there's no point in saying, 'Hey, you're powerful but someone kind of imprisoned you in your own skin,' is there?" There was no remorse in his posture or expression. "I *know* what that's like. It's hell. Better he not know . . . until such time as his path crosses that of someone who can fix it. Like the Lustrata."

"What have I got to do with this?"

"All he does know is that he was prepared for you. He told you that, right?"

"Yeah."

"You must give pieces of your soul to each of them," Beau said. "And take a piece in return in order to maintain the soul balance within yourself. Then you can block WEC from Bindspeaking you. You can also unshackle what's been imprisoned deep inside of Johnny, and—" He shut the briefcase and locked it. "Oh yeah, doll, you can save the world and yourself to boot." He was smiling, but I knew this was no joke.

I just sat there, stunned by his words.

Beau stood. "Come on." He limped through the door. Somehow I managed to stand and follow.

Out in the store, he busily rifled around the shelves. He selected a small, wide-mouthed bottle with clear liquid in it. Uncorking it, he added a peach pit. Scrutinizing the larger jars of herbs, he took down three. By their labels, they were willow, moss, and orchid. He took a pinch from the first two jars, and three dry petals from the orchid jar. After hurriedly replacing those jars, he chose another, took out three holly leaves, and placed them in a small box.

The bells on the door jingled.

"Hi, Maury," Beau called. He recorked the bottle and gave it a shake, then shoved the items into a bag and pushed it to me. "Go now." He ducked back behind the curtain.

Someone knocked on the door of my room at the haven. I opened it expecting to see Johnny. Instead, I found Seven smiling at me. "It's time to get you ready, my lady."

"C'mon in."

"No, for the ceremony you will be entering from the rear of the auditorium. We have a dressing room prepared for you off the lobby. You can dress there and be ready for your entrance. Menessos has provided you a gown and accessories."

"What about Johnny?"

"Please advise him to shower and be ready. Mark will deliver his attire in half an hour."

"Johnny's not here." After Mountain had escorted me back, I'd paced and thought. Beau's charm was on a long, thin gold chain around my neck, but hidden under my clothes. I needed to talk to Johnny and Menessos about what Beau had told me—*before* the ceremony.

"Where is your pet?"

I shook my head. "I don't know. He went to work. Was supposed to get off at six." It was six forty-five now. The ceremony would begin at eight.

"I'm sure he is simply stuck in Friday-evening traffic."

She was probably right. He normally rode his motorcycle and doubtlessly weaved illegally through traffic as needed, but today he'd taken my car.

The new heavy red velvet stage curtains were drawn in far enough to frame an opening in the center the width of the black dais. Three steps up from stage level, the dais was set with three regal chairs: the ornate, high-backed one I'd seen earlier was flanked by a similar but smaller chair to its right and a feminine divan to its left. Beside the divan was a large red velvet pillow. *For Johnny to sit on, like a pet on the floor.*

"Seven, is it possible to give him something less like a sissy dog bed?"

She lingered atop a new set of red-carpeted steps leading from center stage down to the house. "I have a large black pillow of wormy silk, if you would rather . . ."

Johnny would prefer black. "If you'd exchange them, I'd be grateful."

"Consider it done," Seven said tersely, then led me down the steps onto more red carpeting. It made an eight-foot-wide crimson aisle that reached through the center of the black marble-tiled area and extended to the doors to the auditorium. The marble floor was now set with tables decked in black cloths and black candles in gold-crackled globes. The chairs were wrought iron and I wondered if they would scratch the high-gloss marble. Glossy and slick. Although the ever graceful vampires would have no problem with it, the marble could be dangerous for a mortal in the wrong shoes.

That reminded me of the Hallowe'en costume Menessos had sent me. While I'd worn the top, I'd replaced the skirt and stilettos with pants and boots. I hoped he hadn't included similar shoes for tonight.

She took me through the lobby area. The walls were covered in gathered silk. Gold wall sconces may have been original, but had been cleaned and restored to working order. "It's lovely."

Seven stopped at a hallway leading off the lobby. Pushing back a bit of the fabric on the wall, Seven revealed new particle board beneath, and staples hidden under the fabric to make it pleat. "You're amazing," I said.

Seven let the fabric fall back into place. "And here I

thought you were the amazing one." Her words had an edge of dryness, as if there were sarcasm in there.

"Why me?"

"The Boss has kept few court witches. He is so powerful himself, it was not necessary."

In case she was one of those concerned about his power—and something had her in a snit—it would be better not to feed any suspicions. "A vampire executive must have many responsibilities. I guess he decided that it suits him to allow another to help carry this aspect of court life."

"He once enjoyed the magic, displaying his power before us all and for other vampire *executives*." She said the last word with distaste.

"Maybe he's impressed everyone he cared to impress. My nana used to collect snow globes—you know, the ones with water in them you shake to make the fake snow swirl? But when I was in high school she stopped. Then, while I was away at college, she gave the whole collection away. She'd just lost interest in them. Maybe he's done everything magically he ever wanted to do and now it's lost its thrill for him."

Proceeding down the hall, she gave a backward glance at me. "He's lost something. I'll agree with that."

Oh, hell. Change the subject. "Have you been with him long?"

"Centuries."

"Vivian had quite a long life because of her mark. Do you know who preceded her?"

"The last witch before her was in the sixteen hundreds. I do not remember her name."

Perhaps Menessos's mention of court witches and their apprentices meant *other vampires* customarily kept them, but not him. "That is a long lapse, I guess."

"Here we are," she said, and opened the door for me.

I preceded her inside. It was a wood-paneled room, with a door on the opposite end. Rose-scented candles ringed a wide claw-footed tub in the center. Petals floated on the water, red roses, deep purple violets, and white daisies.

Behind me, Seven shut the door and locked it. "Now, it's just you and me." She took my arm and squeezed hard enough to take my blood pressure. Her tone was harsh as she continued, "I may not be privy to whatever arrangement you and Menessos have concerning the handsome wærewolf, but your skin reeks of your pet." She spat that last word.

Reeks?

"You've used soaps you must have brought with you."

"I did. I like Ivory. It floats." *Damn. And I thought she liked me yesterday.* "I didn't know it was a big deal."

Her fingers squeezed tighter; I resolved not to wince or whine as long as I could fight it. "While here, you will use what is provided you. We're not naïve; we know and expect that your pet is more than a servant, but to flaunt your pleasure and parade around smelling of your coupling as you did earlier is unwise. It creates an undercurrent of disrespect toward Menessos. And *that* I will not abide."

"I didn't know."

"So I'm telling you. If you have any questions, ask them now."

The pain in my arm had harnessed my focus and I couldn't think of any questions though I was sure I had several. I said, "There really needs to be a textbook for Erus Veneficus etiquette."

"There isn't. But I hear you're a journalist. I expect you'll keep fine notes and write one for whoever will follow you." It was an unsubtle reminder that Menessos was timeless and I wasn't.

"Can I get a rain check and ask some later?"

"How about you take some advice: make certain you 'pet' the wolf in private. Never show him affection in front of another member of this haven. They must all see that you are utterly loyal to Menessos. There must be no flaws in their perception of this." She released me with a shove; her vampire strength put me back three steps. "He has given you a position of honor, and I will not watch you make him a laughing stock before his own court. I will not allow you to destroy what he's built. Even if it costs me my place." Her lip curled enough that I saw fangs.

"Your *pointed* threat is understood." I couldn't begrudge her wanting to protect those she cared for; Seven was a lot like me in many ways. In other ways, of course, we weren't at all similar. *Like the fangs.* "The mistakes I'm making are out of ignorance, Seven. How can I keep from breaking rules I don't know exist? Who can? He won't tell me. Or can't or . . . I don't know. Every time I ask, it results in a show of power. I learn a single lesson in the time that he could have told me a long list of rules."

"A show of power?" Her tone remained sharp. "Do you not see the obvious?"

I didn't know what to say, and couldn't guess what answer would satisfy her. I couldn't tell her we were struggling for dominance and defining our roles. I couldn't explain about being the Lustrata. The risks kept me from confiding in anyone. I longed to talk to Xerxadrea. Or even Nana.

"Get your bath. I'll be in that room waiting when you are finished." She left. After the door shut, I heard her mutter, "Foolish woman!"

My skin was scented with rose soap, and my body and hair were wrapped in two of the softest, thickest towels I'd ever touched. The necklace had come off while I soaked, but it was around my neck again, charm under the top of the towel. I didn't want to take any chances. This evening was the public ceremony and WEC might try something.

I exited the bathing area by the same door Seven had used. The room beyond was candlelit, with a single beauty-salon-style chair centered in a U of granite countertops. To either side sat vases of roses and scented candles. Long garment bags hung from hooks to the right of the door.

Seven sat in that salon seat facing me. As I was clad only in a towel with my hair turbaned up in another, my entire bare neck was on display—fang marks and all. Her eyes were neon bright, focused on the puncture marks. She made small circles with the wine glass in her hand. Dark red fluid swirled in its bowl. "I know what you are," she said plainly. "And I know why you are being made EV."

Claiming she knew and actually knowing were two

different things. And Seven was shrewd. I was determined not to give up any information, but I decided not to play dumb, either. "And?"

"And!" She flew from the chair and stood before me, panting with anger. The crystal glass trembled in her hand, but she did not spill a drop. "And Isis weeps for me, as I cannot cry out my mourning myself," she whispered.

I stayed very still. "Why do you mourn?"

"He will not find what he is seeking."

"What does he seek?" I was pretty sure we were talking about Menessos.

"I have seen him struggling to re-create what came before. It cannot be done." She inhaled my scent again. Her look of disdain indicated that, in spite of the flowery perfumes, she'd found the fragrance of a fool upon me yet. "I have been the object you are about to become."

"You were Erus Veneficus?"

"No!" She withdrew from me. "This was before VEIN or its earlier version, before any such hierarchy started trying to brand vampires, before there were peripheral titles or even a parliament!" Shaking her head, she spat the words at me. "Long ago, I was *Isis* for him. A goddess for him." She turned away. "It was not enough. And neither will you be."

Isis? "I'm not trying to be anything but myself. If you did . . ."

"What?" She turned back. "If I did, what?"

"Maybe that was your mistake."

She *hmpf*ed. "He's altering and amending you already." She gestured at the garment bags. "And you cannot resist it."

"Should I? Shouldn't I?"

"You cannot be Una!"

Oh, hell. "I'm not trying to be Una!" I'd even told Menessos as much.

"Don't you understand? *That* is what he wants! He wants you and the wærewolf to complete the trio he once had!"

Beau's ritual might bring us close.

Seven sank into the salon chair. "I could not love him as he needed to be loved. I tried. I care for him deeply, but I do not love him as I love Mark . . . never have I loved anyone as I love Mark."

"Seven, you say that like it means you failed. Loving someone isn't a failure."

"And what of *not* loving someone who deserves it? Of not being able to be what they need you to be?" She stood and tore the fastener from her braid, ripping her fingers through her long, black hair. It fanned out behind her, full and loose, crimped from the twisting. "Do you know who I am?"

I nodded and my voice came soft, "You're Seven."

"I was once the Lustrata."

I gaped at her. *She* was my predecessor?

"Long ago," she added.

"You're a vampire."

"I am *now*." Her tone was rueful. "He could not bear to lose us."

"Us?"

"Mark and I." She delayed before continuing. "I failed. Horribly. We both failed him."

"How?"

Her gaze went downcast. "I grew blinded by my love. My heart wanted to do the right thing."

For the right reason?

"I was proud. And I was selfish. I could not give up what I had and follow his course. Love blinded me to what must be done."

"Whatever I have become, I am yet a Greek, Persephone. Like you. I used my position, my power, to achieve what was best for my people. When all I had fought for was lost, my heart was broken and my will shattered. When Mark stood before these eyes again, restored and immortal, my judgment grew clouded. *Love* led me to make choices for *him* . . . choices that failed Menessos and the balance of the world." She fixed those bright irises on me. "You must not fail. Not even for your wærewolf."

"Then tell me what to do."

"Love him, Persephone. Love Menessos as he loves you."

My throat clenched up and nothing would come out, neither would any air go down. *Love? She said* love? "He doesn't love me."

Seven crossed to the door. "Risqué will be here soon to do your hair and makeup." She left.

I stood there for a full minute, staring at the closed door, hearing "Love Menessos as he loves you" echo over and over in my rattled brain.

Her final words eventually silenced the echo: *Risqué* was going to do my hair?

CHAPTER TWENTY

I was thinking on what Nana had once told me about there being two previous Lustratas when Risqué came in wearing a slip dress of shiny orange fabric and clear high-heeled shoes. The skirt was so short there was a potential peep show in her every move, and the zippers over her breasts promised one. She should have been at the Playboy Mansion, but it was common knowledge they had something against the not-quite-human. Still, her attire hadn't surprised me, though the suitcase she carried did.

"Let's get your hair done first." She set the case on the counter.

"You know, I can do this myself. You don't have to go to the trouble."

She ignored my resistance. "Boss said to make you elegant. Goliath suggested an updo with hanging tendrils. Said he'd seen your hair up at some concert thing and that it suited you."

"That's what I'll do, then."

"Honey, Boss gave me orders. Not even you can alter them. Now sit down." She patted the chair and actually smiled. Sort of.

I sat.

The suitcase held all the tools and supplies she needed to make me into a red-carpet statement. She even had a pair of lights; she set them up on the counter first. The next twenty minutes passed blow-drying and hot-rollering my hair. I couldn't see what she was doing, but she seemed to be an expert hairdresser. "Let's get your dress taped on now."

Taped?

"We'll do your makeup and then I'll take those rollers out and pin your hair up."

Although Risqué was on her best behavior—no rudeness or apparent animosity—I still had the distinct impression that she was imagining shoving actual pins into my head like a voodoo doll.

Risqué unzipped the first garment bag and I knew this was going to be bad. She took out a pair of boots, set them to the side, and reached for the next garment bag.

"Wait," I said.

The glossy red boots were thigh high, laced up the front and had multiple buckles. Santa might wear them— if he were a drag queen. The five-inch heels—as in two inches of platform and an additional three inches of heel—made me wince. I'd be nearly as tall as Johnny in those. "I can't wear those."

"You must."

"Not."

Risqué scowled. "This is what the Boss has provided you. It's all there is."

She needed to think I was motivated by his orders, so I reconsidered the boots. They were stripper sexy, but I wasn't sure I could walk anywhere in them without breaking my neck. At least the chunky heel was not a stiletto. "Show me the clothes."

She unzipped the second bag and brought out a red dress.

The skirt was at least longer than hers, but slitted over both thighs. The top draped to enhance, and the back was nonexistent except for a few strings that would keep the front from revealing too much. I gulped. Audibly. Thank the Goddess there were matching dance briefs, high cut on the thigh, but still offering coverage if I did take a tumble in the boots.

"Off with the towel, Miss Modesty."

Nearly an hour and several strips of double-sided tape later, Risqué had proved that, in spite of her lack of people skills, she did have cosmetology talent. She wanted me to remove Beau's charm, but I insisted it stayed on. When my clothes, hair, and makeup were done, she presented me with a wrapped and beribboned box from the bottom of the last garment bag. "Boss said to give you this, and to leave you alone with it. I will wait in the bath chamber, and escort you to your place in time for your cue."

Upon opening the box, I found another gold-bordered note.

Xerxadrea sent these.—M

Pushing back the tissue paper, I saw a row of seven red jaspers—a stone known for its protection against night hazards, for promoting the courage to speak out, and for physical energy. The number of stones and the fact that each one had a means for securing it—gold chains or hairpins, some affixed to scatter pins with clutch backs—

I knew these were meant to coincide with my chakra points.

Taking the first from the box, I immediately felt its empowerment. I slid it into my hair at the very top of my head. The updo hid it, but a tremor pulsed over my aura. The second hung centered on my forehead from a chain secured in my hair with pins. The third was the center-piece of a choker on a thin golden chain. The fourth, fifth, and sixth fastened at my heart, my solar plexus, and at the upper edge of the skirt in the back.

The seventh was trickier. I pinned it to the front of my dancers' panties.

The stones did not warm to the same degree as the charm, but each jasper worked with the others to create an extra shield for my aura and amplified the strength of it. My body felt energized.

Risqué had declared me ready—a word I was heavily weighing the definition of as I stood alone in the lobby outside the auditorium doors. I guessed they'd cleared it of malingerers before Risqué escorted me to my place. I wondered if latecomers were to be held up somewhere to be allowed in later.

For their purposes, I was: ready (adj.) "completely prepared." Meaning: I was dressed and able to proceed with this ceremony. Taped into a revealing dress—*which would be on the news!*—and coached in how to *not* stomp or march. Risqué had made me practice walking in the damned platform boots until I could move with some measure of confidence and grace.

However, for my own reasons, I was not: ready (adj.) "inclined to start." At least not yet. Johnny still hadn't arrived. *Where is he? Menessos better not have anything to do with his being absent.*

Inside, voices chattered quietly, and music began to play. The voices began to hush. Risqué had told me the doors would open and I'd enter. At the sound and light cue, I was to walk the red carpet to the stage steps. I would take the steps up to center stage where Menessos would await me. She'd not said what I could expect from there.

Damn, damn, damn. I'm about to become a master vampire's court witch, I'm wearing next to nothing and about to be on TV, Johnny's not here, and whoever the WEC traitor is—not to mention other assorted unknown enemies—might try to use this event as a means of attack. Deep breath.

Beyond the doors, the music waned and Menessos's voice called out to address those assembled. My hand strayed to my neck, to the bite. *Love him as he loves you.*

"Vampires mine, honored Offerlings, beloved Beholders, members of the media, guests—welcome, all of you, to our ceremony. In an effort to be open and allow the public to see us . . ." He went on with his prepared opening speech.

Very exposed, I was an image of vulnerability. Bait. But thanks to Beau and Xerxadrea, I was not defenseless.

If only I was calm. For that, I realized, I needed Johnny.

I heard Menessos's voice whisper as if next to me, "Come."

The doors before me swung open.

Everyone came to their feet. In the seconds before the cameras flashing burned out my retinas, I saw a DJ booth (Jaded Jason, according to the logo), and a news crew area (Channels 3, 6, and 43 all seemed to be tolerating each other well). Between the cameras and the stage lighting, I was unable to see anything else.

Fighting to not squint, I found that directly ahead I could see the equally-lit stage where Menessos sat on his throne, across the long hall, and Goliath sat to his right. Behind them, the bank of screens displayed the stylized fang symbol I'd seen on the plywood by the theater's front doors. No sign of Johnny anywhere.

Where is he?

Goliath Kline caught my eye from the stage. Despite Menessos's obvious possession of the stage, Goliath still had considerable stage presence. Tall and Nordic in a supermodel way, with eyes the color of summer for-get-me-nots, he was nothing like his younger brother, Samson, whose spirit was now housed in my protrepti-cus—which rested in a black velvet pouch draped from a belt at my waist. Risqué had fretted over this addition to the Boss's selected ensemble as well, and grouched about my being afraid I might miss a call. I let her grouch. She didn't need to know what it really did.

I heard the music swell slightly. The houselights dimmed a bit, leaving the scarlet aisle more highly illuminated. That was my cue.

Chin level, shoulders squared, I moved forward amid an orchestrated melody of pomp and spectacle. My steps were as confident as any I'd ever taken.

CHAPTER TWENTY-ONE

There were several rows of chairs at the back of the house for less exalted guests and Beholders. I moved past them, concentrating on walking and the stage before me. My eyes were adjusting to the lights and I could make out that the tables seemed to be occupied mostly by vampires and Offerlings. My best guess numbered them at about a hundred. It seemed that, with the exception of Risqué, basic black was a requirement for the ceremony, or they dressed dark all the time, in love with the stereotype. I imagined some mundane humans were there, too: local celebrities, movers-and-shakers, politicos.

But Johnny was still nowhere to be seen. Had he seen his "dog bed" and refused to have any more to do with this event? I couldn't blame him if he had.

Another mental signal from Menessos instructed me to stop several paces from the end of the ramp and turn to face the crowd. *Smile regally.* A follow spot "hit" me—as if I weren't already noticeable. Around me, vampires were breathing me in, murmuring of roses and warmth.

I saw Seven—*my predecessor!*—standing to my left at a table in the row closest to the stage. A ruggedly handsome man, who had to be Mark, stood next to her. He was broad-shouldered and built like a lumberjack, as if muscle and brawn were part of whatever his trade had been in life. At the table to my right, I spotted Heldridge, the local vampire lord and owner of the Blood Culture. With the spotlight in my eyes, I couldn't see any further.

Menessos stood on stage and extended his hand. "I present to you Persephone Isis Alcmedi!"

At my name, Seven zoomed in on me.

"Henceforth," Menessos continued, "she is Erus Veneficus of this haven."

I turned toward the stage and carefully made my way up the steps. Reaching the stage I took the vampire's hand. Menessos twirled me around in a pirouette. That was a move Risqué had not prepared me for; I barely stayed on my feet.

From stage left, Mountain came forward with a large wooden chest. While he held it, Menessos opened the lid. Drawing a blood-red velvet cape from within, he placed it upon my shoulders and adjusted the hood before once again reaching into the chest. This time he held up a much smaller item. Mountain backed away.

"Shall I, Master?" Goliath asked. The others called him Boss, but Goliath always used "Master."

"No. I will display to her, and to you all, the honor I feel at having her here. I will place it upon her myself." With that he crouched before me, carefully *not* going down on one knee. Still, a few gasps were heard. He held the elaborate red garter open and ready. I lifted my foot, somehow retaining my balance on one leg, and he deftly maneuvered the symbol over the boot and up my leg to mid-thigh.

The garter was a symbol of power among witches, and in some traditions it marked the high priestess in a coven. I was certain the symbolism was not lost on the vampires, or at least not on Menessos.

He came to his feet and took me into his arms, dancing me merrily around in a circle. I caught a glimpse of a close-up of our faces in the big television screens. Grinning splendidly, he called out, "Let us celebrate!"

The houselights came up and the music kicked in again but this was not orchestrated. Now, the beat thudded from the speakers like that of a dance club. Waitstaff offered stemmed glasses on trays to the vampires and placed red pillar candles around the room. "My sincerest thanks to Heldridge for providing the beverages," Menessos announced. Cheers filled the theater.

He led me to the divan on his throne's left. When I sat, he gestured to Goliath. After Goliath had taken his place in the smaller chair, Menessos sat in the center.

Risqué climbed the steps—her golden ringlets and shiny orange rear end were probably quite a sight as she ascended—carrying a tray with three glasses. She offered the tray to Menessos first, then Goliath who pinched her bottom. When she offered me the tray, she said, "Yours is strawberry wine."

I scanned the auditorium again. Still no sign of Johnny.

The doors I'd entered through swung open and a body flew through, rolling and twisting in what seemed a gymnast's nightmare, only to leap, arcing up and out, and into a series of spectacular backflips along most of the length of the red-carpeted aisle. When the figure came to stand upright, he hesitated only until polite applause began, then threw his arms out and whips shot up with a crack. He went into a routine I thought might snap the leather lashes across the bodies of the vampires, but none reacted. The crackling sounds worked with the music and I was impressed with how this performer was emphasizing the beat through dance and whip.

He worked his way amid the tables, expertly minding his whips and flicking out the candle flames on the red pillars the staff had just placed.

Rapt, several minutes had passed when I felt a sharp coldness in the pit of my stomach. I felt fine, just *cold*. Cold enough to be distracted from the show. I looked for Johnny again.

Menessos put his hand on mine. "Eyes ahead," he whispered. His voice was tight, though his expression was pleased. "And smile."

I did as he said. "What's going on?"

"I will explain later."

The performer dropped the whips and drew daggers from his belt. Tossing them high into the air, he began to juggle.

Menessos's grip on my hand tightened. The coldness in my stomach grew. Something was wrong.

He lifted my hand and drew me toward him. "Come," he whispered. "Into my lap."

In private, I would have argued, but this was not the place. In an instant, he had me draped across his throne and his lap as if I were a rag doll. He was trembling.

Something bad had happened.

I covered his hands with my own. He needed blood from his master to balance whatever was happening to him. I stroked my throat as if offering it to him, letting him know I understood and that it was all right.

His mouth lowered to my neck, lips gentle on my skin, moving the thin gold chains out of the way. His beard tickled a little, in a way that made me tingle with urgency. My eyes shut, waiting . . . waiting. "The stones," he whispered.

Right! The jasper wouldn't have stopped any vampire from feeding, let alone one caught in bloodlust, but they were protective of me. They were pulsing, drawing mystical energy off me and storing it inside them where they would hold it like a reservoir for me to tap. That, while protecting me, would keep him from getting what he needed. Concentrating, I shoved the protective shielding back within the stones. I held Beau's charm in my palm and envisioned an orb shield momentarily containing its protection, too. *It's okay.*

Menessos's tongue drew across the bumps caressing my flesh. "I would not take from you again so soon . . ." His voice was barely a breath in my ear. "But they are killing her. It pains me to the core." His embrace became a vise. His fangs stabbed into me. My eyes shot open, time slowed.

Killing her? Killing who? They?

Vampires had left their seats and gathered at the edge of the stage to watch their Master drink. Camera flashes twinkled in the distance. And a gleaming line of steel zoomed toward me.

A dagger.

All my protections were disabled.

Goliath's body shot in front of us. I heard the clang of metal on the floor as he deflected the knife. The music stopped. There were gasps and a few screams. Goliath rolled down the three dais stairs and shot up, running. His voice boomed a command across the room.

Vampires surged toward the performer. He tried to flee, but in milliseconds they had him.

"Cameras," I whispered. Menessos withdrew his fangs and repeated the word himself. I knew he was sending that one word as a warning to Goliath, who immediately shouted a new command. Vampires carrying the performer leaped onto the far end of the stage and dragged him into the back.

Stunned silence fell across the room.

Was that dagger for me? Or Menessos?

I heard a thud of doors, distantly, but ignored it.

That is, until Johnny's voice rang across the theater, "Help me!"

CHAPTER TWENTY-TWO

Johnny, two vampire guards trailing him, was walking hurriedly toward the stage from the back of the auditorium. His white shirt was smeared with dark stains. He carried something in his arms. Something small. It moved. *A child?* My heart lurched in my chest.

Menessos came to his feet, and put me on mine. Instinctively covering the wound with my hand, I applied pressure and felt blood smear on my skin. I tried to stand. Dizzy, I stumbled. Menessos caught me and sat me on the divan. "No." I didn't want to sit. "Let me see!" I stood again, and Menessos gave me his arm.

What he carried was blue—*Aquula!* The fairy's mermaid tail fin flared in spasm.

"Make way!" Menessos commanded the vampires. They had toppled chairs and overturned tables in an effort to get to the performer. Beholders had flooded from backstage and were carrying out furniture.

I was at Johnny's side as he stepped onto the stage. "Aquula . . . what can I do for you?" I reached to my pouch for the protrepticus. I'd call Xerxadrea. She'd know—

"Waste not thy effort. Nothing can be done for me." The fairy's voice was little more than a tremulous whisper.

"No!"

"The fire fairy has seen to it." Aquula meant Fax Torris, but saying her name was similar to calling her, and nobody wanted her to show up now. "The poison is slow, but it is certain." Aquula coughed; blood was draining from her mouth and her gills. "I must warn thee."

"Tell us," Menessos said, caressing the top of her head.

"My death is meant to hurt thee, Master. Moreover, the fire fairy has vowed that if Persephone doth not honor WEC's command and deliver you at dawn on Sunday, she will target the child again."

My heart shuddered. *Beverley!*

Aquula convulsed, then continued. Her too large eyes had lost their sparkle. They seemed dim. Her pupils dilated, then contracted and found me. "She will use any means necessary to get around thy protections, and she will not stop there. Thy granddam and the new high priestess will follow." To Menessos, she said, "She will not stop until her bonds are broken." She stretched to touch his face but was too weak to reach him.

"I grieve," Menessos said, taking her hand and bringing it to his cheek.

When she touched him, she whispered, "Remember me well."

"Fondly. Forever." Menessos stroked her glittery blue cheek.

"From an immortal, that is more than enough."

As she spoke, I saw that her teeth were stained with

blood. Her eyes searched around and found mine again. "Take my pearls. I want them to be thine."

Tears burned my eyes.

"It is an honor to die in thy world," she whispered to Menessos. "Ever . . . ever do I love thee." Aquula's hand dropped from his face.

He positioned her fragile arm across her small chest. He was shaking badly.

Johnny saw it, and shot me a questioning glance.

I shook my head.

He scanned the smear of blood on my neck.

"How did you find Aquula?" I asked.

"She was in the parking garage, trying to drag herself to the stairwell. They must have flown over and dropped her on the top level.

"I was just getting here and I can't stay . . . but I wanted to tell you what was going on. Hector called."

"Ig?"

Johnny nodded gravely.

Menessos turned his back to us, moved a half step away.

Aquula's body, I saw, was covered in dark blisters. Perhaps they were from the poison, but they might have been from the proximity of large amounts of asphalt and iron in the city.

"Red, I have to go. Where can I put her?"

I didn't know and Menessos didn't seem to be about to answer. I reached to the vampire's arm, but withdrew realizing Goliath had positioned himself so they could stare at each other. They were communicating. With an almost imperceptible nod, Goliath approached the edge of the stage. "Brethren of this haven, a new EV has been appointed to you, and that is cause to celebrate. Continue your festivities, but pardon our absence as we attend to this matter." He gestured to the DJ and the music blared through the speakers once more.

I felt a ripple on my aura—as if it had been flicked by invisible fingers. Menessos's voice resonated from the speakers, mentioning "minor events must be attended to . . . dance and enjoy." Along with the words, he was giving them all a subliminal push away from any curiosity.

Goliath led Johnny backstage. Menessos was following. I remained where I was, unsure of what to do. Mountain—in a tuxedo!—approached me. "Ms. Witch? The Boss will be needing you."

I took Mountain's arm and he guided me through the backstage maze to the green room. We arrived as Menessos was opening the door to his private chambers, beneath mine. We all filed through the door. Mountain took up a position outside.

The front chamber had a round stone altar table across from the door and leather seating to the right. The latter seemed designed for private meetings with other members of VEIN. Two plush armchairs sat directly across from each other, while two armless semicircular couches would each accommodate six. The walls were stacked stone. On the back wall, two white marble pillars stood on either side of a wooden door with iron studs set into it.

"Here." Menessos shoved items from the circular altar. Stones went flying. His athame clattered to the tile floor. A clay goddess statue shattered on the floor. "Place her here." He cast the altar cloth aside.

Johnny laid Aquula on the stone table. Poisoned purple blood continued oozing from her gills. Menessos adjusted her into a peaceful pose, lovingly folding her fingers together. He lifted her head to remove the pearls and smooth her raven hair, then he bent and kissed her forehead tenderly. When he straightened, he reverently covered her with the silver altar cloth and laid the pearls at her side.

"I have to go," Johnny whispered again.

"Do you need to change?"

"I don't have time to change." He brushed hair from my neck; I felt strands pull, caught in the congealing blood.

He saw Menessos drinking from me. Had he understood?

Or maybe it didn't matter. He was in anguish, losing someone he cared about. So was Menessos. I wanted to be with them both, to comfort them both. "I want to come with you! But—"

"Will you be okay?"

He would tend his mourning alone. It made me want to go with him all the more.

I nodded. Despite Seven's objections to my showing affection to Johnny, only Menessos and Goliath were present and they already knew. I pulled him into my arms and hugged him. "Go, Johnny. I'll be fine."

"Your car's in the parking garage. I'm taking the bike. Friday-night traffic . . ."

"I know. Go. It's all right."

He kissed me quickly, a mere peck, and left. The music pounded in for an instant, then the door shut with a dull sound. The silence seemed empty and sad.

"What can I do, Master?" Goliath asked.

For several seconds, Menessos did not answer him. We waited. "Persephone, contact Xerxadrea. Tell her what has happened and ask her to come to the Botanical Gardens. Tell her I will prepare the body."

I removed the protrepticus from the pouch at my waist and opened it.

"What do you need now, little girl?" Samson's voice grumped.

Peripherally, I detected Goliath's head snapping toward me.

Oh, damn. I flipped the phone shut. "I should do this in my room, and give you some privacy." I headed for the door.

Abruptly, Goliath's wrist encircled my arm and yanked me back. "How is my brother speaking to you?"

"Let go."

Instead, he jerked me to him. Rage made those forget-me-not eyes glow like an ice-blue neon sign. "How?"

Frightened, my only thought was to make him release me. I envisioned and invoked the power pull on him. Instantly, wind swirled up and energy lifted from deep inside him. Electricity crawled over him as it had crawled over Menessos. The sensation of icy water blasted over me.

Goliath recoiled and stumbled, falling to his knees even as Menessos cried out in pain. I shut it down as quickly as I had invoked it. Both gaped at me, but Goliath's surprise quickly mutated into malice.

Holy shit! Beau's charm is a serious *talisman of power.* It had made my ability to tap that energy instantaneous. "I am Erus Veneficus," I declared. "You will not touch me without permission." To Menessos I said, "I will contact Xerxadrea as you have asked. And I will meet you at the gardens." I left.

If I hurried, I could still catch Johnny. I had just made Menessos's situation worse with two thoughtless acts. Maybe I could do better for Johnny.

I twisted through the mazelike passageway, and crossed the stage with urgency but refrained from running down the steps. The news crews were still up there. Winding through the dancing crowd—the center aisle was now thick with revelers—I tripped on a chair leg. *Damn platform boots. Have to overexaggerate every step!*

Someone caught me and I twisted, ready to invoke my power again, but Risqué let go as soon as she had me on my feet. "What's your hurry? Is the poor wære injured?" she asked, almost shouting to be heard over the music.

"Menessos has set me upon an important task," I said to Risqué, and hurried on my way.

Just as I burst through the outermost door, a motorcycle zipped past. I ran across the sidewalk, to watch as it rolled up Euclid Avenue. My shoulders slumped.

The motorcycle squealed to a halt in the middle of the street.

Car horns blared. Johnny gave someone the finger as he twisted to see me.

In a heartbeat, he jumped the motorcycle up on the sidewalk and sped back to me. It being Friday evening, there were plenty of pedestrians forced to dash out of his way. He stopped the bike right in front of me. Worried as hell, bloodied and grieving, time pressing, he'd nonetheless spent the seconds to fetch me.

"You came back."

"Look at you, Little Red Riding Hood. What Big Bad Wolf wouldn't want those long legs wrapped around him?"

The people he nearly ran over had stopped to stare at us. I threw my leg over the bike—as modestly as possible—and sat. As Johnny pulled out onto the street, the same pedestrians cheered.

Sitting at a red light, I got out the protrepticus again. As soon as it opened, Samson scolded me. "That was rude, little girl."

"Can it, Sam. I haven't got time. Get Xerxadrea for me." He grumbled, and I shouted, "Now! And it better be a private line."

The next thing I knew, the Eldrenne said, "Yes?"

"Can I talk freely?"

"This time, yes."

I relayed Menessos's message. "I'm with Johnny right now. We want to join you at the Botanical Gardens, but I don't know how long we'll be. Can you guess how long it will take for Menessos to prepare the body?"

"An hour at best, two at worst. I will contact you when I am leaving."

"Good enough for me," I said. Seeing the light change, I added, "Gotta go," and shut the phone just as Johnny accelerated. It was cold to be on the motorcycle in the thin, small pieces of fabric I wore, so I kept the length of the cape around me and safely away from the wheels. I used the time to try and form a strategy for dealing with Goliath.

Menessos had enough pain at the moment, and I hadn't meant to hurt him more by hurting someone bound to him. The power that came with mastery was frightening, let alone amping it up with Beau's charm. I had to think it through before I acted again.

The Dirty Dog was closed and dark. Johnny turned the Night Train into a narrow alley and parked in the rear of the bar. I unstraddled and followed him. Inside, we marched up the narrow stairwell again and approached the door.

This time, there was no need to knock; the door stood open. One table lamp brightened the tall room, but failed at making it cheery or homey. It had been a dark room during the day when we'd visited, but in the night, that one necessary light illumined what the sun could not. And that was a shame. The dust covered the mantel like a sheer cloth. Soot tags waved in the air like willow fronds. And the couch, so close to the light, was revealed to be not a patterned fabric, but a solid and threadbare one.

The juniper and ambergris aroma had a drop of something else, something almost antiseptic.

Hector sat on the couch, staring at the floor. He didn't acknowledge us, even after we'd entered. An open bottle sat on the floor beside his torn and dirty sneaker. He held a juice glass filled with ice and a clear liquid. I'd located the hygienic odor. The label was on the other side of the bottle, but I'd have guessed gin.

"Has he . . . ?" Johnny asked.

Voices trickled in from the room beyond the pocket

doors, but not live voices . . . I recognized the Coca-Cola jingle. Television or radio, then. I couldn't imagine that would have been left on in the room with a dead man.

Hector shook his head. "No. I just . . . I can't be in there." His voice was hollow.

Johnny crouched before the big man. "I need you to be in there. I need you to see something."

"You're gonna . . . ?" Hector swallowed, but he remained intent on some spot on the floor. He shook his head like a felon with a nervous twitch and his face pinched up. "I can't watch." He still hadn't met Johnny's eyes.

"Hector. You have to see this. You'll have to tell the others."

He shook his head again. "Todd's the one who'll need convincing anyway."

"We don't have time to wait for—"

"He's already in there. He knows I called you."

Johnny stood. "If he—"

"Don't worry," Hector said. "I told him that if he touched Ig he'd not make it out of this building alive." For the first time, he looked up from the floor. His eyes settled on Johnny. "Ig wanted you. And you it will be."

Johnny nodded. He went to the pocket doors. After a deep breath, he slid them open. When he entered, the voices from the TV were silenced. Hector drained his glass.

I started across the room, but Hector's soft voice stopped me. "Where does your allegiance lie?" When I didn't answer quickly enough he added, "I was in there earlier." He pushed an elbow toward the pocket doors.

"I saw the news. Does Johnny and the pack he's about to acquire have your loyalty? Or do the vampires?"

I thought stating "both" would lack validity, so I decided to point out what I *wasn't* as it might have more impact. "I'm not an enemy to either."

"And who is your ally, then?" he pressed.

"Justice."

From the bedroom I heard, "Don't come any closer."

Leaving Hector for the doorway, I saw Johnny and another man were glaring at each other. The other man—obviously Todd—stood between Johnny and Ig's bed. Everything about him, from his posture to his scowl, screamed that he was furious. Blond, broad, and built like a brute, if he wasn't a pro wrestler, it meant they had a height requirement. Todd was maybe five-foot-four. In boots. The bulging weight-trained muscles were his means of compensating his lack of height. His eyes darted around, dark and cunning, with an edge of bestiality and instability.

"I've busted my ass for years as his second while you fucked off playing rock star. And regardless of that ulti-mate irresponsibility of yours, and in spite of the total loy-alty I showed, he still wants you to take his fucking place. *You!*" His fervor made it clear his pain and anger could merge immediately and violently, and that he was teeter-ing on that edge right now.

"Todd—"

"Don't! Don't you fucking try to rationalize it! You've been nothing but a fucking letdown and a traitor to this pack. Ig doesn't want to see it, but in an hour, what Ig wants won't matter. I can wait that long. I'll fight that long." He took a fighting pose and, for the first time, became aware of my presence. "Huh." He gestured at me and added a contemptuous smile. "Brought a witch for backup? She doesn't scare me." He inched closer to Johnny. "I've seen the news. She's nothing but a blood whore."

Johnny threw a punch, a left. Todd ducked, but Johnny countered and, crouching into nearly a squat, landed a right in Todd's gut. While Johnny's arm was down, Todd thrust his fist into Johnny's jaw. It didn't have nearly the sting and power Todd wanted it to. Clasping Todd's arm as he followed through, Johnny rose to his full height, and used the other man's momentum to throw him to the floor. "Mind your mouth."

Todd sat up. "You were there! I saw you! They had live coverage." He got his feet under him and stood, moving slowly to the foot of the bed. Johnny was nearer Ig's head. "The vamp fed on her, she bled into him while the whole fucking world watched. And after years of absence you want to come in here like some damned prodigal son, with *her* on your arm, and make a claim for the pack? Fuck you, Johnny! Fuck you."

Ig groaned behind them. He could not speak.

Johnny landed a punch to Todd's right eye; it snapped his head back and Todd stumbled three steps back to keep from hitting the floor.

Hector came up behind me at the door. "Todd," Hector said huskily.

"No. I'm not letting him take what's mine!" He posed as if his feet were rooted in that spot.

"Todd," Hector said again. I smelled juniper. Definitely gin on his breath.

Todd spat on the floor. "Over my dead body, Hector. Over my dead fucking body is this deserter gonna put the whole pack in danger with his witch-bitch!"

Johnny roared in anger. I felt a flare of energy surge off him unlike anything my aura had ever detected. His body trembled, his hands unclenched and rose up, turning dark even as he kicked off his boots and tore off his already ruined shirt. I backed up, into Hector, who didn't budge.

Todd retreated also, but came up against Ig's bed and his legs bent, sitting him on the edge as Johnny went into a full transformation. He stripped out of his clothes just in time, and glanced toward me even as his skin darkened and his snout pushed out. It was horrific and yet fascinating to watch as his skin rippled, his shape changed, and fur sprouted.

As he fell on all fours, a triumphant howl filled the room.

Ig was grinning.

Johnny growled at Todd, who shook his head. "Not possible. This isn't possible." He pointed at me. "You did something."

I shook my head emphatically side to side.

"And it didn't affect either of us?" Hector asked. "She didn't do anything."

Johnny growled again, lips curling back and hackles rising.

Ig began chanting. It sounded like, "Now. Now. Now."

Todd's feet came under him and he stumbled backward to the wall, staring. Johnny's haunches gathered and he leaped up onto the bed gracefully, lightly, straddling Ig, who continued chanting, "Now, now, now." Ig lifted his arm and gripped the black wolf's hackles, encouraging the animal toward his neck.

Johnny's neck arched back and a mouthful of jagged teeth bared as he prepared for the strike. I didn't want to see this. My eyes squeezed shut.

"Now, now, nnuh—"

As the wet sound of a torn throat met my ears, I pressed my face into Hector's chest. Despite his fear of me at my previous visit, he put an arm around me comfortingly.

CHAPTER TWENTY-THREE

I g was dead.

Johnny leaped down and lay upon the floor beside the bed, head and tail low. He gave a single whimper. The flash of power that had hit me earlier now seemed to *whoosh* back into him. Fur retracted, dark skin lightened, and bones and shape reverted.

He was still, cheek on the floor, eyes shut, blood-smeared face stuck in a grimace.

With my head downcast to keep the image of the throatless body on the bed from making its way to my nightmares, I left Hector and went to crouch with one knee down beside him. "Johnny." I touched his shoulder; his skin was heated.

At my touch, he stirred. His eyes caught the edge of my skirt; from his angle he could see the dancer undies. It changed the grimace entirely.

"Johnny," I repeated—with a dash of scolding in it—and put my other knee down.

He sat up as if his body weighed more than the world itself. I started to help him, then stopped myself. He'd just revealed to Hector and Todd who and what he truly was. Seven had taught me that, especially with these other-than-humans, appearances conveyed valuable messages of strength and respect and status.

I stood and backed away as Johnny, naked, gained his feet. He was dirty from the floor and his chest, like his chin, was stained with dark blood. It was a morbid scene, a ravaged dead man, sheets coated bright red, and the tang of fresh blood in the air.

It was a rite of ascension, it was a mercy killing, and it was murder. Yet, it was not unjust. I felt no urge to take action and right this, for this had not been wrong.

Todd pushed off from the wall. He went forward and stopped beside Ig and in front of Johnny. He said nothing. I held my breath.

When Todd reached into the gore on the bed and removed the wolf's-head necklace from Ig's body, though, tension filled the room in an instant. Todd was taking the symbol of leadership of the pack.

He made no immediate move to put it on, however. He just studied the bloodied herringbone chain and rubbed his thumbs over the Y-shaped centerpiece. His bruised eye was swelling.

I expected a swing, a kick, a punch, harsh words, anything. Anything but Todd dipping his fingers into Ig's open throat.

I choked on my held breath, unable to form words.

With fingers coated in syrupy fluid—and wearing the deep frown of a man resolved to an unhappy fate—Todd reached out and drew a long Y on Johnny's chest, stylizing the snout and ears of a wolf.

It reminded me of the ankh Menessos had drawn on

my sternum with his blood when he'd marked me. *That seemed like so long ago . . . much more than a month.*

Lowering himself on bended knee, Todd offered the necklace up to Johnny. "This pack has no crown to offer, but our leadership is yours, Domn Lup."

Johnny squared his shoulders, and accepted the wolf's-head, chains dangling and dripping the blood of his predecessor. He considered the token, weighing its meaning for the space of several heartbeats before lifting it and securing it around his neck. Though he was still naked and dirty, all I saw was the king of wolves, a lean and muscular man with dark hair and a haunted blue gaze fixed on me.

He'd just claimed his mantle. For all the symbolism, for all the promise it held for us, it had cost him. And I already understood the price that must be paid more than I wanted to.

"I'll call the pack." Hector left us.

Don Henley's voice erupted from my bag with the chorus of "Witchy Woman." The protrepticus.

"Yes?"

"Xerxadrea is leaving for the Botanical Gardens now," Samson said.

"Thanks." I lowered the phone, biting my lip. I needed to be on my way, but I didn't have a ride. Johnny couldn't take me, he had to address the pack. "I have to go." I put my hand on Johnny's arm. "I'll call a cab."

"I . . ." He didn't finish. He wanted to come with me, but he needed to stay here. We both knew it.

I nodded. "I know. We'll figure out how to manage without you."

"Can you do that again?" Todd asked. "The change?"

Johnny nodded tiredly. "If I have to."

"They'll need to see it."

Once his tattoos were unlocked, as Beau said, he'd be able to transform without such effort. That he could defy the magic and do it at all meant that the ink spell was weakening. Or that Johnny was more powerful than anyone knew. We had to find the person who had tattooed him. But until Johnny, Menessos, and I all shared pieces of our souls, we couldn't proceed with that. *I'll have to dig in his memories. Sharing souls must grant the shareholders an All Access Pass.* I was going to have to talk to my spirit guide, a jackal named Amenemhab.

On the phone, Samson cleared his throat loudly. I put it back to my ear. "Yes?"

"The Lustrata doesn't take cabs, honey. Especially not dressed like Superhooker. Your broom is leaning on the bad boy's motorcycle."

I'd left it at the haven. "How—"

Sam rolled his eyes, literally, around in his head. "Do you really need to ask that, witch?"

Riding the broom, I discovered another problem with the boots. The high wedge heels made it impossible to sit a broom properly with my feet tucked under my bottom. *Menessos and I are going to have a long talk about shoes before he has the chance to send me any others with the expectation that I'm going to wear them.*

Flying over the gardens, I scanned for any movement or people. The moon was waning, only a few days past full, but clouds were diffusing its light. So I had to rely on the street lamps lining Wade Oval and the soft glow they cast through the leafless trees. Still, I saw no one moving inside the gardens. So I steered lower and skimmed along the perimeter. I saw two shadows in tailored suits on East Boulevard and recognized Menessos and his next in command.

Damn it, Goliath's here.

Menessos sprang over the Botanical Garden's fence and landed beside a white oak. The fence wasn't incredibly high, but I was impressed that such fine suits could endure that kind of activity without damage.

Goliath passed what had to be Aquula's wrapped body to him, then vaulted into the gardens himself before taking the bundle back.

I considered waiting until Xerxadrea showed, but my conscience reminded me that I was the Lustrata. Being a coward around Goliath wouldn't cut it. So I intentioned myself under the branches—brooms steer on intentions—and landed on the pathway behind them. Maybe giving him the higher ground would show my lack of hard feelings.

Menessos came forward. Goliath, holding the little body as if it were a swaddled infant, wore indifference like a mask *Though I put him on his knees, he's likely assuming I'm foolish to give him any advantage.*

"The rose garden," Menessos said. "She would like that."

I'd been to the gardens a few times, and having just done a flyover, I led the way. After a few steps I realized this was silly. The vampires could find their way in the darker garden interior better than I could, and with me having to contend with the impractical boots, I just slowed our progress. I followed inset stone stairs that, as the pathway steepened, gave way to railroad timbers. At the bottom, going around a spindly fir tree, we passed a hedged container bed and arrived at a concrete path with rounded steps and two stone masonry columns supporting wrought-iron gates.

In the summer, hostas lined this pathway with their broad and lush leaves, but the gardeners had evidently been preparing the beds for winter. In the dark, the empty patches were ominous in this solemn place, too quiet without crickets.

We emerged at a clearing with a tall red oak. I spotted Xerxadrea flying over. We hurried down the stone path and stopped at the edge of the rose garden. The roses, trained over the arches in the summertime, had also been trimmed back for the winter. The main bed held sad remnants of red and orange mums, and the water feature was drained and dry.

I knew this place could be so much more. To find it lacking just now, with the sad duty we had before us, made holding back my tears more difficult.

Xerxadrea stood before one of the stone benches. She wore white robes, and her hair, parted in the center, fell loose about her shoulders. Single white strands rose on air currents and afforded an extra measure of mystery to her magical countenance.

In one hand she held her broom; the other was just removing a black velvet sling bag from her shoulder. When she settled, Ruya landed where the bag's strap had lain. "Water is the element of the west, and this is the western bench," she said. "Come summer, it will overlook the spray of water, but be in the shade of roses."

"Perfect." Menessos moved into position beside her at the stone bench. She furnished him with items from inside the velvet bag and he quickly arranged the bench as if it were an altar. As he worked, I studied him. He was dressed in a suit as stylish as any he wore, but next to Xerxadrea's ceremonial garb he almost seemed incongruous.

He lit a pair of illuminator candles and placed a dried starfish in the center, made a ring of eight white candles around it, and ended by creating a ring of aquamarines and tiny shells outside of that. Xerxadrea passed the velvet bag to me to hold. As an afterthought, I slipped it over my head and underneath one arm as Xerxadrea had carried it. She must have been distracted not to simply do this herself.

Menessos removed his suit jacket and he passed it to me. I shoved it quickly into the bag. The candlelight showed a subtle white-on-white pattern to his shirt. He and Xerxadrea now seemed more compatibly attired, enough to perform a funeral rite.

At Menessos's signal, Goliath came forward and held out the bundle. Menessos took the swathed body into his arms and cradled it, saying,

> In this world, so far from your birth,
> Your precious life has ended.
> So I offer your body to the earth
> In this garden, expertly tended.

Menessos lifted Aquula up high and went on.

> May your spirit pass into cool blue waters,
> Finding your way beyond the veil
> To join the ocean's daughters.
> Someday, perhaps, I will see you there.

His aura pulsed, sending out energy he didn't have to spare. In response, just behind the bench, the rich black earth writhed. At the roots of a rosebush, the ground opened up to accept what Menessos had offered. Roots reached up, waving in the air in a manner that had me thinking of an octopus. Leaning over the bench, Menessos placed her into those waiting arms. Suspended there, Menessos blew out each candle and took up the aquamarine and shell before it, tucking them inside the swathing. Lastly, he took up the starfish, inserted its topmost and bottommost points under the wrappings, and whispered, "Until then."

The body sank as the ground received her and conveyed her deep enough not to be found by the groundskeepers.

I intended to let this moment of grief pass, and offer some of my energy—not blood—to him soon. After all, I had my bloodstone back at the haven. I could draw some energy for myself out of it if I needed.

Xerxadrea faced the sky and whispered something to Ruya, who took to the air, clutching something in her talons. I had to wonder what. Curiously watching the Eldrenne, I saw her flip her broom bristle side up—and the night was pierced by a sudden, shrill whistle.

Xerxadrea stamped the wooden handle end of her broom onto the stone pathway and cried out, *"Afflatus!"* Air whooshed outward from her, shoving the vampires and me backward, knocking away leaves, and propelling small, unanchored things like fairies into the air, tumbling as if shoved.

Fairies!

In the next instant, Xerxadrea had settled onto her broom and seized Menessos by the arm. "Come!" He fell across the broomstick and they shot into the air.

I straddled my broom and glanced at Goliath. I couldn't leave him. The fairies had already killed one of their own to wound Menessos, they'd surely kill Goliath if they could. "C'mon!" I shouted.

He didn't move.

The broom lifted me aloft and as much as possible I tucked the toes of the boots up behind me.

A fireball zoomed through the air toward me. Beau's charm grew warm against my skin. The fiery blast shifted and hit the stone pathway. Luckily, Goliath had leaped clear the opposite way, and crouched beside the next bench. I heard the skittering laughter of fairies. That fireball meant one thing: fire fairies. *Fax Torris is here!*

"Now!" I shouted, gliding swiftly in to get him and concentrating on drawing protective energy back out of the jaspers and into my aura.

From the tree, fairy shot filled the air like a gray cloud descending on Goliath. He stood and ran toward me, but not before one of the little arrows slammed into his cheek.

Another bolt of fire flashed in just as he leaped for the broom.

The charm warmed again.

Menessos still dangling, Xerxadrea zoomed by—and the fireball was gone.

Goliath latched onto the broom handle. It didn't even dip under the new weight. He heaved himself up like a gymnast on the uneven bars, doubling himself over the broom. Not a pretty position, but it worked. We flew up, but before I could rocket away Goliath pointed at a large jagged circle of broken glass and bent steel below us. He shouted, "They went into the Glass House!"

Intention sent us speeding back to it. I gauged the size of the hole. "Tuck your feet up."

"Fuck that! Drop me in and you follow!"

I didn't have time to make two passes. Leaning low across the small of his back, I took hold of the hem of his pants and yanked so his legs came alongside the broom. It rolled him uncomfortably on the broom handle; I didn't care.

He swore, but knowing I was doing this my way, he twisted more to comply. He reached for my ankle and lined his torso along the broom's other side. We were as lean as we could get.

I angled straight down and dropped through the broken greenhouse roof, intending the broom to level off at the base of the huge Strangler Fig tree. We landed.

Goliath smoothed his suit as he stood. The fairy shot, which resembled a barbed toothpick, was still stuck in his cheek. He jerked it loose, swore, and announced, "We can't stay here."

"Duh." I could hear the alarm buzzing in the hallways beyond the area.

"Incoming!"

As we scurried under the tree, I realized the steel structure and the iron mesh in the glass panes would keep the
fairies out, but standing under the hole open to the sky
made us easily accessible targets.

The fireball hit the edge of the gaping hole in the
structure above us. Some sparks showered down, but
mostly it stuck there and burned.

Strategically, I wasn't sure why we were here. The fey
could have flown and followed us in our retreat, so shel-
tering here had the merit of stopping pursuit. But now all
they had to do was wait until the alarm brought human
authorities who would escort us out—probably in hand-
cuffs.

*Was their plan to get the police to arrest us for breaking and
entering? The discredit might amount to something, but how
would that help them?*

Into the darkness of the Costa Rican exhibit, Goliath
called, "Master?" loud enough to be heard over the din of
the alarm and the waterfall.

"Here."

They were waiting on the other side of the waterfall.
Goliath and I sprinted across the little wooden bridge.
Well, Goliath sprinted. Sprinting in these boots was
ridiculous and impossible. I walked quickly.

Menessos was huddling over Xerxadrea, and when
I saw that her broom lay in two pieces beside them, my
heart seemed to stop.

Her robes smoked like the mist that sometimes surrounded her when she had to climb stairs. But it lacked
the guided quality it usually had.

I rushed to her side. When I saw how ashen her skin had become, my steps faltered.

"Perseph . . ." she said. The din of the waterfall right behind me made it hard to hear. So did a second set of alarms going off.

"I'm here, Eldrenne." I crouched at her side. "Tell me, what can I do?"

"Seal the gateway. Seal the fey out of this world. The fire fairy . . . she's gone mad."

"What can I do to help *you* right now?"

"Nothing."

"Eldrenne—"

"Fairy fire," Xerxadrea said. She gestured at her robes. "Is not like regular fire."

The fireball was meant for me. The charm had diverted it and it had hit her.

It was not mist floating around her; her robes were smoldering. The new alarms were smoke detectors. "Xerxadrea!" *No!* "I'm so sorry. The charm, it—"

"The fire fairy doesn't miss. She knew what you had and adjusted her spell."

"But—"

"I have foreseen this, child."

"What? You knew?" *She dived in. She took it knowingly?* "Then why did you come?"

Her lips were blue, but twisted into a wry smile. "Better me than you."

My throat tightened with a lump so big I could hardly breathe. I remembered her—in my cellar—saying the reverse about me being the Lustrata: "Better you than me."

"Problem is," she went on, "WEC's going to blame

you." Her eyelids fluttered shut and for a second I feared the worst, but she opened them again. "Vilna most of all. But there's a silver lining . . ."

"Eldrenne." I could hear sirens. Police and fire would be here soon.

"I'd have reinstated you into my *lucusi*."

"I know." It hurt to say anything, my throat was constricted by that lump.

"I'd have kept you from being Bindspoken."

My eyes stung, but those desperate tears didn't fall. A cold, cold breath filled my lungs and seemed to ease the lump a bit. "I'll stay ahead of them." I squeezed her hand reassuringly. "We're working on that already."

"They can't catch you. You're too crafty." She smiled, weakly. "Even now, I see your mantle . . . glowing soft around you like a nimbus. Don't forget the silver lining." She took a deep breath; her last. "Was my honor to know you both."

"Oh, Xerx," Menessos whispered.

"I'm crossing that bridge, Persephone. Hold my hand while this world fades."

I am holding her hand. Can't she feel it?

"Go, Xerxadrea," Menessos whispered. "Linger here no more. Summerland's gates are just across that bridge." He sounded strong, not sad.

I took strength from his words, too. The lump in my throat faded and I found my voice. "The Lord and Lady are waiting, Xerxadrea. Into those bountiful arms, with you."

CHAPTER TWENTY-FOUR

Xerxadrea was gone.

She sacrificed herself for me.

I hadn't known her for long, and though I genuinely liked her, we hadn't grown very close. Yet all I knew was grief, the tightness in my chest and the profuse flooding of tears. I could think no thoughts. It hurt but letting the emotion out felt right, the release of it felt good. Then came the heat of Menessos's touch on my arm.

"Come." He pulled me to my feet. "We must go."

"Can't leave her." *She died to save me.*

"We cannot take her, either. She will be identified and given to her own."

I shook my head. "No." It was cruel to leave her—

"Will the broom allow me to ride it, Persephone?" Goliath asked.

His tone and direct calling of my name snapped me back into myself, and into the realization that we weren't out of danger yet. What remained of my grief was displaced. "I don't know," I said, wiping my face. "What are you thinking?"

"If it will hold me, I can wear the Eldrenne's cape and

fly out, diverting the fairies from you two making a real escape." He held out his hand for my broom.

I gave it to him. He positioned it, then gingerly lowered his weight onto it. It did not rise, and wouldn't hold him. He held it out to return it to me. "What do you want me to do, Master?"

"Wait," I said.

I put my hand beside Goliath's as he held the broom. "Awaken ye to life, and fly Goliath as he bids this night." The broom tingled in my grip and the bristle end skittered toward his feet. "Take my cape," I added, removing it from my shoulders, tugging it free from the velvet sling bag Xerxadrea had given me. "They'll know they hit her, and the red one may mean more."

I put it on him, hood up, and spied the opening above. I had an idea. "If I give you the Eldrenne's robe, do you think you can cover that hole with it?" I pointed at the roofline.

"Why?"

"So the butterflies and birds don't escape."

"A waste of time," he declared.

Menessos added, "This garden can import more birds and butterflies. I cannot as easily replace Goliath."

"You're right." It was true; I conceded.

"Goliath, go up to the second level, stay hidden, and leave only once the police arrive, but before they see you. This will give us time to get into position. Hopefully, you'll draw most of the fairies away, but I doubt all of them will follow."

"Yes, Master."

"Goliath," I added, "that thing flies on intentions, so intend to go fast."

He actually grinned and showed fang. "Good to know."

Menessos and I left the rain forest section of the gardens, passing through the mirrored exit where people made sure no butterflies had landed on them and were in danger of riding out. We did not stop to check.

"What's your plan?" I insisted.

"We have to get back downtown, where there are no trees to shelter the fairies from the effects of their allergies."

If the blisters on Aquula had been any indication, their allergies to asphalt were immediately intense. They must have come straight down from the sky into the gardens and the abundance of vegetation there shielded them. Bad thing was, there were trees all over this area. "On foot?"

"No. We're going to steal a vehicle."

"There are no vehicles around except those of the response teams."

"Precisely."

"You mean we're stealing a police cruiser?"

"We cannot call a cab."

"If we could make it down the street a ways—"

Menessos dragged me into the men's restroom and around the privacy wall. It was pitch-dark except for emergency lighting filtering through the vented bottom of the door. "We cannot risk being under the trees," he whispered hotly. "The roads in this area are lined with them! We must take whatever is parked conveniently to their doors."

"That could be a fire truck!"

He shrugged and put a finger to his lips, moving me into the stall. "Stand on the toilet," he whispered.

My vision had adjusted to the dimness and I complied, sort of. I placed one of the platform boots on the side of the toilet seat. "What are you going to do?" I whispered back.

Menessos shut the stall door. I reached out and reopened it.

"What will you do?" I demanded.

"Whatever is necessary to get us out safely."

"Menessos. You don't have to kill an officer."

He arched a brow poignantly. "Did I say I needed to kill?"

The bathroom door opened and Menessos quickly joined me in the stall. Gripping the upper edge of the partitioning, I hauled myself up, standing on one side of the toilet, and allowed him to do the same on the other side. Squatting down to keep my head out of sight, fighting to keep my balance on the tapered seat—damned boots—and doing it all silently wasn't easy.

On the plus side, the officer had a flashlight, and the glow of it made it easier for us to see each other.

The stall door opened, and in an instant Menessos had ripped it back and pinned the officer against the painted cinderblocks beyond. He'd also taken the man's flashlight. Menessos managed to hold him and still keep the beam illuminating both of their faces.

"Hear me, mortal, I will not hurt you. You must merely comply with my orders."

The man sighed, eyes glassy. "Yes." His voice slurred and his jaw went slack.

"You will take us out to your car—"

"Others might see," I interrupted. I'd been recognized

a lot tonight already. And without the cape I was showing a lot of skin again.

Without breaking the visual connection, Menessos said, "I must keep him in sight to maintain control. I haven't the strength to send him on a mission."

"I do." I gripped Menessos's arm and called energy up from the jaspers and out of me, preparing to transfer it to him.

"No," he said.

"Tell him to bring a patrol car down into the garage, and open the trunk for us there. He must drive us a mile down the road then park somewhere secluded and let us out."

"It will drain you!"

"It will drain only the jaspers Xerxadrea gave me to wear." The "only" part was a lie.

"Then you will be unprotected!"

"Not true." I wagged the chain with Beau's charm at him. "I can't mesmerize people. You can." Before he could protest further, I poured the energy into him.

After we exited the trunk of the police car and the officer drove away, Menessos quickly flagged down a cab. Once we climbed inside, the obvious question came. "Where to?"

"Public Square," Menessos answered.

The cabbie asked, "You want the Holiday Inn Express or the Hyatt Regency, my lucky friend?"

Menessos gave me the once-over and laughed out loud.

"Just take us to Public Square," I snapped.

"Oh, yes. Trixie's late for work," the accented cabbie grumbled.

Though Menessos had said it was unlikely the fey would follow us in the open city, he inspected the sky through the back window. In spite of the fact that he was still chuckling, I was glad he checked and found the sky satisfyingly fairyless. He settled into the seat and took my hand.

"You and I are going to have a long talk about shoes and what I wear," I said.

"Whatever you want, Persephone, you shall have."

I laid my head on his shoulder. "Sensible clothes and sensible shoes." I was glad he didn't argue. Due to my energy dump, it felt like I'd been awake for days and had just run a marathon. Yet this night was far from over. I had to talk to Menessos and Johnny, together, about what Beau had said. I'd have to see the Codex, decipher the spell, and prepare. Having Nana around at this moment would have been helpful, and yet I had no desire to inform her of what I was facing now. If I had to guess, soul-sharing was not an idea she'd get behind.

I just needed the support of Johnny and Menessos. If they were both willing we'd have to perform it as soon as possible. The fey and WEC were expecting me to deliver Menessos Sunday morning at dawn.

Xerxadrea's dead. Her plan is lost. We're on our own. My insides pinched with grief, but I denied it again.

According to the cab's clock, it was nearly midnight now. So we had a little more than thirty hours. Thirty hours to prepare and perform the soul-sharing spell, to make plans for the fairies and implement those plans. Some of those precious hours would be spent unproductively sleeping. Being well rested going into a spell like that was simply common sense. But how could I sleep now?

Because I just poured energy into Menessos.

I had something else to add to my endless to-do list: Xerxadrea had said I needed to shut the door between the worlds. I needed to find out how Menessos, Una, and Ninutra opened the door before I could close it. I couldn't ask Menessos in the cab though. No telling who the cabbie might know.

The fairies were expecting Menessos to be delivered at dawn. The vampires would be, literally, dead to the world. Useless. And the witches were out.

We were going to need the wærewolves.

"Wait." I sat up and leaned toward the cabbie. "Take us to The Dirty Dog instead."

In the rearview mirror, he confirmed this new destination with Menessos, who nodded his assent.

"The Dirty Dog it is," the cabbie replied. He changed lanes and hit the turn signal.

"Do you have my jacket?" Menessos asked as the cab rolled onto a familiar side street and slowed, then stopped. I had forgotten about Xerxadrea's velvet sling bag, still draped over my shoulder. As I understood that I had something of hers, tears threatened to spill yet again, but I dug into the purse's silver interior, removed his jacket, and passed it to him.

Producing a money clip from the inside of his suit coat, Menessos provided the cabbie with a hundred-dollar bill and said, "Wait wherever you want, but return to this spot in thirty minutes and I'll give you another one of those for that ride to Public Square."

"You got it," the cabbie said enthusiastically.

We exited the cab. I shivered. Maybe the cold night air would firm my resolve to be tear-free. Menessos draped his jacket around my shoulders. Smiling my thanks, I stuck my arms through the sleeves.

It seemed like much more than a few hours since I'd left Johnny here in the darkened building with a dead body and a pair of men from the pack. Now, every window in the upper floor of the building glowed with light, and cars lined every inch of the street, preventing any hope of nearby parking. Arriving in a cab was the best thing we could have done.

The bar was now open, with light trying valiantly to push beyond the grimy front windows, and the buzz of music rattled the panes. However, the bouncers at the bar door—and the scent of pine as thick as sap in the air— heralded the idea that not all patrons were welcome inside tonight.

So I wasn't surprised when the nearer of the two—a bald wære with ebony ear gauges—raised his hand in the universal stop gesture. "Private party tonight."

I walked right up to the Mr. Clean wannabe anyway.

"I'm here to see Johnny Newman."

"Even dressed to kill and hot as you are, I can't let you in," he insisted.

"Then get Todd. I only need a moment."

He sniffed and knew I wasn't wære. "Droppin' names will get you nowhere tonight."

I was too damned tired for this shit. "I'll go around back," I said, and moved away.

The bouncer caught my arm. "You can't go inside tonight."

"She must be deaf," the other bouncer said. While not as tall as Mr. Clean, the wiry Asian guy had arm bulges that were just as impressive. He gripped the other man's shoulder and plastered on a fake pout. "Ain't that sad?" His pout evolved into a smirk.

Menessos drew his foot lightly across the sidewalk, making an unsubtle scraping that drew to him the attention of both the Overactor and Mr. Clean. "This lady usually gets what she wants, boys. One of you be a sport and ask the man who signs your checks to get his ass out here, or both of you will be in danger of not getting paid ever again."

"We won't get fired over this," Overactor said.

"Unlike vampires, wæres don't collect checks after they die," Menessos clarified.

Both bouncers growled menacingly.

"Does your master reward obedience?" Menessos lifted another hundred. "I do. Now, who's going to go ask?"

"We don't fetch for fang-faces," Overactor said.

"Only pack tonight," Mr. Clean said.

"There were five members of your pack at my party tonight," Menessos touted back. "No exclusivity on my part."

Mr. Clean reevaluated Menessos, perhaps just recognizing him. He crossed his arms. "This is different."

We didn't have time for this. "I know Ig's dead," I blurted. "Let me speak to Johnny, then we'll be on our way."

Mr. Clean and the Overactor exchanged shrugs.

I stomped my boot. "Somebody go ask!"

"This isn't an issue of permission," Mr. Clean said. "We're keeping you out for your own safety."

"I can handle myself around wæres," I snarled and pushed past. This time, neither made a move to stop me.

The bar was packed with people laughing, drinking, and dancing—a pair of women were dancing on this end of the bar. One of them could barely stand, and the men around them made no effort to hide the fact that they were staring up their short skirts.

Making my way toward the far end of the bar, I didn't see Johnny anywhere. The more crowded my path became, the more my pushing lacked courtesy. By the time I'd fought my way to the middle of the room, my patience had run out. The odor of ale and whiskey and pine burned in my nose, ruining that last bit of sympathy I held for their loss.

Do wærewolves always mourn like this? I wondered.

"Witch!" someone shouted.

Stillness abruptly spread across the room. People backed away from me. A man nearby howled approval, but it was cut off by a woman elbowing him hard in the ribs. The jukebox had been silenced.

"Where's Johnny Newman?" I demanded.

"Witch, witch, witch." It started as a whisper, but it was soon picked up by many mouths and a chant ensued. The pack crowded close, encircling me but leaving an arm's length open all around.

They were responding with pack traits: grouping, surrounding, snarling as if to make me cower. I didn't blame them for reacting with a show of force; a witch has the power to send them all into life-ruining partial changes simply by stirring up energies.

Lucky them, I was too tired to stir any.

Lucky me, they didn't know that.

Trump card: they were all at least half drunk, and I'd have bet a high percentage of them were well past the halfway mark. It didn't take much for wæres to get drunk or high or overmedicated. That meant they weren't likely to be thinking clearly. They might do something stupid.

"You're Johnny's witch girlfriend?" came an irritated but lilting voice behind me. Sounded like she wasn't sure if she was making an accusation or asking a question.

It was one of the women who'd been dancing on the bar. The other dancer clung to her to keep from falling off the bar. As they both faced me, I realized they were twins.

Sammi and Cammi Harding, bank heiresses. They were the ones who had pawed Johnny after Lycanthropia's set at the Rock Hall showcase. "I didn't recognize you without your leather pom-poms."

The one who'd spoken put her arms out and stepped off the bar. The men nearby caught her and made sure she had her feet under her. Her sister toppled down with less grace but the men helped her, as well. The first pushed her way through the crowd and gave me the once-over.

The two of them were identical physically, but they didn't dress exactly alike and they displayed different personalities. This one was more aggressive and I pegged her as the one who had planted the lip-lock on Johnny.

She exuded only contempt, until she spied the boots. I

recognized the covetous gaze of a window-shopper. "Bet you're almost his height in those."

Her sister stumbled up behind her. Her mascara was smeared at one end and she could hardly stand. "Oooo. Pretty. Bitch to walk in, aren't they?"

"Where's Johnny?" *And where is Menessos, for that matter?*

The first sister bared her teeth; it was too vicious to be a smile. "Busy."

I'd read some puppy manuals when Nana got Ares. Maintaining eye contact was always key and using firm, low tones was important for reprimanding inappropriate behavior, so I did both. "Get him for me."

"Eat shit."

The bank heiress has a foul mouth? I knew better than to back down. She was trying to assert her dominance over me. "Now."

"Or you'll what? Spank me with a newspaper?"

A man in the crowd growled, "I'll spank you, Cammi."

She ignored him. So did I.

"Don't make me rub your nose in it." *Oh, for a wære-safe charm that would make her pee herself right now.* If I had known a spell for spontaneous incontinence, one that wouldn't send her into a partial change, it would have been impossible to resist using it. Pressing her face to this grimy floor would leave no doubt of my dominance. Trouble was, if I did that, the rest of the pack would likely jump on my back and do worse to me. Tactically, I needed to posture more aggressively than she did.

A deep, deep growl erupted beside us. Cammi looked away first, as a huge black wolf leaped onto the bar and stalked down the length of it.

Johnny.

Cheers rose up around the bar. "Hail the Domn Lup!" People held their beverages aloft. The people crowded around me were mostly without their beer cans and shot glasses, so pumped their fists in the air. Johnny lifted his muzzle to the sky and howled loud and long. His cry ended to more drinking, shouting, and fist pumping.

Cammi thrust herself into my personal space and said, "With all that he is, he deserves a pack bitch, a *haita catea,* not a *sange stricata* like you . . . blood whore."

A pair of women nearby heard and gasped, then burst into laughter. They were laughing at me. As I stood in The Dirty Dog, dressed in taped-on clothes and glossy red boots, after everyone saw Menessos drinking from me broadcast on TV and online, did I have any right to be surprised?

Moving forward, pushing into Cammi's personal space, I put myself nose to nose with her. The move brought an end to the cheers around us as ears strained to hear. I could smell the bourbon on her breath. "He chooses to spend his time with me, so you're going to have to find another bone to chew—but remember this: 'all that he is' has gone unnoticed. You and this pack are only aware of the truth now because he is *allowing* you to know. And there's a reason I knew first."

She tried to slap me. From the bar, Johnny barked and snarled. I caught her wrist and held it. Either I was able to restrain her because she was half drunk or his reaction had stopped her. It didn't matter which, really; it reminded me that wærewolves only respect the power that dominates them.

"Give me a reason," I shouted. A challenge.

She jerked free of my grip and in doing so compromised her tenuous balance. She backpedaled. "Don't threaten this pack!"

With her small retreat, the scales had just tipped in my favor. I took up the distance. "I'm *not* threatening the pack! I simply came to speak to Johnny and you're threatening *me*. I won't tolerate it."

She recognized the concession inherent in her move was a mistake and tried to correct it by planting her feet. But it was too late. She'd given ground and I'd taken it. "If you try a spell, witch, you'll be dead before you can call enough energy to damage us all."

"I don't intend to 'damage' anybody, but if you don't get out of my face, whatever the consequence, I *guarantee* you'll be a half-formed bitch. You'd probably be more likable that way."

CHAPTER TWENTY-FIVE

Johnny's hand encircled my arm. I hadn't detected the *whoosh* of power as he'd reverted to man form.

He pulled me away from Cammi and led me toward the back. People scurried to make way for us, well, for him. "Out," he said to the few wæres milling around this room. He guided me near the door.

I stared through the glass, focusing on the mesh in the screen door. A loose weaving of wire. *"And there she weaves by night and day a magic web."* I thought the lines from Tennyson's poem. Orderly little empty squares on the screen, but trapezoids in a spider's web. One kept the flies out; the other trapped them for nourishment. My life needed a screen door to keep out the bugs, but what I had was a web. I didn't see how all these things that were sticking to it were supposed to nourish me.

My rage back in the bar, I realized, was my grief, my fear and loss and pain hunting for a way out. It couldn't stay bottled inside, but I didn't intend to give it a release through violence, either. Now, almost alone with Johnny, those tears burned again. *Damn it, I'm not going to cry.*

"Red?"

"Yeah." I returned from my weary, zoned-out state. Johnny stood beside me, naked.

"Don't let her get to you."

"It's not her." I clenched my jaw to steel myself.

He must've thought I was angry. "Hey, I'm glad you came back"—he tweaked my cheek—"but this isn't the best place for you right now."

"I know, but I had to come. I had to tell you." *You can say these words. You can do it without tears.*

"Tell me what?"

I blurted, "Xerxadrea's dead."

"What?" His jaw dropped, then his arms encircled me.

Again, the tears threatened to come. Not here. The wærewolves would hear sobbing. They'd never respect sobbing. "After we buried Aquula, the fairies attacked."

He jerked back and examined me again. "You're all right?"

"I'm fine. I'm fine because Xerxadrea sacrificed herself."

The tears won. I pressed my face into his naked chest and he held me so tight. I squeezed my reaction, being as silent as I could, telling myself this was just a little over-flow. *Let a little spill out and then I can seal them off again. That's not all I need to tell him about.*

A moment later, in his safe arms, I found the strength to staunch the waterworks, quashing tears down hard. On to the bigger thing we had to deal with. "Johnny, she was working on a plan, but whatever strategy she had, left with her." I wiped my face with my hands. His embrace diminished but he didn't fully let me go. I went on, "We have about thirty hours to come up with something. I know you have to be here, to let the wærewolves mourn, but . . ."

"They mourned Ig for about a half an hour. That"—he gestured to the bar—"is a celebration of being the pack that can claim the Domn Lup."

The drinking and dancing made more sense now. I nodded.

"I'll come back to the haven as soon as I can, okay?"

There were so many other things I needed to tell him right now, but they would keep a little longer. I didn't want to pass through the wærewolf throng again, so I reached for the knob of the back door. "I'll go this way, and walk around."

"I'd go with you but it's cold and I don't know where my jeans are. I'd be humiliated if you witnessed the inevitable shrinkage."

I smiled and whispered, "Please, please, don't ever change."

Johnny pulled me into a sudden kiss, and I clung to him, very unheroinelike. His soft lips pressed to mine. I felt tingly and velvety static crawled over my skin. His arms were like a security blanket around me, making me safe and grounded. I didn't ever want to be parted from him.

When his tongue slipped to mine he tasted like something I couldn't name, something oaky sweet, and when the kiss ended, his lips rose to my forehead. The tinglies subsided. "What's that flavor?"

"Todd toasted me, opening Ig's bottle of eighteen-year-old Laphroaig."

"La-froyg?" I repeated.

"A single-malt scotch. Made on some island called Islay off of Scotland."

Interesting. "Where is Todd?"

"Upstairs listening to Erik and Celia and Theo's account of what you did to them, how they keep their man-minds."

"Is it a good idea to let him know about that?"

"I think it's something in our favor, something we can use in our planning. I'll explain more when I get to the haven."

I squeezed him tight, then exited out the back door.

The party was still going full tilt with the vampires, Offerlings, and Beholders. We could hear it when we entered. Mountain was waiting for us to get back, sent to the ticket booth by Goliath. "After coming in with a broom," Mountain reported, "he hurried off to question that guy with the daggers." Mountain took Menessos and me the back way around, down the service elevator, and across the backstage area.

Menessos dismissed Mountain, then called my name. "Before you retire to your bed, would you please come with me?"

A nod was the best response I could muster. I was drained of energy, and filled with emotion. I needed to reverse that.

He opened his door; his room had been tidied and cleaned since we'd brought Aquula here. "Wait here." He passed through that heavy, iron-studded door to his private room, and quickly returned with a small wrapped present. "It is traditional to give the Erus Veneficus a gift after the induction ceremony. Of course," he said as his expression went sly, "that tradition dictates that the witch be bedded and her family taken hostage. She is to be given a ruby ring to remind her of the family blood that would be spilled if ever she disobeyed. I was certain you would object to such traditions, and I have no desire to put any of my people through the agony of holding your grandmother hostage again. I selected something more modern instead. I hope you will enjoy it."

Curiosity piqued, I ripped into the paper and lifted the lid of the palm-sized box. What I saw was a sharp reminder that Xerxadrea was dead, that my protrepticus was useless, and that Samson was gone. "A cell phone?"

"This is actually *more* than a cell phone. It is connected to a private satellite network, directly linked to others with similar phones. The lines are scrambled for assured privacy." He took it from me and opened it, hit a button or two. "I took the liberty of programming my own number and a few others in there for you, including this one." He handed it back. The letters read: NANA.

Almost giving myself whiplash snapping my head up so fast, I started to ask but he answered my question before I could. "Yes. I thought after the ceremony you would want to speak with her. I had not guessed that so much would happen before I had the chance to present it to you."

My finger poised, ready to hit the dial button, but in the corner the time read one-twelve. "She'll be sleeping."

"If my guess is correct, she'll be sleeping with her phone right beside her." He pushed hair back from my shoulder and neck, appraising the bite marks he'd made. "Take this to your chambers, call if you wish, but rest."

"You'll tell me what Goliath found out from the performer?"

Menessos sighed. "We removed weapons from two others at the door, and refused admittance to another we suspected. That was close."

"Which of us was the target?"

"When I find out, I will let you know."

With that, I left. If there was any doubt of my exhaustion, climbing the metal stairs confirmed it. My finger touched the SEND button of my phone before my chamber door had shut. Nana answered on the third ring. "Seph? Is that you?"

"Sorry it's so late, Nana."

"Forget the hour! Are you all right? I saw the news, I saw him bite you! Saw that scrawny blond vampire divert a blade—"

"The bite was just for show, Nana." The lie tumbled out so easily when I heard her fear and worry trembling in her voice. "The other . . . the culprit is being questioned. We're all fine. I'm okay, really. What's happening there? How's Beverley?"

Nana sighed and I could hear her relax in the sound of it. "She got a perfect score on her spelling and vocabulary semester test, so we went to the movies to celebrate."

What? Doesn't she know how dangerous it is to take Beverley away from the safety wards of the house? But they couldn't stay inside forever. According to Aquula, Fax Torris's threat stated she'd go after Beverley if I didn't deliver Menessos at dawn on Sunday. We had a little time.

The first part of the plan had to make sure the fairies thought we were complying with that. Then they had to be stopped once and for all.

Then it hit me: Aquula's death meant that severing

the ties to Menessos was as easy as killing the remaining two fairies. Our plan had to utilize that, and somehow strengthen Menessos against that dual loss.

". . . left Ares out," Nana was saying. "I thought he'd be okay, but he chewed up one of your couch pillows. I'll replace it. And I promise we'll remember to crate him before we go out again."

"Good." *If only the worst of the problems I faced was a teething Great Dane.* I unbuckled the boots.

"And the men came to install the security system this morning. Done and gone in three hours. Said it secured the house against intruders as well as the painting. And while they were here, a contractor showed up to give a quote on renovating the dining room into a bedroom. He said that it would actually be better to just add a whole room and a bathroom than to take away the dining room."

"What about the cellar entry?" I dropped the first boot aside.

"He drew a picture on that grid paper to show you what he means."

"I'm anxious to see it." I considered. "With just a crawlspace under it, we may have to put heated flooring in to keep your room from getting too cold in the winter." I wiggled the second boot off.

"This quote isn't cheap, Persephone, and I don't think any heated flooring was included in his estimate."

"You're worth it, Nana. How are your knees feeling?" *I never got the chance to ask Xerxadrea to teach Nana how she did that mist trick.* I wished I could tell Nana about Xerxadrea's death, but—if she knew an Eldrenne had died, she'd be even more worried about me. I removed the pouch from my belt. I almost took out the protrepticus to see if it worked, but didn't. I set it aside, unzipped the skirt, let it fall. I peeled the dual-sided tape from my skin. Ick.

"Steady." She paused. I sank on the bed and drew covers over me, threw them down again, rose up and got the bloodstone. "What was it that Johnny carried in? The cameras never got a clear shot of that."

The sigh that left my lips must have sounded like a yawn through the phone. "The fairy. Aquula. She died, Nana."

"Oh." She was silent a moment. "I'm sorry."

"Me, too."

"You must be worn out."

"Yeah. I am." I held the stone tight and let it bleed energy into my palm. "And Nana, please don't go anywhere. Threats have been made. I'd feel better if you'd promise me that you won't take Beverley away from the house and wards this weekend."

"But—"

"No buts, Nana. This is serious. The fairy made a threat against Beverley again. And you. Promise me?"

She delayed. "I promise."

"Thank you, Nana. I . . . I love you." I didn't tell her that nearly as much as I should.

"I love you too, Persephone."

I was asleep as soon as I closed the phone; the bloodstone was still in my hand.

When I woke, Johnny was beside me. The clock read five-nineteen.

My first thought was to wake him and find Menessos and tell them about the soul-sharing. My second thought reminded me Johnny had done at least two full transformations yesterday. Disentangling his arm from around my waist, I decided that since he didn't even stir that meant he needed more rest. I left the bloodstone on the bedside table.

In the tub, when the water temperature was just right, I relaxed in the heated fluid and steam surrounding me.

> Mother, seal my circle
> > and give me a sacred space.
> I need to think clearly
> > to solve the troubles I face.

I flipped my meditation switch to on and hit my alpha state—my meditation mode. Visualizing the grove of old ash trees beside a swift-flowing river, I imagined walking toward the water.

My skin seemed dim. As if the sunshine here weren't touching me.

Proceeding with my method of cleaning my chakras, I sat on a rock and stuck my toes into the water. My shields begged to be let loose, to be eased for just a short time. Here, alone, it was safe to let go. I gave in and tried to loosen that protection the same way a flexed muscle relaxes. But the shields seemed cramped in place, and would not lower.

Typically, if my body was clothed when I meditated, I was clothed here within the meditation. If, like now, I meditated in the tub, I showed up here naked. So, I scrutinized my exposed skin. All of me was coated in something *murky*.

The coating was all the emotions my life path had cultivated. The ones I didn't want, like despondency, panic, shame, fear, and grief. The ebb and flow of emotions was healthy, but I'd been shoving all these feelings down and tucking them far away. Tucking them here. They weren't released, so they didn't recede naturally. Instead, these emotions were dammed up. And they stagnated.

Like mold on past-ripe fruit, this darkness was the rot of what was meant to nourish me. This was the apathy I'd protected myself with while, like an emotional anorexic, I avoided the buffet of negative feelings my life had served me lately.

Sure, I'd devoured the laughter and the happiness, the contentedness. But, to be the Lustrata, to be balanced, I had to ingest the negative emotions, too. I had to consume all of it to truly own my life and my destiny.

That's part of the cost.

I'd thought that, to accomplish all I had to do, a barrier around my emotions would be helpful. And this was the apathetic wall I had to show for it. I'd been building up my shields in the last few weeks, taking them down less and less, strengthening them by constant use. With Menessos bouncing all over my emotional trampoline, and my being absent from this place of cleansing and release, I'd been reinforcing these shields with the mortar of pain, guilt, denial, and mourning.

But strength had to be balanced with vulnerability. Closing off to the negatives meant not being open to the positives.

I understood what I'd done now, but undoing this damage would not be easy. *Nor should it be.*

I leaned over the water and looked at my reflection.

I could leave this murky shield alone. Let it get thick and so solid it would never come down.

My eyes adjusted to see through that reflection, to the things under the surface, the stream bed, the stones.

Nana once told me how if you peer into a stream during the day you see your reflection. But if you look in the stream on a moonless night, you'll see the stream bed. She'd said, "You've been exposed to the dark, so you're seeing below the surface, now, Persephone. You're seeing the beauty in the smooth stones, but you must also feel the slime covering them. Slime that, if you're not mindful of your footing, will cause you to slip . . ."

I'd slipped. There was slime on me that would make me someone I didn't want to be. I didn't want to be unable to care, to be cold and indifferent. I'd rather be strong *and* vulnerable.

In that instant I stood and clawed at the murky surface of emotion. Rending a hole, I released those feelings I'd resisted and fought against. Sobbing and staggering further into the river, I tried to use those emotions, to convert them into anger and rage, to fuel the destruction of that barrier. But the wave of anguish was too strong, the barrier too thick. The more I dug at the shield, the deeper the emotion became. Relentless, I tore until my fingers, in the meditation, were bloody.

There, in the middle of the river, as the grief and fear and loss and doubt and pain poured out of me in a flood down my cheeks, I stumbled. The current caught me and threw me under the surface.

CHAPTER TWENTY-SIX

The river dragged me, yanking me desperately along, mocking me, heaving me to my feet and permitting me to slosh a few steps toward the bank. I retched and gagged. Then another wave pounced, shoving me under the surface again. I fought to rise above it, but the water quashed me, twisted and wrung me, stifling every attempt.

These emotions are too powerful. You don't want them.

Immersed, drowning, I grappled with the rushing current, too stubborn to surrender. Surfacing amid white rapids, I gasped once before plummeting over a high falls. I was pinned at its base, buried under the weight of the water pouring down on me.

Yes. I. Do. They're mine!

All I had left was this fight. I curled into a ball and scrabbled for the edges of large rocks to hold on to. Using them, I wrenched myself away from the imprisoning, crushing weight of the falls. Then the current plucked me loose and whisked me away again. This time it wouldn't let me surface.

I thought of what I'd said to Menessos about being his

master, about accepting it. The good and the bad. But I hadn't accepted the good and the bad emotions of my own life. How could I balance a world if I couldn't balance myself, couldn't accept the good and the bad of what I had, inevitably, to face?

I kicked my feet and stretched for the bottom, raking already bleeding hands along the riverbed searching for something heavy enough to anchor me. I clung to the first large stone I could keep a grip on.

The current tugged at me, wrenching me and the stone free, dragging me slowly along the bottom, scraping my fingers against other rocks. But still, I would not let go.

I will not be swept away. Not by any emotion! I accept what it means. The good and the bad. The good and *the bad!*

The river hurled both the stone and me onto the muddy embankment. I landed on my back. My arms flew over my head guiding the stone to *thunk* into the soft ground there.

A tree leaned over me, branches low. I started to sit up, but the stone rested heavily on a portion of my hair. After slithering around in the mud, struggling without enough leverage to roll away the offending rock, I finally managed and sat up. I wanted to rise and stomp away, but the branches of this mighty tree made standing up impossible.

I lingered, considering. The river had deposited me under a willow tree laden with some kind of wispy moss. As my awareness of the area spread further, what I saw before me was no longer a river, but a lake with water so blue and smooth it made me calmer just to see it. The picturesque lake was framed by distant forested moun-

tains. The sharp shapes revealed a particularly jagged gla-
cier had carved this land.

Nearer to me, a craggy, sun-bleached face of stone
thrust up from the water like a giant's spearhead rammed
into the earth. The white reflection of the bare stone on
the water's surface was the only break in the blue, like a
single cloud in the sky.

"Fancy meeting you here."

I twisted in the mud. "Amenemhab!"

"Hello, Persephone. Needed a change of scenery?"

I crawled out from under the low branches and sat near
the jackal who served as my totem animal. "I hear mud is
supposed to be good for your skin, but I can't say I like
it." I couldn't wipe my face clean, my hands were covered
in it. I tried to get one hand mostly clean with the other.
It wasn't working. With a glare at the placid and benign
surface of the lake, I decided not to attempt washing it off
just yet.

"I'm putting this to memory so I can always remember
you this way."

"Naked and covered in mud. Gee, thanks."

"I see you more as bathed in the element of water, and
coated with earth for good measure." His nasal-haughty
and matter-of-fact tone meant he was being literal; totems
aren't typically sarcastic. Didn't keep me from letting
loose my own cynical humor, though.

"You make it sound like some hallowed initiation.
Like a baptism. I didn't think lofty spiritual conventions
were supposed to include this much muck."

He laughed.

I gave up trying to be cleaner. For now. "I'm not sure

why I'm in a new place." The sun was dipping across the lake preparing to set. Fingerlike rays stretched through the moss and the slender willow branches. It was a peaceful scene and, although I was caked with mud, it evoked serenity in me. Or maybe I felt *grounded* because I was covered in it.

"Examine where you are."

"The mud capital of the world," I muttered.

Amenemhab turned away, muzzle closed. Totems didn't suffer fools who evaded answering their questions.

"By a lake. Near a willow tree. There's moss. And a rock that nearly smashed my skull."

He sat patiently.

"The river, now a lake, threw me out." *And the stone.*

I pushed back the curtain of lance-shaped leaves. A snapping sound preceded the dropping of a small branch onto the stone. "Sorry," I mumbled to the tree. I hadn't meant to break anything.

Shadows swung across the surface of the rock as the breeze rustled the drooping branches on the other side. There was a texture to the stone, mostly hidden under the mud. Dropping to my knees, I crawled under the low branch again to examine it better. The fallen branch had landed across the rock, and pieces of moss wound around the stick's length. I reached out and pushed it from the stone top.

My fingers tingled.

I touched the stone lightly again. Nothing. I laid my palm on it. Nothing. "Hmmm." Drawing closer, I wiped at it, smearing the mud over it. After cleaning it as best I could, I saw that the dark matrix of interlocking cubes binding it together was obvious, but the color was lost to the mud. The stone's roughness meant it hadn't been a river stone for long. I tilted the stone toward the light.

It didn't help.

I wondered if the water would have thrown just me out if I'd let go of the stone, or if it was meant to be ejected, as well.

Laying the stone over on the ground again, intending to see its underside, I brushed the fallen branch again. The tingle returned.

Intrigued, I lifted the branch. It buzzed happily in my palm, warm and friendly. It was nearly straight and resembled a wand. But I already had a wand.

The happy energy settled into a pulse, not unlike the purr of a cat.

I resumed my spot beside Amenemhab. His ears pricked expectantly.

"It's a willow branch."

"And? The symbolism?"

"Willow is a very emotional wood." The events of the last few days had frequently elicited shielding against my natural emotions, to be strong and emotionally uncluttered, in order to keep moving forward.

But emotions are fluid; they kept rising like floodwaters. *Water.* "Of course, water is the metaphor. That's what the suit of cups in Tarot is all about. How the cups are placed, how the water is contained, or not, means something. If fluidity is absent, you have apathy. And apathy isn't me; it scares me. So I fought."

"Fought what?"

"I've been stifling my emotions."

"What represented your emotions?"

I thought about it. "The stream. When I destroyed the shield damming me, it became a gushing river."

"So the emotions, the current, grew stronger."

"Yes."

"When you set your sights on something, Persephone, you are not removed from it. Your will is iron. Willow respects that, enhances that."

"I held back tears tonight, because of the wærewolves. Because they would see it as a sign of weakness. I want to be strong enough to not fear the repercussions of letting my true feelings show." I was fighting for my right to have my emotions without being deemed weak.

He cocked his head. "Ah. As I recall, the last time we spoke feelings were at issue then, too."

"This time people have died. Good people."

"I told you the hurt you felt over Johnny would fade or fester depending on how you chose to feel about it. Correct?"

"Yes." I'd been reeling, thinking Johnny had used and betrayed me. Amenemhab had reminded me that this was who I'd been chosen to be and that all of my experiences, even the hurtful ones, had been creating and would continue to hone the warrior I must become to be the Lustrata. He'd made me understand when and how I had transformed the vampire stain into a hex. There was some divine influence to that, to be sure, but I still had the choice. I chose to bear the pain and remain true to who I was. *Who I am.*

"And how did you choose to feel about it?"

"I let it go. I suppose you're going to tell me to do the same thing this time?"

"Did you? Or did you deny it?"

"I denied it the ability to hurt me. It's faded."

Amenemhab watched me.

I searched my heart. He was right. "Fine. I wanted to dish out some just 'desserts,' as in Retaliation Pie, when I knew it was Cammi confronting me at The Dirty Dog. She was challenging me. Sure, her motive had been Johnny's new status and making an opposing stand over a witch getting the Domn Lup's affections. That was a territorial pack thing. Not specifically a Cammi-versus-Persephone thing. I could have been anyone and it would have been the same."

"You have accurately accounted for her motive. What was yours?"

"I didn't seek her out, but when I had the chance, I was glad to give her some comeuppance."

"What had she done?"

I knew what the jackal was digging for. To shorten this conversation—there was no avoiding it anyway—I gave it to him. "She challenged me. Not a challenge to the Lustrata, but a challenge to me personally, a challenge to my heart."

"Just making sure you recognize it. We're likely to do a lot of work on this before we're through."

I swallowed, hard.

"And where are you now?" he asked.

"By a lake."

He waited, ear pricked.

It hit me: *a bigger body of water.* "A larger pool of emotions."

"This lake is fed by mountain streams. By *old* water. It is not dammed, but it is surrounded by wilderness."

I looked around me more closely than I had before.

"You were given a trial by fire," Amenemhab continued. "You fought for who you are, saved the core of yourself from being burned at the stake. I daresay that was the moment the fire forged your iron will." He put a paw on my thigh. "Now, you have experienced a trial by water. The mirrorlike surface shows us what we know, what we are conscious of. But that water can be deep under the glassy surface wherein lies the subconscious. You broke the dam. You dove in. You chose to drown in your negative emotions rather than to let them pull you along. You made quite a statement."

My attention fell to the branch in my lap. It was perhaps nine inches long, finger thick and tapered at the end. I reached to clear the moss off it.

"Don't."

"Why?"

"Moss is protective. Do you know its other name?"

He wouldn't mean the scientific name, he'd mean the witch name. I could think of no such name for Spanish moss. "Bat's wool refers to the short green kind of moss."

"There's still a mental moss connection there. Bats represent what?"

"They reveal secrets. Through those revelations, initiation and transition occur." That was how it was worded in my Book of Shadows.

His paw lifted from my thigh to gesture at the branch I held. "The very essence of magic lives in willow wood, a wood strong with the element of water—"

My thoughts flashed on Aquula.

"—and of the element of spirit. This tree has honored

you because you honored yourself and matured beyond your old emotional stream, to be born at her feet into a deeper emotional world."

When I roused, still in the tub, I instantly raised my hands so I could gauge how long I'd been in here by how pruny my fingers were. I forgot all about the time, however, seeing I held a willow wand with moss coiled around the length.

CHAPTER TWENTY-SEVEN

I woke up to Johnny calling my name softly. He was on his knees beside the couch. "Why'd you move out here?"

Fog lifting slowly, I sat up. "I couldn't sleep so I took a bath. Then"—after I'd stashed the wand in the bed table with the spell items Beau had given me—"I had the thought that it would be rude to climb into bed beside you with wet hair." I unwound the towel from my head and finger-combed my hair. "What time is it?"

"Just after nine."

So my three hours of sleep had expanded to about six. *That should be enough.*

Johnny yawned and stretched. My eyes rested on his shirtless chest, on the half-dollar-sized pentacle on his sternum. Wings spread from it across his pectorals, and the tail caressed the top two of his six-pack abs. The wings were black, and white ink created highlights, with a deep blue seeming like a sheen on the feathers. The seven-pointed fairy star was lower down. Next, my attention shot to the Celtic armbands, stylized dogs. Or wolves.

"What is it?" he whispered, fingertips stroking the line of my jaw.

"The place I had to go yesterday. Wolfsbane and Absinthe. Beau, from The Dirty Dog, he runs it."

"I thought you were going to a witch supply shop?"

"It *is* a witch supply shop."

Johnny went still. "But he's not a witch."

"Well . . . not exactly."

"What does that mean?"

"He used to be, but he isn't anymore."

Johnny rubbed sleep from his eyes. "I don't understand. How does somebody stop being a witch?"

I studied his Wedjat tattoos with an all-new wonder. *What was that ink keeping from him?* "Beau was Bindspoken."

"Bindspoken," he repeated, rising from the floor. I bent my legs up to make room for him on the couch. "Still. Why would a Bindspoken witch hang with wæres?" His warm hands rubbed down my lower leg and tickled across the top of my foot, then slid upward again.

"The witches can't associate with him; my touch had a shocklike effect on him. Maybe it's camaraderie, a sense of being a social outcast he shares with wæres."

Johnny shrugged. "Did you get what you needed?"

"Yeah. More than I thought I would."

He grinned merrily. "That's what happens when women go shopping."

Spoiling anyone's good mood first thing in the morning was terrible, but I had to tell him. No delays. "Johnny, he told me something about you that you don't know."

"What?"

I sat closer to him, wrapping my arms around my bent legs, trapping his hand under mine. "He said someone long ago must have figured out that you were the Domn Lup. He suggested that this person had you tattooed as a means to make your magic relinquish its power into the art and colors of the pictures, thereby locking that power up. He said we'd have to find out who did it and persuade them to unlock it."

He let that sink in.

"Is my memory locked up, too?"

"He didn't mention that specifically, but it seems logical to think so. If all of this is unlocked, it could come back along with your ability to change at will without the struggle and pain."

"Why didn't he tell me?" His voice was clipped.

"Beau said that, being Bindspoken, he knows what it's like to have your power cut off from you. He said it was pointless to tell you until someone who could help you, someone like the Lustrata, showed up."

"He knows that's you?"

I nodded. "I'm supposed to be able to help you figure this out." Gripping him tighter, I went on. "He said there's a spell in the Codex that we must do."

"A spell?" he echoed indignantly.

"Yes. Magic is not the same threat to you since you're Domn Lup. Beau said that's because you *are* magic. And the 'we' I referred to is you and Menessos and me."

"Why's the vamp got to be involved in finding out who did this to me?"

I bit my lip. "This won't directly find out who did your tattoos. That's going to be a multistep process. This is step one."

Johnny snorted disapproval. "What does this spell do—wait, let me guess. There's binding involved."

"It takes from each of us two pieces of our soul—"

"Soul?" Johnny stiffened.

"Beau said that in order to maintain our own 'soul balance' within ourselves, we'd have to take pieces of each other even as we gave up pieces."

Johnny stood, his hand falling away from mine as he strode across the room.

I bit my lip waiting, studying the dragon and foo-dog tattoo on his back.

Finally, he paced back. "I'll do anything you ask, but don't tell me I'm supposed to give part of my soul to the vamp, and take part of his in trade."

"I'm not going to ask you to do this. I'm going to tell you what's been presented as the solution. Either you volunteer, or you don't. If the three of us don't agree on this, it won't happen at all."

"And if this spell doesn't happen?"

Having to be the one to present him with the first of his unpleasant choices of real leadership hurt my heart. "If this doesn't happen, then I can't stop WEC from rendering me Bindspoken. If I can't tap into the energy and magic, then I can't help you find the person who tattooed you, and your power and your memory may stay locked up forever."

He sighed heavily and paced away again.

"I'm sorry, Johnny. I know. Doing this will cost you; not doing it will cost you. You just have to decide which of these two evils is more acceptable than the other."

"This is why I didn't want to be pack leader," he muttered. "This shit sucks even on small-time local pack levels." He didn't return for a long, long minute. "How does this stop them from harming you?"

"If I'm correct, then if pieces of my soul are elsewhere, as in my soul is incomplete, they cannot bind it down. Like they can't close the door because there's other things in the way, the pieces of yours and Menessos's souls." Instantly, I was willing to bet that the gateway the fairies used, the one Xerxadrea wanted me to seal shut, worked on the same principle.

"Why wouldn't they just work their Bindspoken ritual on us all?"

"How would wæres everywhere react to learning that WEC had damaged their Domn Lup?"

"Good point." He resumed his place on the end of the couch and drew my legs across his lap. He draped one arm over the couch back, ran the fingers of the other up and down my shins. "But how will wæres everywhere react to learning that their Domn Lup is bound to some vampire?"

"He's not just any vampire."

"Oh, right. He's the lord of the northeastern quarter of the U.S.A."

"He's more than that."

His mouth crooked up on one side, unimpressed. "Oh, yeah?"

"Do you want to bear the burden of another ultimate secret that cannot be revealed unless *he* reveals it first?"

Johnny studied me, silently earnest. His hand rested on my knee, heavy and hot.

Yes, I haven't told you everything.

Then Johnny looked away.

Yes, you know what a burden a secret can be. Do you want the knowledge, and the responsibility?

I waited. It was his decision. I wondered if Johnny,

through the deeper bond Menessos had implemented between Johnny and me, had somehow heard those thoughts. I could almost hear him weighing the pros and cons of his answer: he didn't want to know anything more about Menessos. But I needed him to voluntarily agree to soul-sharing with the vampire.

And the stakes are too damn high to even consider making that decision without knowing all the facts.

He shifted, brought down the arm draping the couch back. "Tell me."

"He is the original vampire and he is yet alive."

I watched him struggle with this information. Surprise. Disbelief. Waiting for the punch line. Suspicion rose, followed by doubt. Rejection of the idea came next. Then deliberation. Concession of plausibility. Conversion. Acceptance. "You've got to be fucking kidding me."

"I'm not."

His hands were both in motion then, stroking me, knee to ankle. "Not centuries old. Millennia old?"

"And alive. That's why he doesn't smell like the rest of them."

"And how he moves around during the day!"

I nodded. "He doesn't die. He really sleeps."

He covered his face with his hands and groaned. "That's just . . . mind-blowing."

"Johnny, do you see what the three of us are to each of our own respective kinds?"

"Oh, I see it." His hands fell limp into what little of his lap wasn't covered by my legs. "I see a binding between the three of us makes it all tidy, and this soul-sharing is the means to force us to work together as we have pieces of our very souls lodged in each other. I can never strike at him, and he can never strike at me.

"Menessos and I will be each side of the scales the Lustrata must balance. You'll always be in the middle." I couldn't tell if he was just working it out audibly or if he was getting angry, so I stayed silent. "This isn't just about today, either. I mean, sure, it's about the needs we have right now. But this will project into the future. It *keeps* us from striking at each other. And what if the day comes when we need to? You said the old witch claimed the red fairy was mad. What if the vamp goes mad? We'd be stuck."

"You're right." I hadn't thought in fast-forward. I put my feet on the floor and scooted closer to him, took his hands in mine. "You have a valid point. I'll give it some more thought. I wish we had more time."

He squeezed my hands. "Do you want this? Do you want to be rooted between the original vampire and the king of wærewolves?"

"I am already there. It's inevitable. I didn't want to leave my home and leave Nana and Beverley behind. I didn't want to out myself to the world, or become Erus Veneficus. I didn't ask for any of this, but it was appointed to me and—"

"I'll do it," he said softly.

"What?" *I hadn't even gotten to my usual spiel yet.*

Johnny looked at me with the weight of the world in his eyes. "Your needs come first."

My heart broke. This was changing him. *I* was changing him.

He said, "It's the right thing for the right reason."

• • •

Two hours later, I sat in church.

Not just any church. This was the Pilgrim Congregational Church. The interior was very theatrical with seating fanning out from a pulpit in one corner. Rounded arches rose to a central stained-glass dome, the space under it unbroken by supporting columns. For all its grandeur, it was practical, too. Lower walls could be raised into upper walls to open Sunday school rooms to the sanctuary and expand the seating. Johnny pointed out the historic pipe organ and the original Tiffany stained-glass windows flanking it. He concluded his little guided tour with a grand view from the balcony. I was speechless, but that was more due to the fact that the pews filling up below me on this Saturday afternoon were filling exclusively with wærewolves. It smelled like a forest in here.

"Why do they gather in a church?" I asked.

"No vamps. Any sanctified ground is magically protected. Vamps can't be on your Covenstead grounds without permission, right?"

I nodded. "It's a sacred space, set aside and protected by our magic. Christian churches, Islamic mosques, Jewish temples . . . they have inherent protections, too."

"It's kind of a tradition for wæres to meet here."

"So do they own this place or rent it or what?"

He made a face. "They've worked out an agreement that benefits both parties."

"Ahhh." Meaning I wasn't getting details I didn't need. Fine with me.

There were perhaps sixty wærewolves assembled. I saw Celia and Erik, Theo. Hector sat in the back, Todd in front. The Harding twins sat in the middle of the right section, and the rows around them, unsurprisingly, were filled with young men. For a pair of wærewolves they sure had cougar opportunities.

"I'm going downstairs. When I start speaking, would you make your way down, so that when I call you, you can come forward?"

"Sure." He had told me what his plan was, but neither of us would dare to predict how the wæres would react. Not even with double innuendo points on the line.

I sat in the balcony, waiting. Being in a church made me think of the Reverend Kline. I took the protrepticus out of my jeans pocket and flipped it over and over. Surely, with Xerxadrea dead, it was no longer functional. But one never knew. I kept it with me, but I hadn't opened it yet. Nor had I figured out what to tell Goliath about his dead brother speaking to me from it. For now those answers could wait.

We were here to ask for help. According to the news, the body found inside the Botanical Gardens had not yet been identified. But it would be. Xerxadrea had warned me Vilna-Daluca would blame me. I couldn't expect them to offer any aid, no matter what plans might have been in the works.

Minutes later, when the flow of people into the building had ebbed, Todd took to the stairs before the pulpit. He did not stand behind it like a pastor, but remained in front.

"Welcome. This gathering has been called by our new *dirija*, our Domn Lup, and your presence is noted by your signatures in the Book of the Ascribed. I will remind you that what is discussed here is pack business and goes no further than pack ears." He gestured and Johnny came up the steps to join him. "And now, the Domn Lup." Todd went back to sit in the front pew.

The silence that followed was probably a formal show of wære respect, but I'd seen Johnny take the stage to vast applause and screams of excitement. The quiet did not befit him as well.

He nodded to them. "Hello." Pausing to draw a breath, a charming grin came to his face. "I trust that after last night's festivities, none of you awoke with a hangover."

It won him a few snickers.

"No wolf worth his howl ever admits to a hangover, right?"

Howls went up around the room. When they faded, Johnny began. "I called this meeting to tell you something, and I trust that you will be patient with me in the telling." A few seconds ticked by as he seemed to decide on his wording. "The witches have a legend about a witch who will bring balance to this world. They call her the Lustrata. All of their lore confirms that she is real and active."

I remembered I was supposed to go down and be ready. I left my seat and quietly descended, then waited in the back of the church, leaning against the wall.

". . . in order to achieve that balance, she must make tough choices. And she has made some. She has chosen to align herself with both wærewolves and vampires. To charge both with managing their portion of balance. Each side must do their part."

"Vamps can't be trusted!" someone interjected.

Johnny regarded the man who had shouted. "A few weeks ago, I was in complete agreement with that statement."

"Bah!" someone else shouted.

"I'm not saying I've done a full about-face on it, either. But I've seen a few things that have made me reconsider. That said, one thing I *am* a hundred percent certain of is that I trust the Lustrata. She has generated the loyalty of a most powerful vampire and—"

"We know who you mean!" the first man said. "And what she did to generate that loyalty!"

"Her blood!" another added.

Johnny wasn't hassled by their outbursts. "The mundane humans cannot comprehend our world, so open your eyes, and see things as they are, not as the reporters see it. We are on the brink of a war, and you must hear this!" Johnny was many things, including a musician. He knew the value of silence, and when he stopped and let silence fall, it only served to emphasize his next words. "Her blood sealed his loyalty! 'The Lord of Vampires will drink the Lustrata's blood.' That is what the vamp's own bards wrote in the eighteenth century."

News to me.

"She is aligned with the vampire who will rule them all, and she is aligned with me."

Cammi Harding stood. I wasn't sure she'd changed her clothes since last night. Perhaps her closet was filled with short skirts and shirts with plunging necklines. "How did she generate *your* loyalty?"

Johnny appraised her, and it wasn't kind appraisal. "In ways you cannot."

A few men howled their Neanderthalish approval.

"She has shown me loyalty and respect, and undeniable power. The Domn Lup acknowledges power." He beckoned me forward.

My heart was thudding in my chest, but I walked toward him. *Hell, I've strutted about in the stupidest shoes on the planet. I can walk up there in sneakers, no prob.* As I passed certain rows, the growls weren't hidden. *Keep going.*

"I present to you the Lustrata," he said.

I surveyed the crowd as I stood one step below Johnny and saw hardened, unconvinced faces.

"We are on the brink of a war," I said, "and I have asked your Domn Lup for aid."

They were all worried now. If Johnny said, "Jump," they were supposed to ask, "How high?" and immediately comply.

The gathered wærewolves fidgeted uncomfortably in their seats or made other restless moves. Cammi remained standing. She tossed her head and crossed her arms, deepening her cleavage.

"Tomorrow at dawn," Johnny said, "the fairies are coming to dole out their vengeance upon a vampire. The vampires cannot defend their own in the sunlight. We have been asked to stand in and fight for them."

The interjections that came were, "Fight for vampires? Are you out of your mind?" and, "Let his Beholders defend him!" and, "You can't ask us to fight for vampires."

"I have not," Johnny interjected there, "asked you to do anything but gather here and listen." That shut them up. "The Beholders will be there, but our future also teeters on this one sunrise."

"*Our* future?" Cammi asked.

"The fairies gave the witches an ultimatum: deliver the vampire or face war."

Cammi sneered. "Let the witches fight!"

"I am," I said.

"Right." She moved into the aisle. "They're sending just one little witch?" Something about church aisles made people move as if decorum were required, or so I thought. Cammi managed to stomp down the aisle in four-inch heels. "Their commitment seems lacking."

My chin leveled. "I am the Lustrata."

Cammi stopped, even with the first pew.

I wouldn't risk touting the aid of witches who weren't likely to show up. I just hoped none of the wæres knew the witches were divided on the subject of supporting me. "Will you be there?" I asked Cammi.

She didn't answer, but she clearly didn't want to have to rise to that challenge. She might get dirty. Scuff her shoes. Break a nail.

"If this war happens," Johnny went on, "it will spill into the life of every creature on this planet. The mundane humans have been waiting for an excuse to demand the extermination of the rest of us. This could easily be that excuse." His voice changed then, passion filled his words as when he sang. The heartfelt rawness of his plea shone through. "If you fight, you fight for the world. Many of you have children. They will still inherit this world from you. What world will you give them? The one in which you're an embarrassment that was eradicated? Or the one in which you stood up and declared your bravery and fairness as you chose to fight for *all* people?" He searched the room as he spoke, acknowledging his pack members individually.

Cammi shifted her weight and tossed her head. "Out with it already! Are you ordering us do this, Domn Lup? To risk our lives in protection of a single vamp while the rest of the undead remain safe in their haven and WEC sends a single witch to represent their interests?"

Here it was, the moment when the responsibility of leadership became the Hand of Fate that slapped him in the face. The first hard question of his rule had been asked. This was what he didn't want: his decision risking people's lives.

Would he cower, bruised by Fate's inescapable hand?

Would he fight back?

His answer would characterize the kind of leader he would be. The pews were silent as if the wæres present collectively held their breath.

Into the fallen hush, Johnny stood unmoving. Solid.

As he considered, he conveyed calmness to his pack. He demonstrated he did not make snap decisions. He established he was not an insensitive autocrat. Their lives mattered, and he would not recklessly risk them. He showed me that he was willing to lead, that he could bear this mighty authority and its cost, that he could be accountable, and be in command of the situation.

Goddess, I love him.

He filled his lungs, ready to answer. "I am not going to command you do this," he said. "I have told you what is at hand and I have presented my solution. I know there's been no time to prove I deserve your trust. But you know what I can do. You know what I am. You know what *my* course of action will be. And I'm giving you the choice. Either you volunteer and stand at my side, or you don't."

He was using my words. I was flattered he thought them worthy. He nodded to me, a signal.

I faced the crowd again. "There will be a reward for anyone who takes this risk." It was time to tell them all. Some already knew, but Johnny wanted me to tell the rest here, now. "I saved the life of a friend of mine, a member of this pack. Theodora Hennessey. Erik and Celia Randolph were also there and involved. I used magic, a powerful spell provided to me by the very vampire whose life is now threatened and needs your aid. Because of this spell, Theo's life was saved. And now, she, Erik, and Celia all claim to retain their human minds while in wolf form. They have spoken of this to Todd. I promise, when this is over, I will repeat that ritual and give all volunteers who wish it that same gift."

"Todd, I charge you with sharing the details," Johnny said, "but only with those who take oath not only to be there and assist, but to keep secret those details." He came down a step to stand beside me. "You all have a decision to make. Do you choose to be spectators, and let the fate of the world happen as it will, or do you choose to shape the future with your own hands?" He took my hand, put it on his arm to lead me out as an equal. He brushed past Cammi and hit her shoulder with his for emphasis.

CHAPTER TWENTY-EIGHT

We arrived at the theater and were met by Mountain. "Boss says for you two to come to his chambers." He escorted us.

The big door thudded shut, sealing us in a room spared from utter darkness only by a single red pillar candle on the otherwise bare altar. Calla lily incense permeated the air. It was the scent of mourning. In the meager light, the stacked stone walls were believably subterranean, threatening and imprisoning. The two white marble pillars glowed like rigid ghosts, and the door between could have been the black chasm to Hell.

On the far side of the room, I spotted Menessos in one of the high-backed leather chairs. He could have easily blended into the night the room had become. He was clothed in black, and I could discern no details save the stern set of his downcast gaze and his hand curled thoughtfully at his chin.

"Goliath questioned the performer," he said softly.

"And?" I went to him. Johnny followed.

Menessos waited until we were seated on the half-circle

bench beside him, but he did not look up. "He confessed to attempted murder."

Johnny sat forward, creaking the leather. "Which of you was his mark?"

"I was."

Relieved, and yet not, I asked, "Where is the performer now?"

"By law, I have the authority to detain him twenty-four hours for questioning, but if local law enforcement intervenes they have the right to remove him into their custody—which they always do if the prisoner is human. This one was no exception. We gave him over before dawn."

"Who sent him?" I asked. "Or was he self-appointed to the task?"

He put off voicing that answer as long as he could. "Heldridge sent him."

I was too stunned to comment, but my memory of how Menessos had subdued Heldridge at the Eximium remained fresh.

"Evidently he was opposed to my headquartering my court in his established area. He should have been honored to host my sector authority here. Quarter-lords always improve the local economy. Chicago's lord begged me not to leave . . ."

He was rambling, and his voice was distant. It gave me the impression that he was holding this conversation while his thoughts were truly far, far away. "What else?"

"Hmmm?"

"Tell me." I put a hand on his knee.

Those sharklike eyes lifted then, and locked on me. "Heldridge was at the Eximium. Perhaps he told the fairies of the hanky. If he wanted to be rid of me, that is logical. But he cannot call the fey or stir the energies. No witch in her right mind would do so for him. That means the fairies contacted him, probably after I confirmed moving the haven here. Riling him. They've been working against me with my own kind."

"Where's Heldridge now?"

"He's fled. His haven is in distress. I must send his people to other lords. I dare not take them into my own haven, though it is customary. With you here . . . I cannot afford to risk it."

We sat in silence, the brooding gloom of the room taking hold.

"I sent scouts to the beach. They will ascertain the lay of the land. Their report will be useful to Mark as he begins strategizing at dusk."

"That is so little time," I said.

"There will be some wæres who will aid," Johnny offered. "I can't say how many, but I should have an indication by dusk."

Menessos bowed his head toward Johnny. "Congratulations on your ascension, Domn Lup."

Johnny nodded back.

Menessos turned to me. "What did you think of Wolfsbane and Absinthe?"

"It was more than I expected."

"Beauregard explained, then, the need for the soul-sharing?"

I nodded.

"And you, Domn Lup, you agree to its necessity?"

"Yeah, but . . . I have questions."

Menessos inclined his head slightly, acknowledging that Johnny should continue.

"I'm a fan of the one-body one-spirit concept. So tell me—honestly"—he glared pointedly at the vampire—"how will it alter our conscious selves?"

"Are you conscious of your soul now?" Menessos asked back.

"I'm self-aware."

"That is consciousness, yes, but do you feel your *soul*?"

Johnny considered it. "I don't know. I don't know what it would feel like to be alive and soulless."

"If you were alive and soulless you'd be a zombie," Menessos said plainly. "Many think vampires are soulless, but I say not. It is why we do not rot as zombies do. I say vampires' souls leave them at dawn, yet are tethered to them still, and return at dusk bringing consciousness back."

"Like astral travel?" I asked.

"Similar, but in astral travel the soul is aware like a dream. Vampire souls are simply dormant."

"And while the soul is dormant and absent," Johnny pressed, "what do your people claim the experience of that is like?"

Menessos's head snapped toward me sharply.

Johnny's words had implied that Menessos wouldn't know himself. "Yes. I told him you're alive." I defended my actions, saying, "No one should go into this ritual without knowing the truth."

Johnny snorted. "She did swear me to secrecy first."

The vampire was nonplussed, but it was done. I hoped he could concede that my logic was valid.

"They claim it is a second of nothingness," he said.

"Vampires die, and they 'instantly' awaken knowing hours have passed but without a true sense of them. It renders the impression of near-constant life."

"And sharing souls? How does it work?"

"I have not experienced it before," Menessos said irritably as he rose and paced.

"If I had to guess"—Johnny came to his feet—"I'd say that psychic stuff like telepathy touches on what we're attempting, but what we're doing is more permanent."

Menessos stroked his chin contemplatively.

"And," Johnny continued, "I don't want either of you in my head."

I had a thought. "This ritual is in the Codex, right? Didn't you perform it with Una and Ninurta?"

"Una would not."

"Why?"

"She feared the repercussions. She thought that souls are the handiwork of the gods and that, should we play at separating and dividing our essences, we would all die."

Guardedly, I asked, "What do you think?"

My question lingered, unanswered. Then Menessos disappeared into the black chasm doorway. A minute later, he came back with the Trivium Codex and placed it into my hands. "A silver ribbon marks the proper page. If, after studying the ritual, you still wish to perform it, return here an hour before dusk."

Wordlessly, I pleaded with him to answer.

He stroked my cheek. "I think the goddess favors you above all others." Then he departed into that blackness again.

I followed Johnny out.

• • •

I couldn't call Nana to decipher this for me. So, I called Dr. Geoffrey Lincoln. It being Saturday afternoon, the veterinarian was out of the office. The recorded response supplied an "emergency number" which I promptly dialed and left a message. After answering Johnny's "where'd you get that phone?" questions, I worked translating things via the Internet, doubting the accuracy of every syllable. A half hour later, as Johnny served up lunch, I'd succumbed to the idea that the doc wasn't going to call back. I commenced an internal dialogue of how to broach the subject with Nana.

Then the phone rang.

For the next two hours, I read passages to Dr. Lincoln, Johnny snapped phone photos and e-mailed them to him, and slowly we interpreted and deciphered the ritual. Dr. Lincoln promised to bill me.

I sat down to study the actual spell. Though I knew how Beau's ingredients would work, I didn't see how the willow wand fit in.

An hour before dusk, we gathered in Menessos's chambers around the altar table where Aquula's dead body had lain.

It was just after four in the afternoon. The sun would set at the startlingly early time of five-nineteen. Tomorrow would be the first Sunday in November, and daylight saving time would officially kick in at two A.M. tonight. *All things considered, we have about fifteen hours.*

The altar held the Trivium Codex—open to the proper page—the supplies Beau had provided, and the standard supplies, too. My wands, old and new, marked my place at the table. Menessos's was marked by his black-handled athame. For Johnny, Menessos had placed an onyx carved in the shape of a howling wolf. Though he would not call or shape the magic, Johnny would be a participant in this spell, and it was a nice gesture on the vampire's part. I was pleased that Menessos had respected him enough to consider it.

We were all here. *Ready or not.* I reached for the salt to get this ritual under way. Menessos beat me to it, taking the salt neatly before I could. He walked around casting about this representation of the element of earth and cleansing the space.

I picked up the paper with the sigils for the spell, studied it once more, then set it to one side. Johnny picked up the corked bottle I'd been given at Wolfsbane and Absinthe. "What is this?" he whispered.

"Something Beau gave me."

Johnny lifted the bottle, tilting and examining it. "Is this made with water or whiskey?"

"Water." *I hope. I hadn't opened it.*

"Is that a peach pit?"

"Yes. For love and wishes."

"And the other stuff floating in there?"

I thought back.

Menessos replaced the salt on the altar, then smoothly took the incense and a feather and cleansed the space with the element of air.

"Moss, willow, and orchid petals," I said to Johnny, fingers trailing along the secondary wand, the willow branch with moss. "Moss is for luck, and is protective. Willow is for love and protection."

"And the orchid petals?"

"Love."

"And?"

"Just love."

"There's a lot of love in that bottle."

My cheeks warmed.

Menessos put back the incense, then made a trek around the circle with a red candle, cleansing the space with fire.

"Protection, too," I said, holding up the prickly holly leaf. "Protection and luck."

Johnny cocked his head a little. "Do we need that much protection, luck, and love?"

"For what we're about to do, yes."

He shot a glance at Menessos, then shifted back to me with brows raised, as if silently asking, *Him too?*

Making my expression entirely soft and full of compassion, I nodded.

He pointed to the paper on which I had drawn. "Those?"

"Sigils and symbols. The cross-number-two thing is the symbol of Saturn, and since it is Saturday we'll tap the humility, authority, and respect associated with this day. However, we are at a crossroads here, so we'll also call on the energy of Scorpio, the current zodiac house, and since the moon is waning we'll concentrate on being rid of the dangers and doubts and . . ." I let it trail off. Johnny's eyes had kind of glazed over, as if I'd started speaking Chinese or something.

Menessos replaced the red candle and took up the sea-shell filled with water.

Johnny studied the lines and curves of the next, a sigil, and gave me a polite nod.

"You're thinking it's just a scribble, right?"

"Actually, I was thinking it's like fan blades that have had Silly String sprayed on them."

Maybe he won't change after all. "You've sprayed Silly String on a fan before?"

"Of course. Haven't you?"

"No." Inspecting the sigil again, I had to agree it was as good an interpretation of the lines as another. "Your 'fan blades'"—I traced with my finger—"are two *S*'s, see?" I'd drawn them with glue and silver glitter, one at a forty-five-degree angle, the second ninety degrees from the first so they crossed in the center. "They represent soul sharing, which is what we are doing. These are each of our initials, *M, J,* and *P.*" These were centered among the glitter. Purple and red ink from standard office-supply Sharpies highlighted the drawing.

Menessos finished with the cleansing, opened the altar energies, and lit the illuminator candles. With a nod at me he said, "Your turn."

Taking the pail of sea salt, I drew a large circle encompassing much of the room, chanting, "Where circles are cast in salt . . . there, magic is called." Then I redrew it with my usual crystal-tipped wand. "Where cross the paths of fate . . . there, magic is made." I drew it a third and final time with the new willow wand. "Where three pieces make one whole . . . there, magic is the soul." A triple-cast circle always made me feel safer.

"Two wands?" Menessos asked.

"This one is new." I laid the willow wand on the table.

"Oh?"

"A present."

"From?"

Who? The Goddess? A tree? "My meditation."

He thoughtfully studied where it lay on the altar.

When I spoke the quarter calls, north and the earth element came first. The coarse sea salt marking the circle shifted as if to acknowledge that presence. The second call stirred the air in the room like a sighing breath. With the third call, the candle flames flickered down low in unison, then shot up in a single blast of greeting. When I called water, the seashell on the table rocked, making ripples across the water's surface. Most impressively, the fluid in the bottle Beau had given me swirled as if shaken, forming a tornado effect with bubbles and debris being pulled down in the center.

I nodded to Menessos. "Backatcha."

He shook his head. "No. You will invoke deity."

"But—"

"No buts. They like you better."

I thought of Hecate at the Eximium. "She told you to be forgiven."

His chin leveled. "Still, you are Her chosen."

"And you are not?"

In one sharp, sideways glance, Menessos told me he didn't feel comfortable discussing this around Johnny. His posture stiffened as emphasis to that point.

I took up the bottle and uncorked it. To Johnny I said, "Bare your chest, please."

"You first."

I smirked.

He unbuttoned his shirt. Taking a holly leaf from the altar, I allowed the mixture to drip onto the prickly leaf. It was neither water nor alcohol, but a thin oil. The fragrance was pleasant. After setting the bottle on the altar, I smeared my fingers through the oil from the leaf and I traced the pentacle tattoo on his sternum. Above it, I drew the sigil of our combined initials, *MJP*. I replaced the holly leaf on the table beside the onyx wolf.

Making certain I moved clockwise, deosil, around the circle, I went to Menessos and repeated the actions on him—minus the tattoo to use as a pattern. I opened his shirt a bit more to check the spot where Samson had tried to stake him. It was perfectly healed. No scar. I clasped his hand. "She forgave you. Can you not forgive yourself for whatever it was that caused the rift?"

His resolve was strong. "I want you to call Her." He squeezed my hand for emphasis.

Having pushed as hard as my conscience would allow, I relented. We couldn't risk negative energies tainting the sacred space we'd created. Releasing him, I shifted to the side, not resuming my former place.

"Who gets to mark you?" Johnny asked.

I removed my shirt, but remained modestly covered by my bra. They each gave a man-growl indicating their approval, then Johnny tried to outstare Menessos.

"Both," I said. "Menessos draws the pentacle, you draw the sigil." I moved Beau's pendant so it hung down my back, leaving drawing room on my skin.

Menessos went first. He poured the liquid onto the

holly leaf, and dipped his fingers in it. Solemnly meeting my eyes, he touched my skin.

When first he'd marked me with his own blood, he'd drawn an ankh on my sternum. It was against my will and he knew it, but I was engulfed in his power. Now, he drew not the symbol of his alchemy. He drew the symbol of my magic. Slowly.

He painted the pentacle with tenderness and burning certainty. It wasn't innocent. It wasn't chaste. Not because his fingers strayed—they stayed right where they were supposed to be—but because of his eyes. The gray was simmering like quicksilver.

Seven wanted me to love him. But this wasn't the countenance of love. It was covetous. Lecherous. Hedonistic. It made my heart race. It summoned that warmth deep inside of me that only he could stir. And it beckoned to my darkest desires . . . the kind good girls never admit having.

Menessos stepped aside and held the leaf out to Johnny.

I had to take a pair of cleansing breaths.

Johnny wiped his fingers over the holly and extended his hand toward me. "Does it matter which order I draw the letters?"

"No."

He drew the *J* first, and I could feel the trembling in his fingers. He covered the *J* with a *P*. I watched his face, so serious, intent on getting it right. *For me.* He added the *M* last, and nodded. *His first magic circle; his first sigil.*

With shoulders squared and voice strong and firm, I said, "I call upon She who is the Three and the One. The crone who has been the maiden and the mother. You have been the Past, You are the Present, and You will be the Future. Queen of Heaven, Earth, and Underworld. *My Goddess.*"

Taking a pause to consider that we three were, from a certain point of view, about to become one, I felt the hair on the nape of my neck rise.

A presence hovered on the periphery of reality. Observing. I had seen the darkness coalesce and become the night alive, sparkling like black diamonds. I had seen it become Her. I had felt Her touch before.

Hecate was here.

CHAPTER TWENTY-NINE

I did not call Her into me, as I would have when Drawing Down the Moon. After our last meeting, I wasn't sure I'd have the nerve to do any such thing ever again. She'd said—

My heart skipped a beat.

She'd said She would see me when I was ready to see my own soul. That I would find Her at the crossroads. *I'd said to Johnny we are at a crossroads . . .* And this was all about my soul. And theirs.

From the ethereal, a hand stroked my neck, through my hair, causing it to prickle more stiffly. The hand caressed my skin so subtly, intangible but undeniably touching me.

"Hecate!" I whispered Her name, reverently, fearfully.

Her fingers trailed down my spine, nails sharp and scraping my flesh. Like a warning. It set the charm at my back swinging.

"Our purpose," Menessos said, "is *Sorsanimus,* to share pieces of our souls, each with the others. For our own protection. For balance."

When he spoke, it seemed the Goddess's attention shifted to him. I sighed in relief. *This is it.*

I took Johnny's hand in my right, and I took Menessos's hand in my left. Then I waited. They had to work this out. Each had to come to the moment when he was ready to hold the other's hand. But of course, they were men. While I had my suspicions that Menessos and Ninurta had been intimate, that was long, long ago. Johnny wasn't the kind of man who held other men's hands.

So, this was difficult for them both, but in different ways.

At once, both reached, then stopped, holding back their hands as if expecting the other to concede to the undergrip.

Then I realized it was more than I feared. Their hesitation was about more than pressing their palms together. It was about who would, literally, have the upper hand. Who got the overgrip, the undergrip.

Matter-of-factly, Menessos said, "I am the oldest."

"It's my people coming to save your ass."

"And they are so motivated because of *my* Codex giving them the ability to retain their man-minds."

Johnny was unimpressed and unmoved. "It's still your life on the line, man." He wiggled his fingers. "Show me how grateful you are for the chance to keep it."

Menessos didn't have a comeback for that one. Slowly, he turned his hand.

Johnny's mouth curved up slightly.

I held my breath, waiting for the sarcastic remark that would make both release my hands as they came to blows again. But Johnny said nothing.

And Menessos let a small smile of his own slip through.

It's a miracle. Then it hit me that they were being men again. Though Menessos had conceded the upper hand, both were waiting to see who would take the other's hand.

I sighed exasperatedly.

Johnny grabbed Menessos's hand.

"Three. Two. One. Three of us. Two male. One female. Three. Two. One. Three lives. Two sigils. One purpose. Three. Two. One." I spoke softly, rhythmically. It was not a part of the spell, it was a reminder.

"Tres. Duo. Unus. Tres fieri unus. Sorsanimus," Menessos said. "A piece of my soul I offer to each of you. I accept a piece of your soul in return."

I repeated the words, then Johnny did.

"Vieo nexilis trini."

It was the chant that would achieve our goal. That is, if we could convince a higher power to grant us this mutual intercession.

In ritual, the ability to focus is crucial. Right now, concentrating on my intention was as important as keeping my eyes on the road when driving one hundred miles per hour. Menessos knew this. In discussing the ritual with Johnny earlier, I had advised him it was imperative that he maintain his thoughts precisely on what we were doing, his willingness to participate, and to not let his thoughts go roaming.

Taking my own advice, I turned my inner "meditation switch" halfway and edged toward alpha. I imagined that through my voice I poured into the chant all the hopes I had for this spell. I poured in my need to block the Witches Council from rendering me Bindspoken and thwarting my destiny. I added my need to help Johnny unlock his power—which he would require as Domn Lup. And I included my need to save Menessos from the fairies . . . *in about thirteen hours.*

Around us, wind howled like a wolf. The sea salt marking the circle's barrier was lifted into the air like dust particles, thrown into the fray to whirl and dance. I was the only one of the three of us facing the table now, and I saw the candle flames flickering, but not as harried by the rushing air as I would have expected. In fact, the flames sank low to the wicks and sporadically flashed high. Within the salt-strewn air at the circle's edge, flashes of light erupted, coinciding with the candle bursts. Water rose up from the seashell, somehow expanding to become much more than a few drops. An umbrella of water formed over our heads, more water than the seashell actually held. Each flash of light created a ripple on the water's surface.

Menessos was rapt, resolute. Seven's words, *"Love him as he loves you,"* flickered through my mind, but I cast them out and checked on Johnny. He stared up, fascinated by the magic, but maintained the chant.

The power was present, but it was holding back. The chant had gone on too long for nothing to be happening. It had built, and was building no more.

Was one of them resisting? Was Johnny? *I need this! For all of us!* I pleaded.

That intangible hand reached through me, then, and turned my switch all the way to alpha.

I stood on the shore beside the willow tree, toes sinking into muck. Regardless of my state in the circle outside this meditation, I'd been delivered here naked.

Amenemhab was nowhere to be seen. Out of nowhere, the buckskin mustang raced by the tree at a full gallop and splashed into the lake, ruining the tranquil surface with splashes and ripples.

Oh no you don't. My need was such that She must not get away. But the horse kept going.

I rushed into the water. The cold fluid tugged at my ankles, jerked at my knees, and my vivid memory of my last visit made me hesitate. *A deeper emotional world.*

She was swimming toward the white spearhead-shaped rock.

If I wanted this soul-sharing to work, I was going to have to earn it or prove it or something.

"Fine."

Stomping forward, I leaped in and swam. I tried not to think about how far it was, how deep the lake might be, and what else might be in the water. *Just keep swimming.* I twisted into a backstroke. *What a beautiful sky, like a web of stars over my head.*

I was finding a sense of calm when the fin arose in the water beside me, just gliding smoothly alongside. If it had been a sharklike fin, I probably would have panicked. But this was spiky, like the dorsal on a walleye or a bass. Only this was a couple hundred times bigger.

Panic was trying to set in anyway.

The fin angled sharply away and headed out and around the lake. I flipped over to watch it go, just to assure myself that the lake creature wasn't going after the horse, and that it was far, far away. My efforts to get to shore redoubled.

Across from me, on the narrow shore, the horse

climbed from the water and shook Herself, then turned to me. She flicked Her tail and cantered around to the farside of the rock island.

Soon, my kicking feet brushed the pebbly offshore mix and I swam a few more strokes, then stood.

Muck between my toes wasn't any more preferable on this side of the shore than on the other. I wrung out my hair and hurried along the shore the way the horse had gone. At the far end the stone jutted out into the sea. Hoof marks in the sand and pebbles became human footprints and entered a crevice in the stone. *A doorway.*

I approached the crevice and entered a cavern through it. Dim inner light showed the single pathway immediately split into three, each ending at the opening to a tunnel.

The crevice I had entered abruptly disappeared. Darkness surrounded me. It would not have been the way out anyway, it was the way deeper in. Deep enough to see my soul.

For a long minute, I stood, paralyzed. I hadn't checked to see if there were damp footprints leading to any of the tunnels.

The dark closed in on me, suffocating me like obscurity and insignificance.

Cleansing breath in, doubt out.

Which way felt right?

Johnny still held my right hand, physically and outside of this meditation. And the right-hand path seemed to smell of cedar and sage. To the left, my senses found it cinnamon-and-coppery sweet, like blood. Menessos. So the center path : . . that must be my darkness.

My breath caught. At the Witches' Ball, before I told the *lucusi* I was the Lustrata, I had a vision of Hecate. She had said, "You will find Me in the darkness. In *your* darkness. I am there. When you are ready to see your own soul . . . I'll be waiting."

As my fingers scrubbed along the chilled, damp wall, my toes slid cautiously forward. My progress was slow, but certain. A dozen paces in, my heart leaped as I felt no floor before me. Crouching to inspect, I felt nothing.

My first thought was to go back. But I knew that I could not choose between Menessos and Johnny. This was ridiculous. *My* path was not a dead end. Was not a path into darkness that led to a bottomless pit. It couldn't be. I was the Lustrata. I was the bringer of light and justice. *Light.* Lustrata implied luster, a glowing sheen.

The mantle!

Calling my armor, calling on the light, that gentle gleam brightened the area around me. Little by little, a vast cavern appeared, a place giants—*Titans*—had carved into the foundation of the earth. I stood atop a grand stairway, each step five-feet high and thirty feet wide. Pillars stood like skyscrapers across the endless hall before me.

Crouching on the edge, I leaped down, step after step, and counted thirteen in all.

I lingered on the last. Stalactites dotted the ceiling between the enormous pillars, and their companion stalagmites disrupted the floor below. I searched to define a path. Feeling rather like a mouse in the Titan's house, and wary that there might be a giant cat waiting to pounce, I peered into the distance before easing down.

My feet did not scrape over more stone, but struck wood.

I dropped to the ground. Here, at the foot of the giant stone stairway, was a wide arched door that looked like a cartoon mouse might live behind it—if the mouse were tall as a human. *Have to be careful what you're thinking in here.*

The vast hall was an expanse of rock except for a single human-sized door. That made for an easy decision of what to do next.

I pushed the knobless door and it gave with a groan. As I passed through, I emerged into the night. This wasn't the lake area. I stood on solid, dry earth topped with fall's dry grass brittle under my feet. The door was attached to a giant—*no, I'll use that word sparingly now*—a mature elm tree. It stretched up like a black silhouette, leaves unnaturally still.

As I brought my focus down from the limbs, I checked the sky for a clue to my location. The night was moonless. None of the constellations were ones I could name. The sky didn't help me at all.

Then the aroma of raisin and currant cakes filled my nostrils. A dirt road stretched before me. I stepped onto the path. Perhaps a dozen yards ahead, two more roads joined it. One on either side. In the center where the three roads intersected, stood an old woman robed in black, face hidden in the depths of a hood. She grasped the handles protruding from the curved shaft of a scythe. The blade's tip rested on the dirt. Hecate of the Crossroads.

"You have come," she said in the voice of Time Eternal, the voice of the Depths of Nothing and Everything, the voice of The Crone.

Leaving the elm behind, I asked, "Do I have to see my own soul?"

"Only if you want control over what pieces of it you share."

I stopped about ten feet away from Her. She was armed, after all. I hoped She didn't actually take part in this ritual and cut away pieces of souls with that scythe. It didn't look very precise. Or sanitary. "What's the risk if I don't?"

She shrugged Her bent shoulders. "You may have your choice or your desire."

Choice or desire? Sounded redundant, as if they should be the same thing, but I knew they were not. If asked to make a choice, people had to consider the possibilities. If given their desire, it might reflect a base, instinctual need without conscious thought attached to that selection.

I respected Johnny's concern not to have us in his head. That encouraged me to pick *choice,* so he could decide what he shared.

If Menessos had that same opportunity to choose what to share and what not . . . it could be far more dangerous. And yet, letting his desire take some piece of my soul didn't sound like the best option, either.

The root question was: do I trust my mind and heart to decide what was best, or my subconscious?

"Now I know why Una didn't want to do this," I muttered.

"Why do you utter such?"

"One I would give his choice. The other . . . is hard to trust with either option."

The old woman laughed. "Why do you trust Menessos less?"

"I didn't say it was him."

"You don't have to."

Fine. "He would know better than Johnny or me how to manipulate the situation to his gain."

"Has his gain been so unkind to you?"

"No."

"Then decide which gift you give him."

Choice or desire. *Both.* "I will allow Johnny to take what he desires, but I will choose what Menessos receives."

"So it will be done. Come, child, and kneel before me."

Even though She had chosen me to be the Lustrata, getting that close to the armed Crone was unsettling. Still, I could not refuse. I walked forward and knelt before Her, naked except for the Lustrata's mantle.

Instantly She was in motion, Her age-spotted and gnarled hands swirling the scythe in overhead arcs and wide sweeping motions. The blade whistled as it sliced the air; the wind of the motion stirred my hair. I didn't flinch, but pondered Her face, hidden in the dark of Her hood. Her eyes, I remembered, were haunting.

Suddenly, Hecate cried out and the scythe point embedded in the ground before me, so the widest part of the blade was waist high. "Cast your eyes upon this blade!" She commanded. Her hood fluttered and fell back, exposing Her wrinkled face, loosening gray hair, and terrible eyes that had stared into the sun for eons. "Stare into the silver and see your own soul."

CHAPTER THIRTY

I peered at the blade, but saw nothing. No reflection at all.

Where am I?

My hands rose to the blade, to be sure it was real, and that the angle was right. The surface was shiny enough . . .

The side of my finger skimmed along a fraction of the keen blade. Pain sliced as my skin split. I jerked away. A single glistening drop of too-red blood ran slowly down the razor edge. The shiny blade shimmered and there I was, appearing surprised in my reflection. Then my image faded like smoke.

What remained glowed softly, nearly invisible, a stereotypical ghost from the movies. Yet my senses overloaded at the sight. My mind went strange, as if perception had become tactile. My skin could see. I observed all that was around me at once. What was my previous sense of vision now examined the surface of the blade as if with intangible fingers. *Tentacles? No, more like arcs of electrical current, searching, feeling, discerning with energy.* The blade felt like radio static.

For one perfect moment, my awareness was redefined as a gentle light that surrounded me, as heavy as a knight's armor yet nebulous as a cloud. It permeated my skin and my aura. It pulsed with energy like a venous system filled with a lifetime of flowing memories rather than blood. All that made me the person I was, created this synthesis.

My soul!

The revelation was astounding, amazing, and so vivid that—

I blinked and it severed me from this place.

No! I'm not done—

I was free-falling, rushing back into myself with break-the-sound-barrier speed.

I wanted Menessos to have my first memory of the Goddess. So he would know why I was in that cornfield, why I was running. And so he would know the comfort and solace that found me and changed my life forever . . .

A piece of my soul was torn from me.

The ache that claimed me was deeper than the heartbreak of my mother abandoning me, sharper than the rejection suffered when Michael and I broke up, and more miserable than the still-fresh grief of Xerxadrea's death. Sorrow engulfed me and I choked on uncontrollable sobs.

I wanted Johnny to have his desire.

Another piece ripped loose. As it left me, I forgot what it was.

I felt emptier than I ever had. This was complete misery and despair. This was utter depression. This was hopelessness so absolute that life was not worth living anymore—

And then, where the pieces were torn away, pieces were added like a soothing balm.

My emptiness was gone. My despair subsided. My hopelessness faded away.

As master of the vampire, I had chosen what he would get and what I would take. As equal of the Domn Lup, I allowed him to choose what to take, and what to give. And when it was done, I collapsed into their strong arms.

I awoke.

There were voices, but not close by. I was in the dark. Waiting, I listened.

". . . they'll come in from the lake," Menessos said.

The lake. The tunnel. Hecate. I sat up. The voices continued:

"You could make use of the sand. His people go out, lie down, and cover up with tarps then sand. The last one makes sure the others aren't obvious."

"What if the fey are watching the beach tonight?"

"Of course they are. *We* are."

"Is there any means of magically detecting them?" I recognized Johnny's voice saying this.

"It would have to be done prior to the arrival of your people. By the time the wæres arrived the situation could change. The fey might be monitoring it for magic and that action might give them cause to inspect."

I didn't recognize all of the voices. But I knew both Menessos and Johnny were nearby. I identified the big iron-studded door across from me as the one to Menessos's private chamber. That meant I was in Menessos's bed.

Black silk. The cinnamon smell of him was all over the bed. Invigorated by it, warmed from the inside out, I breathed it deep again and again. *Mine*.

My mind flashed on a memory. Something new and unclear. A whisper of music—plucked strings, hollow drums, a flute—I'd never heard before; the murmur of a male voice, the soft laughter of a woman. I tried to hold on to that remembrance, to relive it and know—

The studded door swung farther open. "You've roused. Join us." Menessos gestured to the room beyond.

The recollection was gone. I rose from the bed, put on my boots, and followed him into the front chamber where Johnny, Goliath, Seven, and Mark were gathered around the altar table where we'd performed the ritual. Johnny mimicked my smile of greeting. My mind flashed on another new memory—a howl of profound alone-ness—and I tripped, but recovered, seeing Mark steadying Johnny.

"Are you two all right?" Seven asked.

"They are fine," Menessos affirmed, taking my arm to escort me the rest of the way.

Seven wasn't convinced. She asked me directly, "What did you do?"

She'd already made it clear she wanted me to honor Menessos more than Johnny. From what she'd told me it was easy to see she believed her mistake as Lustrata was not giving the vampire enough of herself. Perhaps telling her—in private—of the soul-sharing would reassure her.

"What do you mean?" I hoped that, despite my embarrassment-warmed cheeks, I conveyed innocence.

"We need to update Persephone on our strategizing," Menessos redirected.

"Our plan is simple: kill the fire fairy and the earth fairy." Mark pointed to the table, indicating a spot on a map spread out on it. "This is Headlands Dunes. We are relatively certain the fairies will come in from Lake Erie, as it is less offensive to their allergies than the land. When they appear, Menessos must call them to him, as if to guard a circle. They will be drawn to him and, from the lighthouse here, the wærewolf sniper—safely away from the magic—uses iron-tipped bullets to kill the earth fairy. Menessos kills the other himself."

"And what do I do?" I was supposed to be right there with Menessos.

Mark said, "Stay out of the way."

"Hold on," I said to Menessos. "They are bound to you and it hurt you when I killed Cerebrosus, it hurt you when Aquula died. What will happen to you if the remaining two are killed at once?"

"It will hurt," he said plainly.

I made an irritated face at him that Seven copied. "If the sniper takes out the earth fairy, will you be able to take the fire fairy? I think you'd better plan on me"—even as the words left my mouth, I was stunned to hear myself saying them—"taking her out. She might compromise you if, at a critical time, the sniper acts."

The weight of the stares directed at me made my heart race.

"You're right," Menessos conceded.

"How will you combat the effect of these two deaths?" Seven asked him.

"Mountain volunteered to fight. His bulk will be hard to hide, so let's plan to have him nearby, ready when I need to feed."

Everyone nodded. I added, "Okay, but this whole battle is all about them stopping you from calling them ever again. I may be supposedly delivering you to them, but they will anticipate you might use your summoning power. They will be ready for that."

"Yes, I expect they will be."

The calm in his voice bothered me. "You're betting your life on the ability of a sniper to take out a fairy before they can strike."

"Kirk's the shooter," Johnny said. "You met him last night, bouncer out front of The Dirty Dog."

"The Mr. Clean wannabe?"

"No, the Asian guy."

"The wiry overactor?"

Johnny nodded happily. "Yeah, him. He's ex-military. Expert marksman. He can make the shot."

"Do you fully trust him not to shoot Menessos?"

Johnny's positive demeanor faded and he crossed his arms defensively, but I thought it was a legitimate question. "I do. He will shoot as instructed."

"How many wæres do you have?"

"Twenty."

I was able to stop myself before I blurted, "That's all?" and changed it to an even, "Okay." Twenty wæres were about as formidable as fifty or so men, I reminded myself. I addressed Menessos next. "You're the master of the fairies. There's some compulsion in that bonding, right? Will you be *able* to strike them?"

"Servants bear something of a benevolent compulsion toward their masters—"

I snickered, but he continued on, unaffected.

"—more so than masters feel toward them. Consequently, it is much easier for a master to strike a servant."

Good to know. I guess. "How many Beholders will you bring, Menessos?"

"Forty-five. Fifteen will remain here as guardians."

So we had less than seventy people to bring to this war. *Kind of downgrades it to a battle, huh? With the war coming after, if we lose.* Seventy people didn't sound like much, but it was better than two. Technically Menessos and I were the only ones supposed to show up. "Any idea how many fairies will come?"

"I am guessing forty or fifty," Menessos said, "but the fey royals may want to show off. Especially if they are anticipating that we are bowing to their demands. They will want many of their underlings to see it."

He had the most experience with the fey, so no one argued with his assumption. I certainly wouldn't. "I can't believe we might pin the hopes of this whole thing on one guy with a rifle. Is there a backup plan?"

"That's where the wærewolves and Beholders come in." Mark squared his shoulders. "The light infantry will be hidden in the switchgrass, and, hopefully, avoiding the cocklebur. They will wait for the signal and then storm the beach."

Light infantry? I waited. "And?"

"And fight."

"I'm no grand strategist, but isn't that sparse on the

planning? Fight with what? In formations or something? Or is this just a bar brawl?"

The men reacted with amusement, as if the silly waitress had just asked if they'd mind having another round of beer and wings for free.

"Have you ever seen wærewolves in an all-out bar brawl?" Johnny asked.

"No."

"We don't need formations and we don't need weapons, we use what's at hand."

"There won't be barstools and beer bottles on the beach. And even it there were, you need iron not broken glass. You're fighting fairies who can change their size and fly. *And,* they're magic. You're bringing wærewolves."

That reminder sobered him.

Goliath had taken up pacing on the far side of the room. He was listening, but not participating. He would be dead while all this happened. His master was heading into danger and, for all his expertise as an assassin, he'd be missing it.

"I can get you iron weapons," Mark said.

Seven asked thoughtfully, "What about buckshot?"

Mark shook his head. "A shotgun has a range of fifty yards or less. For the wærewolves it would be risky. That's close, energywise."

"But buckshot is smaller pieces," she countered, "meant to spread out to hit small flying targets like birds. If we make them *iron* pieces it'll stop the fey and at least interfere with spell casting."

"Good idea," I said.

Mark addressed Johnny. "Your people shoot?"

"Yes. Most have experience hunting in the woods in human form. Deer and pheasant."

"Perfect. I will get some men to round up shotguns and make some iron buckshot." Mark left.

I stand with Menessos as if to deliver him to them, he calls them to him for a magic circle. The sniper kills one and Menessos kills the other. I'm to help him if, weakened by the death of the other, he cannot accomplish it. Then the Beholders and wærewolves come over the dune and, if necessary, fight off other fairies if they don't retreat. If anything goes wrong, the wærewolf cavalry—wait, that's light infantry—comes to our rescue immediately.

I wondered if Xerxadrea's plans would have inspired more confidence.

Xerxadrea!

"Menessos." I rested my hand gently on his arm. "The Eldrenne told me to seal the gateway before she died."

"I'll get the Codex." He left us to enter his bed-chambers.

Around the table, only Seven, Johnny, and I remained. To the wærewolf I said, "Guess I'll be making a rather late call to Doc Lincoln."

"Why do you need a doctor?" Seven asked, obviously puzzled.

"I'll need the spell translated. Menessos has other business to attend to and Latin isn't my best subject," I admitted. Not to mention doing a spell of this magnitude without days or weeks of preparation would be strenuous, let alone the possibility of performing it in the middle of a raging beach battle.

"Well, you're in luck." Seven grinned, flashing fang. "Latin *is* one of my best subjects."

Menessos entered the room carrying the Codex. She approached him and put her hand on his forearm. "You need to address the Beholders. Mark will also have to discuss strategy with them. I assume the Domn Lup will need to brief his people, as well."

So she knows he's more than just another old wærewolf. They must have discussed that before I awoke.

Seven continued. "Perhaps the Lustrata and I should go to my chambers? It will be quieter there for what we must do."

Menessos approved with a single nod.

But I was left warily wondering if "what we must do" included more than Latin lessons—like my predecessor giving me any more advice on love.

CHAPTER THIRTY-ONE

I followed Seven across the backstage and down a spiral staircase not far from the service elevator. Silently, I began preparing a short homily in case she was still harboring her concern for the improvement of my emotional attachment to Menessos.

The rooms she shared with Mark were as large as my own, with sheer white drapery separating the spaces. The main chamber had taupe walls, olive and gold accents. Pieces of a stone frieze were hung along the left wall over three shadowboxed pieces of carved stone artwork and a gilded display case, softly lit. I wandered near, saw little ruby scorpions and amethyst scarabs placed around a diadem with a lapis lazuli cobra head. To the other side was a hand mirror. The tarnished round of silver was attached to a base displaying the head of Hathor, and a handle of obsidian.

Like Menessos's office, this was reminiscent of a museum.

As I perused the art, the centermost piece held my attention. It was of a *ba,* the body of a bird and head of a person. Not quite the ancient Egyptian equivalent of a soul, but at least one of the essential parts of what made a human human. In this carving, the *ba* sat in the branches of a distinctive tree. "Is that a willow tree?"

"Yes," Seven answered. "Do you like it?"

Thinking of my meditation wand—which Menessos must have cleared away with all the other magical items after the ritual—I asked, "What is the significance of the *ba* sitting in this particular tree?"

"That is Osiris."

"The Egyptian god of the Underworld," I murmured.

"Willow is believed to have sheltered Osiris's body and his *ba* sat in its branches."

"That's interesting."

Seven crossed her arms and threw her hip to one side as she said, "Actually, what's interesting is your being named for both the Greek and Egyptian goddesses who were consorts to gods of the Underworld." Her eyes narrowed just slightly as she scrutinized me, but they did not take on that stalking brightness. That made it easier to not flinch under her inspection.

I was choosing my words carefully, trying to craft something acknowledging our discussion of Menessos prior to the Erus Veneficus ceremony, when she said, "Let us sit over here." She pointed toward a small table with two padded red leather chairs. I placed the Trivium Codex on the marble-topped table and opened it to the pages that Menessos had marked this time.

Just after midnight, the translation was complete and we had rehearsed it a few times. Seven had been nothing but charming, using friendly, lilting tones that put me at ease. She hadn't brought up Johnny or pressed me about why we'd both needed steadying in the same instant. Trying to keep that going, I told her, "I'm completely impressed with your knowledge of Latin."

"When it became clear that I had an aptitude for language, I was taught many. In addition to English and Latin, I am fluent in Greek and several other ancient languages as well as the major Romance languages and Russian."

I almost said, "What? Not Chinese?" but resisted letting my inner smart-ass run my mouth. *She could tell me off in a dozen languages.* "Did this talent come before you were the Lustrata?"

"Yes." Her features were alight as she said, "I grew up with the best tutors available and an amazing library at my disposal. What about your childhood?"

"Hmmm. What I had at my disposal growing up was a demanding grandmother."

Seven didn't laugh, as I had expected she might. Instead, she relaxed into her seat. "She must have made quite an impact to be the one thing you compare to my library and tutors."

"She raised me." I had an urge to check on Nana and find out if she and Beverley had stayed safely home and planned to continue staying at home until they heard from me tomorrow. But I had already asked her to; so she would. Right now seemed like an opportunity to find out more about the previous Lustrata. "Tell me about your library. What was your favorite book as a child?"

Seven became wistful. "My library is gone. And there were scrolls then, not books. So much knowledge was lost."

"Lost?"

"Yes, but despite what legend may say, it was not destroyed by Caesar in my day. Nor did Mark give me the plundered library of Pergamon as a wedding gift."

Wait. According to some accounts, Julius Caesar was responsible for burning the library at Alexandria. That was during the time of . . . that would mean that Seven was . . . *No! She was the Lustrata?* "You're—you're not—"

"But I am."

"Cleopatra? And," I pointed at the other section of the chamber though he was not here, "Mark is Mark Antony?" *No wonder he was the one Menessos counted on for strategizing.*

She conveyed a mixture of sadness and determination in her nod.

I was dumbfounded. My head was filled with so many questions and I could not speak one of them.

Finally she said, "The bite of an asp is not so different from the bite of a vampire."

"An asp bite won't transform you into an asp."

"Neither will the mere bite of a vampire remake you into the same, but to someone in those times, physically the bites look much the same." She was silent for a heart-beat longer, then, "If the bards and historians only knew how wrong they have been about so much."

"But Mark Antony died on his w—"

She cut me off with an imperial—I realized now it came naturally—wave of her hand. "As I said: bards and historians are wrong about so much." Seven stood. "They are also wrong about war. War is not romantic. It is brutal and ugly. Cities burn and the wind carries the stink of failure." She closed the Codex and held it out to me. I was being dismissed. "Don't fail."

I stood and accepted the book.

As I left, she added, "Remember. You cannot shut the door until both fairies are dead. Only then will the bonds that are keeping the doorway open be severed. It cannot be shut until then, so make no attempt until you are certain they are both dead."

I quietly closed the door of the last queen of Egypt.

Just before five A.M., I entered my chamber to get my coat. I had fifteen minutes until I was supposed to meet Menessos at the front entrance. We were going to take my car and leave for Headlands Beach. The rest of them had left an hour before.

The fairies knew I would show up with Menessos. WEC had sanctioned it. Of course, the fey had to have a plan ready in the event that we didn't just easily surrender. But what kind of plan?

I had my coat in my hands and had started back to the door when I stopped short, captured somehow by the painting on the wall. I stared at *The Charmer* as if I'd never seen it before.

The lute-playing woman in the picture was peering down at the fish that were drawn to her by the music she played. Or was she? Far more intent on the water, she didn't seem to see the fish. I could imagine her using the water to examine her emotions, as I had, but from the safety of the shore. Perhaps she was using the surface of the water to scry into her future.

I rushed to the closet and retrieved my suitcase. Throwing it open, I took out the shoe box with Nana's scrying crystal. Shutting off all but the dome's starlight, I drew a circle on the floor with my broom. I sat cross-legged within the circle, facing the closet to keep the light from reflecting on the surface of the crystal globe. While making my quarter calls, I used my T-shirt to wipe my fingerprints from the crystal.

Cradling the heavy ball in my hands, I grounded and centered. Gazing softly on the clear surface, I let my mind hit alpha. In seconds the crystal grew cloudy. Keeping my breathing even and steady, my mind receptive, I waited for the images.

Nana was more accomplished at this, but I was not entirely unskilled. I just preferred the stable symbolic images of Tarot. My interpretations seemed stronger with the cards than with the fluctuating fluidity of scrying.

I quickly settled my intention on seeing something to help me know if we were prepared for what would come to pass.

The murk within the crystal thickened and lathered into seafoam. It receded, showing me the wet sand. No, this was not the sea, it was a lakeshore. Another wave crashed, foam stretching . . . the splash of bodies falling into the water, screams.

My breath caught and held.

A flash of red. A lick of flames. The face of Fax Torris, the fire fairy, laughing. At her feet lay a man. Naked. His back . . . was that sand sticking to his skin, making patterns? She kicked him, rolling him over.

Johnny!

CHAPTER THIRTY-TWO

Menessos and I stood on the beach, shoulder to shoulder. With my hand up to block the wind, I watched for any sign of the fairies. Lake Erie was veiled in mist, yet the air was gusty onshore. Weather wasn't supposed to work that way. "The fairies are creating this mist."

"Yes. They wouldn't dare arrive without making it a spectacle," Menessos said.

Magic mist or not, it was chilly. I wore a tank and a tee under a hoodie and my blazer. A pair of thermal leggings under the jeans would've helped. Of course, I'd made sure Beau's charm was on its long chain around my neck. I wished it would kick in and warm me up as it had when I'd first touched it.

"It wouldn't surprise me," Menessos added, "if the fairies painted the mist different colors just before they appeared."

"I'm more worried that they're hiding something in there, not just making a grand entrance."

"You may be right," he said, "but it is too late now for us to alter our position, our strategy, or our numbers."

If the mist came ashore, the sniper in the lighthouse wouldn't be able to see us. If everything we couldn't see was going according to plan, then Johnny and the other wæres and Beholders were in the switchgrass, a disturbingly far distance behind us.

"Is this wind going to be a problem?"

"The conditions are not perfect for what our outlying friend does."

It had been explained to me that snipers don't aim directly at their targets, but have to calculate a height above the target based on distance and how the bullet will drop, as well as calculate a distance to the side of the target based on wind direction and speed. So snipers basically shot at nothing and hoped the bullet landed where the math said it would.

"So maybe once you call the fey we should prostrate ourselves like we're worshipping them and let the guy get his shot off."

Menessos touched me. "Persephone."

My hand was visibly shaking. I let it fall to my side. I hadn't told anyone that I'd gotten out the scrying crystal, or what I had seen. How could I? Uttering the words would make it more real. But I was ready. I had my own plan. *I've never gotten a chance to tell Johnny that I love him.* "What?"

"Do you know what it meant to me, the night you destroyed the stake, to take that walk alone?"

I shook my head no, not trusting my voice.

"I was utterly *alone*."

He sounded happy about it, so I waited to see where he was going with this before I cut in, asked anything, or interrupted.

"I hadn't felt so alone since I buried Una and . . . I revisited my greatest fear."

He put his hands on my arms; even through the layers, I could feel the warmth in his hands. It steadied me.

"I knew what you had done. I knew the Goddess had touched you and lifted you up, declaring that She had chosen you over me. I was terrified. It meant I had been bested. I feared you would learn this and be compelled to destroy me . . . and my family."

I shook my head again. That had been Johnny's first thought. Not mine.

"In the nights since then, Persephone, I have struggled with what it means, struggled with how to proceed. I had been so accustomed to being the master of all around me . . ."

Yeah, being top dog for a few thousand years tends to give a guy a definite attitude.

". . . that I could not see the truth. Everyone else looked up to me. It should have been easy to pass that reverence on to you, but it was not. It finally hit me. Last night during the ritual."

During?

"The memory you gave me, Persephone." He stood straighter and lifted his face to the sky, inhaling deeply as if relishing the lakeshore breeze that lifted his hair in a mesmerizing dance of curls. "I can see you in my mind, so clearly. A child. Innocent and afraid. Yet defiantly *alone*." He brought his face down again. "And She chose you. She lifted you up with Her power, lifted you high above the stalks. She kissed you with stardust, bathed you with moonlight, and swaddled you with destiny. It was a revelation," he whispered.

My memory of that was gone, but as he shared it

with me, it was restored. It came back to me completely, totally. I hadn't remembered floating up in the air that night, hadn't remembered the touch of Her grace upon me, but as he said it, I knew it was true.

A chill ran through me. It seemed the only warmth in the whole world radiated from his hands on my arms.

"When you burned the stake, you unshrouded the destiny that had always been right in front of you, hidden, waiting for you to be ready, waiting for you to claim it. Sparing me, you fastened your grip on the reins of your future. And"—his hands fell from my arms down to hold my hands—"you held in these fated hands, my own life. My future." He let his statement stand for a heartbeat, then added, "I detected something special in you from the very start. I feared it at first. Now . . . now *I* look up to you for it."

"Being the Lustrata?"

"No. Heroism."

I swallowed hard enough to be heard.

"What I have learned from all these long years is that everyone who knows what I am has expected *great things* from me. And it is the same with you." He touched my cheek. "It will never end. The demands only grow. The stamina to provide . . . that is harder to maintain. To be successful, I have had to stay ahead of the demand, to anticipate it. And sometimes, to squelch the ungrateful and those whose demands are exorbitant." His expression became the saddest smile I'd ever seen. It conveyed tiredness and inevitability and it made me want to cry.

I looked toward the lake again. *Must watch for the fairies.*

"The people you have surrounded yourself with, they are

your family. You love them and you will never stop doing all you can to protect them. You sacrificed what *you* wanted in order to become what you must be, but not for yourself. You did it for them. There are rewards within that, but those are not the kind of goals you would set your sights on and make you seek *this* path. You wear the mantle of a heroine, Persephone, and not because you want it. You wear it because, like Cinderella's slipper, it fits no other."

I twisted back to him. "Damn it, don't make me cry right now. I have to be able to see when the fairies arrive!"

Menessos's arms—and his conviction—enveloped me and I let my tears fall, unashamed. There weren't many, but I didn't hold them in. That heat within me flared to life. Warmth and reassurance spread through me. He held me in silence, both of us staring out over the water as the night abated.

As the sun rose, the mist became shadowed, as if the fairies neared the edge of it. For an instant the haze glittered silver and gold, then the prows of a line of ten boats appeared, elongated keels rising up like swan necks fore and aft. They were palest ivory and the golden hues of oak. Sails billowed with unearthly winds, banners snapping atop their masts. At first they seemed ghostly, unreal—but as they cleared the veil of mist, another row appeared like the first. And another. Solid and frightening.

A larger vessel followed. At first I thought it was black and red, but as it became clearer, it was seemingly made of coals flickering with inner heat. Instead of rails, a line of flames framed it bow to stern. And Fax Torris stood on the bow. Her skin was crimson. Her hair, rising stiffly from her scalp in odd peaks, was also shades of scarlet. A wreath of yellow and orange flowers helped create the illusion of a blaze atop her head. She was clothed in shreds of her fiery colors, stirred by the winds into a flickering semblance of flames.

Just to her port side sailed a ship of timber with branches woven to create an intricate railing with yellow and brown leaves flapping. Lucrum stood at the bow of this ship. His face was the green of new leaves, his brown hair tousled thick with brambles. He wore a surcoat of wheat-field tan, a vest and breeches of mud brown. The large jeweled brooch heavy on his lacey cravat was familiar; he'd worn it when they kidnapped Beverley.

At the stern of these two ships came three rows of something like canoes, but fatter on the bottom. Each of these smaller boats carried one or two fairies, and they were dressed for a show, not for battle. That, however, didn't mean much with the fey.

Behind the last three rows was a pair of tugboats, pulling something large, flat, and threatening. What it carried, though, the mist effectively secreted.

The smaller boats and canoes began fanning out.

"On this humble world," Fax Torris shouted, "on this great day, witness as we are liberated from our bonds! Long have we been shackled by this great insult. But no more!" Her voice seethed through the air. "Before us stands the source of our abuse. We answered his call, we aided him in his plight, and with cruelty he reacted. With malice he laid a trap. With malevolence, he sprung it. But this day we will be freed."

While listening, I studied the distant craft, holding my breath and waiting to see it revealed, only to realize they had no intention of showing it—unless needed. It was the surprise threat meant to ensure our submission.

I scanned the smaller boats again. "Are they taking up viewing points, or are those war formations?" I whispered. *Mark would know. Does Menessos?*

"That's precisely what I was pondering. Perhaps I should not delay any longer."

Menessos sank to his knees, in the circle he'd drawn in the sand. It was my cue to get behind him a few feet, but still within the circle. It appeared he was offering himself without resistance. But he whispered the chant, calling the two remaining royal fairies. A call neither could resist. A call that would tear them from their ships and thrust them through space/time to materialize within the circle.

Lucrum, the earth fairy, should appear before Menessos, to the north. Fax Torris would appear behind the vampire, in the southern position allotted to fire. Kirk would take Lucrum. I had a short iron dagger taped up the left sleeve of my blazer. I was ready to rip it free and stab her in the back. *There will be no scene of Johnny lying at her feet.*

Menessos completed the first line of the chant in seconds. I felt the stirring and studied the fire fairy closely. I wanted to know when she felt it, too.

In a flash of flames, Fax Torris leaped from her ship toward Lucrum's. Wings of fire sprouted from her back. I glimpsed her raised arm, saw the glint of a blade. Lucrum saw it coming. His cry of horror carried across the water to the shore, vibrating like the dull thudding impact of boulders in a landslide. Fax Torris had murdered him.

Menessos doubled over and fell to the sand in pain, unable to finish the call.

CHAPTER THIRTY-THREE

I fell to my knees beside Menessos. "Finish the call!"

"I cannot!" His voice was ragged.

I wrapped my arms around him protectively. *He's mine and he's hurting. Hurting because of* her.

"Treachery!" Fax Torris cried. "That monster has forced my actions! Forced me to slay my own brother! His control over me must be ended! Kill him," she sobbed. "Kill him!"

It didn't surprise me that she would twist it and blame Menessos for her own murderous actions.

Beneath me, Menessos groaned and shivered. A spasm rocked him. He whispered, "Call Mountain!"

I turned to the tall line of switchgrass far behind. Wærewolves and Beholders were already racing forward from their hiding spots. "Mountain!"

The big man cleared the tall grass at a jog.

That was when the first shot was fired.

I twisted toward the shore again. The fairies from the small boats were taking to the air, wings speeding them ashore or fleeing into the sky. Of those ready to fight, colorful balls of energy flashed from their palms, magic meant to do harm. A multitude of shots followed in quick succession and their magic died in the iron-filled air. Booming gunshots echoed under the screams of fairies. The caustic odor of gunpowder surrounded me. *People are dialing phones right now, reporting gunfire. Police will be here in force in ten minutes . . . They will have to stop. It'll end before anything can happen to Johnny.*

Mountain dropped heavily beside us. "I'm here, Boss." He offered his wrist to Menessos. Instantly, the vampire lurched upward and took Mountain at the throat, sucking and slurping like a desert wanderer finding the oasis pool. It was beastly and grotesque. It wasn't anything like the tenderness he showed me. Horrified, I scrambled back.

The scene across the water was macabre. So many fairy bodies dropping on the lake, their frilly costumes rippling on the waves for an instant before body and all disintegrated into slime. Fax was raging, screaming with her scalding voice, demanding Menessos's head. Injured fairies fluttered ashore.

The buckshot was apparently gone, but it had done its job. If not mortally struck, with iron embedded in their skin, the fey could not work magic. Additionally, blisters were rising, limbs swelling in allergic reaction even as I watched. They could not summon their magical weapons, but clearly a few had summoned theirs before being injured. The wærewolves—I saw the Mr. Clean wannabe and Hector among them—and Beholders clashed with this pitiful fey force, swinging shotguns like baseball bats. It was all carnage.

"Stop," I whispered.

Menessos lifted his face away from Mountain, but I

wasn't talking to him. I didn't want to see this anymore. We were winning. We didn't have to keep killing.

Menessos left Mountain and the big man collapsed to the sand, one hand applying pressure to his neck. Menessos crawled toward me. "Fax isn't dead, Persephone. They cannot stop until she is dead!"

I stared at the blood smeared across his face. My horror must have been clear. He wiped at his face with his sleeve.

The fire fairy's voice bellowed, "Elementals!"

The vapors concealing what was behind the tugboats began to dissipate. From the flat surface, dozens of creatures rose up and swarmed toward the shore.

"She brought the elementals!" Menessos whispered.

Unicorns became warhorses, galloping atop the water and racing toward the beach, slashing their horns like swords. Dragons, with broad fan-gilled heads and fanged jaws wide, roared as their eellike bodies slithered into the water behind the unicorns. Griffons sprang to the air crying like hawks and flashing talons, ready to rend flesh. Phoenixes joined them, sparks falling from their feathers like glittering firework trails.

"They all have collars," I said. Links of chain dangled from each.

"It was bad enough the fey stole them from us," Menessos growled, "but so much worse for such enchanted creatures to be enslaved."

Fax Torris fell onto the back of a phoenix, her flaming wings making the bird even more regal. With a flick of her hand, the collar twisted—the bird reacted with a cry of pain and its long wings stuttered in their motion. The chain slapped into Fax Torris's palm, and the bird flew around the others, as if coming to the front of the horde.

"She's controlling them with those collars." My eyes searched the beach for Johnny.

That was when I saw the witches.

Brooms rocketing in from the west, maybe twenty-five in all.

"Do you know if Xerxadrea's body has been identified yet?"

"What?" Menessos asked sharply.

I pointed to the fast-approaching women, wands at the ready. "Are they coming to our aid or to do more damage?"

The wærewolves noticed the threat of magic zooming in on them. I knew by the uneasy voices calling for Johnny. That, at least, helped me locate him. He was running toward us from the east end of the beach.

He stopped a dozen yards away, shouting, "Do they know wæres are down here?"

"I don't know," I answered.

"What about those creatures? They're magic, too, aren't they?"

I nodded.

Menessos called to him, "You know what you must do, Domn Lup."

Johnny and he locked eyes. They shared something. I tried to reach Johnny through the connection Menessos made. I had a sense of the memories they had shared. I heard a whisper, Xerxadrea's voice. He was remembering what she had said to him in my kitchen: "Perhaps you would learn a few things if you would but try to see beyond your own conflict and see his."

Johnny nodded, turned, and ran.

I reached for Menessos. "Can the Beholders get the collars off those elementals?"

"Good thinking."

Johnny gathered the wæres to the east. He must have given them the option of leaving. Over half of them fled the beach. Menessos, for his part, must have given a mental order to the Beholders. They formed a phalanx on the beach before us, four rows deep, ten abreast, and a handful around the circle. All held iron weapons at the ready. Unfortunately, they had no shields. The animals charging them, unlike storybook depictions, were not dainty and frail.

Long pikes would have been better weapons against them, not that I wanted to see unicorns die.

The witches hovered beside us, in formation. Vilna-Daluca sat at their lead. The four members of the *lucusi* that I had already met were all with her, and nearly two dozen more. "It doesn't appear the two of you are alone or that you intend to deliver the vampire as WEC commanded."

"We tried that," I said. "Apparently there are plenty of sneaky people who thought that was a bad idea."

"*Riiiight.*" Vilna winked.

"Your wands-at-the-ready scared off half the wærewolves," Menessos added.

"I think we can handle this."

"Where's Xerxadrea?" he pressed.

It was a good cover move. I hadn't thought of it.

Vilna's features flickered with worry, but she covered instantly. "She's too old for a fight like this. She sends her blessings."

The unicorns were nearly to the shore. Fax Torris and her phoenix were coming up fast on the outside. These beautiful creatures had served to guard our circles, in spirit form, for decades. Fighting them was so wrong.

Vilna-Daluca nodded. "Witches!" she called. The hair on the nape of my neck rose as they called on the power of the ley and it answered. The crystal tips of their wands flared to life and settled into a subtle glow. Vilna raised her arm to signal.

"Remove the collars," I shouted to her.

She paused, considering this, then nodded.

Before she could complete the gesture that would send the witches against the elementals, however, I saw a black wolf race along the beach and leap at the phoenix carrying Fax Torris.

The witches flew past our heads, but I didn't care what they did now. I could not look away from the wolf.

Fax Torris wrenched the phoenix's chain and leaned back hard. Her wings fanned out as she stood and used her feet to press the phoenix's body into an angle that put its talons slashing forward.

While the avian's claws were not as long and sharp as those of a griffon, they were dangerous nonetheless. They raked across the wolf's chest. His teeth sank into the phoenix's neck. The fairy's wings beat furiously, dragging them farther out over the water. Then the wolf yanked the phoenix's neck to the side, snapping it. All three fell into the water, disappearing beneath the surface.

"Johnny!" Only Menessos's grip on my arm kept me in the circle. "Let me go!" My hand clawed at his. I jerked free and headed out of the circle.

Menessos shouted, "You *must* stay! You have to shut the gateway!"

Damn it!

I held my breath, shifting my weight, as the seconds ticked past. I scrutinized the water where they had plummeted. They'd been down too long without surfacing for air. *Maybe they'd struggled away from where they went under and I didn't see them come up.*

With the melee raging before and around me, there was too much to see. When I watched something to the left, I missed something happening on the right. My gaze constantly returned to the water, scanning the surface.

Witches thrust bursts of ley energy from their wands—bolts like glowing bullets of white and magenta. As the bursts struck the unicorns, shrill neighs pierced the air. Two bolts in quick succession struck the collar of the unicorn centermost in the charging front line. The collar fell away. The beast immediately shifted its path to our right, pushing the animals down the line veering that way as well. The second row followed them.

The other half of the front line, however, stayed true to their course.

The Beholders held their ground.

Even as the witches tried desperately to make double strikes on the magic collars, not all of their bolts hit their marks. When they succeeded, the unicorns fell out of attack mode. Those that missed, though, seemed only to enrage the animals and they charged onward more furiously. Beholders were run through, lifted, and tossed to the air. Spiraled horns once flecked with gold came free smeared with blood. Hooves pounded . . . until an iron weapon rammed through a chest and white fur was stained red with blood.

Someone shouted, "Just touch the collars with iron! They fall free!"

In seconds, a handful of the freed unicorns had formed a line before us, rearing and neighing, flailing their hooves as if to ward off the other elementals. Huge dragons slithered ashore roaring and snapping, obliterating Beholders and unicorns—collared and uncollared alike. Griffons and phoenixes engaged the witches in aerial acrobatics. Wands flashed; scintillating specks of flame fell and caught broom thatch.

And over all the noise, I heard a crackling laugh.

Fax Torris stood at water's edge. She dragged Johnny's naked body behind her. With a jerk, she hauled him farther onto the beach. She dropped his arm like a filthy rag, and kicked him so hard he was lifted into the air, rolling, and landed hard. He didn't move. I couldn't tell if he was breathing or not.

My heart froze, hard and heavy, a block of ice in my chest. I jerked the dagger from my sleeve. I turned to Menessos. "Call her!"

He shook his head. "Lucrum's death, the Beholders' deaths. I haven't the strength."

Trembling with rage, I took his chin roughly in my free hand. "Say the fucking words!" I shouted even as I shoved energy at him.

He recoiled from me before I could transfer it, throwing himself backward to the sand. "You must not!"

"Fax must die!"

"You have to shut the gateway! You need your energy to do that!"

"I'll use the ley. But she has to die first!"

"You can't use the ley to shut the door."

That stopped me. "Why not?" I felt deflated, lost and scared. So angry. Failed.

"We didn't know about ley power when we opened it. You have to shut it as we opened it. All we had was our own power. Our desperation. Our hope and resolve. Our pain and our loss." He moved onto his knees, so weak. Jerking up his pant leg, he released something concealed there.

I'm not the only one hiding backup plans on their person.

The willow wand.

He offered it to me. "There's another way."

CHAPTER THIRTY-FOUR

F ax Torris's fire wings had carried her and her scalding laughter out over the lake. She was gathering some of the collared phoenixes to her, a new formation for a new attack.

Unicorns with broken legs or bleeding stab wounds sprawled around me. Their pitiful noises told me they'd have to be put down. Griffons struggled in the surf, trying to come ashore. They didn't seem able to swim and twisted at odd angles. One, already ashore, had lost an eye and the talon tips from the claws of one foreleg; it hobbled around stretching its beak down to other griffons that lay unmoving on the sand. A smaller dragon was curled protectively around the head of another dragon that was coughing blood on the sand. The small one whimpered.

Those that still wore collars continued fighting the handful of Beholders who remained.

The witches had regrouped and were attempting some sort of airborne offensive against the griffons. My attention strayed to Johnny. Was he dead or alive? Mountain was crawling toward him, trying not to gain the attention of any collared elementals.

The air prickled with another calling of the ley. As I felt it crawling over my skin, I knew Fax was drawing heavily on the line. The fire fairy pushed her hands down before her, wrists together, and opened herself like a conduit. Her wings flared like flamethrowers, engulfing nearby phoenixes like burned offerings. She was creating an energy reservoir within herself. The accumulation of ley line magnitude caused the air underneath her to shimmer. The swell of her power triggered something in Beau's charm. It answered with a glow that thawed my frozen indecision, emboldened me and warned me.

This is going to be bad.

A white-hot beam of energy flashed into existence beneath her. Twisting up from the lake, a waterspout instantly turned into steam. Fax glowed an eerie red; her eyes were radiant white orbs. Her hair and clothing whipped around her in a cyclonic turbulence of steam.

Tapping the ley in normal usage was dangerous and potentially addictive, but she was taking in more power than I could even imagine. That she could hold that much power and not explode was amazing.

Fax Torris angled her wrists, moving the beam toward the shore, filling the air with steam. Her fingers splayed wide, broadening the beam. It seemed a heavy burden, difficult to move. Hard to control. She guided it in the direction of the fighting dragons and Beholders. None of them were aware of what was coming at them.

"Get out of there!" I screamed. My voice was lost to the lashing wind. "All of you run away. Run now!"

The beam came ashore. Where the beam touched sand

its progress was slowed, and a dark strip of something glossy was left in its wake.

Glass. The temperature required for that—

The beam ran across the middle of the dragon coughing up blood—it was cut in half and left nothing in its wake! The superheated light was incinerating nearly everything it encountered.

The Beholders ran—the young painter with the broken demeanor of a pit-fighting dog was among them. He stumbled. Clawing at the sand, desperate to get up, he managed to rise to one knee just as the beam struck his still-extended foot. He lurched forward and sideways. Relentless, the beam passed over his legs. His scream was unlike anything I'd ever heard: pure agony enunciated. When the beam moved on, his legs were just . . . gone. His clothes were consumed in flames.

Fax Torris guided the beam, keeping it trained on those fleeing. The molten light destroyed two more. Then the fire fairy seemed to notice Mountain. And Johnny.

She shifted the death-bringing radiance toward them.

Menessos, taking my dagger from me and casting it to the sand, put the willow wand into my hands. "The sacrifices you have made, you made only to see that things are done right," he said.

He aimed the tip of the wand at his chest. "Do this," he said. "It is the right thing, for the right reason."

"No." Horrified, I backpedaled. Limp fingers let the wand fall to the sand.

"There isn't time to debate, Persephone! I cannot call her. This is the only way to sever the bonds so you can seal the gateway."

"No," I whispered.

Menessos took up the wand and staggered to his feet. My legs were jelly. He placed the wand—*a stake!*—into my limp hands, curled my fingers around it. "Let's give her what she wants. Free her. Let her go home and take her madness with her."

"Menessos." I drew a breath. My words came back to haunt me. *When have I not accepted the responsibility thrust upon me? When have I drawn the line and said "No, this is too much"?* "No. No. Here, at *this,* I'm drawing the line," I said. "*This* is too much."

"You are my master, Persephone. I accept what that means. The good and the bad." He stood straighter. "For you, I will experience death." He opened his shirt and bared his chest.

I beheld Arthur. My hero and king.

I thought of Seven. She'd chosen love over destiny. Seven believed herself a failure for her choice. Johnny might be dead already. And Menessos was telling me to kill him, as well. Destiny sucked.

"Take pity, Persephone, do not draw this out."

I nodded, once.

But I couldn't do it.

I grabbed him into my arms and I pressed my lips to his.

A rush of heat blossomed around me. *Was it Menessos's heat or the charm redirecting something dangerous?*

The charm.

Screams erupted to my right. I broke the kiss to see two witches taken by the beam, reduced to nothing in an instant. They were trying to stop Fax Torris, drawing the beam away. But she was back on target.

Menessos whispered, *"In signum amoris."*

Staring into his eyes, I drew on our bond, just enough. I held him in my mind because I could not hold him in my arms.

"By your hand, let it be done."

My heart thudded once and my world slowed as battle-heightened senses went dull. I heard only my own tardy heartbeat in my ears, the shift of fabric as I drew back my arm.

Johnny. And now Menessos.

Seven was right. There was no romance in war.

I accept the good and the bad.

I staked Menessos.

I didn't look away from his eyes, even to see his crimson life leaking away. The drops splattered warm across my hand, and spilled down his chest in a gush that should not have been possible. I felt the life leaving him, fleeing him almost as if his heart had seized up, forcing all his blood out at once to make a quick end. He made no sound. He drew no breath, let none escape. But his set jaw slackened.

I knew a choking thick darkness was swallowing him.

His knees gave. But his gray eyes never left mine.

All the threads that held us were taut; stretching, threatening to snap. I felt the cords grow thin, frayed with his dying. The friction of my will against this inevitable death grew white hot. All at once it snapped.

My hands shot out, fisting in his shirt, clutching his body. I went down on my knees, too . . . and still he was slowly slumping away from me. I pulled him back into my arms. *I will not let go*. His head fell forward to rest on my shoulder. Clinging to him, I wept.

I will not *let go*.

Wiping my hand across my face, my tears mixed with the blood on my fingertips. I drew the five-pointed star on his forehead. A witch's symbol. "You are mine."

Even with my lids shut tight, I could not dam the flow of more tears.

"Element of Earth! I call you to my circle." My voice cracked and I choked. "Element of Air! I call you to my circle. Element of Fire! I call you to my circle. Element of Water! I call you to my circle." My words were bitter, mumbled sobs, as I gave in to the grief and cradled Menessos to me.

Such a long, long life, and so devastating that it should end this way, over fairies he had only sought in desperation to find the end of his curse. A curse that made him all he now was. I was bringing to fruition the ending Ezreniel intended from the start.

Eyes still shut—I could not look at him—I raised my head high and cried out, "Goddess! Hear me!" My voice was clear and defiant.

> This guarantee, sealed by me,
> by your blood and by my tears.
> This guarantee, sealed by me,
> the promise of many more years!

I yanked the wand from his chest. On my end of our severed bond, frayed edges became taloned claws. *Mine.* The claws surged into the receding dark, grasping for the threads. *Mine.* I willed more strength down the line, to coil about the cords and refasten them, stronger than before. *Mine!*

And my second hex filled Menessos.

"As I will, so mote it be!" I whispered.

A quartet of odd sounds answered. My eyelids parted a crack. Blinking away tears, I peered around me. A tremulous sigh escaped as I assured myself what I was seeing was real.

Around my circle, what remained of the elementals stood poised and regal, watching me. They had come at my call, stood at my circle.

The unicorn nickered, bowed, then craned his graceful neck toward the shore as if to say, *Can we finish this now?*

The gateway!

Slipping from under Menessos's body, I assured myself that Mountain had Johnny. The big man was on his knees still, dragging the inert body of the Domn Lup farther onshore. He gave no indication that Johnny was alive. With all that was going on, all I'd just done, my senses and emotions were overloaded. I did not dare try using our bond to confirm my fears. I had to finish this.Someone was running down the shoreline from the lighthouse. Kirk.

I tore off my blazer and hoodie, covering Menessos against the rising sun.

Vilna-Daluca and a handful of other witches continued to battle Fax Torris.

The bonds were broken. The fairy was free and she had to know it. Still, she made no effort to fly away, no attempt to flee. She *wanted* to fight.

Vilna-Daluca had said they could handle this, but at

what cost? Even as I watched, that beam claimed another witch's life.

Let her take her madness home with her.

No. She wasn't going to get away. This was one fairy who wasn't going to go home and live happily ever after.

I took up the bloody wand in my hand again. Grounding and centering, I sought alpha. Menessos, Una, and Ninurta had used astral travel to find the fey. Witches could similarly send their spirits out to journey for knowledge, tethered by a silver cord of light. Many even visited other worlds by this nonphysical means. I was going to find the gateway the fey were using to this world. Then I would shut it. For good.

Letting my spirit project, I rose up over Lake Erie and followed the silver cord that Fax Torris was using as a tether to her own world while manifesting herself here.

I followed it, speeding across Earth to the place where the portal originated. This was where Fax Torris's line led me. No other cords were using the gateway. The other fairies were dead or had fled home.

Calling the glowing mantle of the Lustrata—given me by Hecate herself—to my spirit shoulders, I touched the badge with the balanced scales over my heart.

Fax Torris has done enough damage to both worlds.

With steadfast will, I visualized the gateway and, raising the wand with Menessos's blood, I demanded it slam shut. My own power poured into that plea and, as Menessos said, I added my desperation, hope, and resolve. Lastly, I offered my pain and loss.

The door started to swing shut.

When finally it closed, her cord snapped back to her.

Severed. I hoped that she realized the chance at freedom she'd lost. I hoped she panicked. And I hoped Vilna-Daluca was the one to strike her down. *For Xerxadrea.*

For several minutes I remained engulfed in the astral world, creating seals—I visualized steel bank-vault doors and thick concrete. When I had erected what I believed to be an impenetrable blockade, it was done.

Fax Torris wasn't going to escape back to her world. One way or another, she was going to die in mine.

CHAPTER THIRTY-FIVE

By the time I returned from the astral plane to the circle on the shore and released the elemental quarters, the witches were flying in low from the lake. The red fairy was nowhere to be seen.

What remained of the elementals had gathered around the circle. Without the magic collars, they were no longer ominous. The unicorns' eyes had softened and they pawed at the sand as if bored. The griffons lay down like a herd of cattle before the rain. The phoenixes preened themselves. The dragons had curled up like coiled snakes.

Thirty yards away, Kirk was crouched before Johnny and Mountain who were both sitting on the sand.

Sitting. Alive! Thank you, Goddess.

Two others I recognized as Beholders sat with them.

I eased away from the circle, using a soothing voice to say things like, "Good griffon, stay. Pretty unicorn, don't step on the vampire."

When I was clear of the animals, I ran toward Johnny, shouting his name.

With Kirk's help, he stood. He wasn't naked; Kirk must have retrieved Johnny's clothes for him. When I reached him, I almost knocked him down, wrapping him in my arms that urgently. Holding on so tight, I squeezed him like I'd never let go.

He was gasping and flinching. I jerked back. "What's wrong?"

Johnny let me go to clutch at his chest. It took a few heartbeats before he found his voice. "Phoenix cut me."

"He needs stitches," Kirk announced. His rifle was slung over his back.

Johnny's shirt was black. Other than being damp, it didn't show blood.

Vilna-Daluca's voice came from behind me. "Is the gateway shut and sealed?"

I twisted around. "It is. The fire fairy?"

"Slain." She didn't say it proudly.

There were perhaps eighteen witches with her. Most had visible wounds on them. I had seen three incinerated. From Vilna's expression, I didn't need to ask what had happened to the others.

The distant wail of sirens was heard.

Vilna-Daluca mounted her broom. "What are we going to do with *them*?" She gestured toward the elementals.

"Excuse me," Mountain said. He had managed to stand as well. Blood stained his ripped football jersey, but the flow from his bite had apparently stopped. Truthfully, he seemed steadier than Johnny. "I have an idea."

"What?"

"Well, you have all that land . . . If you and the others can find a way to transport them, I'm sure the Beholders can build you a barn."

I put my hand on his arm. "There aren't many Beholders left."

"We lost twelve, but the Boss has all of Heldridge's people to deal with. This can be used as a test to evaluate them with. It'll work, Seph. They can have it up in a day or two."

We weren't at the haven and he used my name. It made me smile. I remembered he'd grown up on a farm. "Someone will have to tend them. Do you think the Boss would let you? Would you want to?"

"If you ask him, yes."

"I'd be glad to." *If he wakes up. Goddess, please, let him wake up tonight. Let him be what he's been meant to be for so long.*

Into the approaching wail of sirens, Vilna-Daluca spoke. "Jeanine, take a group and contain the elementals for now. We'll deliver them to Persephone later." Jeanine called out some names and immediately the group left to gather the animals. In moments, the elementals—some being assisted by the witches—were retreating out over Lake Erie. The griffons and phoenixes flew low, as she did, the dragons swam, and the unicorns did their walk-on-water trick.

"The rest of you," Vilna-Daluca instructed, "clean the beach of guns, casings, anything with fingerprints. Call in some waves to remove the broken brooms, the dead elementals, and other debris." All jumped to action.

Kirk and the Beholders helped Johnny to my car, then the Beholders got into their own vehicle and sped off. The police would be arriving momentarily.

The wæres who'd fled earlier had taken their wounded

with them; of those that remained to fight with Johnny, two had lost their lives to the beam. The Beholders had lost a dozen to the incinerating deathbeam. Someone had removed the Beholder with the eyes like a mistreated dog—I didn't see him anywhere. The dead fey weren't a problem. They disintegrated into goo.

Vilna turned back to me. "Anything else, Persephone?"

"Thank you."

"Blessed Be, Persephone."

"Blessed Be, Vilna-Daluca." She swooshed out over the lake to join Celeste.

Kirk came back across the sand. "Domn Lup sent me for the vampire."

"He's dead."

"Duh. It's cloudy, but the sun's up," Kirk said. "Johnny didn't figure you'd leave the body."

Putting every ounce of hope into the idea that Menessos would rise tonight, I said, "Please help me get him to my car. He should be safe from the sun in the trunk."

Yeah. Because the risk of leaving the scene with a guy toting a rifle isn't enough. It'll be a better headline if there's a dead body found in my trunk.

EPILOGUE

A semitruck had jackknifed, for no apparent reason, without injury to the driver or much damage to the vehicle, on Lakeshore Boulevard and delayed the first land responders. A mysterious fog on Lake Erie had slowed the Coast Guard. We—Mountain, Johnny, Kirk, and me—were able to leave the area without even seeing a police car. Mountain was riding shotgun, filling the front space of my car, the seat all the way back and partially reclined. Johnny was in the back middle with Kirk beside him. Kirk's rifle and Menessos were in the trunk.

Nobody spoke.

Of course my mind was still racing. *Mountain thinks the Beholders can build me a barn to house the unicorns, griffons, dragons, and phoenixes. He says they can do it in a day or two even. Depending on the kind of job they do, I may ask them about Nana's room addition.*

Mountain didn't ask me about his boss. He knew that Menessos had the ability to be up and move around the haven during the day, yet we'd just dumped his body in the trunk. While vampires are *supposed* to be dead during the day, Mountain wasn't stupid, either. I was certain his thoughts were racing as well.

I headed toward I-77 South. I knew I couldn't go back to the haven. I didn't intend to drag Menessos's body through the theater with whatever Beholders and Offerlings remained to see.

I was going home. *Home.*

I almost didn't recognize Nana. She'd gotten a haircut. A major one. I stood there in the doorway staring. She ran a hand through the fluffy layers on top. It lay beautifully in natural waves. The sides and back were shorter. She smiled. "Saw myself on TV. Looked like a stump full of granddaddies."

She'd always compared someone's messy hair to a spider's nest. "It really looks good, Nana." I went forward and hugged her tight.

Johnny came in behind us and Kirk helped him upstairs. I gathered the Ace bandages from the bathroom and took them to the attic bedroom even as I called Doc Lincoln and left a message requesting a house call. After Johnny was wrapped in the bandage, Kirk and I brought down the mattress from my bed and put it on the living room floor for Mountain, who immediately crashed. Ares plopped right beside him. Both the big man and Nana's Great Dane pup were snoring loudly within minutes. Then Kirk and I removed Menessos—wrapped in blankets—from the trunk of my car. Kirk let me know in no uncertain terms that he did not need a woman's help to carry the vampire to the cellar. When he finished that, he wanted to call for a ride. I told him—also very directly—that he wasn't going anywhere until he could be debriefed by his Domn Lup. So he went upstairs to wait with his king.

I promised Nana—who'd had the nerve to gripe about the sand we were tracking through the house—and Beverley that they'd hear the full story after a nap of my own. I stretched out on the couch. Nana busied herself in the kitchen. Beverley curled up beside me, watching cartoons and keeping the volume low. "I'm so glad you're home."

I squeezed her. "Me, too."

A few hours later, Beverley woke me. A pair of semis had pulled into my driveway. By the time we made it to the porch, Vilna-Daluca had opened the back of one and a flurry of phoenixes filled the air. Griffons leaped out and paraded by. Some of them had wounds. The one that had lost an eye and the talons from his foreleg was among them.

Beverley, overjoyed at the sight of the glorious creatures, was barely able to contain herself. Even as the dragons slithered by she was shifting her weight and almost dancing. The unicorns, however, stunned her to slack-jawed stillness.

Once unloaded, the creatures headed straight for the grove, drawn to the ley line's power.

I guess that's where we'll put the barn.

From my front porch, I watched the semis drive out and head down the road.

It was just after noon.

Nana called Beverley to lunch. The kid went in chattering and excited. "Demeter, did you see them?"

I stayed on the porch.

I had to wait for Johnny to wake up. I had to wait and see what the nightfall brought for Menessos. Heldridge was still out there somewhere, and whether or not he was the one who'd given the fairies info about the hanky, he had it in for Menessos.

Tomorrow would be Monday. I was sure Xerxadrea's body would be identified. Then I'd have to deal with Vilna-Daluca and WEC. I also had to help Johnny unlock his tattoos. And speaking of wærewolves, though they had fled when the witches arrived, they had shown up at the beach and most had survived. They'd been promised the ritual to retain their man-minds. I had to perform it again. Then there was whatever Beau was going to want me to do before the next full moon.

And Beverley's birthday party.

Still so much to do.